RENEGADES

Books by Marissa Meyer from Macmillan

Heartless
Renegades

First published in the US 2017 by Feiwel and Friends
First published in the UK 2017 by Macmillan Children's Books

This edition published 2018 by Macmillan Children's Books
an imprint of Pan Macmillan
20 New Wharf Road, London N1 9RR
Associated companies throughout the world
www.panmacmillan.com

ISBN 978-1-5098-7643-3

1 3 5 7 9 8 6 4 2

A CIP catalogue record for this book is available from
the British Library.

For Jeffrey, the first hero I ever had

CAST OF CHARACTERS

THE RENEGADES: SKETCH'S TEAM

SKETCH — Adrian Everhart
> *Can bring his drawings and artwork to life*

MONARCH — Danna Bell
> *Transforms into a swarm of monarch butterflies*

RED ASSASSIN — Ruby Tucker
> *When wounded, her blood crystallizes into weaponry; signature weapon is a grappling hook formed from a bloodstone*

SMOKESCREEN — Oscar Silva
> *Summons smoke and vapor at will*

THE ANARCHISTS

NIGHTMARE — Nova Artino
> *Never sleeps, and can put others to sleep with her touch*

THE DETONATOR – Ingrid Thompson

Creates explosives from the air that can be detonated at will

PHOBIA – True Name Unknown

Transforms his body and scythe into the embodiment of various fears

THE PUPPETEER – Winston Pratt

Turns people into mindless puppets who do his bidding

QUEEN BEE – Honey Harper

Exerts control over all bees, hornets, and wasps

CYANIDE – Leroy Flinn

Generates acidic poisons through his skin

THE RENEGADE COUNCIL

CAPTAIN CHROMIUM – Hugh Everhart

Has superstrength and is nearly invincible to physical attacks; can generate chromium weaponry

THE DREAD WARDEN – Simon Westwood

Can turn invisible

TSUNAMI – Kasumi Hasegawa

Generates and manipulates water

THUNDERBIRD – Tamaya Rae

Generates thunder and lightning; can fly

BLACKLIGHT – Evander Wade

Creates and manipulates light and darkness

RENEGADES

W E WERE ALL VILLAINS *in the beginning.*

For hundreds of years, prodigies were feared by the rest of the world. We became hunted. Tormented. Feared and oppressed. We were believed to be witches and demons, freaks and abominations. We were stoned and hanged and set afire while crowds gathered to watch with cruel eyes, proud to be ridding the world of one more pariah.

They were right to be afraid.

Hundreds of years. Who would have stood for it?

Ace Anarchy changed everything. He united the most powerful prodigies he could find and together they rebelled.

He started with the infrastructure. Government buildings torn from their foundations. Banks and stock exchanges turned to rubble. Bridges ripped from the sky. Entire freeways reduced to rocky wastelands. When the military sent jets, he plucked them from the air like moths. When they sent tanks, he crushed them like aluminum cans.

Then he went after the people who had failed him. Failed all of them.

Whole governments, gone. Law enforcement, disbanded. Those fancy bureaucrats who had bought their way into power and influence . . . all dead, and all in a matter of weeks.

The Anarchists cared little for what would come next once the old world crumbled. They cared only for change, and they got it. Soon, a number of villain gangs began to crawl out from society's ashes, each hungry for their own slice of power, and it wasn't long before Ace Anarchy's influence spread across the globe. Prodigies banded together for the first time in history, some full of wrath and resentment, others desperate for acceptance that never came. They demanded fair treatment and human rights and protection under the law, and in some countries, the panicking governments hastened to cater to them.

But in other countries, the rebellions turned violent, and the violence dissolved into anarchy.

Chaos rose up to fill the void that civilized society had left behind. Trade and manufacturing ground to a halt. Civil wars erupted on every continent. Gatlon City was largely cut off from the world, and the fear and distrust that prevailed would go on to rule for twenty years.

They call it the Age of Anarchy.

Looking back now, people talk about the Anarchists and the other gangs like they were the worst part of those twenty years, but they weren't. Sure, everyone was terrified of them, but they mostly left you alone as long as you paid up when it was your due and didn't cause them any trouble.

But the people. The normal people. They were far worse. With no rule and no law, it became every man, woman, and child for themselves. There were no repercussions for crimes or violence—no one to run to if you were beaten or robbed. No police. No prisons. Not legitimate ones, anyway. Neighbors stole from neighbors. Stores were looted and supplies were hoarded, leaving children to starve in the gutters. It became the strong against the weak, and, as it turns out, the strong were usually jerks.

Humanity loses faith in times like that. With no one to look up to, no one

2

to believe in, we all became rats scrounging in the sewers.

Maybe Ace really was a villain. Or maybe he was a visionary.

Maybe there's not much of a difference.

Either way, the gangs ruled Gatlon City for twenty years, while crime and vice spread like sewage around a backed-up pipe. And the Age of Anarchy might have gone on for another twenty years. Fifty years. An eternity.

But then, seemingly overnight . . . hope.

Bright and sparkling hope, dressed up in capes and masks.

Beautiful and joyous hope, promising to solve all your problems, rain justice down upon your foes, and probably give a stern talking to a few jaywalkers along the way.

Warm and promising hope, encouraging the normal folks to stay inside where it was safe while they fixed everything. Don't worry about helping yourselves. You've got enough on your plate, what with all the hiding and moping you've been doing lately. You take a day off. We're superheroes. We've got this.

Hope called themselves the Renegades.

PROLOGUE

NOVA HAD BEEN COLLECTING SYRINGES from the alleyway behind the apartment for weeks. She knew her parents would take them away if they found out, so she'd been hiding them in an old shoe box, along with an assortment of screws, zip ties, copper wires, cotton balls, and anything else she thought might come in handy for her inventions. At six-going-on-seven years old, she'd already become aware of how important it was to be resourceful and thrifty. She couldn't exactly make a list and send her dad to the store for supplies, after all.

The syringes would come in handy. She'd known it from the start.

She attached a thin plastic tube to the end of one and stuck the opposite end of the tube into a glass of water she'd filled up in the bathroom sink. She pulled up the plunger, drawing water into the tube. Tongue sticking out through the gap where she'd recently lost her first tooth, she grabbed a second syringe and affixed it to the opposite end of the tube, then dug through her toolbox for a strip of wire long enough to secure it to the pulley system she'd built at the top of her dollhouse.

It had taken all day, but finally she was ready to test it.

She tucked some of the dollhouse furniture onto the elevator's platform, picked up the syringe, and pressed in the plunger. Water moved through the tube, extending the second plunger upward, and setting the complicated series of pulleys into action.

The elevator rose.

Nova sat back with a grin. "Hydraulic-powered elevator. *Success.*"

A cry from the next room intruded on the moment, followed by her mother's cooing voice. Nova looked up at her closed bedroom door. Evie was sick again. It seemed she was always running a fever these days and they'd run out of medicine for her days ago. Uncle Alec was supposed to be bringing more, but it might be hours still.

When Nova had overheard her father asking Uncle Alec if he might be able to find a children's ibuprofen for the baby's fever, she'd considered asking for more of the fruit-flavored gummies he'd given her on her birthday last year, too, or maybe a pack of rechargeable batteries.

She could do a lot with rechargeable batteries.

But Papà must have seen the request brewing in her eyes, and had given her a look that silenced her. Nova wasn't sure what it meant. Uncle Alec had always been good to them—bringing food and clothes and sometimes even toys from his weekly spoils—but her parents never wanted to ask for anything special, no matter how much they needed it. When there was something specific, they had to go into the markets and offer up trades, usually the things her father made.

The last time her dad had gone to the markets he'd come back with a bag of reusable diapers for Evie and a jagged cut above his eyebrow. Her mom stitched it up herself. Nova watched, fascinated to see that it was exactly like how her mother sewed up Dolly Bear when her seams came open.

Nova turned back to the hydraulic system. The lift was just shy of being level with the dollhouse's second floor. If she could increase the capacity of the syringe, or make some adjustments to the lever system . . .

Beyond her door, the crying went on and on. The floorboards were squeaking now as her parents took turns trying to comfort Evie, pacing back and forth through the apartment.

The neighbors would start to complain soon.

Sighing, Nova set down the syringe and stood.

Papà was holding Evie in the front room, bouncing her up and down and trying to press a cool washcloth against her flushed brow, but it only made her wail louder as she tried to shove it away. Through the doorway into their tiny kitchen, Nova saw her mom digging through cabinets, muttering about misplaced apple juice, though they all knew there wasn't any.

"Want me to help?" said Nova.

Papà turned to her, distress shadowing his eyes. Evie screamed louder as he forgot to bounce her for two whole seconds.

"I'm sorry, Nova," he said, bouncing again. "It's not fair to ask you to do it . . . but if she could just sleep for another hour or two . . . rest would be good for her, and Alec might be here by then."

"I don't mind," said Nova, reaching for the baby. "It's easy."

Papà frowned. Sometimes Nova thought he didn't like her gift, though she didn't know why. All it had ever done was make the apartment more peaceful.

He crouched down and settled Evie into Nova's arms, making sure her hold was secure. Evie was getting so heavy, nothing like the tiny infant she'd been not quite a year ago. Now she was all chubby thighs and flailing arms. She'd be walking any day now, her parents kept saying.

Nova sat down on the mattress in the corner of the room and stroked her fingers through Evie's baby-soft curls. Evie had worked

7

herself into a tizzy, big tears rolling down her plump cheeks. She was so feverish that holding her felt like holding a miniature furnace.

Nova sank into the tossed blankets and pillows and placed her thumb against her sister's cheek, scooping away one of the warm tears. She let her power roll through her. An easy, gentle pulse.

The crying stopped.

Evie's eyes fluttered, her eyelids growing heavy. Her mouth fell open in a shuddering O.

Just like that, she was asleep.

Nova looked up to see her dad's shoulders sink in relief. Mom appeared in the doorway, surprised and curious, until she spotted Nova with the baby tucked against her.

"This is my favorite," Nova whispered to them. "When she's all soft and cuddly and . . . *quiet*."

Mom's face softened. "Thank you, Nova. Maybe she'll feel better when she wakes up."

"And we won't have to start looking for another place to live," Papà muttered. "Charlie's kicked people out for less than a crying baby."

Mom shook her head. "He wouldn't risk angering your brother like that."

"I don't know." Papà frowned. "I don't know what anyone would or wouldn't do anymore. Besides . . . I don't want to be in Alec's debt any more than we already are."

Mom retreated into the kitchen to start putting away the cans and boxes she'd scattered across the linoleum, while Papà sank into a chair at the apartment's only table. Nova watched him massage his temple for a moment, before he squared his shoulders and started to work on some new project. Nova wasn't sure what he was making, but she loved to watch him work. His gift was so much more interesting than hers—the way he could pull threads of energy out of the air, bending and sculpting them like golden filigree.

It was beautiful to watch. Mesmerizing, even, as the glowing strips emerged from nothing, making the air in the apartment hum, then quieting and darkening as her father let them harden into something tangible and real.

"What are you making, Papà?"

He glanced over at her, and a shadow passed over his face, even as he smiled at her. "I'm not sure yet," he said, his fingers tracing the delicate metalwork. "Something . . . something I hope will put to right some of the great injuries I've caused this world."

He sighed then, a weighted sound that brought a frown to Nova's face. She knew there were things her parents didn't talk to her about, things they tried to shelter her from, and she hated it. Sometimes she would overhear conversations between them, words passed through the long hours of night when they thought she was asleep. They whispered about falling buildings and entire neighborhoods being burned to the ground. They murmured about power struggles and how there didn't seem to be any safe place left and how they might flee the city, but that the violence seemed to have consumed the whole world now, and besides, where would they go?

Only a week ago Nova had heard her mother say—"They'll destroy us all if no one stops them . . ."

Nova had wanted to ask about it, but she knew she would get only vague answers and sad smiles and be told that it wasn't for her to worry about.

"Papà?" she started again, after watching him work for a while. "Are we going to be okay?"

A figment of copper energy spluttered and disintegrated in the air. Her father fixed her with a devastated look. "Of course, sweetheart. We're going to be fine."

"Then why do you always look so worried?"

He set down his work and leaned back in his chair. For a moment she thought he might be on the verge of crying, but then he blinked and the look was gone.

"Listen to me, Nova," he said, slipping off the chair and crouching in front of her. "There are many dangerous people in this world. But there are also many good people. Brave people. No matter how bad things get, we have to remember that. So long as there are heroes in this world, there's hope that tomorrow might be better."

"The Renegades," she whispered, her voice tinged with a hint of awe.

A wisp of a smile crossed her father's features. "The Renegades," he confirmed.

Nova pressed her cheek against Evie's soft curls. The Renegades did seem to be helping everyone these days. One had chased down a mugger who tried to take Mrs. Ogilvie's purse, and she'd heard that a group of Renegades had broken into one of the gangs' storehouses and taken all the food to a private children's home.

"And they're going to help us?" she said. "Maybe we can ask *them* for medicine next time."

Her father shook his head. "We don't need that sort of help as much as some other people in this city do."

Nova's brow furrowed. She couldn't imagine anyone needing that sort of help more than they did.

"But," her father said, "when we need them . . . when we *really* need them, they'll be here, all right?" He swallowed, and sounded more hopeful than convincing when he added, "They'll protect us."

Nova didn't question it. They were superheroes. They were the good guys. Everyone knew that.

She found Evie's pudgy fingers and started to count off each knuckle, while running through all the stories she'd heard. Renegades pulling a driver from an overturned delivery truck. Renegades breaking up a gun fight in a nearby shopping district. Renegades rescuing a child who had fallen into Harrow Bay.

They were always helping, always showing up at just the right moment. That's what they *did*.

Maybe, she thought—as her father turned back to his work— maybe they were just waiting for the right moment to swoop in and help them too.

Her gaze lingered on her father's hands. Watching them mold, sculpt, tug more threads of energy from the air.

Nova's own eyelids started to droop.

Even in her dreams she could see her father's hands, only now he was pulling falling stars out of the sky, stringing them together like glowing golden beads . . .

A DOOR SLAMMED.

Nova awoke with a start. Evie huffed and rolled away from her.

Groggy and disoriented, Nova sat up and shook out her arm, which had fallen asleep beneath Evie's head. The shadows in the room had shifted. There were low voices in the hallway. Papà, sounding tense. Her mom, murmuring, *please, please* . . .

She pushed off the blanket that had been draped over her and tucked it around Evie, then crept past the table where a delicate copper-colored bracelet sat abandoned, an empty space in the filigree waiting to be filled with a precious stone.

When she reached the front door, she turned the knob as slowly as she could, prying the door open just enough that she could peer out into the dim hall.

A man stood on the landing—stubble on his chin and light hair pulled into a sleek tail. He wore a heavy jacket, though it wasn't cold outside.

He was holding a gun.

His indifferent gaze darted to Nova and she shrank back, but his attention slid back to her father as if he hadn't even seen her.

"It's a misunderstanding," said Papà. He had put himself between the man and Nova's mom. "Let me talk to him. I'm sure I can explain——"

"There's been no misunderstanding," the man said. His voice was low and cold. "You have betrayed his trust, Mr. Artino. He does not like that."

"Please," said her mom. "The children are here. Please, have mercy."

He cocked his head, his eyes shifting between them.

Fear tightened in Nova's stomach.

"Let me talk to him," Papà repeated. "We haven't done anything. I'm loyal, I swear. I always have been. And my family . . . please, don't hurt my family."

There was a moment in which it looked like the man might smile, but then it passed. "My orders were quite clear. It is not my job to ask questions . . . or to have mercy."

Her father took a step back. "Tala, get the girls. *Go.*"

"David . . . ," her mother whimpered, moving toward the door.

She had barely gone a step when the stranger lifted his arm.

A gunshot.

Nova gasped. Blood arced across the door, a few drops scattering across her brow. She stared, unable to move. Papà screamed and grabbed his wife. He turned her over in his arms. He was trembling while her mom wheezed and choked.

"No survivors," the man said in his even, quiet voice. "Those were my orders, Mr. Artino. You only have yourself to blame for this."

Nova's father caught sight of her on the other side of the door. His eyes widened, full of panic. "Nova. Ru—"

Another gunshot.

This time Nova screamed. Her father collapsed over her mom's body, so close she could have reached out and touched them both.

She turned and stumbled into the apartment. Past the kitchen, into her bedroom. She slammed the door shut and thrust open her closet. Climbed over the books and tools and boxes that littered the floor. She yanked the door shut and crouched down in the corner, gasping for breath, the vision of her parents burned into her thoughts every time she shut her eyes. Too late she thought that she should have gone for the fire escape. Too late.

Too late she remembered—

Evie.

She'd left Evie out there.

She'd left *Evie.*

A shuddering gasp was met with a horrified cry, though she tried to swallow both of them back. Her hand fell on the closet door and she tried to gauge how fast she could get out to the living room and back, if there was any chance of snatching the baby up without being seen . . .

The front door creaked, paralyzing her.

She pulled her hand back against her mouth.

Maybe he wouldn't notice Evie. Maybe she would go on sleeping.

She listened to slow, heavy footsteps. Squealing floorboards.

Nova was shaking so hard she worried the noise of her clattering bones would give her away. She also knew it wouldn't matter.

It was a small apartment, and there was nowhere for her to run.

"The Renegades will come," she whispered, her voice little more than a breath in the darkness. The words came unbidden into her head, but they were there all the same. Something solid. Something to cling to.

Bang.

Her mother's blood on the door.

She whimpered. "The Renegades will come . . ."

A truth, inspired by countless news stories heard on the radio. A certainty, patched together from the words of gossiping neighbors.

They always came.

Bang.

Her father's body crumpling in the hall.

Nova squeezed her eyes shut as hot tears spilled down her cheeks. "The Renegades . . . the Renegades will come."

Evie's shrill cry started up in the main room.

Nova's eyes snapped open. A sob scratched at the inside of her throat, and she could no longer say the words out loud.

Please, please let them come . . .

A third gunshot.

The air caught in Nova's lungs.

Her world stilled. Her mind went blank.

She sank into the mess at the bottom of the closet.

Evie had stopped crying.

Evie had stopped.

Distantly, she heard the man moving through the apartment, checking the cabinets and behind the doors. Slow. Methodical.

By the time he found her, Nova had stopped shaking. She couldn't feel anything anymore. Couldn't think. The words still echoed in her head, having lost all meaning.

The Renegades . . . the Renegades will come . . .

Doused in the stark lights from her bedroom, Nova lifted her eyes. The man stood over her. There was blood on his shirt. Later, she would

14

remember how there had been no regret, no apology, no remorse.

Nothing at all as he lifted the gun.

The metal pressed against her forehead, where her mother's blood had cooled.

Nova reached up and grabbed his wrist, unleashing her power with more force than she ever had.

The man's jaw slackened. His eyes dulled and rolled up into his head. He fell backward, landing with a resounding thud on her bedroom floor, crushing her dollhouse beneath his weight. The whole building seemed to shake from his fall.

Seconds later, deep, peaceful breathing filled the apartment.

Nova's lungs contracted again. Air moved through her throat, shuddering. In. And out.

She forced herself to stand and rub the tears and snot from her face.

She picked up the gun, though it felt awkward and heavy in her hand, and slipped her finger over the trigger.

She took a step closer, one hand gripping the doorframe as she left the sanctuary of the closet. She wasn't sure where she should aim. His head. His chest. His stomach.

She settled on his heart. Got so close to him she could feel his shirt brushing against her bare toes.

Bang. Her mother was dead.

Bang. Her father.

Bang. Evie . . .

The Renegades had not come.

They weren't going to come.

"Pull the trigger," she whispered into the empty room. "Pull the trigger, Nova."

But she didn't.

"Pull the trigger."

She couldn't.

Minutes, maybe hours later, her uncle found her. She was still standing over the stranger's sleeping form, ordering herself to pull the trigger. Hearing those gunshots over and over every time she dared to close her eyes.

"Nova?" A plastic bag dropped to the floor, taking a plastic medicine bottle with it. Nova startled and turned the gun on him.

Uncle Alec didn't even flinch as he crouched before her. He was dressed as he always was—the black-and-gold uniform, his dark eyes barely visible through the copper-toned helmet that disguised most of his face. "Nova. . . . Your parents. . . . Your sister. . . ." He looked down and reached for the gun. Nova didn't resist as he took it from her. His attention turned to the man. "I'd always thought you might be one of us, but your father wouldn't tell me what it was you could do. . . ."

He met Nova's eyes again. Pity and, perhaps, admiration.

With that look, Nova fell apart, throwing herself into his arms. "Uncle Alec," she wailed, sobbing into his chest. "He shot them . . . he . . . he killed . . ."

He picked her up, cradling her against his chest. "I know," he murmured into her hair. "I know, sweet, dangerous child. But you're safe now. I'll protect you."

She barely heard him over the noise in her head. The tumult pressing against the inside of her skull. *Bang-bang-bang.*

"But you can't call me Alec anymore, not out there. All right, my little nightmare?" He smoothed her hair. The handle of the gun bumped against her ear. "To the rest of the world, I'm Ace. You understand? Uncle Ace."

But she wasn't listening. And maybe he knew that.

In the midst of her cries, he squeezed her tight, aimed the gun at the sleeping man, and fired.

CHAPTER ONE

——■—■—**■**—■—■——

TEN YEARS LATER

THE STREETS OF DOWNTOWN GATLON were overflowing with fake superheroes.

Kids ran amok in orange capes, screeching and waving Blacklight-branded sparklers over their heads, or shooting one another with Tsunami-themed squirt guns. Grown men had squeezed themselves into blue leggings and painted shoulder pads to look like the Captain's armor, and now sat clinking glasses together inside the roped-off beer gardens that dotted the main street. Gender-swapping was a big thing this year, too, with countless women having shown up in risqué versions of the Dread Warden's signature bodysuit, and plenty of men having strapped cheap replicas of Thunderbird's black-feathered wings to their backs.

Oh, how Nova despised the Renegade Parade.

The street vendors weren't any better, hawking everything from cheesy light-up wands to tiny plush versions of the famous Renegade quintet. Even the food trucks were celebrating the day's theme, with Captain Chromium funnel cakes and Tsunami fish'n'chips baskets and one sign advertising DREAD WARDEN'S FAVORITE POPCORN CHICKEN—GET SOME NOW BEFORE IT *DISAPPEARS!*

If Nova had had an appetite to start with, she was sure she would have lost it by now.

A great cheer rose up through the crowd and the noise of a marching band broke through the din. Trumpets and drums and the steady thumping of hundreds of synchronized musicians moved through the street. The music grew louder, bearing down on them now. Cannons blasted overhead, dousing the crowd with confetti. The children went nuts. The adults weren't much better.

Nova shook her head, mildly disappointed in humanity. She stood at the back of the crowd, unable to see much of the actual parade, which was fine by her. Arms crossed defensively over her chest. Fingers drumming an impatient rhythm against her elbow. Already it felt like she'd been standing there for an eternity.

The cheering turned suddenly to loud, exuberant boos, which could only mean one thing. The first floats had come into view.

It was tradition for the villain floats to go first, to really get the crowd riled up, and to remind everyone what it was they were celebrating. Today was the ninth anniversary of the Battle for Gatlon, when the Renegades had taken on the Anarchists and the other villain gangs in a bloody fight that had ended with dozens of deaths on both sides.

The Renegades had won, of course. Ace's revolutionaries were defeated and the few villains who didn't perish that day either crawled away into hiding or left the city entirely.

And Ace . . .

Ace Anarchy was dead. Destroyed in the explosion that leveled half of the cathedral he had made his home.

That day officially marked the end of the Age of Anarchy, and

18

the start of the Council's rule.

They called it the Day of Triumph.

Nova looked up to see an enormous balloon, spanning nearly the width of the street as it floated between the high-rises. It was a cartoon-like replica of the Atomic Brain, who had been one of Ace's closest allies before the Renegades had killed him nearly fifteen years ago. Nova hadn't known him personally, but she still felt a spark of resentment to see the balloon's treatment of him—the bloated head and grotesquely disfigured face.

The crowd laughed and laughed.

The tiny transmitter crackled inside her ear.

"And so it begins," came Ingrid's voice, wry and unamused.

"Let them laugh," Phobia responded. "They won't be laughing for much longer. Nightmare, are you in position?"

"Roger," Nova said, careful to move her lips as little as possible, though she doubted anyone in the crowd was paying attention to her. "Just need to know which rooftop you want me on."

"The Council hasn't left the warehouse yet," said Phobia. "I will alert you once they do."

Nova glanced across the street, to the second-level window of an office building, where she could barely see Ingrid—or the Detonator, as the public knew her—peering out through the blinds.

The booing of the crowd started up again, more enthusiastic than before. Over the heads of the spectators, Nova caught glimpses of an elaborate parade float. On it was a miniature-scale version of the Gatlon skyline and standing among the buildings were actors wearing over-stylized costumes meant to resemble some of the most well-known members of Ace's gang. Nova recognized Rat and Brimstone, both killed at the hands of Renegades, but before she could be offended on their behalf, she spotted a dark figure near the top of the float. A surprised laugh escaped her, easing some of the anxiety that had been building all morning.

"Phobia," she said, "did you know they were going to put you on the villain floats this year?"

A hiss came back to her through the ear piece. "We are not here to admire the parade, Nightmare."

"Don't worry. You look good up there," she said, eyeing the actor. He had donned a long black cloak and was carrying an enormous plastic scythe with a bunch of rubber snakes glued to the handle. But when he opened his cloak, rather than being consumed by shadows, the actor revealed a pale, skinny physique wearing nothing but lime green swimming briefs.

The crowd went berserk. Even Nova's cheek twitched. "They may have taken a few liberties."

"I think I like it better," said Ingrid with a snort, watching the parade from the window.

"It certainly inspires terror," agreed Nova.

Phobia said nothing.

"Is that . . . ?" started Ingrid. "Oh my holy bomb squad, they have a Queen Bee this year."

Nova looked again. At first the actress was concealed on the other side of the cityscape, but then she moved into view and Nova's eyebrows shot upward. The woman's blonde wig was twice the size of her head and her sequined black-and-yellow dress could not have been any gaudier as it sparkled in the afternoon sunlight. She had black mascara running down her cheeks and was embracing a large stuffed bumblebee to her bosom, wailing about the unfair treatment of her little honey makers.

"Wow," said Nova. "That's actually not a bad impersonation."

"I can't wait to tell Honey," said Ingrid. "We should be recording this."

Nova's eyes darted around the crowd for what might have been the thousandth time. Standing still made her edgy. She was wired for movement. "Are you offended they don't have a Detonator?" she asked.

There was a long pause before Ingrid said, "Well, I am *now*."

Nova turned back to the parade. She stood on her tiptoes, trying to make out if any of their other comrades were among the costumes, when a loud crash startled the crowd. The top of the tallest building on the float—a replica of Merchant Tower—had just blown upward, and a new figure was emerging, laughing madly as he raised his hands toward the sky.

Nova clamped her jaw shut, the moment's amusement doused beneath a rush of fury.

The Ace Anarchy costume was the closest to reality—the familiar black-and-gold suit, the bold, iconic helmet.

The audience's surprise passed quickly. For many, this was the highlight of the parade, even more of a draw than seeing their beloved Council.

Within seconds, people had started to reach for the rotten fruits and wilted cabbages they'd brought with them for just this purpose. They started pummeling the villain float, shouting obscenities and mocking the villains on board. The actors took it with remarkable resilience, ducking down behind the buildings and screeching in feigned horror. The Ace Anarchy impersonator took the brunt of the attack, but he never dropped character—shaking his fist and calling the children at the front of the crowd *stinking rascals* and *little nightmares*, before he finally ducked down into the hollow building and pulled the top back over himself, setting up the surprise for the next street of onlookers.

Nova swallowed, feeling the knot in her stomach loosen only once the villain float had passed.

My little nightmare . . .

He had called her that, too, all those years ago.

The floats were followed by a band of acrobats and a Thunderbird balloon gliding overhead. Nova spotted a banner being propped up on tall poles, advertising the upcoming Renegade trials.

BOLD. VALIANT. JUST. DO YOU HAVE WHAT IT TAKES TO BE A HERO?

She faked a loud gagging sound, and an elderly woman nearby gave her a sour look.

A body crashed into her and Nova stumbled backward, her hands instinctively landing on the kid's shoulders and righting her before she fell onto the pavement.

"Watch it," said Nova.

The girl looked up—a domino mask over her eyes making her look like a smaller, scrawnier, girlier version of the Dread Warden.

"What was that, Nightmare?" Ingrid said into her ear. Nova ignored her.

The girl pulled away with a muttered sorry, then turned and wove her way back into the teeming crowd.

Nova adjusted her shirt and was just about to turn back to the parade when she saw the kid crash into someone else. Only, rather than set her right as Nova had done, the stranger stooped low, grabbed the girl's ankle, and turned her upside down in one swift motion.

Nova gaped as the stranger hauled the girl, screaming and swatting his chest, back in Nova's direction. He was roughly her age, but much taller, with dark skin, close-cut hair, and thick-framed eyeglasses. The way he strolled through the crowd made it seem more like he was carrying one of those cheesy Captain Chromium plush dolls rather than a ferocious, flailing child.

He stopped in front of Nova, a patient smile on his face.

"Give it back," he said.

"Put me down!" the girl yelled. "Let me go!"

Nova looked from the boy to the child, then took a quick scan of the nearby crowd. Far too many people were watching them. Watching *her*.

That wasn't good.

"What are you doing?" she said, turning back to the boy. "Put her down."

His smile became even more serene and Nova's heart stammered. Not just because he had one of those easy smiles that made other girls swoon, but because there was something unsettlingly familiar about him, and Nova immediately began racking her brain to figure out where she knew him from, and whether or not he was a threat.

"All right, Mini-Magpie," he said, somewhat patronizing, "you've got three seconds before I send in a request to put you on probation. Come to think of it, I'm pretty sure the janitorial crew has been needing some help lately . . ."

The girl huffed and stopped struggling. Her mask had begun to slip and was close to sliding off her brow. "I hate you," she growled, then reached into a pocket. She pulled out her hand and held it toward Nova, who uncertainly extended her own.

A bracelet—*her* bracelet—dropped into her palm.

Nova looked at her wrist, where a faint tan line showed where the bracelet had been worn every day for years.

Ingrid's voice rattled in her head. "What's happening down there, Nightmare?"

Nova didn't respond. Tightening her fist around the bracelet, she fixed a glare on the child, who only glared back.

The boy dropped her with little ceremony, but the girl rolled easily when she hit the pavement and had sprung back to her feet before Nova could blink.

"I'm not going to report this," said the boy, "because I believe you are going to make better choices after this. Right, Magpie?"

The girl shot him a disgusted look. "You're not my dad, Sketch," she yelled, then turned and stomped off around the nearest corner.

Nova squinted at the boy. "She's just going to rob someone else, you know."

Ingrid's voice buzzed in her ear. "Nightmare, who are you talking to? Who's getting robbed?"

"—can hope it will make her rethink her options," the boy was saying. His eyes met hers briefly, then dropped down to her closed fist. "Do you want help with that?"

Her fingers clenched tighter. "With what? The bracelet?"

He nodded and, before Nova realized what was happening, he had taken her hand and started peeling open her fingers. She was so stunned by the action that he had freed the bracelet from her grip before she thought to stop him. "When I was a kid," he said, taking the copper-colored filigree into his fingers, "my mom used to always ask me to help with her brace—" He paused. "Oh. The clasp is broken."

Nova, who had been scrutinizing his face with wary bewilderment, looked down at the bracelet. Her pulse skipped. "That little brat!"

"Nova?" crackled Ingrid's voice. "Have you been compromised?"

Nova ignored her.

"It's okay," said the boy. "I can fix it."

"Fix it?" She tried to snatch the bracelet away from him, but he pulled back. "You don't understand. That bracelet, it isn't . . . it's . . ."

"No, trust me," he said, reaching into his back pocket and pulling out a fine-tip black marker. "This wrist, right?" He wrapped the bracelet around Nova's wrist, and again, the sensation of such a rare, unexpected touch made her freeze.

Holding the bracelet with one hand, he uncapped the marker

with his teeth and bent over her wrist. He began to draw onto her skin, in the space between the two ends of the broken bracelet. Nova stared at the drawing—two small links connecting the filigree and, between them, a delicate clasp, surprisingly ornate for a drawing made in marker, and perfectly matched to the style of the bracelet.

When he had finished, the boy capped the pen using his teeth again, then brought her wrist up closer to his face. He blew—a soft, barely there breath across the inside of her wrist that sent goose bumps racing up her arm.

The drawing came to life, rising up out of her skin and taking physical shape. The links merged with the ends of the bracelet, until Nova could not tell where the real bracelet ended and the forged clasp began.

No—that wasn't entirely true. On closer inspection, she could see that the clasp he'd made was not quite the same coppery-gold color, but had a hint of rosiness to it, and even a faint line of blue where the drawing had crossed over one of the veins beneath her skin.

"What about the stone?" the boy said, turning her hand over and tapping his marker against the empty spot once intended for a precious gem.

"That was already missing," stammered Nova.

"Want me to draw one anyway?"

"No," she said, yanking her hand away. Her eyes lifted just in time to catch a flash of surprise, and she hastily added, "No, thank you."

The boy looked about ready to insist, but then he stopped himself and smiled. "Okay," he said, tucking his marker into his back pocket again.

Nova twisted her hand back and forth. The clasp held.

The boy's smile took on a subtle edge of pride.

Obviously a prodigy. But was he also . . .

"Renegade?" she asked, making little effort to keep the

suspicion from her tone.

"Renegade?" cried Ingrid. "Who are you talking to, Nova? Why aren't you—"

The crowd burst into a new frenzy of hollers and applause, drowning out Ingrid's voice. A series of fireworks shot upward from the parade float that had just emerged, exploding and shimmering to furious cheers from the people below.

"Looks like the headliners have arrived," said the boy, somewhat disinterested as he glanced over his shoulder toward the float.

Phobia's voice crackled. "West station, Nightmare. West station."

Purpose jolted down Nova's spine. "Roger."

The boy turned back to her, a small wrinkle forming over the bridge of his glasses. "Adrian, actually."

She took a step back. "I have to go." She turned on her heel and pushed her way through a group of costumed Renegade supporters.

"Renegade trials, next week!" one of them said, shoving a piece of paper at her. "Open to the public! Come one, come all!"

Nova crumpled the flyer in her hand without looking at it and crammed it into her pocket. Behind her, she heard the boy yelling, "You're welcome!"

She didn't look back.

"Target now passing Altcorp," said Phobia as Nova ducked into the shadows of an alleyway. "What's your status, Nightmare?"

Nova checked that the alley was empty before lifting the lid of a dumpster and hauling herself up onto its edge. Her duffel bag greeted her, resting at the top of the heap.

"Just grabbing my things," she said, snatching up the bag. She dropped back to the ground. The dumpster lid crashed shut. "I'll be on the roof in two minutes."

"Make it one," said Phobia. "You have a superhero to kill."

26

CHAPTER TWO

———■———

NOVA SLUNG THE BAG over her shoulder and reached for one of the weighted ropes she'd set up in the alley the night before. She wrapped her arm around the rope and untied the sailor's knot from the weights holding it to the ground.

The weights attached to the opposite end dropped, dragging it through the pulley on the rooftop above. Nova jerked upward, holding tight as the rope whistled past the building's concrete wall.

The second set of weights crashed into the ground below.

She stopped with a shudder, her hand only a few inches shy of the pulley, her body swinging six stories in the air. Nova threw her bag onto the rooftop, then grabbed the ledge and hauled herself over. She dropped down into a crouch and riffled through the bag, pulling out the uniform she had designed with Queen Bee's help. She slung the weaponry belt across her hips, where it hung comfortably, outfitted with specially crafted pockets and hooks for all of her favorite inventions. Next, the snug black hooded jacket: waterproof and flame-retardant, yet lightweight enough to keep from inhibiting her movements. She zipped it up to her neck and tugged the sleeves past her knuckles before pulling up the hood, where a couple of small weights stitched into the hem held it in place over her brow.

The mask came last. A hard metallic shell perfectly molded to the bridge of her nose that disappeared into the high collar of the jacket, disguising the lower half of her face.

Transformation complete, she stooped and pulled the rifle and a single poisoned dart from the bag.

"Where are you, Nightmare?" Phobia rasped.

"I'm here. Almost in position." She approached the edge of the building and looked down on the celebration below. It was quieter up here—the noise of the crowd dulled beneath the whistle of the wind and the hum of rooftop generators. The street was a mess of confetti and color, balloons and costumes, laughter and music and cheers.

Nova loaded the dart into the gun's chamber.

Ingrid had concocted the plan, and it was beautiful in its simplicity. When she'd told the group, Winston had griped about not being included, but Phobia had sagely pointed out that Winston, who most people knew as the Puppeteer, wasn't capable of keeping anything simple.

So it was only the three of them on the field today. They didn't need the others. Nova had one dart handcrafted by Leroy Flinn, their own poisons master. She only needed one. If she missed, she wouldn't get a second chance.

But she wouldn't miss.

She would kill the Captain.

Once he was hit, Ingrid, the Detonator, would emerge from hiding and hit the Council's parade float with as many of her signature bombs—made from a fusion of gasses in the air—as she could launch. Phobia would focus on Thunderbird, as she usually took to the air during a battle, giving her a frustratingly unfair advantage. They'd heard that Thunderbird was deathly afraid of snakes, which was one of his specialties. They were banking on the rumors to be true. Worst-case scenario: Phobia startled her long enough for Nova or Ingrid to take her down. Best-case: He gave her a midflight heart attack.

And that was it. The Council—the five original Renegades—all eradicated at once.

But it started with Nova getting past Captain Chromium's supposed invincibility.

"Say . . . Nightmare?"

"I'm *here*, Detonator. Relax."

"Yeah, I can see you up there. But I'm pretty sure Phobia wanted you at the west station?"

Nova froze. She glanced at the rooftop behind her, then across the gap to the apartment building on the other side of the alleyway, where her second weighted rope sat waiting, unused. She squinted up into the midday sun and cursed.

Phobia drawled in her ear, "Tell me she didn't get on the wrong building."

"I was distracted," she said through gritted teeth.

Phobia sighed heavily.

"She can't hit the target from the west rooftop?" asked Detonator.

After a brief silence, Phobia said, "She might have a fair shot at Tsunami or Blacklight, but not Captain Chromium. The parade route will have them turning before she's in alignment." He hummed thoughtfully. "She can end one Council member, and we shall have to concern ourselves with the others at a later date."

"Our priority was the Captain," said Ingrid. "This entire mission was built around taking out the *Captain*."

"One Renegade is better than none."

"It still makes this mission a failure."

Licking her lips, Nova looked across at the opposite rooftop, estimating the distance over the alley. "Everyone calm down. I can get to the other side. Phobia, how much time do I have?"

"Not enough."

"*How much?*"

"Ten seconds before the float enters your prime target area, then perhaps forty-five to make the shot."

Nova picked up the duffel bag and heaved it across the gap. It landed with a thud on the other rooftop.

Phobia's voice crackled. "This seems inadvisable."

"Let her try," said Ingrid. "It will be her own fault if she falls."

"I won't fall," Nova muttered. She slung the rifle onto her back and released a pair of gloves from a hoop on her belt. She shoved her hands into them and buckled the cuffs, securing them in place, then pressed her thumbs into the switches on her wrists. A jolt of electricity shot through the black fabric, forming pressurized suction cups on her fingertips and palms.

She reviewed the distance one more time. Paced back to the far edge of the building. Inhaled.

And ran.

Her boots thudded. Air whistled past her ears, knocking back her hood. She planted her right foot and leaped.

Her stomach hit the ledge of the brick wall on the other side of the alley. Pain jolted through her bones. She groaned and pressed her palms against the concrete to secure herself in place before she started to slip.

Ingrid whooped shrilly in her ear.

Phobia said nothing until Nova had hefted her body onto the east rooftop, and then merely, "Four seconds to visual."

Nova switched the pressure on her gloves, letting the suction cups recede into the fabric, and pulled her hood over her face again. She slung the gun off her back as she walked past the building's utility elevator, coming to stand at the edge as her pulse thrummed through her veins. Though she couldn't see the Council's float, she could tell from the increased excitement in the crowd that it was close.

Ignoring the throbbing pain where her stomach had hit the wall, she knelt onto one knee and propped the barrel of the gun on the rooftop ledge. She checked the loaded dart. "Ready."

"Well done, Nightmare," said Detonator.

"She hasn't done anything yet," said Phobia.

"I know, but isn't it nice to have a shooter on the team again?"

"She hasn't shot anything yet, either."

"Would you both zip it?" Nova growled, peeling off the gloves and shoving them back through the hoop on her belt.

Below, the Council's parade float rolled into view. It was an enormous tiered structure with five pedestals rising from a dark storm cloud. A literal thunder-and-lightning-filled storm cloud, like they thought they were gods or something.

Strike that. They definitely thought they were gods.

Thunderbird—the inimitable Tamaya Rae—stood on the first pedestal, her enormous black wings spanning the full width of the parade float and the wind catching in her long, dark hair, making her look like the proud mascot on the mast of a ship. She occasionally sent bolts of lightning to further ignite the cloud at her feet.

Not to be overshadowed, Blacklight was on the second tier shooting fireworks and flashing strobe lights into the air as the crowd gasped and squealed. With his red beard and tightly curled mustache, Nova had always thought Evander Wade looked more like a six-foot-tall leprechaun than a superhero, but supposedly he had a dedicated fan following, and the giddy shrieks from the crowd seemed to support the theory.

Above him, Kasumi Hasegawa might not have been aware she was in the middle of a parade at all. That's how Tsunami always looked though—caught up in her own world, a cool, secretive smile on her lips. While she stood barely moving with her arms extended, the stream of fish-filled water she was manipulating moved around her like a ribbon in a mesmerizing dance. A jet of foam and spray and angelfish spinning, twirling, spiraling in all directions.

The fourth pedestal appeared, at first glance, to be empty, which meant that's where Simon Westwood was standing. And sure enough, as Nova watched, the Dread Warden flickered into view, posing like the Thinking Man. A second later, he vanished again, only to reappear posed in a handstand, which then turned into a one-handed handstand. A second later, he went invisible again. The crowd roared in laughter when he reappeared, not on his own pedestal, but on the fifth and tallest platform on the float, using his fingers to give bunny ears to Captain Chromium.

Beside each other, they were like night and day. Simon Westwood had olive-toned skin, a close-trimmed beard, and dark, wavy hair, while Hugh Everhart, the city's beloved Captain, was the picture of boyish charm, complete with golden hair and dimples.

Captain Chromium rolled his eyes and glanced at the Dread Warden over his shoulder. They shared a look that was disgustingly endearing.

Nova had been too young to notice if there was any shock or scandal when two of the original Renegades announced they were in love, or if there had been any announcement at all. Maybe they just *were*, from the start. Either way, she suspected the world had been dealing with too much devastation to really care back then, and these days Captain Chromium and the Dread Warden were practically the world's favorite sweethearts. The tabloids were forever going on about whether or not they were planning to adopt another child, or if they were going to retire from the Council and move to the tropics, or if a dark, hidden secret from the past was threatening to tear them apart.

From their smiles, though, Nova highly doubted there was much substance to those rumors, and it made her teeth grind.

Why should *they* have such happiness?

She eased herself into position, calculating the distance and angle as the gun warmed in her hand.

The Dread Warden disappeared again and returned to his own pedestal, leaving the Captain alone, a king before his doting subjects. He was as familiar to Nova as her own reflection. Yellow-blond hair curling against his forehead. Blue shoulder pads jutting out from a broad, muscled chest. A winning smile with teeth so white they gleamed in the sun.

Then, as the crowd's cheers reached a deafening crescendo, he reached for the display stand at his side. His hand wrapped around a tall metal pike, and he lifted it overhead. One of Blacklight's fireworks burst then, lighting them all in a hue of coppery gold.

Nova's stomach dropped.

"Is that . . . ?"

"Don't dwell on it," said Phobia.

"Dwell on what?" asked Ingrid.

Nova swallowed around the lump in her throat, unable to respond.

Captain Chromium, beloved superhero and adored Renegade, had Ace Anarchy's helmet skewered at the top of his pike. It had been driven through the skull, fracturing the bronze-tinted material that had once been dragged from the air by her own father's fingertips, years before Nova was born.

The Detonator's voice came through the headset again, an understanding "*Oh . . .*" as the parade float entered her view. Nova barely heard her.

She was six years old again. Afraid. Devastated. Staring up into the eyes behind that helmet, throwing herself into his arms.

The Renegades had not come, but he had. Maybe not soon enough to save her family, but still, he had come. He had saved *her*.

"You're dwelling," said Phobia, his voice almost a taunt.

Nova squared her shoulders. "Am not."

Phobia didn't respond, but she could feel a haughty response in his silence.

"It's all right, Nightmare," said Detonator. "We're doing this for Ace, aren't we? Use that anger. Use it to avenge him."

Nova didn't respond. The world became still. Serene. Black and white.

She looked through the scope, lining up the sights.

It had to be in the eye. Anywhere else on his body and the tip of the dart would snap on the layer of chrome beneath his skin, and the poison would never make its way into his system.

Her aim had to be perfect.

And it would be.

She'd been preparing for this moment for years.

Use that anger.

It wasn't just to avenge Ace, though that might have been enough all on its own. It was to avenge her family, too, who the Council could have saved, but hadn't.

It was to revitalize Ace's vision. His dream of freedom for *all* prodigies, not just those who were willing to pander to the self-appointed Council and their autocratic laws.

It was because Nova knew that the Council was failing the people—was failing them even now—but no one was brave enough to say it.

Society would be better off without them.

The street below seemed to fall silent, blanketed by the purpose drumming inside her head. The Captain's eye came into focus. Shocking blue and bearing faint wrinkles in the corner as he smiled. He wasn't young anymore, like when he'd first formed the Renegades. The Council were getting older, passing their legacy on to a new generation.

"Pull the trigger," she whispered to herself. *Inhale.* The trigger pressed against her finger.

They were getting older, but they still held all the power. All the control. More, perhaps, than they ever had when they'd prowled the streets at night, searching for criminals and villains.

More than when he'd taken that helmet from its rightful owner. *Exhale.*

"Pull the trigger, Nova."

The Renegades will come.

Nova flinched.

"What's wrong?" asked Detonator.

"Nothing." Nova licked her lips. Lined up the sights again. The float was turning the corner now. Soon it would pass out of sight. Soon he would turn away from her, his smile and charm greeting the next street of worshipers.

This was the best opportunity they would have to take down the Captain, and soon, the rest of the Council would follow.

While the Renegades scrambled to replace the Council, the Anarchists would rise again. Without the villain gangs interfering this time, they would show the people of this city what anarchy was meant to look like. True freedom. True independence. For *everyone*.

All she had to do was pull the trigger.

A bug fluttered in the corner of her vision. Nova shooed it away.

She found her target again.

The Captain shifted, turning his head slightly in her direction.

It was the best shot she would have.

Nova started to squeeze.

Something landed on the end of the rifle. Nova lifted her eyes, focusing on the gold-and-black butterfly, its wings opening and closing as it perched on the barrel.

Nova's gaze lifted skyward.

A swarm of monarch butterflies clouded overhead—hundreds, perhaps thousands of vibrant wings fluttering as they clustered above her.

"We have company."

A beat of silence was followed by, "Renegades?"

She didn't respond. The float was turning. Five seconds, maybe less.

Nova looked through the sights and found the Captain, found his perfect hair, his perfect smile, his perfect blue eyes—

A bundle of balloons passed between them, each emblazoned with the iconic Renegade *R*.

She waited, frozen in time, sweat dripping down her neck.

The balloons passed.

Captain Chromium shifted his gaze upward, looking almost *right at her*.

She fired.

The Captain turned, just a hair.

The dart struck him in the temple. The needle tip snapped off.

Captain Chromium jerked to attention, searching the rooftops, signaling the others. Nova let out a stream of curses as she ducked behind the ledge.

A red hook flew from the side of her vision, attached to a thin wire. It wrapped around the gun and snatched it away.

Nova leaped to her feet.

A teenage girl, pale and freckled, stood at the corner of the roof, holding Nova's gun in one hand and the glittering hook in the other. She wore the Renegade uniform—form-fitting charcoal-gray Lycra from her neck to her boots, piped in red and emblazoned with a small R over her heart. Her hair was a mix of bleached white and pitch-black, pulled into a shaggy ponytail.

The butterflies swarmed beside her, cycloning until their wings became a blur, then solidified into the body of a second girl, wearing an identical gray bodysuit, with long blonde dreadlocks framing her face.

Red Assassin and Monarch.

Nova had met them once before, when they tried to stop her from robbing a small pharmacy for supplies Leroy needed, but there were more of them that time.

Nova lifted an eyebrow. "Where's everyone else? Living it up in the beer garden?"

As soon as she said it, she heard a *ding*, and the metal grate over the utility elevator squealed open.

A third Renegade emerged from the elevator—a boy with light brown skin and thick dark hair. He walked with a slight limp and a cane, faint tendrils of smoke following in his wake.

Smokescreen.

The corner of Nova's mouth curled upward. "That's a bit more like it."

Detonator's voice crackled in her ear. "What's happening up there?"

Nova ignored her.

"Nightmare," said Smokescreen, with a subtle incline of his head. "Long time, no see."

"You're about to wish it had been longer." Nova reached for her belt and unclipped two of her heat-seeking throwing stars, an invention she had worked all last summer to perfect.

She threw them both at Red Assassin, knowing how dangerous she could be with that hook of hers. Red dodged. Monarch burst again into a swarm of butterflies.

A bolt of black smoke struck Nova in the face. She stumbled back, blinded.

"Nightmare, report," said Ingrid.

Snarling, Nova reached for the transmitter behind her earlobe and shut it off.

She forced her burning eyes open and saw a blur of yellow, then Monarch was beside her. A knee collided with Nova's side and she fell to the concrete, rolling from the force of the blow. Nova used the momentum to jump back to her feet, shutting out the pain in her ribs, blinking through the stinging tears that blurred her vision.

Something hooked beneath her chin, pulling tight against her throat—Smokescreen's cane. He yanked her against him. Though he wasn't a big guy by any means, his arms felt like iron as his cheek pressed against the side of her hood. "Your days of villainy are over, Nightmare."

She scoffed. "You sound like you've read too many comics."

"You sound like you think that's a bad thing," he retorted.

She felt around for his hands on either end of the cane, but the gloves of his uniform overlapped with his sleeves, leaving no vulnerable skin exposed.

Smokescreen's hold on her tightened. "Are you working alone?"

In front of her, Red Assassin caught one of the throwing stars on her wire, flinging it at a heat vent. It stuck with a metallic clang. The second star boomeranged over the alleyway and zipped back toward her. She pinwheeled the ruby hook in front of her and stabbed the star into the concrete with the gem's point before it could rise again.

Red Assassin wrenched her gem free and turned to face Nova and Smokescreen, panting. She started to twirl the wire-tethered ruby like a lasso over her head.

Nova scowled. So much work, wasted.

Monarch formed again, arms crossed over her chest. "I believe Smokescreen asked you a question."

"Oh, I'm sorry," said Nova. "I was busy daydreaming about your funerals."

She grabbed the cane and kicked back her hips, launching Smokescreen over her head. He landed on his back with a grunt.

Snagging the cane from his hands, Nova struck the backs of Monarch's knees, knocking her off her feet.

Red Assassin threw the gem at Nova. The wire wound around her ankle, yanking her to the ground and dragging her across the gritty rooftop. Nova tried to dislodge another throwing star from her belt, but before she could get ahold of it, Red pulled a dagger cut from the same red crystal as her hook and pressed her knee on top of Nova's chest. She dug the point of the dagger against Nova's jugular.

"Who," said Red Assassin, with careful enunciation, "are you working for?"

Sensing her own heartbeat against the gemstone, Nova couldn't help smiling behind her mask. "Your worst nightmare," she said,

39

jamming her fingertips into the cuff of Red's boot and finding the skin of her ankle. Her power rolled through her. The blade dug into her throat, but then Red Assassin's eyes closed and she collapsed beside her.

A wave of hazy white mist rolled across the rooftop. Nova looked around, but the mist was already too thick to see Smokescreen. Sitting up, she unwound the wire from her leg and grabbed the dagger. It was lighter than any knife she'd ever held and looked like it had been cut from a single ruby, though she knew a real gemstone would have been much heavier.

Whatever material Red Assassin used for her specialized weaponry, it was sharp, and that's all Nova cared about.

On her feet again, she peered into the shroud of odorless smoke, listening for any sign of Smokescreen or Monarch. Her senses felt dulled in the fog. Infrared goggles would have helped. She would have to work on those next.

She spotted a dark shape—her duffel bag. With one more glance around, she bolted for the bag and threaded her elbow through the handles.

Monarch appeared from nowhere, her dreadlocks whipping behind her as she aimed a jab for Nova's head. Nova ducked and rammed her shoulder into Monarch's abdomen. The Renegade bent forward and Nova stabbed upward with the dagger, but the moment she felt the blade pierce the flesh of her upper leg, Monarch exploded into fluttering wings.

The smoke was beginning to clear, and Nova spotted a rickety fire escape on the next building. Tucking the dagger into her belt, she sprinted toward the edge of the roof and jumped. Catching the fire-escape rail, she vaulted herself over it and onto metal stairs that shuddered and clanged beneath her.

Smokescreen's voice cut through the fog. "Monarch!"

Nova paused long enough to look back and see Monarch reappear, though she immediately collapsed and pressed a palm over the cut in her thigh. The gray fabric of her uniform was darkening with blood.

Nova swung the duffel bag over her shoulder and hauled herself up the winding stairs, taking the risers two at a time.

She reached the roof and ran for the far side.

She was halfway across when a large figure leaped up from the street below, clearing the rooftop by a good twenty feet. Nova skidded to a stop, her panting breaths warming the inside of her mask.

The form landed in front of her with a clang.

Rather than a charcoal-gray bodysuit, he was dressed in something akin to armor—every limb protected, every muscle sculpted into the rigid shell, his face disguised behind a helmet and dark-tinted visor. The Renegade *R* was emblazoned on his chest, but the armor wasn't like any Renegade uniform she'd ever seen.

Though she couldn't see his eyes, she could feel them watching her. Nova took half a step back, scanning the figure from head to toe. There was no skin to be seen, only narrow seams between the armored plates that might be vulnerable to more traditional attacks.

"You must be new around here," she said.

His head tilted. "I've been around long enough to know who you are . . . Nightmare."

Nova's fingers skimmed along the top of her belt, though she wasn't confident any of her weapons would be effective. "Should I be flattered?"

Before the figure could answer, a bout of high-pitched laughter echoed off the high-rise buildings, pealing through the streets and alleys of downtown Gatlon. The sound was grating, shrill, and far too familiar.

Nova grimaced. "What is that idiot doing here?"

CHAPTER THREE

———■—■—■—■—■———

THE ARMORED STRANGER turned his head toward the laughter, just as the curve of a hot-air balloon rose into view over the parade. The balloon was decorated in black-and-white harlequin, with an enormous acid-green Anarchist symbol painted over it. Its wicker basket carried one occupant—a man with wild orange hair, painted red cheeks, and deep lines drawn from the corners of his mouth down his chin in mimicry of a marionette.

The Puppeteer stood on the rim of the basket in a checkered suit, gripping the upright bars as it bounced and swayed beneath him.

"Oh, *Reeeeenegades*," he shouted in a singsong voice. "Doesn't anyone want to play with me?"

The cheers below turned to screams of fright, and he cackled again, holding one hand out over the crowd, tilting so far forward it seemed he would topple from the basket. "Eeny, meeny, miny . . . *mo!*"

Eight shimmering gold strings cascaded from his fingertips into the crowd, and though Nova couldn't see where they landed, she knew he would be seeking out children in the chaos below. Those who were touched by his strings would turn into puppets he could control. After all these years, she still wasn't sure if his power only worked on children, or if he just preferred them because a mindless, rabid four-year-old was so damned creepy.

"Tag!" the Puppeteer bellowed. "You're it!"

The screams grew louder.

"Friend of yours?"

Nova glanced sideways at the armored figure. "Not exactly."

The Puppeteer laughed again, and the stranger's fists tightened. Nova couldn't fault him for his irritation. She wasn't exactly Winston Pratt's biggest fan, either, and she'd been technically on the same side as him since she was six.

In one movement, Nova pulled the duffel bag around to her front and reached inside for the netting gun she'd engineered from a toy bazooka when she was eleven. The figure turned toward her at the same moment she lifted the gun and pulled the trigger, sending a net of nylon ropes soaring toward him. Its eight points spread out like an octopus. The stranger stumbled back in surprise, lifting a hand to defend himself as the net descended.

He dropped to one knee. The net wrapped around him, tangling around his limbs. The helmet twisted from side to side as he struggled to pull the ropes away, but every movement only drew them tighter.

"It was nice to meet you," said Nova, tossing the bazooka back into the bag. She jogged past him, scouting out the next rooftop before making the easy jump.

"We're not done."

She glanced back. The stranger's shoulders were hunched. He wrapped his gloved fingers around the knotted ropes, and smoke started to wisp between his fingertips.

The ropes caught fire. Flames licked along the nylon, blackening the net until whole portions of it crumbled away into ash.

When enough of the netting had been burned off, he tore a hole in it and stepped out of the bindings, leaving the rest to smolder on the concrete roof.

He walked to the edge and peered down at Nova.

She smirked, unimpressed. "Another fire elemental. How quaint. Not exactly a rare breed, but it's hard to criticize a classic."

He bent his knees, lowering himself into a slight crouch, then sprang upward, lobbing his body clean over her head. Nova followed his trajectory through the air, a full arc that carried him onto the rooftop behind her. Though his landing was graceful, the weight of his armor made the floor shake beneath them.

Nova's smile faded.

A fire elemental with a fancy anti-gravity suit . . . or a prodigy with superior speed and strength, who just happened to also be able to burn things . . . or, a superhero with both powers? She'd never heard of such a combination before.

"You can't escape me, Nightmare," he said. "I'm taking you into custody, and you will answer for your crimes."

"Lovely as that sounds, I actually had other plans for this afternoon."

A shadow passed over them—monarch butterflies slowly merging into a girl's shape.

As Monarch took form, Nova looked between her and the stranger. She was trapped between them.

She didn't like being trapped.

Monarch frowned at the armored man. A hasty bandage had been wrapped around the wound in her thigh, cut from gray cloth. "Who are you?"

The stranger didn't speak for a moment, and Nova was sure his voice deepened when he responded, taking on an air of righteousness. "I am the Sentinel."

Nova laughed. "Seriously?"

The Sentinel angled his head in her direction, and she couldn't tell whether she imagined the way his chest expanded defensively.

"Friend of yours?" Monarch said, glancing at Nova.

She tightened her hands around the strap of the duffel bag. "I'm really not that friendly. Besides, he's wearing *your* trademark."

Monarch's eyes narrowed as she took in the *R* on the Sentinel's chest.

Losing interest in Monarch's confusion, Nova heaved the bag at the Sentinel's head, then reached behind her for the red dagger. She swung the blade toward Monarch's abdomen but hit only air as she dispersed again into the swarm. Snarling in frustration, Nova swung again and again—finally slicing a single butterfly in half.

She let out a breath and glanced down at the faint brush of wing dust on the blade.

Two arms wrapped around her, securing her elbows at her sides. If Smokescreen had been strong, this guy was iron and steel.

Or perhaps it was the suit.

Nova clenched her jaw and pushed backward. He yelped but didn't release her as his foot hit the low rail along the building's ledge.

With one more shove, Nova sent them both plummeting over the side. For a moment they were airborne, his arms locked around her.

They hit the next roof with a jolt that reverberated through Nova's bones. Something beneath them crunched and shattered.

Though her body ached, she forced herself to roll off him, shoving his arms away from her as she collapsed, trembling, onto a rattan mat. Nova looked around. They were in a small rooftop garden, surrounded by wicker furniture and potted plants—one of which was now pinned beneath the Sentinel. A water fountain gurgled against the wall they had just fallen from.

She caught a glimpse of the Puppeteer's balloon drifting along the street. There were flashes of strobing red lights brightening the sides of the buildings along the main avenue. Blacklight, perhaps, trying to distract the Puppeteer with fireworks and flashes, or maybe Thunderbird throwing one of her lightning bolts in an attempt to take down the balloon . . . or electrocute the villain. Maybe both.

The butterflies returned, forming a dark cloud overhead. The Sentinel had rolled onto his side and was attempting to push himself up.

"Hey, Sentinel," Nova said, tightening her grip on the dagger.

He glanced up.

She plunged the knife into the space between his chest and shoulder plates.

The Sentinel roared and shoved her away. He crumpled, planting one palm on the ground, while the other lit up, suddenly engulfed in orange flames. He hauled the hand back.

Nova ducked, pulling her hood down as a column of flames rushed over her back. She *knew* adding a flame-resistant coating to her uniform had been a good idea.

A cry of pain hit her ears.

Nova peered up from the shadow of her hood as the swarming butterflies converged back into the body of Monarch. The flames had hit a cluster of the orange insects, and the remaining wisps of ash seemed to melt into the girl's left side, from her ribs to her hip.

Her uniform was blackened and smoking, and the stench of burned flesh permeated the air.

The fire escape rattled and clanked off the side of the building. Smokescreen appeared on the ladder, hooking his cane over the rooftop edge to help pull himself up. He was breathing heavily, his dark hair matted to his brow as he took in the scene. His eyes widened. "Monarch?"

Something clattered at Nova's feet. The ruby dagger, its blade darkened with blood.

Nova didn't bother to look back at any of them as she turned and ran again, scaling the burbling stone fountain and hauling herself back to the rooftop they had fallen from. Behind her, she could hear the Sentinel ordering Smokescreen to help Monarch, and an incredulous Smokescreen demanding, "Who the hell are you?"

The Puppeteer's wicker basket drifted back into view.

"Catch!" Nova yelled.

The Puppeteer glanced in her direction, but made no effort to catch the duffel bag as Nova tossed it into his basket.

"Good afternoon, tiny Nightmare," said Winston. "What a delightful surprise this is. I was just out for a little . . . float." He tossed his head back and started to laugh, the marionette lines on his face making it even creepier than it already was.

His hands were still held out over the crowd, golden gossamer strings toying with the helpless children below. Nova glanced down long enough to see a pigtailed girl chomp hard on the ankle of a gray-haired man . . . possibly her own grandfather.

Grimacing, Nova climbed onto the ledge of the roof. "Toss me a rope."

The Puppeteer fell silent and peered at her with emotionless eyes. "You have a tagalong."

A hand grabbed her elbow, spinning her around. Fingers closed over her throat, tilting her backward, squeezing just tight enough to keep her from plummeting to the street below.

"You tried to assassinate Captain Chromium," the Sentinel growled. "Why? Who put you up to it? What else are they planning?" The visor of his helmet was a blank canvas, but his voice was furious. Nova imagined she could still feel the heat from his flames seeping through his glove.

"You Renegades sure ask a lot of questions," she said, white spots flashing in her eyes.

He moved so close that his visor almost clicked against her own face mask. "You'd better start answering them."

"You think I'm afraid of a pompous neophyte in a toy suit?"

The fingers at her throat seemed to loosen, just a bit. "Neophyte?"

"It means amateur. You're obviously new to this game."

"I know what it—" The Sentinel made an annoyed sound. "Look, I don't really care whether or not you're afraid of me, but I'm willing to bet you're at least a little bit afraid of dying, like we all are." The fingers tightened again, and Nova felt herself being forced backward. The change was minimal, but just enough so she could feel the shift in her balance, the slight pull of gravity.

She fought off the need for air and forced out a laugh, though it came out more like a wheeze. "You know what they say . . . one cannot be brave who has no fear."

He jerked back as if she'd struck him. In the same moment, Nova reached forward and pressed her hand against his chest, digging her fingers into the sliced fabric where the knife had penetrated. It was hot and sticky with blood and it was all she needed. Flesh and tissue and a heartbeat that thundered underneath.

"What did you just—"

She drove her power into him, a sledgehammer into his chest.

His breath hitched, and he stood immovable for a moment. Then the grip loosened around her throat. Nova cried out and grabbed his forearm, pulling her center of balance toward him as he fell backward, landing with a bone-jolting crash.

Nova's heart ricocheted inside her chest as she stared down at him, still feeling the drop in her stomach when, for a split second, she'd thought she was falling.

"*Niiiiiightmare . . .*"

Rubbing her throat, she turned in time to catch the shimmering gold threads the Puppeteer tossed to her. Though her legs had begun to shake, Nova forced herself to gather together any last shreds of strength. She wrapped the strings around her wrist and leaped, swinging out over the street, where people had scattered and a parade float had crashed into the side of a hair salon.

She hauled herself up the ropes and into the basket, landing in a heap on its floor.

"Thanks, Winston," she gasped.

He didn't respond—already he was focused again on his puppets, his mad laughter shrieking over the noise of the propane burner above them.

Once Nova had caught her breath, she wrapped her hands around the edge of the basket and forced herself to stand.

The street below was in chaos. The Puppeteer's gossamer strings littered the pavement, some still wrapped around children's throats and wrists, though many of his puppets had been discarded and were crumpled against buildings or in the middle of the street. A number of onlookers were injured, their bodies sprawled out on the sidewalks and streaks of blood trailing behind them as they attempted to crawl to safety. Winston had four children still enthralled, the strings like nooses around their necks as they threw marching band instruments through shop windows, ripped parade floats to pieces, and hurled street food at the Council members who were trying to stop them without actually hurting them.

The Dread Warden, of course, had gone invisible, while Tsunami kept trying to trap the puppets in a frothy tidal wave—except the spellbound children didn't seem to care that they might drown as they plunged into the wall of water.

Nova searched for Captain Chromium but couldn't find him in the uproar.

All the while, Winston's grating cackle echoed through the city. He could have been at a circus for all his apparent glee.

Nova reached behind her ear and turned on the transmitter. "Nightmare checking in. Detonator, Phobia, where are you?"

Phobia's voice came back to her, even and dry. "Where have you been?"

Nova glanced back to the rooftop, now half a block away as the balloon drifted along the street, but she could no longer see the Renegades or the Sentinel.

"I made some new friends," she said.

A roar dragged Nova's attention upward in time to see Thunderbird's enormous black wings spread out against the blue sky. Her face was twisted with fury, one hand gripping a crackling white lightning bolt.

Nova cursed.

Winston giggled. "Hello, birdie bird!"

Thunderbird lifted her free hand and thrust her palm toward the balloon. The air boomed, shoving the balloon backward. The basket crashed into an office building. Nova ricocheted off the side and landed on the floor again.

Winston hoisted himself up, one hand gripping the upright bar as he pulled on the golden threads around his fingers, making the children below do who-knew-what.

"Ah-ah-ah," he said with a childish titter. "It isn't polite to hit. You should say you're sorry."

"Release those children now, Puppeteer," growled Thunderbird, lifting the lightning bolt over her shoulder.

Nova pulled open the duffel bag and grabbed the netting gun. Exhaling, she popped up over the edge, using the basket's side to steady her aim, and fired.

The ropes entwined around Thunderbird's body. One side tangled around her left wing and she cried out in surprise. The lightning bolt struck a rope and the whole net lit up, crackling with electricity.

Thunderbird screamed.

Then she was falling, falling. Toward the street, toward the pavement—

Right into Captain Chromium's waiting arms.

He set her down, then turned his blue eyes skyward. No longer was he smiling. No longer did he look like an overhyped imbecile on a gaudy parade float.

His eyes met Nova's, and she swallowed.

"What's happening down there, Detonator?" she said. "We could use some assistance."

"Puppeteer wasn't a part of this operation," came the dry response. "He wants to act on his own, he can die on his own."

Down below, the Captain grabbed the metal pike he'd been holding earlier. Nova watched as he ripped Ace Anarchy's helmet from the top and tossed it away. The helmet rolled across the street, coming to rest in a storm drain.

"It's not just the Puppeteer now," she said. "I'm up here, too!"

"Good luck, Nightmare. This mission is over."

The faint crackle over the ear piece went silent.

Captain Chromium hefted the pike over his head, holding it like a javelin, and threw.

Though the balloon was hundreds of feet in the air, the pike did not waver as it soared straight for her.

Nova ducked.

The javelin struck the balloon's heater with a deafening clang, disconnecting the propane line. The flame spluttered and went out. The pike ricocheted off the metal and fell back down to the street.

The effect was instant. Though the balloon continued to drift from momentum, its upward course began to slow.

Nova looked around. They would have cleared the next set of buildings easily, but with the change of propulsion, she doubted they could make it now. Without the heater warming the air in the balloon, they would soon be sinking, and then crashing, right into the hands of the Renegades.

Winston cocked his head and peered down at Nova. "Uh-oh."

Nova held his gaze, considering.

If they could lose some weight, they might still be able to clear the next block, gaining enough distance to make a getaway before the Renegades caught up with them.

She turned her attention to the duffel bag, and all her weapons and inventions. All her efforts. All her work.

Winston whined in sympathy. "Sacrifices must be made sometimes, mini-Anarchist."

Nova sighed. "You're absolutely right."

Then she hooked her arm around Winston's ankles and pulled. He yelped, arms flailing, and toppled over the edge.

Nova didn't wait for his screams to fade as she hauled herself up onto the uprights and inspected the heater. The balloon barely cleared the rooftop, giving her just enough time to reaffix the propane line. She toggled the lighter switch a few times, and the flame burst to life.

The balloon drifted into the sky.

Nova released a weary, relieved groan and dared to look down at the street.

The Puppeteer had landed on a parade float. He was covered in confetti and flowers as Captain Chromium hauled him to the ground.

Winston didn't fight. His gaze lingered on Nova the whole time, his expression contorted into that same delirious grin.

Nova lifted her arm and waved.

CHAPTER FOUR

———■—■—■—■—■———

ADRIAN WOKE UP feeling like his head had been stuffed with
wool. He groaned and tried to roll onto his side, only then
remembering that he was still wearing the armored bodysuit.
The hard material dug painfully into his back.

Everything ached, but it was his shoulder that hurt the worst.
Throbbing and burning and sticky with blood.

He couldn't believe she had actually stabbed him. He wasn't sure
why it was so surprising, except . . . that just wasn't how prodigies
fought. They fought with superpowers and extraordinary skills, but
that had been a plain old dirty attack.

He would have to remember for next time. Nightmare didn't
follow the same rules as the rest of them.

But then, he supposed, neither did he. Not anymore. Not when
he was the Sentinel.

He managed to sit up. Though it was still daylight, the sky was
darkening and the shadows from the next building had eclipsed the
rooftop. He must have been unconscious for five or six hours. He

was lucky she'd knocked him out up here, where it was unlikely anyone would find him. Though it was clear he'd been undisturbed, it made him uncomfortable to think of himself lying prone and vulnerable for such a long time.

Prone and vulnerable and useless.

Why hadn't Oscar come looking for him?

No—that was a stupid question. Why would he have? Oscar didn't know Adrian was beneath the Sentinel's armor, and besides . . . Danna had been injured, and maybe Ruby too. Oscar had other matters to deal with. They would have gone straight back to headquarters. Were probably there still.

Adrian checked to be sure no one was peering down from any nearby windows, then pressed his fingers into the center of the suit's chest piece.

The armor clunked and hissed, folding in on itself like origami, rolling inward along his limbs until the suit was no bigger than a crushed aluminum can. He tucked it into the skin over his sternum and pulled up the zipper tattoo he had inked there more than a month ago.

He started to button the front of his shirt, but his shoulder screamed at him to stop. He looked down. His shirt had a gash through the fabric, and though the compression of the suit seemed to have slowed the bleeding, one glance told him he had lost a lot of blood. His entire side was damp, the fabric of his shirt nearly black where the blood had congealed. He wondered if that was why his brain seemed to be struggling to function or if it was a result of being knocked out by Nightmare.

Perhaps it was a combination of both.

He cursed her every way he could think of as he peeled the fabric away from his skin, then cursed himself as he pulled the shirt over his head.

That girl had a bunch of low-tech gadgets and a power that only worked through skin-to-skin contact. How had she beaten him?

He grimaced, recognizing his own pathetic attempts to defend his pride. But who was he kidding? He had underestimated an opponent who should not have been underestimated. She was strong. She was clever. And most of the low-tech gadgets he'd seen her use were actually pretty impressive.

Shaking his head, he started to laugh, wryly at first, but it quickly grew with real humor, even if it was at his own expense.

So much for being the city's next great superhero.

"Next time," he whispered to himself. A promise.

He would keep training. He would get better. And there *would* be a next time.

Pulling the marker from the back pocket of his jeans, he sketched a water faucet on the rooftop's concrete ledge and pulled the drawing into three dimensions. With a twist of the knob, cool water gushed forward.

He used the clean half of his shirt as a rag to wipe away as much of his blood as he could. The injury didn't look quite so devastating once it was clean. His heart was still beating and his arm was working, so she couldn't have hit anything too important.

After close inspection of the wound, he placed the tip of the marker against his skin and drew a series of stitches, gathering the skin together. Once he was finished, he capped the marker and tucked it away, turned off the water, then sat tracking his thumb around the tattoo on his left forearm. A spiral of flame in bold black ink, its edges fading away into his own dark skin.

Fire manipulation. Perhaps it wasn't rare, but it still remained one of the most coveted powers among prodigies. Between that and the armored suit and the springs he'd inked into the soles of his feet, he'd been confident he could do anything, stop anyone.

But Nightmare had barely bat an eye.

Not just that. She'd *mocked* him.

With a groan, he climbed to his feet and rallied the courage to look down onto the street where the parade had passed that morning. The celebration had been replaced with a sullen quiet as cleanup crews swept away the confetti and the food wrappers along with the broken glass and destroyed parade floats and looted merchandise left behind from the Puppeteer's attack.

Nightmare had asked the Puppeteer to throw her a rope. Were they working together? Was she an Anarchist?

It made sense, in a way. They were one of the few villain gangs who hadn't vanished completely over the past decade, and they despised the Renegades more than anyone, especially the Council.

And that's why she'd been up here, wasn't it? She'd been going after the Council. She'd been going after the Captain.

Adrian pressed his glasses up on the bridge of his nose. On the street below, a little girl was being dragged from beneath a tour bus, where she must have been hiding all afternoon. She was sobbing hysterically, and even from so high above, Adrian could see a string of gold thread still tied around her throat. He wondered what the Puppeteer had made her do.

His jaw clenched.

Most of the Anarchists' identities had been known for years. Winston Pratt. Ingrid Thompson. Honey Harper. Leroy Flinn.

But *Nightmare* . . . she was new. A mystery. And a threat.

When he closed his eyes, he could see her, the slightest glint of her eyes visible in the shadow of her hood. Without expression.

Without remorse. Without *fear*, even as she'd said those words—the words that had haunted him for years. Even now, he couldn't be sure whether he'd imagined her saying them. That it hadn't been part of a dream played out while he'd been unconscious.

One cannot be brave who has no fear.

He released a shuddering breath. It hadn't been a dream. She had said them.

It couldn't be coincidence.

"Nightmare," he whispered, and it felt like the first time he said it. The first time he said the name and it meant something to him. She was no longer just another villain to be stopped. Another blight on their city to be dealt with. Now she was someone who might have answers. "Who are you really?"

—◼—◼—◼—

THE DULLNESS OF HIS THOUGHTS had mostly evaporated by the time Adrian made his way back to Renegade Headquarters. He had drawn a new shirt for himself, with long sleeves to hide the tattoos, his chest and shoulder still throbbing and tender beneath the fabric.

He pushed his way through the rotating door of the main entrance and paused on the landing that looked out over the expansive lobby. It was a vast gathering space that was forever humming with activity and chatter and heavy boots thudding across the enormous *R* inset into the center of the floor. Renegades in gray-and-red uniforms passed doctors in lab coats and mingled with administrators in crisp suits. People rushed between the various departments, gathered in groups, stared at the screens that lined the walls as they replayed scenes from the Puppeteer's attack again and again.

Hugh and Simon sometimes joked about how all this had started in the Dread Warden's basement. They'd been teenagers—friends since childhood, both with extraordinary powers, both sick of watching their city being run by Anarchists and criminals. Until one night when they decided to do something about it.

As their escapades grew in boldness and publicity, four more prodigies joined the crew of vigilantes: Kasumi, Evander, Tamaya, and Adrian's own mother, Georgia Rawles. The incomparable Lady Indomitable.

It was Evander who gave them the name that would solidify their place in history. *The Renegades.* Back then, as Adrian understood, they'd had no money, no headquarters, no influence. Nothing but a profound determination to change the world for the better. And they had done it all while subsisting on boxed macaroni and cheese and wearing cheap homemade costumes and taking turns sleeping on one another's moth-eaten couches.

Though the original six were still considered the core group that had started the Renegades, their numbers continued to grow: more vigilantes joined the cause, more prodigies dared to fight against the villains who had torn their world apart.

Seeing headquarters now, it was almost impossible to imagine how it started in that basement, all those years ago. A couple of teenagers and a desire to change the world for the better.

And now—this. Eighty-two stories and eight sublevels of the world's most comprehensive government and law enforcement facilities.

Okay, most of those floors actually didn't have anything on them, but Hugh often talked about how glad they would be for all the extra space when they needed to expand. The tower had been built to be the main office building for an international bank or something equally dull, but now it held high-tech facilities and virtual-reality simulators, where Renegades could train both physically and mentally inside a variety of programmable situations. There was a full armory, where an assortment of weapons was kept behind a series of ever-increasingly impenetrable defenses, plus an entire floor dedicated to the storage and preservation of superpowered tools and artifacts. There were two floors dedicated to city surveillance and investigative work; the always-busy call center; prison cells for housing prodigy criminals who were too dangerous to be put into the regular city prison; lounge areas for off-duty Renegades; research laboratories; a full-service medical wing; and—their crowning glory—the Council Hall on the highest floor, where the Council passed laws and made decrees designed to strengthen the society they'd liberated from anarchy and protect the world from another collapse.

The Council acted like the only direction society could move was forward, away from those terrible years of chaos and crime, but Adrian sometimes had the feeling that the foundation of order the Renegades had built was more precarious than anyone wanted to admit.

Straightening his spine, he started down the grand staircase to the main floor and cut across to the elevators, heading for the medical wing. A few of the overhead screens switched to an image of Nightmare, waving down to the crowd from the basket of the hot-air balloon, her face eclipsed by the hood.

Renewed determination surged through Adrian at the sight of her. His mind started to replay the moment when Nightmare had stabbed him, with Ruby's own blade, no less. He'd lost control. He'd thrown that flame, intending it for Nightmare, but he'd been blinded by rage, and he hadn't been thinking about what might be behind her.

She called him a neophyte and she was right. It was an amateur mistake.

From the moment he heard Monarch's scream, he knew she was

badly hurt. He hadn't been holding back, and much as he wanted to blame Nightmare for it, he couldn't. The flames had been from his hands—the result of a power he'd barely explored. He had been cocky and careless and Danna was suffering for it.

When he reached the medical wing, he spotted Tamaya Rae—Thunderbird—through the windows of the first room. She was sitting on the edge of a bed while a healer tended to one of her black-feathered wings. She looked enraged, though all he caught were the words *Puppeteer* and *balloon* and *pathetic fishing net!*

He found Danna in the third room, lying on her side, unconscious. Much of her uniform had been cut away, revealing extensive burns along her left arm and torso. A mask was over her nose and mouth, probably filling her lungs with an elixir that would keep her body from transforming while she was unconscious, as sometimes happened when her brain went into fight-or-flight mode. She once told him that it happened to her a lot when she'd had nightmares growing up.

Nightmares.

Oh, the irony.

Adrian's gut sank. He hadn't had time to stop and see how bad her burns were during the fight, and now he was struck with the full weight of guilt from what he'd done.

Oscar and Ruby were there, too, sitting on a bench in the corner. Ruby's head was resting on Oscar's shoulder, and for a moment Adrian thought she might be asleep, but then her eyes peeled dazedly open. She spotted Adrian and sat up. The briefest flash of disappointment crossed Oscar's face, but it was gone so fast Adrian thought he might have imagined it.

"Oh, *now* he shows up," said Oscar, standing. "Dude, where were you?"

"I'm sorry," said Adrian, feeling the apology down to his core.

"I got your message about Nightmare and I was making my way to you guys when the Puppeteer showed up and I was stuck trying to get this group of kids to safety. There must have been a hundred of them there on a field trip. It was chaos." He lightly scratched his wounded shoulder through his shirt, surprised by how easily the lie had come. "But I still should have been there with you. I'm so sorry. Is Danna . . . ?"

Oscar blew out a frustrated sigh. "She got burned really bad in the fight."

On the bed, Danna inhaled a shuddering breath. A machine on the wall beeped faster for a second, then fell again into a steady rhythm. Adrian walked closer, forcing himself to lift one of the cold compresses that had been draped over her burn wounds. Forcing himself to take in the damage he had done.

How much pain had she been in? Or had her body immediately gone into shock? Setting the compress back over her burns, he rubbed the flame tattoo through his sleeve. Though it had been healed for weeks now, he imagined for a moment that he could feel it, like the flame was alive, like it was burning his skin.

He turned back to Oscar and Ruby. "Have the healers been to see her yet?"

Oscar nodded. "Yeah. They say she's going to be okay, but it'll take some time. It's really bad."

"Danna is our eyes when we're on patrol," said Adrian, scratching the back of his neck. "We'll be at a huge disadvantage without her."

"The really weird thing," said Ruby, "is that wasn't even Nightmare's doing. That"—she pointed at Danna, then drew quotes in the air—"was 'the Sentinel.'"

Adrian flinched at the venom in her tone. The small part of him that wanted to tell his team that he was, in fact, on the roof with them that day, quickly evaporated. "Who?"

"Some guy who showed up mid-combat," said Oscar. "Faced off against Nightmare. He had an *R* on his suit, but . . ." He shrugged. "None of us have ever seen him before."

Adrian kept his brow tight with confusion. "The Sentinel?"

"That's what Monarch said, before they put her under. He was a fire elemental, I think." Oscar frowned. "But it definitely wasn't Wildfire."

Wildfire was the only fire elemental they currently had on the Renegades, at least in the Gatlon City branch. Adrian had gotten most of his ideas for how to handle fire manipulation from watching him in the training halls.

Ruby yawned. "I don't think it was that Islander prodigy, either. The one who trained here last year. Magma, was it? This Sentinel guy was fully covered, head to toe. Someone caught a photo of him from street level so they're starting to circulate it, to see if anyone knows anything."

"He also had superior jumping," said Oscar, "and this suit, like something straight out of a comic book. Honestly, I think he might be from research and development—like maybe some sort of new super-soldier they've been working on down there, and it's too classified for them to admit it yet."

Ruby gasped and leaned forward excitedly, like she'd just uncovered a clue. "Or he could be a villain, masquerading as a Renegade. Maybe he's trying to hurt our reputation. Maybe it's all part of some complicated scheme that will lead to our ultimate downfall!"

Adrian and Oscar stared at her.

Ruby shrugged. "Maybe?"

"Maybe," Oscar agreed.

Collapsing back onto the bench, Ruby threw an arm over her eyes, as if this outburst had sapped her last bits of energy. The bloodstone on her wrist reflected the room's light, turning her cheek a rosy red. "That's my theory and I'm sticking to it."

"But he was fighting Nightmare at first," said Oscar, "before he attacked Monarch. Or maybe that was a mistake. Who knows?"

"Was anyone else hurt?" asked Adrian.

"Nope," said Ruby, with a hint of defensiveness. "We're grand. Positively stellar."

"Nightmare got to her," explained Oscar. "Put her to sleep." He reached down and pet Ruby on the head. It was one of the most awkward gestures Adrian could recall him ever making, and Oscar could be a pretty awkward guy at times.

"Tattletale," Ruby grumbled, swatting him away. "In case anyone's wondering, I currently feel like someone's filled my head with concrete."

Adrian bit back the impulse to say he knew exactly how she felt. "That makes the fourth time this year a Renegade team has come in contact with Nightmare. She can't be working alone."

"She escaped on the Puppeteer's balloon," said Oscar. "Could be a new Anarchist."

"But," said Ruby, thrusting a finger into the air, "she threw the Puppeteer overboard. That's not exactly a friendly greeting."

"That's their thing though, isn't it?" said Adrian. "Even when they're supposed to be working together, they still believe in trampling the weak to make way for the strong."

Oscar shrugged. "Makes no sense to me, but then, they are villains. Who knows how they think?"

"On the bright side," Ruby said, opening her eyes and flashing a mischievous grin, "I got Nightmare's gun."

Adrian lifted an eyebrow.

"They took it upstairs to have it inspected," said Oscar. "She fired off one dart at the Captain, came this close to hitting him in the eye." He pinched his fingers together. "That dart is being looked at too. Maybe they'll be able to trace it back to wherever she got it from."

Adrian looked away. He didn't know how much information they could garner from the gun or the dart she'd used, but it was something. It was a start.

That morning, he had cared only about proving his abilities as the Sentinel. He had been excited to show them all what he could do. He had fantasized about taking off the Sentinel's helmet and revealing himself to his team and the rest of the Renegades.

But he hardly cared about any of that anymore. One sentence from Nightmare had changed everything.

He had to find out who she was. He had to find out what she knew.

He had to find her.

CHAPTER FIVE

---◼️◼️◼️◼️◼️---

DRIAN WAS BECOMING ANXIOUS, though he wasn't sure why. Thunderbird had been brought to headquarters hours ago to be treated for her injuries, but the rest of the Council still wasn't back. He would have known by now if they were hurt, so that wasn't it. Maybe he was curious if they'd heard about the Sentinel. What they thought. If they were able to see right through him.

He spent some time making his way around the medical wing, checking on others who had been hurt in the fight against the Puppeteer, before heading upstairs to visit Max, who was probably feeling cut off from all the activity, like usual.

Max's quarantine was built into a sky bridge that extended over the main floor of the lobby. It was quite possibly the fanciest room in the place—practically a luxury suite—with floor-to-ceiling windows that offered a breathtaking view of the river, and private quarters tucked out of sight with a master bedroom and bathroom complete with a soaking tub, though Adrian had the feeling Max didn't use it all that often. Max didn't seem to spend much time back there at all. He was always out in the main space of his enclosure. Always working on the glass city he'd been painstakingly constructing over the last four years.

When Adrian approached the quarantine, he spotted Max sitting cross-legged inside his model of City Park—one of the few spots of empty floor he could comfortably sit down on anymore. His eyes were glued to the screens outside his enclosure, watching the footage from the parade. His fingers were toying with one of the little glass figurines Adrian had made years ago—a horse-drawn carriage like those that took tourists through the park.

It had started as a game. Max was still a toddler when the quarantine was built for him, and Adrian was determined to try to make him feel as comfortable as possible. He'd seen how much Max loved building with a set of interlocking blocks the Captain brought for him, so he started making blocks himself, using his marker to draw new designs onto the glass and pushing them through to Max's side.

As he got older, Max started making requests. He wanted blocks that mimicked tall spires and domed ceilings, or cables he could use to construct a bridge. Before Adrian realized what the kid was trying to accomplish, he saw the familiar skyline evolving before his eyes.

Max was ten years old now and the miniature city was mostly complete. It was a marvel, taking up the entire floor of the circular room. A nearly exact replica of Gatlon, created entirely of shimmering clear glass. But just like the real city, it was always changing. Being torn down, rebuilt, edited, and refined as the kid worked to make it authentic to the real Gatlon, a city he could only imagine being a part of.

Max caught sight of Adrian approaching and held up a pad of

paper for Adrian to see. He had done his best to draw the Council's parade float.

"Can you make that?" Max said, his voice muffled by the glass.

"What, no 'hello'? No 'glad to see you weren't killed by a psychotic villain today'?"

Max lowered the sketchpad. "Reports have been circulating all afternoon, with most of the focus on Thunderbird, though I know Monarch and a few others also sustained injuries. The news is also providing updated reports on civilian casualties every few minutes." He paused, before adding, for clarity's sake, "Obviously, I would have known if you were hurt."

Adrian grunted and lowered himself to the floor. "In that case, yeah, sure, I can make that, but the cloud's not going to have actual lightning coming out of it. You'll just have to use your imagination. You want some street food vendors too?"

Max's eyes lit up. "Yeah. And the villain float. And the marching band?"

"What do I look like, a figurine factory?" He took out his marker and began to sketch the float, making it as detailed as he could recall from memory, though he'd been distracted when it had first come into view, caught up in trying to fix that girl's bracelet.

He paused, the float half finished.

With everything that had come after, he'd nearly forgotten about the girl and the way she'd looked at Adrian when he'd fixed the clasp: not like his handiwork was the most amazing thing she'd ever seen in her life, but like she was trying to figure out if this was a con artist's trick she needed to be wary of.

Maybe there were too many prodigies flooding into the city these days. The novelty of seeing someone with superpowers must be wearing off.

He finished drawing the float, adding wheels beneath it so Max could push it around the streets if he wanted to. "Here you go," he said, pressing his hand against the drawing and forcing his will into the glass.

The drawing emerged on Max's side of the window. A crystal-clear replica of the parade float, complete with rotating wheels.

The glass wall itself was left unchanged, the drawing wiped clean in the transition.

Max held his hand out, his face tensing in concentration. The miniature float began to tremble, then lifted and hovered in the air. It bobbed slowly but steadily through the city, along Raikes Avenue, around the corner onto Park Way, before clunking down beside him.

He exhaled and opened his eyes. "Thanks."

"I think you're getting stronger," said Adrian. "That was steadier than usual. I'm pretty sure."

"No, I'm not," said Max in a matter-of-fact tone that would have disguised his disappointment from just about anyone else.

"Well . . . some telekinesis is still better than none, right?" Adrian scratched his temple with the capped end of the marker. "Did you want figurines of the Council to go on top?"

Max shook his head. "I still have the ones you made last year." He glanced around. "Somewhere." His expression darkened as he turned back to Adrian. "Did someone really try to assassinate the Captain?"

Adrian hesitated, but there was no reason to keep Max from the truth. He was a smart kid, and too observant for his own good. He watched the news more than he ever watched movies or cartoons, and even being stuck in this glass prison, he always seemed to know more about what was happening in the world than Adrian did.

"Yeah," he said. "A villain who goes by Nightmare."

"You've fought her before."

"Not me. Oscar and the others had a run-in with her a few months back, and some of the other teams have seen her before too."

"Why would she want to hurt the Council?"

Adrian started doodling marching band characters onto the glass. A drummer and a tuba player. A whole line of trombones. "Some people liked the way things were before the Renegades took over."

"Back when everyone was always stealing things and stabbing each other?"

"I don't get it, either. But I guess the people in power back then would have been living pretty good, right?" His brow knit together as he tried to picture the intricate coils on a French horn. Giving up, he gave the musician a trumpet instead.

"Do you think this new guy wants that too? To give the city back to the villains?"

"New guy?"

Max pointed at the screens. Adrian followed the look and a chill swept down his spine. The news was showing a photo of the Sentinel. It was a grainy image of him lobbing himself between rooftops, taken from the ground a hundred feet below. Captured in that moment it almost looked as though he could fly.

Though the picture quality was terrible, it was the first time he'd seen himself in the suit, and it was both eerie and comforting.

There was no way to tell it was him. There couldn't be. No one had to know that he was the one who had failed to catch Nightmare. He was the one who had hurt Monarch.

"I don't think . . ." Adrian hesitated. "We don't know that he's a villain. He might have been trying to help. He fought Nightmare, and they say he wears an *R* on his chest."

"But he's not one of us, is he?"

Adrian started pushing the marching band through to Max, one musician at a time. "I don't know. Oscar thinks maybe he's some secret weapon they've been developing upstairs."

A commotion on the main floor drew Adrian's attention to the bright entryway. The Council had finally returned, dragging the Puppeteer between them, wrapped in chromium chains. The Captain pushed the villain off to one of the waiting teams, giving orders for him to be taken up to the prison block. Tsunami went with them, holding a wall of water at the ready, should Winston Pratt try anything. He seemed to be in too much giddy awe being inside Renegade Headquarters to formulate an attack, though.

Blacklight slapped both the Captain and the Dread Warden on their backs, and even from up here Adrian could hear his boisterous voice saying something about Thunderbird as he, too, made his way toward the elevators.

Adrian stood. Captain Chromium glanced up toward him and his face softened, perhaps with relief, though there hadn't been much reason for him to be concerned. As far as he knew, as far as *anyone* knew, Adrian had been down in the crowd watching the parade the whole time, and he could hold his own against a handful of brainwashed kids.

Still, he couldn't help but smile back as he lifted one hand in a welcome-back salute.

He turned and knocked twice on Max's window. Max waved good-bye without looking up, already organizing the band in front of the parade float.

Adrian made his way to the ground floor. The Captain weaved through the crowd that had gathered around him, everyone shouting questions about the attempted assassination, the Puppeteer, Nightmare, the Sentinel, but they all went ignored. The Captain met Adrian at the bottom of the steps and wrapped him in a quick hug, before pulling away and gripping Adrian's shoulders. Adrian grimaced as he felt his stitches pull against the wound, but did his best to cover it with a smile.

"We weren't sure if you were at the parade when it started," said Captain Chromium.

The Dread Warden appeared beside them and gave Adrian a sideways embrace. "We're glad you made it back safely."

To the world, they were Hugh Everhart and Simon Westwood. Superheroes. Councilmen. Founding members of the Renegades.

But to Adrian, they were mostly just his dads.

He rolled his eyes toward the ceiling. "Knock it off. You guys are embarrassing me."

"Not for the last time, I'm sure," said Simon. "Were you involved in the fight?"

Adrian shook his head. "I was a few blocks away when it started. Spent most of my time playing traffic controller to a few busloads of children."

"It's a tough job," said Hugh, "but someone has to do it."

"Has an investigation started yet?" asked Adrian. "The Puppeteer wasn't acting alone. More Anarchists might have been there too—and Nightmare was on the rooftops." He frowned at Hugh. "She was after *you*."

"I'm fine," said Hugh, scratching his temple. Adrian knew that's where the dart had struck him, but there wasn't even a mark.

"I can see that," he said, "but still, she tried to assassinate you today—and she almost succeeded. *And* she took down Thunderbird. This girl . . . she keeps cropping up, and I really don't think she's working alone."

"Neither do we," said Simon. "We're looking into it, but so far there's no solid evidence that Nightmare is with the Anarchists or any other gang affiliation, new or old. She could have just gotten lucky to be able to use Winston's balloon for a convenient getaway. And without evidence—"

Adrian muttered dully, "—it's against the code to go after them."

"If we don't mind the rules, then we'll be just like them," said Hugh.

Adrian didn't respond. Back when the Renegades had first formed, they didn't have to play by any rules—there were no rules to play by. They were more like vigilantes than law enforcers, and they certainly weren't law*makers*. They did what needed to be done in order to make the world a better, safer place. Even if that meant blackmailing someone for information, or infiltrating a hideout because they thought there was something suspicious going on— with or without hard evidence.

There were days when Adrian thought things were better that way. When superheroes were left to be superheroes, not leaders.

Maybe that's why the idea of the Sentinel appealed to him. There was a freedom in anonymity. There was power in not having to answer to anyone.

Except, as today had shown, that didn't mean there weren't consequences.

"Try not to worry so much," said Simon, and Adrian realized he'd been scowling. "We had Nightmare's weapon sent over earlier for examination. We'll see if it turns up anything useful."

"She's just a newbie villain, trying to earn herself some credibility," added Hugh. "We've handled a lot worse."

Adrian couldn't argue with that. They'd taken down Ace

73

Anarchy himself, among countless others. Still, something told him that Nightmare wasn't to be ignored. As far as he knew, that one dart had come closer to killing Captain Chromium than anything had before.

Simon looked up at the wall of screens, flashing between images of the Puppeteer, Nightmare waving from the basket of the hot-air balloon, and, every once in a while, the Sentinel.

Hugh followed Simon's gaze, frowning at the image of the armored prodigy. "Speaking of investigations, what do we know about him?"

Though they were surrounded by reporters, assistants, and patrol teams, no one answered.

Adrian scratched his chest, where the zipper tattoo was hidden, where the Sentinel was tucked safely away. "My team saw him when they were facing off against Nightmare. The Sentinel was after her too."

Hugh glanced at him. "Did they see him use any abilities?"

"I . . . think so. Yeah." He swallowed. "Oscar thought maybe he's a product out of research and development?"

"Would be news to me," Simon muttered. "I'll talk to Oscar and Ruby, see what we can figure out." A sudden clarity entered his eyes. "I heard about Danna. Is she all right?"

Adrian stiffened. He could still feel the warmth of his own fire. Could still see those butterflies blackening and disintegrating before his eyes. "The healers say she will be."

Simon squeezed Adrian's shoulder, and he knew it was meant to be fatherly and comforting, but something about it made him feel worse. Not only about Danna, but also because he had already decided he couldn't tell them that *he* was the Sentinel. Not yet.

Hugh turned away, facing the crowd. "Listen up," he said, in that deep, heroic voice that could have made an earthworm stand at attention. "If anyone knows anything about this prodigy who calls himself the Sentinel, bring that information to the Council. As far as we know, he isn't one of us . . ." He paused, his steely-blue eyes cutting across the room, just in case anyone wanted to step forward and confess right then that, *by golly, it was me all along!* Avoiding his father's gaze, Adrian glanced up at Max, who was watching them from the quarantine.

Hugh continued. "But he is using our symbol and our name. I want to know his motives. If he's an enemy, I want to know who he's working with. If he's an ally . . . I want to know why he's not working with *us*."

He turned to Adrian and flashed his signature Captain Chromium smile, the one that, even after all these years, still made Adrian feel like he was looking at a picture on a cereal box. "Who knows? Maybe he'll be at the trials."

"Mr. Everhart, Mr. Westwood." A woman in a white lab coat and sneakers made her way across the lobby, carrying a clipboard. "May I have a moment? We've finished our preliminary tests on the chemical solution that was inside that projectile dart."

Hugh and Simon joined her and started heading back in the direction she'd come from. Adrian followed, pretending he'd been invited, as the rest of the crowd dispersed.

"We don't have a run yet on the physical casing of the projectile," said the woman, flipping a page on her clipboard. "But the solution was nearly identical to poisons that have been traced to Cyanide in the past."

"Cyanide," said Hugh. "Leroy Flinn?"

The woman nodded.

"An Anarchist," said Adrian.

They paused and turned back, and all three seemed surprised that he was still there.

Sighing, Hugh turned back to the technician. "Nothing on the gun yet?"

She started to shake her head, but hesitated. "This isn't confirmed, but it carried manufacturing marks similar to some we've apprehended from nonaffiliated criminals. Black market, if I had to guess."

"Could be a new dealer in the city," said Hugh, stroking his chin.

"Or an old dealer," added Simon, "getting back into the business."

"Who cares where the gun came from?" said Adrian. "Cyanide made the poison and we know he's an Anarchist. Between him and the Puppeteer, that's got to be who Nightmare is working for. Or . . . with."

Simon shoved the edges of his cape back from his shoulders. "The Anarchists have been inactive for nine years. More likely the girl's just some prodigy miscreant trying to make a name for herself on the streets."

"You don't know that," said Adrian. "And what does it matter? They attacked us today—the Puppeteer and Nightmare both. That has to be enough cause to go after the Anarchists, even under the code authority."

"It isn't enough to confirm that Nightmare really is one of them." Hugh smiled then, and there was something so warm and kind about it that Adrian bristled, like his dad was trying to comfort him after a rough day at softball practice. "But maybe you're right. We'll send someone to investigate the Anarchists. Ask a few questions, see what they can find out."

Adrian's left eyelid began to twitch. "Why not send me? *Us?* Oscar and Ruby were on the ground today—they know more about

Nightmare than anyone at this point. Let my team go."

"Your team is excellent at patrol work," said Simon, "but you're not investigators. We'll find someone with more experience to handle it."

Adrian massaged his brow. "I don't think . . . I just wonder if another team is going to take this as seriously as they should. Nightmare showed herself to be a real threat today, and if the Anarchists were involved, then we have to stop thinking of them as harmless tunnel rats. Even without Ace, they're still villains. We can't be sure what they're capable of."

Hugh laughed. "You forget who you're talking to, Sketch," he said, using Adrian's Renegade name, and Adrian couldn't tell if it was endearing or insulting. "Let the Anarchists try to reclaim power of the city. They would never stand a chance—with or without this *Nightmare*. We are still superheroes, you know."

They turned and followed the woman into the elevator bank, and already Adrian could hear them moving on to other topics of Council business—how they would reassure the people after today's attacks, and what to do about Winston Pratt, and how best to track down this alleged black-market weapons distributor.

Adrian watched them go, his arms crossed tightly over his chest. He couldn't help but feel that Hugh Everhart was mistaken. They weren't superheroes anymore—not in the way they used to be. It wasn't because they were getting older or because they hadn't been out on the field so much since they'd assembled the Council and left most of the crime fighting to the younger recruits. It was because they had rules now. Rules that they themselves had created, but that kept their hands tied nonetheless.

The solution seemed so simple to him, so obvious. They knew where the Anarchists lived. Renegade teams raided their stronghold every few months to make sure they weren't harboring illegal weaponry or building bombs or concocting fatal poisons exactly like the one found in that dart. All they had to do was go there and demand that Nightmare be handed over.

Instead they were going to send in some team who would . . . do what? Ask a few inane questions, then politely apologize for taking up their time?

The Puppeteer and Cyanide were both Anarchists who had been loyal to Ace from the start. The odds that Winston Pratt had been working alone today struck Adrian as unlikely, and the idea that Nightmare's usage of his balloon and the fact that her dart had Cyanide's poison in it might be coincidences seemed naïve.

If the Anarchists were growing active again, recruiting new members, plotting against the Council, this might be their best opportunity to stop them, before they were allowed to get out of control.

Because they could not get out of control. Not again. Nine years had passed, yet the world still bore too many scars from the rule of Ace Anarchy.

Adrian wasn't sure they would be able to recover a second time.

CHAPTER SIX

———■■■■■———

THE BALLOON HAD CRASHED into an apartment building just south of Bracken Way. Nova jumped from the basket before it hit the pavement and disappeared into the shadows of a connecting street. Knowing the Renegades would be tracking the balloon and searching for her, she forced her legs to carry her almost two miles through back alleys and empty courtyards before she finally collapsed behind a laundromat and a restaurant that advertised both teriyaki and cheeseburgers. She lay on the concrete, staring up through the grates of the fire escape, through the clotheslines strung with underpants and towels, at the faintest glimpse of sky between the brick facades. Grit dug into her back and every muscle ached, but it felt good to remove the hood and face mask. To breathe in the air, even if it smelled of old grease and garlic and, occasionally, a whiff of wet dog.

Only when a real wet dog came sniffing around her head did she shove its nose away, peel herself off the pavement, and start to make her way back home.

Back to the shadows and squalor of everyday life.

She walked for more than an hour before she made it to one of the defunct subway entrances that connected to the network of tunnels the Anarchists had seized after the Renegades' victory had sent them into hiding. For the last eight years the Council had been saying they were going to get the subway system up and running again, but as far as Nova could tell, there'd been exactly zero progress made. She had serious doubts it would happen anytime soon.

She squeezed past the plywood board and slipped inside.

Darkness engulfed her as she made her way down the stairs. Only when she reached the first landing and turned to face the second did she take the small flashlight from her belt and flick it on. The light danced over familiar scrawls of graffiti and signs advertising books long out of print and stage shows that hadn't toured in Gatlon in more than thirty years.

The subway system had fallen with the government, back at the start of Ace's revolution, and the tunnels had become a refuge for those seeking solace from the upheaval above. They offered shelter and anonymity, at least, and that wasn't nothing. Now the abandoned tunnels belonged to the Anarchists, at least this corner of the labyrinth, with its broken-down train cars, trash-littered tracks, and a darkness that seemed to permeate the very walls.

They weren't exactly in hiding—the Renegades knew where to find them. But years ago, after the Battle for Gatlon, Leroy had offered a truce to the Council. That's what he called it. A *truce*. Though Ingrid said it had been little better than groveling. Still, the Council had accepted his terms. The few surviving Anarchists would be permitted this tiny bit of autonomy, this pathetic little life underground, so long as they never again used their abilities against the Renegades or the people.

Nova wasn't sure what had possessed the Council to accept the offer, when they could easily have rounded them up and put them in prison that day. Maybe whatever sense of righteousness driving them had faded as soon as they watched Captain Chromium emerge from the ruins of the cathedral with Ace Anarchy's helmet on his pike. Maybe they pitied the Anarchists who had lost everything so suddenly—the battle, their leader, their home.

Or perhaps they simply figured that, without Ace, the Anarchists were no longer a threat.

The Renegades still visited them on occasion—raiding the tunnels to ensure they weren't harboring illegal weaponry or "causing trouble," but otherwise, they were more or less left alone.

Nova wondered how long that would last now, after Winston's debacle at the parade. If it had just been her, the Renegades might never have traced the assault back to their group. She could have been working alone for all they knew. Of course, once Phobia and Ingrid had announced themselves, they would have given the Anarchists away, but by that point the Council would have been dead and it wouldn't have mattered.

But the Council wasn't dead, and while Nightmare's alliances might still be a mystery, the Puppeteer's involvement would lead the Renegades straight to them.

She shouldn't have gotten into that balloon. That choice was just one more piece of evidence linking them together.

If it hadn't been for that new guy . . . *the Sentinel* . . . things might have ended very differently.

Nova hit the bottom level of the subway station and made her way across the platform. Rats scuttered nearby as she jumped down to the tracks and headed into the tunnel. She sent the beam of her flashlight over the walls until she found the switch that she'd helped Ingrid install a few years ago. With a flick, a string of dim bulbs brightened and flickered along the ceiling, guiding her home.

Nova clicked off the flashlight and tossed it into her bag, which felt fifty pounds heavier than it had that morning. Her arms burned from exertion. Every muscle in her body was making itself known—each one sore and tired and voicing its complaints.

A few hundred feet down the tunnel, she found Ingrid on their central platform, loading crates of food and supplies into a rusty shopping cart.

Nova dropped the duffel bag on the rails. Ingrid spun around, eyes wide, but relaxed when she spotted Nova.

"You left me there," said Nova, fisting a hand on her hip.

Ingrid flurried a hand toward her and turned back to their shelves, grabbing packs of sardines and cans of chili. "Help me load these up, will you?"

"Like you helped me?"

Groaning, Ingrid turned back and fixed a scowl on Nova. She was still wearing her Detonator uniform—tall boots, slim khaki pants, a blue cropped top, and those metallic blue armbands that spiraled across her dark brown skin, from shoulders to wrists. The only difference from her usual tough villainess look was that she'd tied back her coiled black hair beneath a rhinestone headband, no doubt stolen from Honey.

"Time to build a bridge and get over it, Nightmare," said Ingrid. "You knew the risks of this mission, you knew there'd be no rescue attempts if things went haywire. But, look . . . you're fine, I'm fine, Phobia's"—she gave an exaggerated eye roll—"I don't know, hosting a séance or something, the creepy deadbeat, but whatever, he's fine, too. We're all fine."

"Winston's not fine."

"Winston deserves what he got. To stage an attack like that, right in the middle of downtown! He almost got us all killed. He's the one you should be mad at right now."

Nova's lip curled. She was mad at Winston, too, but it was overshadowed by her guilt, knowing he was caught in part because of her.

"And now we have more pressing things to deal with than that cretin," said Ingrid, "so stop sulking and take this cart down to the storeroom under the yellow line." She started throwing goods into the cart again.

Nova hopped up onto the platform and tossed the duffel bag on top of the goods. "You think there will be a raid tonight?"

"Bet on it. The Renegades will be looking for trouble." She set a few boxes of instant rice on the bottom rack of the cart. "There. They could light up the tunnels, but at least we won't starve."

A faint wailing reverberated off the walls. Nova turned her head. "Honey?"

Ingrid huffed. "Been like that since we got back. Not sure what she's got to be so upset about. Maybe a drone died. I don't know. Ignore her. Here, I'll help you lower the cart down to the tracks." She nudged the cart toward the edge of the platform, its tired, uneven wheels squealing in their ears. "I swear, there are days when I wonder what I'm still doing here with you has-beens. Honey's a lost cause. Leroy's killed off one too many brain cells with all those chemicals he's always sniffing at. And Phobia—he gets weirder by the day, have you noticed that?" She hopped down onto the tracks and held up the front of the cart as Nova eased it toward her.

"Maybe," said Nova, once the cart was secured below, "you stay here for me."

Ingrid guffawed. "Oh, sweetie. You took a shot at the Captain himself today." She clicked her tongue but, for the first time since Nova had come across her on the platform, her eyes did take on a hint of warmth. "You might just be the craziest of us all."

"It was your idea."

"Exactly."

By the time Nova had dropped off the cart of supplies in the storehouse beneath the yellow line, which was overrun with cockroaches and usually went ignored during the Renegades' visits, her arms were vibrating from pushing the cart's wheels over the bumpy tracks. She was glad to finally make it to her own abandoned train car and drop off the duffel bag.

She took a moment to prepare a cup of tea with a small electric kettle. It was one of the rituals that regulated her days. Though the tea never put her to sleep or even seemed to do much to calm her mind, like it was supposed to, it still signaled to her body that the day was over and nighttime was about to begin. It gave her a suggestion of normalcy—something as simple and comforting as a bedtime routine, even if she skipped over the going-to-bed part.

With the mug in one hand, she headed back into the tunnels.

Honey's wails grew louder as Nova approached her utility room, the crying offset only by the buzzing of her hives.

"Honey?" Nova said, nudging open the heavy steel door with her shoulder.

Honey Harper, the infamous Queen Bee, was in one of her moods. She had dolled herself up like she did when things got really bad, with thick, sparkling black eyeliner and blonde curls teased into a gravity-defying bob. She was in a slinky dress that cascaded over her generous curves as she stood in front of a full-length mirror, alternating between admiring herself appreciatively and sobbing into her hands.

She would have been a picture-perfect reflection of a long-ago movie starlet, all dramatic and flashy, bordering on the ridiculous . . . except for the bees.

Besides the room's sparse furniture—a messy bed, vanity, antique wardrobe—every spare inch of space was taken up with hives and nests and the little creatures whose cumulative buzzing could be louder than a chainsaw. Sweet, chubby bumblebees and efficient, hardworking honeybees and hornets and wasps and yellow jackets, some as big as Nova's thumb. Though they came and went from the tunnels, there were always thousands of them in here, working, building, producing. A few dozen were crawling along Honey's dress and skin, and Nova could see that two had gotten caught in the sticky, hair-sprayed strands of her hair.

Nova had once pointed out to Honey that, scientifically speaking, hornets and wasps weren't bees at all, and how was it that she could have dominion over them if her power was supposed to be all about bees. But Honey had just smiled and pet her cheek, murmuring, "It's good to be queen."

Nova had been only a child then—that was before they'd been run down into the tunnels.

When the Renegades had defeated them, Honey had taken it the hardest, feeling that it was a personal assault to force her and her precious subjects into these dark, sunless caves. She truly had lived like a queen in those days, and often pretended she still did. Nova was fairly certain her adamant denial of their new reality had turned her delusional.

"Honey?" she asked again, louder now, to be heard over the buzzing.

Honey spun toward her, cheeks flushing. "What?" she snapped.

Her eye makeup was running, leaving dark tracks along her cheeks, but it didn't make her less beautiful so much as it made her look like a distraught mess that needed fixing. The sort of woman that a lot of guys probably would attempt to fix if it wasn't for the black wasp wandering over her cleavage.

Seeing Nova, she drew herself up to full height, so she could peer down her nose as she gathered herself. A phantom smile crossed her shiny lips. She never wore lipstick, only slathered them with honey—nature's best moisturizer, she reminded Nova again and again, not so subtly suggesting that maybe Nova could use some herself.

"Apologies, darling," Honey said with a sigh. She reached for a martini glass on her vanity, ignoring the bumblebee on the rim as she took a sip. "I didn't hear you come in."

"It's all right. Could I borrow—"

"I thought you were out. It's been quiet around here today. Where has everyone gone?"

Nova pressed both hands into the sides of the mug. It was cold in the tunnels, and the warmth coming through the clay felt good on her fingers. "The parade?"

One heavily penciled eyebrow shot upward. "Was that today? How did it go?"

Nova opened her mouth to tell Honey what a failure the mission had been. She hesitated, though, and instead told her, "They had an actress portraying you on the villain float."

Honey started. The bumblebee slipped into her drink and she reached in and plucked it out without looking, dropping the sodden creature onto the vanity.

"She was really pretty," Nova added. "I mean, not quite on par with"—she gestured at Honey's gown—"but still, she did a good job. Very classy. I don't even think she got hit with any fruit."

Honey looked down into her glass, her long, fake eyelashes brushing against her cheek, and for that moment she looked like a portrait. Sad and forlorn. A queen divided from her kingdom.

"Perhaps they haven't forgotten me, after all."

"Oh, come on," said Nova, bobbing the bag of tea in the mug. "How could they forget about you?"

A faint smile climbed up Honey's glistening lips, just as a yellow jacket made its way over them.

"On another note . . ." Nova held up the steaming mug. "Could I borrow some honey?"

Honey looked at her, eyes shining, and sighed.

The tea was already cooling when she left Honey's room and headed for the fork in the tunnels. Nova passed another abandoned platform, a mural of chipped and grungy tiles marking the stop for Blackmire Station, and again she paused, considering.

The platform was set with three children-size circus tents, each one barely big enough to stand up in. Their wide stripes done in once-vibrant primary colors had been dulled with years of dirt and grime. The tents were connected through flaps torn into the fabric and stitched together with shreds of old sleeping bags and bedsheets, forming a sort of miniature tent-palace. The most striking change, though, was that their pennant flags had been replaced with skewered doll heads, one to each tent, their dull black eyes watching anyone who dared approach.

Nova set down the cup of tea and hauled herself up onto the platform. She peeled back the front flap of the tent and spent a moment letting her eyes adjust to the dimness, and her wrinkled nose adjust to the stark odor of Winston Pratt, who had never been particularly adept at self-hygiene.

Holding her breath, she stepped over the scattered remains of broken windup toys and dried-out paint sets, making her way to the second tent, where a child's wooden kitchenette greeted her, overflowing with food both real and plastic.

She rummaged through the fake refrigerator and cabinets until she found a bag of kettle corn and a candy bar. She stuffed them both into her pockets.

Winston wouldn't be back for them anytime soon.

By the time she reached Leroy's train car, where a lantern was glinting in the window, the tea was lukewarm. Things never stayed hot for long in the damp tunnels.

Nova stepped up to the side door and knocked.

"Enter at your own risk," came the familiar greeting.

Nova pried open the glass door, which had long ago been painted black, and stepped into the car. Leroy, or Cyanide, as the world knew him, was at his worktable, measuring a spoonful of green powder and dumping it into a vial full of yellowish liquid. The concoction crackled and hissed inside the tube.

He looked up at Nova and smiled, pushing his goggles to the top of his head. "You look terrible."

"Just what I needed to hear, thanks." She threw herself into a brown recliner. Though the cushion had once been home to a family of mice and the fake leather upholstery was torn in multiple spots, it still remained one of the most comfortable seats on the entire westbound line. "What are you working on?"

"Just a little experiment," said Leroy. He was a pudgy man, with brown hair that was always matted to his forehead and a face that was a patchwork of scars and discolorations from a multitude of botched experiments over the years. He was missing three teeth and both eyebrows and always smelled of chemicals, but of all the

Anarchists, he had always been Nova's favorite.

"How was the parade?"

She shrugged. "We didn't kill the Council. Or any Renegades, for that matter."

"Shame."

"I think I might have broken one of Thunderbird's wings, though."

Leroy's eyes brightened, impressed, as he lifted the vial. The mixture inside had stopped bubbling. "Were you able to use the dart?"

Her frown deepened. "I tried. I missed."

He hummed, unconcerned. "Maybe next time."

Nova leaned back and the footrest jutted upward. "Winston showed up."

"Oh?"

"He wasn't supposed to."

"I didn't think so."

Nova stared up at the metal bars stretching down the length of the car. The aged yellow maps of the city. The ceiling that had started to crack on one side.

"He was captured by the Renegades." She took a sip of tea. "It might have been my fault."

Leroy didn't respond. Nova listened to the sounds of his work. Measuring, pouring, mixing.

She set her tea down on the floor, then reached an arm upward and folded it behind her head, trying to stretch out the muscles. "I probably could have saved us both, if I'd really tried."

Leroy stoppered one of the vials and wrote out a label for it. "If he'd been stronger than the Renegades, he wouldn't have fallen to them."

It was logical. Anarchist logic. Comfortable, blameless logic.

"Anyway," said Nova, switching to the other arm, "Ingrid thinks the Renegades will raid us tonight, in retaliation, or maybe to find out if any of us were involved."

"I trust you'll be well hidden when they arrive."

"Yeah, but . . . maybe you should put some of this stuff away?"

Leroy's lips quirked to one side, making half of his face go slack with disuse. "Believe it or not, everything I do here is perfectly legal."

Nova couldn't tell if he was joking. "Yeah, well . . . don't say I didn't warn you."

"Warning duly noted, with my heartfelt appreciation." He pulled an empty jar and a funnel from a nearby cabinet. "Were they advertising the trials at the parade?"

"Like it's a national holiday," Nova grumbled, then added mockingly, *Do you have what it takes to be a hero?* Ugh. Stab me with an egg beater."

She took the kettle corn from her pocket, the bag crinkling and squealing as she pried it open. She held it out toward Leroy, but he just shook his head.

"The world needs heroes," he said, lowering the goggles again to transfer the concoction into the bottle. They made his eyes look three times bigger.

"That's what they keep telling us." Nova popped a handful of popcorn into her mouth. "But we both know the world would be better off without heroes. Without villains. Without any of us, getting in the way of normal, happy people and their normal, happy lives."

Leroy's lips lifted in a subtle smile. "Have you ever considered trying out?"

She laughed. "What, to be a Renegade?"

"They don't know who you are, what you look like." He turned the flame of a burner to low and set a glass jar on top. "You would make a promising spy."

"Except there's no way I could pretend to respect those righteous, arrogant, pretentious . . . *heroes* long enough to learn anything useful."

Leroy shrugged. "You could, if you wanted to."

"Not to mention getting through their background check," she continued. "Not just anyone gets to join their clique, you know. You really think they'd let in a girl with the last name *Artino*?"

He waved a hand at her. "Minor obstacles. It's easy enough to get forged paperwork in this city. Are we villains or not?"

"You've given this some thought."

He glanced up. "Only since they started promoting the trials again. Ace always used to say that knowledge is power, and he was right. Unfortunately, these days the Renegades have all the knowledge *and* the power."

Nova picked up her near-empty mug and stood. "In that case, sending me to the trials would be a perfect plan. If only I had a death wish."

"Give yourself more credit, little nightmare," said Leroy. "I know I do."

Nova grunted. "I'll think about it," she said, shoving open the door. "And don't call me that."

Leroy only smiled.

CHAPTER SEVEN

———■-■-■-■-■———

ADRIAN TOSSED HIS FEET onto the coffee table, a bowl of cereal cradled in his lap. It was his standard fare when his dads worked late, which happened more often than not, and after the day they'd had, he didn't expect them home anytime soon.

Grabbing the remote, he turned on the late-night news. Shaky footage of the parade appeared on the TV screen—a video of the Puppeteer's harlequin balloon drifting through the streets of downtown Gatlon while crowds screamed and stampeded to try to get away. The voice from an off-screen reporter was quoting the statistics. The numbers had grown since he heard them that afternoon and now they were saying there were sixty-eight casualties, with fifty-one civilians still receiving treatment at Gatlon City Hospital and two Renegades, including Council member Tamaya Rae, being treated for injuries at Renegade Headquarters. Luckily, there were no fatalities. The perpetrator, Anarchist Winston Pratt, known to most as the Puppeteer, was in custody . . .

Adrian turned his gaze away from the footage and settled his hand on the sketchbook beside him. He opened the cover and used his thumb to flip through the pages until he found his most recent batch of drawings, those he'd doodled hastily as soon as he got home, while the idea was still fresh.

Crunching his way through a mouthful of cereal, he lifted the sketchbook to eye level, inspecting the drawings.

Concepts for a new tattoo.

He hadn't planned on giving himself any more, but then, he'd thought every tattoo would be the final one, and less than two months into this experiment he already had three inked into his skin.

But he'd learned a lot about his abilities up on those rooftops, facing off against Nightmare. Or, he'd learned a lot about the Sentinel's abilities.

There was potential there. Great potential—he knew it. The armor had worked precisely how he'd hoped it would, offering both flexibility and protection, even if Nightmare had managed to find a vulnerability in the suit.

And the springs on his feet had worked like a charm. The first time he'd launched himself from street level up to a ledge three stories high, he'd felt almost as if he'd taken flight.

But the fire . . . the fire was problematic.

It had seemed like a great idea when he'd done it. Had, in fact, been the first tattoo he'd given himself, before he'd even known for sure that it would work. Before he could be certain that the gift of his drawings could transfer into a permanent tattoo and imbue his body with a brand-new, entirely real superpower.

Everyone wanted fire manipulation. It was a classic, and it came with so many applications, from lighting birthday candles to torching an entire warehouse stocked with illegal narcotics.

Not that he'd ever stumbled across such a warehouse, but if he *did*, he liked knowing he could do something about it.

But fire was also unpredictable. It was a force of nature—wild and erratic.

What Adrian needed was something clean and orderly. Something that could be systematically aimed and fired, even by him, who was admittedly not the best shot in the Renegades. He needed something that would be a lot less likely to strike one of his own teammates.

His first thought had been some sort of gun appendage built into the armor, but then he'd remembered a girl who had come to be trained at headquarters a few years back—a prodigy who could shoot narrow beams of energy out of a node in the center of her forehead, hitting any target with percussive force. People had mostly referred to them as lasers, but that's not what they were. Adrian wasn't actually sure *what* they were, but he did know that they hit with enough force to stun an opponent and sometimes even knock them unconscious, without leaving any of the evidence a bullet might have left. No shell, no casing, no open wound.

It was perfect.

The trick was for him to figure out how to incorporate such an ability into the Sentinel's armor . . . and what sort of tattoo would convey such a power. He often found it ironic that he could make absolutely anything come to life when he drew it, if only he could first convince himself that it would make sense in reality. He had to be strategic. Practical.

Springs on the soles of his feet. A swirl of flame on his forearm. A zipper on his sternum that could be opened to release the armored suit.

And now, a laser diode, of sorts. A long, narrow cylinder, this time on his right forearm, that would emerge on the Sentinel's gauntlet, already charged and ready to fire . . .

He set down the sketchbook and crunched through another spoonful of cereal.

". . . and yes, the Puppeteer was caught in the end, but I just don't think it's acceptable that so many bystanders were harmed before he was stopped."

Adrian's eyes skipped back to the television, where two men and two women, all finely coiffed, were sitting around a table inside the news studio.

"Exactly!" said one of the men, leaning over the table and pointing an accusatory finger toward the woman who had spoken, even though he seemed to be in agreement with her. "It's not acceptable. This was a heavily attended public event. Where was the security? And why did it take the Council so long to respond to this threat? It's their job to protect us, but today they seemed more concerned with bad publicity than they did with stopping this madman."

"Now, in the Council's defense," said the second man, raising both hands in a calming gesture, "we do have witness reports telling us that within the first few minutes of the attack, Captain Chromium managed to rescue seven young children from the Puppeteer's control, while the rest of the Council and a number of off-duty Renegades ushered literally hundreds of civilians to safety inside nearby buildings and parking garages." He lifted a silencing hand as the other man tried to interrupt. "*And* this aligns with what the Council has been telling us from the day the Renegades became an official entity—that they will always focus on protecting innocent lives first, and engaging in an attack *second*. They followed their protocols today, and I have to admire them for it. It couldn't have been easy, especially when the Puppeteer was making himself such an obvious target."

Adrian lifted the bowl to his mouth, slurping at the pink-tinged milk.

"Yes," said one of the women, "but how many injuries could have been prevented if they'd just stopped him?"

The man shrugged. "And what if one of those civilians they took to safety had ended up dead? We'll never know."

"What we do know," said the first woman, "is that—casualties aside—Winston Pratt probably would not have been captured today at all if it wasn't for that would-be assassin tossing him out of his own balloon. Can we please talk about the elephant in the room here?" She spread her arms wide, her face contorted in disbelief. "Nightmare! Who is she? Where did she come from? We don't know the first thing about her, except she almost assassinated Captain Chromium today, she took down Thunderbird, and she eluded a Renegade patrol unit in a one-on-three fight. Isn't anyone concerned about this?"

"I am," said the man beside her. "But what concerns me even more than this solo attack—if it *was* a solo attack—is that, for all we know, this could be a sign that more prodigies are going to start coming out of the woodwork, bent on destruction and mayhem all over again. It shows that the Renegades may not have the city under control like they want us to think they do. That new, *villainous* prodigies are still going under the radar. And if that's the case, I'd like to hear from the Council about what they plan on doing about these threats."

"Hopefully," said the woman beside him, "they have a better plan going forward than they had today!"

Scowling, Adrian grabbed the remote and turned off the TV. He leaned back into the sofa cushions and took another bite of cereal. In the sudden silence, the crunching became absurdly loud, the demolition of small artificially flavored rice puffs filling the entire living room.

It was uncanny how much the news anchor's questions mirrored those that had been revolving through his head all day.

Nightmare. The great mystery. And they didn't even know the greatest mystery of all, those words that he could not quiet.

One cannot be brave who has no fear.

Swinging his feet down to the carpet, Adrian set the bowl on the coffee table and grabbed his sketchbook.

The wooden floorboards of the house creaked beneath him as he padded into the main foyer and up the oak staircase to the second floor. It was an old, stately home. Had, in fact, been the mayor's mansion, back when Gatlon City had a mayor. The mayor and his family and even some of the staff had been murdered in this very home in the early days of the Age of Anarchy. When he was younger, Adrian had been convinced their ghosts still haunted the upper floors, which was why he begged to be able to convert the basement into his bedroom. Though he no longer believed the spirits of the dead were still hanging around, he often felt a chill of apprehension when he went up to the second floor, where the master suite and a series of guest rooms branched off a central hallway. He rarely had cause to come up here, though. The basement, the kitchen, the living room—those were his domains.

But what he needed to see now was up here, in his dads' shared home office.

Reaching the landing, he flicked on the hallway light, illuminating the dark wooden doors, the intricate crown moldings, the faded oriental carpets that ran the length of the narrow corridor.

The house had been in terrible shape when his dads decided to move in. It had been a prime target for looters during the Age of

Anarchy, but Simon felt it had too much history to be allowed to succumb to eternal abandonment. It was a symbol of a different time—a peaceful, civilized time, when society had order and rules and leadership.

So they'd all moved in and had been restoring it ever since. Adrian could hardly remember how bad it had been back in those early days, when he'd been mortified at the thought of actually living there, with its piles of trash and cigarette butts, stripped wires left dangling from punctured holes in the walls, thick cobwebs and scrawled graffiti on every surface. But before long, his dads' dream became his, too, and by now he'd done almost as much to restore the place as they had. At least his skills lent themselves easily to the project. When a shutter was broken or a balustrade destroyed, it was easier for Adrian to simply draw them a new one rather than track down an artisan who could mimic the work. The result was that Adrian felt as much pride in the house as he could imagine any of them did, even if he still found himself avoiding the rooms where the murders had taken place.

With his sketchbook tucked beneath one arm, he placed his fingers against the door to the home office and nudged it open. The hinges creaked. The hall light cut through the thick shadows. Reaching into the room, Adrian pressed the top button of the vintage press-button light switch, one of the few that was still original to the home. The chandelier brightened, five small amber lampshades making the room glow in subtle shades of gold.

The desk at the room's center was a mess, the bookshelves behind it equally chaotic. Organizing the room never seemed to become a priority when there was a city to run, and any free time his dads did stumble into was almost always dedicated toward working on the house.

Adrian ignored the random stacks of paper, files and folders, mail and magazines and newspapers. He went straight to the bookshelf, where a series of dusty photo albums were sandwiched between an outdated geographical dictionary and a broken radio.

He settled his hand on the spine of an album covered in a maroon slipcover and pulled it from the shelf. The rest of the albums tipped inward, thudding against one another as Adrian sat down on the large area rug. Stacking the album on top of his sketchbook, he flipped past the first few pages. Though it had been years since he'd looked through this album, he still had most of the photos memorized.

A grainy image of his third birthday party, where he sat in the midst of a pile of boxes and shredded newspapers that had been used as wrapping paper, his mom and Kasumi grinning in the background.

A photo of him balanced on his mother's hip as she stood in front of a collection of bags and boxes overflowing with canned vegetables and boxes of dried pasta. The rest of the original Renegades were all there, too, except for Simon, who had probably taken the photo. Adrian recalled the story of that day, how they had successfully liberated all that food from a warehouse run by one of the villain gangs, who were selling it to hungry civilians at egregious prices.

His mother stopped appearing in the photos after that, and with just a few page turns later, Adrian himself went from a chubby-faced toddler to a skinny eight-year-old kid. His dads standing behind him, hands on his shoulders, grinning proudly. He looked happy that day, though it was hard to recall just how he had felt. It was the day they'd officially adopted him, more than a year after his mother's death. The wounds hadn't healed, but something about completing the paperwork had left him feeling like he was no longer floating away, untethered to any family, detached from any sense of belonging. At the time, it had felt immeasurably important.

In hindsight, Adrian recognized that there really weren't any *official* adoptions. Evander Wade was the one who drafted up the adoption certificate, as there was no legislation in place for that sort of thing. His dads were making up the laws as they went. But maybe they sensed Adrian's anxiety over not having a family to call his own, even if they had taken him in from the start. Maybe they'd known what a few signatures and an official-looking stamp would mean to him.

Adrian flipped past the photos from the adoption celebration, past even that official-looking certificate tucked between pages. A couple more birthdays, a few holiday celebrations, though photographic records became a lesser priority as Adrian aged, and there was virtually nothing from his teen years, which was fine by him. He wasn't really looking for a stroll down memory lane, anyway.

Finally, he found what he was looking for. A shred of newsprint folded up tight and tucked into a plastic page protector near the back of the album. He worked the page out from the sheet. The paper had the faintest hint of yellow to it, which struck him as peculiar. Certainly it hadn't been that long ago—long enough for age to take a toll on the scraps that had been saved. There were days when it felt like it had just happened.

Though, there were also days when it felt an entire lifetime ago.

Adrian nudged up his glasses and unfolded the square of paper, cut from the *Gatlon Gazette*—the only local newspaper that had continued to operate throughout the Age of Anarchy, though there had been years in which journalists were pressured by the gangs to report on some activities in a not-entirely-honest manner.

Nevertheless, *this* article Adrian had every reason to believe was full of truth.

A black-and-white photo showed a picture of her in all her superhero glory—her white-booted feet hovering over the ground, her golden cape whipping in the air, her familiar bright smile as she gave the cameraman an A-OK sign. All in such drastic contrast to the headline at the top, printed in harsh block letters.

LADY INDOMITABLE FOUND DEAD, KILLER UNKNOWN

Adrian had not expected the words to affect him so strongly all these years later. He had read this article so many times, he didn't think it would still hurt to see it. He had come to terms with his mother's death. He had adjusted to life without her. He had accepted that whatever villain had murdered her had almost certainly been killed on the Day of Triumph, and he would have to be content with that small bit of justice, even if the mystery of her death was never solved.

But that had all been before Nightmare had taunted him with those words. That phrase that meant so much more to him than to anyone else. Had she known?

But . . . how could she have?

Adrian scanned the columns of the article until he found the paragraph he was looking for.

> An autopsy revealed broken bones and a fractured skull consistent with having fallen seven stories to the concrete alleyway, and the coroner has stated that this is without doubt the cause of death. Though no additional signs of foul play on the body or at the crime scene have been found, the death being a potential suicide was quickly ruled out due to one piece of evidence: a plain white note card tucked into Lady Indomitable's belt and printed with the

ambiguous phrase: "One cannot be brave who has no fear."

Adrian peeled his attention from the page and stared blankly at the back of the desk.

Someone had killed her. Almost certainly a villain, someone who had managed to circumvent her own superpower—because how does one fall seven stories to their death when they can *fly*?

He shut his eyes, and though it had been years since he'd had nightmares about his mother's body, his imagination supplied the vision all over again. Broken bones. Fractured skull. Though this article didn't mention it, he had heard rumors that when she'd been found, her eyes had been open, her face contorted in a silent scream.

A chill swept down his back.

One cannot be brave who has no fear . . .

What did it mean that Nightmare knew those words? She herself seemed far too young to have been involved with the murder, but was it possible the murderer was still alive? Did Nightmare know who it was? Was she in league with them?

But if she had really joined the Anarchists, then didn't it make sense that his mother's murderer might be one of *them*?

He shoved the album onto the floor and stood, rubbing the back of his head. His feet began to pace, his eyes unseeing as he padded back and forth across the office.

He knew the Council was sending someone to search the Anarchists' stronghold for any signs that they were working with Nightmare, or that more of their members were involved in the attack on the parade. Maybe to arrest Cyanide as an accomplice. A patrol unit would be investigating them tonight, maybe even at this very moment. An "experienced team."

But he was the only one who knew about this connection to a cold case. The ten-year-old murder of Lady Indomitable. An original Renegade. His *mother.*

If her killer was still alive, was still out there . . . then Adrian had to know. And as far as he could tell, the only person who might have that answer was Nightmare.

Swallowing, he brought his hand down to his sternum, where the zipper tattoo lived in secret beneath his T-shirt.

His feet stilled.

For Adrian Everhart to go against a direct order and investigate the Anarchists on his own would tempt far too many consequences— for him, and for his team. Sketch couldn't go by himself, and he wouldn't involve the others. Not until he had something more substantial than a single uttered phrase that no one else had been around to hear.

He knew it was dangerous, and maybe a little stupid. His first go-round as the Sentinel hadn't exactly gone as planned. But he'd already tried asking for permission once; he knew there was no point in trying again.

He would tell the Council everything. About the Sentinel and his newfound abilities. About Nightmare and what she had said. He would tell them soon.

He would tell them the truth, after he had some answers of his own.

CHAPTER EIGHT

THE ONE THING Nova liked most about the tunnels was that there was no night or day down here. Nighttime could be lonely on the surface, when all the storefronts were closed and even the most serious of night owls finally gave in to the lure of sleep as the clock edged its way toward morning. Nova didn't mind being alone, but she got bored sometimes, waiting for the world to wake up and return to its drab, miserable existence.

In the tunnels, the only reminder that Nova had eight more hours to spare than everyone else was whether or not she could hear Ingrid's snores coming from the defunct elevator shaft she called a bedroom. Everything about Ingrid was loud—her bombs, her personality, and evidently, even her dreams.

Nova collected the darts from the target and walked back down the tunnel, setting herself up for practice again. She'd been at it all night. Usually she liked to divide her nighttime hours between tinkering with her newest batch of weaponry and inventions, or practicing meditation and martial arts, or going through a series of exercises to build up her strength and stamina—any skills she might need in her next encounter with the Renegades.

But tonight, she couldn't shake the memory of the parade. Those moments when she'd been on the rooftop. When Captain Chromium had been in her sights.

She could have done it. She, Nightmare, Nova Jean Artino, could have been the one to take out the invincible Captain Chromium.

But she'd hesitated. It had taken her too long to pull the trigger, and she'd blown it.

Never again.

She returned to the line she'd chalked across the tracks and loaded a dart back into the chamber of the gun. Not the gun she'd had on the rooftop that day—Red Assassin snatched that one right out of her hands and she never had a chance to recover it—but another found in Ingrid's collection.

She lifted the gun into her arms. Peered down the sights. Lined up the first target.

She fired.

Again.

And again.

And again, until each of the darts had been unloaded.

She exhaled and went to collect them. Only when she'd gotten close enough to the targets could she evaluate how well she'd done.

Bull's-eyes across the board. A dozen darts stuck into the pupils of a dozen magazine clippings—each one a glossy photograph of the Captain's charming face.

She didn't even smile as she yanked the darts out. This was just target practice. She'd failed when it had actually mattered. When she could have made a difference.

All revolutions come with death. Some must die so that others might have life. It is a tragedy, but it is also a truth.

She could still remember Ace telling her this when she was younger, when she'd asked him why so many had to die so they might have freedom. At the time she couldn't fathom the hatred and violence that had been directed at prodigies in the centuries prior to the Age of Anarchy, but even then, even to her six-year-old mind, Ace's passion had been contagious.

So few people really understood what Ace had been trying to accomplish. He hadn't wanted the world to become what it did. Sure, there had been a lot of brutality and destruction when he first took over, but he was right—there always is during a revolution. Ultimately, he'd wanted a world in which prodigies were no longer oppressed and frightened, belittled and tormented. He'd wanted a world where they could all be free to live their own lives according to their own devices.

It was all the *other* power-hungry people, villains and non-prodigies alike, who had started to vie for control. Who had run amok in a world without rules.

Nova didn't want to go back to the Age of Anarchy. She didn't want innocent people to be slaughtered like her family had been. She just wanted the freedom that Ace had envisioned for her and those like her. She wanted the Renegades and the Council to leave her alone, to leave all the Anarchists alone.

Hell, she wanted the Council to leave all of society alone. Maybe they thought they were doing the right thing by being the end-all, be-all of the ruling elite, but society was barely getting by and they had too much pride to admit they weren't what the people needed.

What the people needed was to learn to take care of themselves, but that would never happen so long as superheroes were running things.

She was making her way back up the tracks when the ground shook beneath her. Nova stumbled, planting a hand on the wall to stabilize herself. Bits of dust and chunks of loose concrete tumbled down the sides of the tunnel in small rivulets. The tracks vibrated under her feet, and for a moment Nova had the uncanny and horrifying thought that a train was coming—and she had nowhere to go.

The trembling stopped. A few more shudders passed underfoot before the earth stilled and quieted again.

Nova glanced down the tunnel, wondering whether it had been an earthquake—one buried deep underground, perhaps even a hundred miles away. Nothing to be concerned with. Surely these ancient tunnels had withstood far worse.

But then the silence was again broken, this time by a crash. The acoustics of the tunnels made it impossible to guess how far away the sound had come from, but it filled Nova with one certainty.

The Renegades were back.

She grabbed the gun and loaded a dart into the chamber, stashing the others into a pouch at her belt. Though Leroy hadn't yet filled them with poison, she figured she could still find a way to make them useful.

She raced back in the direction of the platforms and tunnels where their train cars dwelled. As she neared the main platform, she forced herself to slow. She didn't have her hood or mask to disguise herself as Nightmare, and she knew it would be foolish to give up her identity to the Renegades now.

As she rounded a corner, the walls began to shake again, which was followed by another crash—louder and closer this time.

Nova reached the back end of Cyanide's train car and paused.

She could hear things scattering across the platform and dropping down onto the tracks. A moment later, a small can of baked beans came rolling toward her, striking the side of the tracks only a few steps away from Nova's feet.

"Come on out, Anarchists," trilled a chipper, feminine voice. "It's time for your performance review."

Nova darted behind Leroy's train car and crept to the other side. Peering around the edge, she spotted four figures on the central platform, where many of their rations and supplies were stored. Or had been stored—two of the massive industrial metal shelves had been thrown to the ground, leaving a mess of broken bottles, crushed boxes, and a thick stench of vinegar in the air.

She recognized the Renegade team immediately—one of the most high-profile teams in the city, with a reputation for having taken countless criminals into custody. Their leader, the girl who had spoken, was Frostbite. A few years older than Nova, she was athletic and pretty, with a bob of silver-white hair and silver-white skin that was so translucent Nova could see hints of her blue veins even in the tunnel's dim lighting.

Then there was Aftershock, a stocky man with a dark goatee who must have been the cause of the earthquakes. Beside him stood Stingray, a lanky, beady-eyed boy who moved with as much creepy, slithering grace as the animal he took his alias from, a sleek barbed tail trailing behind him. Last was the giant. Gargoyle, who seemed to be permanently hunched from always having to stoop to fit into places, and whose limbs could shift from human flesh to solid stone in an instant.

"Well," said Frostbite, planting her hands on her hips, "it looks like they're all too cowardly to come say hello." She nodded at Aftershock and Gargoyle. "Search the tunnels and see if you can't draw them out of hiding."

While the two Renegades lumbered down opposite tunnels—Aftershock passing an arm's distance from Nova's hiding spot—Stingray began picking through the scattered supplies.

"Pickled okra?" he said with a sneer, picking up a glass mason jar. "Sounds disgusting." Turning, he threw the jar at the wall, where a mosaic of small tiles spelled out the name of the street above. The glass shattered, spilling more vinegar and green vegetables across the platform.

Nova's grip tightened on the gun.

"And Fruity Rings?" said Frostbite, kicking a box of breakfast cereal that was already crushed on one corner. "I haven't eaten this junk since I was four. It's really better given to the rats." Stalking to the edge of the platform, she picked up the box, opened it, and dumped the chunks of colorful cereal onto the tracks.

That box had actually been Winston's—it was his favorite kind of cereal—so it would be no great loss to the rest of them. Still, the waste of it made Nova's jaw clench. Anyone who remembered the Age of Anarchy at all knew that wastefulness was an unforgivable crime, no matter which side of the battle they fell on.

On the opposite side of the train car, a door clunked open. Frostbite and Stingray spun toward the car. Nova ducked back into the shadows, listening to the sounds of Leroy's footsteps as he paced down the steps and onto the tracks. She caught a glimpse of Frostbite's disgusted look as she took in Leroy, with his scars and discolored skin.

As Leroy passed into Nova's line of vision, she saw that he was wearing his worn bathrobe over tattered sweatpants and slippers. His feet crunched through the pile of cereal as he made his way to the steps beside the platform.

"Oops," Frostbite said in a saccharine voice. "Did we wake you?"

"Oh no," said Leroy, coming to stand a dozen paces from the Renegades. "We were expecting you, after what happened today. It is nice to see you still living up to expectations. Although . . ." He sighed heavily and gestured toward the fallen shelves and the mess that took up a quarter of the platform. "I question the point of all this."

Frostbite's face turned swiftly from arrogant to enraged. She closed the distance to Leroy, a long shard of crystalline ice forming in her fist. "The point is to remind you freaks that anything you have, whether it's food or water or even this pathetic little hovel in these cockroach-infested tunnels, is because *we allow it*." She lifted the shard, tucking the point beneath Leroy's chin and forcing him to lift his face. "And if we decide you don't deserve such charity, then we can take it away."

"Charity?" said Leroy, his voice even despite the ice digging into his jaw. "The Renegades have given us nothing. Everything we have has been bought and paid for—or fairly scavenged, just like everyone else."

"Scavenged," said Stingray. Turning his head, he hacked up a glob of spit and sent it onto the platform. "We wouldn't all still be scavenging for goods if it weren't for your lot, now would we?"

Leroy lifted an eyebrow—or the muscle where an eyebrow would have been, but had been burned off ages ago. "If it wasn't for *our lot*, then the boy with the barbed tail almost certainly would have been slaughtered at birth, his remains stuffed into a jar of formaldehyde for further examination."

Stingray's face contorted with anger, but Leroy went on, "Your Council has had domain over this city for almost ten years. If they haven't managed to restore your economy, perhaps you should ask them what's taking so long, rather than wasting your time blaming us."

Frostbite dragged the ice shard to the side, leaving a thin cut beneath Cyanide's chin. He flinched, but only slightly.

"Maybe if the Council wasn't having to defend the people of this city from mindless attacks, they could focus on cleaning up the mess that villains like you made of this world."

"Maybe," said Leroy, "with so many prodigies brainwashed by their tutelage, they could stand to update their security measures."

The ground rumbled again and Aftershock appeared at the entrance to one of the tunnels, each step he took sending mild quakes into the earth. "Nothing down that way but a bunch of moldy books." Planting one hand on the ledge of the platform, he vaulted himself up to stand beside Stingray.

"You must not have looked very hard," came a dry voice. Aftershock spun to see a dark form emerging from the tunnel he'd just left—Phobia's pitch-black cloak forming as if made from the shadows themselves, the blade of his long scythe catching on the dim overhead lights. No loungewear for him, of course. Of their whole group, he was the only one Nova never saw outside of his uniform—the hooded cloak, the mask of shadows, the scythe that arced over his head. Also unlike Ingrid and Honey, Winston and Leroy, Phobia was the only member of the Anarchists whose given name remained a mystery. Sometimes Nova wondered if he had been born so terrifying from the start that his horrified parents had settled on *Phobia* even back then.

"They really are pathetically unobservant."

Nova glanced up, to where Ingrid was sitting on the narrow pedestrian bridge that crossed over the tracks to the opposite platform, her long legs dangling through the rails.

"I've been up here this whole time and not once did they think to look up. Honestly, it's amazing this city is functional at all with you people in charge."

Frostbite snarled. "Get her down."

Aftershock lifted one knee and stomped—hard. A fissure opened in the concrete, arcing toward the staircase. The ground split apart beneath the steps, a gap opening in the earth. The stairs slumped downward. The bridge tilted sharply. Ingrid leaped to her feet moments before the bolts holding the metal rails pulled free and the bridge careened to one side—half of it sinking into the chasm that Aftershock had made, the rest crashing down onto the tracks. Ingrid jumped clear of the bridge at the last moment, diving into a roll and coming to a crouch not far from Leroy's train car.

"That's better," Frostbite said breezily, one hip jutting to the side.

Sparks flashed in Nova's eyes. Taking a step back, she lifted the rifle, turning the barrel toward Aftershock. But no sooner had she found him in the sights than a figure moved between them.

She lowered the gun. Ingrid stood between her and the Renegade, her back to Nova. She reached back with one hand, sweeping her fingers in Nova's direction.

Nova glared, annoyed at being shooed away like a pestering child.

She would have been even more annoyed, though, if a part of her didn't know that Ingrid was right. It would be careless to give herself away, and what was she going to do with this gun and a handful of darts? Without any poison, an offensive attack would serve only as a minor annoyance.

"I recommend caution," said Phobia, his raspy voice as patient as ever. "These are old tunnels with old foundations. You wouldn't want us all to be buried alive, would you?" He spun his scythe overhead. "I wouldn't mind so much, but I doubt that was your intention when you came to interrupt our repose."

With Ingrid still blocking her view, Nova sank back between the wall and train car. She reached the metal rungs on the side of the car and, gripping the gun in one hand, scampered to the top. She stretched out on her stomach, inching forward until she could see the platform below.

"I think what Phobia's saying," said Ingrid, blue sparks flickering at her fingertips, "is that sometimes showing off can have negative effects."

Frostbite smirked. "I wouldn't know."

Screams of hysteria echoed up from the far tunnel. Nova planted one hand on the rooftop of the car, craning her head upward. At first Honey's wails were indistinct cries of panic, but as they grew nearer, they began to merge into desperate words.

"Put them back! *Put them back!* You don't know what you're doing!"

Moments later, Gargoyle lumbered out from the overhang of the tunnel, his arms cradling close to two dozen bee hives of various sizes and states of completion. The swarms of angry drones were buzzing all around him, creating a black writhing mass that engulfed his torso, but he had turned his entire body to stone and their vicious stings appeared to have no effect.

Honey came marching after him, dressed in a pale pink negligee, her hair rolled in curlers. "You have no idea the work that goes into those, you giant chunk of rubble!"

When Gargoyle continued to ignore her, she started to run and launched herself at him, grasping for his thick arm. She dangled from his elbow, her pale legs kicking vainly at his side.

Irritated, the Gargoyle gave one powerful shake of his arm, sending Honey skidding across the platform. She crashed into the pile of supplies, her shoulder smacking the toppled metal shelf. Though momentarily dazed, her eyes were vicious when she raised them again.

Gargoyle came to stand before Frostbite, who seemed to tense, her eyes darting warily around the cloud of wasps and hornets, some of which had bodies as long and thick as Nova's thumb, and venom that could burn like hot pokers.

Frostbite jutted a finger toward Honey. "Call them off," she demanded, her voice dulled by the buzzing all around her. "Send them away or this will be treated as a use of prodigious abilities against an active Renegade."

Honey pushed herself up to sitting. "I will as soon as he puts those back where he found them!"

"Puts them back?" Frostbite said, her tone laced with amusement. She turned to Gargoyle. "Where did you find them?"

"She's got a room a few hundred feet down that way," he said. "An old storeroom of sorts. Was brimming with these."

"Well, for a prodigy with control over bees," said Frostbite, cocking her head, "that sounds like harboring deadly weapons to me."

Honey let out an aghast cry. "Those are my babies! And you've just taken their homes—the homes you have no right to!"

"And I'm telling you to call off your babies, now," said Frostbite. "Or else *your* next home will be a prison cell at Renegade Headquarters."

Honey fixed a glare on her and Nova could see her shaking. Her eyes flashed and the air seemed to hum around her—though perhaps that was the incessant buzzing as the bees continued to throw themselves at Gargoyle's impenetrable skin.

Nova could see temptation written across Honey's face, coupled with indecision.

Perhaps she couldn't harm Gargoyle, but Frostbite would be plenty vulnerable to the stingers of her most deadly wasps. Nova had to admit, seeing Frostbite writhing in pain from a hundred venomous stings seemed very appealing at that moment.

But it would last only seconds before Gargoyle reached Honey and either killed her or arrested her.

This tiny revenge wasn't worth it, Nova knew, and Honey seemed to realize the same thing. Drawing herself up amid the toppled cans and boxes, she squared her shoulders and flung her arm wide.

As one, the swarming insects cycloned into the air, then turned and retreated back into the tunnel.

Once they had gone, Frostbite nodded at the Gargoyle. "Destroy them."

Nova gasped, but the sound went unheard behind Honey's shriek.

Gargoyle dumped the hives onto the ground and began stomping through them, crushing them one by one beneath his massive stone feet.

Honey's cries turned from enraged to heartbroken as she watched the destruction being wracked upon the hives—many with drones and worker bees still inside. Honey's body was ravaged by sobs as the destruction grew. Papery walls scattered across the platform, and the corpses and detached wings of bees smashed into the concrete.

All the while, the Gargoyle was grinning. It was the smile of a child who had just discovered the sadistic pleasure of crushing beetles beneath his heel.

Nova ground her teeth until her jaw hurt. She swung her attention from Honey to Ingrid, Cyanide to Phobia, but no one moved to stop the Gargoyle.

Any attempt to stop him would be seen as an attack on a Renegade and would be cause for arrest. The Renegades had made it quite clear when they accepted Cyanide's truce all those years ago that the Anarchists would not be given any third chances.

Finally the Gargoyle was finished. He kicked aside the remains of the last hive. It skidded across the platform and tumbled onto the tracks, not far from where Frostbite had dumped out Winston's cereal.

"Well, now that we're all accounted for . . . ," said Frostbite sweetly, twirling the shard of ice like a baton. "We have some business to attend to."

She turned and, before Nova could guess her intentions, heaved the ice like a javelin at Phobia. It struck him through the chest and his body dispersed into black smoke, wisping back into the shadows of the tunnel.

In the same moment, Stingray spun and lashed his barbed tail at Honey. The venomous spines caught her in the side and her cry of surprise turned to one of pain as her body went rigid and collapsed. In almost the same motion, Stingray swung the tail back toward Leroy, stinging him in the shoulder as he tried to back away. Leroy froze, then tipped backward, landing hard on the concrete.

Nova pulled the gun closer, this time targeting Stingray. But his attack had already ceased, leaving Honey slumped awkwardly over the fallen shelving unit, and Leroy motionless except for his eyes, which were blinking rapidly as he gaped toward the low ceiling. Nova was not exactly sure what sort of venom Stingray had in his tail, but they both appeared paralyzed, motionless but for twitching limbs as the venom rushed through their veins.

Ingrid roared and charged toward the platform, a sphere of blue energy swirling in her cupped palm. Frostbite thrust her hand toward

Ingrid's feet and a stream of ice shot out from her skin, forming a small glacier around Ingrid's legs. Ingrid cried out in surprise and barely caught herself, her momentum carrying her upper half forward while the ice held her feet cemented to the tracks. The bomb she'd been crafting evaporated as her focus transitioned from fury to bewilderment.

"You seem to be the last Anarchist standing," said Frostbite, nonchalantly popping off a few ice crystals that had formed on her knuckles and letting them fall to the ground. "For now, that is. Humor me—is there any reason why we shouldn't kill you all after what happened at the parade today?"

Ingrid snarled. Blue energy began to hum around her hands again. "I wasn't at your stupid parade," she said, and even though Nova knew it was a lie, she found it to be a shockingly convincing one.

"I don't care," said Frostbite. "Winston Pratt led an attack against the innocent people of Gatlon City, and it's my job to make sure that's the last time our civilians will ever be terrorized by an Anarchist."

"Winston Pratt attacked your parade, and to my knowledge, you now have him in custody," said Ingrid. "So what do you want with us?"

Frostbite snorted. "You expect me to believe that imbecile was working alone?"

"That's exactly what I expect you to believe," Ingrid said. She seemed to relax, her snarl turning to a cool glare. "And you and I both know you don't have any evidence to suggest otherwise, because if you did, we wouldn't be having this chat while you wait for me to say something that will incriminate myself or the others." She started to toss the glowing bomb into the air, catching it easily every time it came back down. "I've seen your Council's edicts. *No one shall be found guilty by mere association*, right? So don't threaten

117

us, sweetheart. And good luck finding something that will connect us to the Puppeteer's crimes. He was on his own today. We had nothing to do with it."

Frostbite moved forward until the toes of her boots hung over the edge of the platform. "I don't need to connect you to the attack on the parade," she said, waggling her fingers. A new stream of ice shot toward Ingrid. The block of ice around her legs grew larger, expanding over her thighs and hips. "To attack a Renegade is an offense of the highest order. With your temper, it won't be that hard to get you to lash out. Sort of like poking a rabid dog, now that I think about it."

Ingrid hissed as the column of ice made its way over her abdomen. She had stopped tossing the bomb and was gripping it in one fist.

"I know what you're thinking," said Frostbite. "You'll insist it was self-defense. Except . . . without anyone being here to witness it, who's going to believe your word over mine? An Anarchist versus a celebrated Renegade." She clicked her tongue in feigned pity. "It seems you have a decision to make. Attack me, and we'll arrest you. Or confess your involvement at the parade today, and we'll still arrest you, but we'll be a bit nicer about it." She shrugged. "Or do nothing. What do you think will kill you first? The cold or suffocation? I'd bet on the latter, myself."

The ice made its way over Ingrid's chest and began to climb over her shoulders. Soon she would have no use of her arms, or her bombs, at all.

Nova squeezed her eyes shut, trying to think clearly despite the way her veins were pulsing, hot and steady.

These were the superheroes the world idolized? Maybe Ingrid wasn't wholly innocent. Maybe none of them were, but then, the Renegades weren't, either. Here they were, torturing Ingrid, trying to force a false confession. They had ruined Honey's hives, caused destruction in their tunnels, torn through the supplies they needed for survival, all in an effort to find a *legitimate* excuse to have them imprisoned.

Her finger slipped over the trigger. She opened her eyes and her vision seemed suddenly clear. Her mind free of obstructions.

She found Frostbite through the scope.

Maybe the darts weren't poisoned, but that didn't mean a well-targeted shot couldn't do plenty of damage.

She focused on Frostbite's eye, which was pale blue. Lighter than Captain Chromium's, but not by much.

The trigger pressed into her finger.

She had just begun to squeeze when a cascade of fire, bright and blazing, roared across the tracks.

CHAPTER NINE

━━■ ■ ■ ■ ■━━

N OVA GASPED AND PULLED BACK, peering over the edge of the train car.

The tracks were on fire.

No—it was a column of flame shooting out from the shadows. In seconds it had burned through the channel of ice between Ingrid and Frostbite.

Frostbite cursed and drew back, spinning toward the tunnel as heavy footsteps clanged off the walls.

Nova's jaw dropped as he came into view, his armored suit somehow more ominous emerging from the darkness than it had been beneath the sunshine on the city's rooftops.

The Sentinel.

"Much as I would love to see each of these villains behind bars," he said, his voice steady and low, "something tells me the Council wouldn't approve of your methods for arresting them."

"And who are you?" Frostbite said, curling her fist and forming another long shard of ice. "The Council's lapdog?"

"That's funny," said the Sentinel, without humor, "I've often thought the same of you."

Nova relaxed her hold on the gun. She could see her suspicions mirrored on Frostbite's face. His words suggested that he knew her, and not in a generic has-seen-her-in-the-papers sort of way.

"We are here on official Renegade business," said Frostbite. "If you try to stop us, we'll be plenty happy to arrest you too."

A gauntlet of orange-tipped flames began to lick around the Sentinel's left hand. "You're not the only one on official Renegade business. The difference is that I take my orders direct from the Council itself."

Nova scooted forward, not wanting to miss a word. She found herself staring at the chest plate of his armor. Was it a trick of the dim lighting in the tunnels, or the angle from the top of the train car? From here, it appeared that the gash in his shoulder armor was gone.

Her frown deepened. She'd stabbed him, right between the shoulder and the breastplate, yet she couldn't see any sign of damage there. No blood dried onto the suit's exterior. He wasn't even acting wounded. Perhaps a little stiff in some of his movements, but not nearly as incapacitated as he should have been after a wound like that.

It was yet one more mystery about the so-called Sentinel, and one more shred of evidence that he was *not* a normal Renegade. That he was something new. A soldier? An assassin? A weapon created by the Council, to be used for missions too nefarious to be assigned to a typical superhero?

"Direct from the Council?" said Frostbite, barking a laugh. "Do you think I'm an idiot? No one at headquarters has even heard of you. You're an impostor. And that"—she lifted the shard of ice over her shoulder—"makes you an enemy."

"Or it means you're too low on the pay scale to be told everything we've been working on," said the Sentinel.

Frostbite seemed to hesitate, and Nova could see a tinge of doubt creep into her face.

"Whereas I," continued the Sentinel, "know that you were sent here for two reasons: to determine whether or not any other member of the Anarchists were involved with the Puppeteer's attack, and to find out their connection to Nightmare." He tilted his head, and Nova had the impression he was glancing at Ingrid, who was still encapsulated in ice from the neck down. Her teeth were chattering. "I take it you haven't learned much."

Frostbite's nostrils flared.

The Sentinel suddenly sprang upward, smashing down on the platform feet away from Frostbite. She stumbled back a step but quickly regained her balance. Behind her, Gargoyle, Aftershock, and Stingray all stood, defensive and ready to attack, though no one had moved. It was clear that the Sentinel's claim to be there on the Council's orders had given them all pause.

"Release the Detonator," he said, opening his fist. The flames extinguished. "Then you and your team are free to leave. I am taking over this investigation."

Frostbite let out a disbelieving laugh. She twirled the ice shard once, but then let her arm fall, planting the shard like a walking stick into the cracked concrete. "If the Council wants to call us off, they can tell us themselves."

"They did," said the Sentinel. "Too bad the reception down here is so horrible. You could have saved yourself this embarrassment."

Frostbite only looked more suspicious, but Stingray and Aftershock glanced down at the identical black bands that snaked around their wrists. Nova bit her lip. She had often wondered about the bracelets that Renegade patrol units wore. Were they some sort of communication device?

"As it is," continued the Sentinel, "I'll refrain from informing your superiors about the many, *many* codes you've broken tonight. But not if you waste any more of my time."

Fingers drumming against her shard of ice, Frostbite shifted her gaze from the visor to the red *R* imprinted on the Sentinel's chest. Her face turned sour, but no less haughty. "Fine," she spat. "There's nothing more to be learned here anyway." She tossed the ice shard to the side. It shattered against a wall.

Striding past the Sentinel, she gestured for her team to follow her.

"Release the Detonator," called the Sentinel.

"Release her yourself," she retorted. "And if she repays you by blowing a hole in that fancy suit, don't come crying to me about it."

Nova watched the Sentinel as the four Renegades disappeared into the tunnel that would lead them back to the surface. She desperately wished she could see his face—to know if he was relieved or angry, annoyed or grateful. But she could read nothing in his posture, which was the picture of comic-book heroism. Tall and stoic, shoulders peeled back, hands clenched at his sides.

Slowly, he shifted his head to look at Ingrid and let out a frustrated huff. He seemed to consider his options for a long, irritating moment, before he finally stretched his hand out and released a thin, steady stream of flames toward the block of ice. He aimed for the thickest parts around her feet, letting it slowly melt away.

Nova's mind reeled. She couldn't help but feel just the tiniest bit grateful that he had come when he had, but still, despite his obvious dislike of Frostbite and her crew, she wasn't naïve enough to think that he had suddenly become an ally.

He was a Renegade, and one working for the Council. A top-secret project that the rest of the organization was unaware of.

Something told her they might have just traded one threat for an even bigger one.

When enough ice had melted away, he pulled his arm back, extinguishing the flame. With a pained groan, Ingrid forced one knee to break through the thin layer that remained. A sheet of ice crashed onto the tracks and she fell forward, landing on her hands and knees, shivering. When she could sit back on her heels, she started to rub her hands together, trying to return warmth to her extremities.

The Sentinel said nothing, watching her, motionless. Nova had the distinct impression that he was debating about something, and every now and then she would see a halfhearted flame sputter between his clenched fingers, like he was contemplating lighting a fire to warm Ingrid.

But he never did.

Instead, when the chattering of her teeth had quieted enough that it seemed she would be able to speak, the Sentinel paced to the edge of the platform. "I'm here for Nightmare," he said. "Where is she?"

Ingrid fixed him with a look of utter contempt. "Nightmare *who*?"

"Yea tall?" said the Sentinel, holding his hand at a level that was surely a mockery of her actual height. "Black hood? Tried to kill Captain Chromium today?"

Ingrid flexed her fingers, testing the blue sparks she could draw from the air, before forcing herself back to her feet. Nova could tell she was weak, though she was trying hard to hide it. "Oh, that Nightmare." She shrugged. "Haven't seen her."

The Sentinel's voice darkened. "Perhaps you know where I can find her."

Behind the Sentinel, Leroy groaned and rolled onto his side. The Sentinel spun around, flames bursting from his palm, but he seemed to relax when he spotted Leroy struggling to sit up.

Leroy coughed into his elbow, then peered up into the Sentinel's mask. "She isn't one of us." His words were as evenly paced as if he were giving directions to City Park. "We have no affiliation with the girl who calls herself Nightmare, therefore, we cannot possibly tell you where to find her."

The Sentinel strode toward him, his steps measured and intimidating. "Then explain to me, Cyanide," he said, crouching so he was almost eye level with Leroy, "how one of your signature poisons came to be in the projectile she used to try to assassinate the Captain."

"One of my poisons?" said Leroy. "Truly? What a coincidence."

The Sentinel grasped Leroy by his jaw, turning his face upward. Nova's fingers curled, recognizing how the tactic was so similar to the way he'd tried to intimidate her atop the rooftop.

Top-secret, high-tech Renegade experiment or not, he was still nothing but a mindless bully. Just another brainwashed minion for the Council.

"You can't expect me to believe you aren't connected with her," he growled.

"I don't care what you may or may not believe," countered Leroy. He had begun to sweat—his blackened skin glistening. "As for my poison being found in her projectile, well . . . I've been selling practical poisons in this city for decades." He smiled, revealing chipped and missing teeth. There was an aura of pride in the look. He might have been bragging about being a world-renowned tulip grower. "From pharmaceuticals to ridding one's home of vermin, there are a thousand reasons one might have had one of my poisons, and not *all* of those reasons are nefarious or illegal. Have you considered that perhaps this Nightmare, whoever she is, might have purchased that concoction from one of my distributors?"

This, Nova knew, was all true. The poisons that Leroy made were, by and large, legitimate and useful. His side business remained the primary source of income for the Anarchists. A boon when it was getting harder and harder to scavenge or steal even basic necessities in this post-Council world, which was something Frostbite and her goons had undoubtedly known when they decided to go after their food supply.

"This wasn't a mere pesticide," the Sentinel growled.

"And how am I to know that? All you said was that it was one of my signature poisons, which hardly narrows it down."

"Okay, Cyanide, try one of your signature poisons intended to—" The Sentinel pulled up short, interrupted by a quiet hissing sound. He recoiled, pulling back the hand that had been gripping Leroy's face.

Nova clamped a hand over her mouth to stifle a giggle. Even without being able to see the Sentinel's expression, his disbelief was written clearly into his body language. His arm fully extended, his head pulled back as if trying to escape from his own limb, where the fingers of his right gauntlet were coated with a sticky, dark substance that had just oozed from Leroy's pores and was now eating away at the glove's metal surface.

Climbing to his feet, Leroy tightened the belt of his robe and tucked his hands into his pockets. "You were saying?"

"He was saying," said Honey, trying to shake off her lingering paralysis as she leaned against one of the fallen shelves, "that he has as much evidence of criminal activity as that irritating ice girl did. Which is to say, none at all." She pulled one of the curlers from her hair and began rewrapping the blonde lock around it.

"You're right," said the Sentinel. "We don't have any evidence . . . yet. But I know you were involved with the attack today. I know the Anarchists want to see the Renegades destroyed."

"Of course we wish to see them destroyed," came Phobia's haunting voice, like a boom of thunder echoing from every corner of the tunnels. The Sentinel spun around, searching the darkened tunnels. "But wanting something is not a crime, not even under *their* laws."

The shadows behind the Sentinel solidified and Phobia stepped out as if from nowhere, gripping the scythe in both hands. "We have tolerated this invasion of our home for long enough."

"I concur," said Leroy. "If the Council believes we are in violation of our agreement, let them make these accusations themselves. Until then, we demand to be given the privacy we were promised."

Small flames began to crackle around the Sentinel's clenched hands. "You have been given privacy only so long as you adhere to the Council's laws. When we have reason to believe otherwise, it is within our rights to investigate. Today, an Anarchist was arrested for terrorism and assault. Today, an Anarchist concoction was found to be involved in an attempted murder."

"And if that were enough to arrest us all," said Ingrid, who was on her feet again, arms crossed defiantly over her chest, "we'd all be in custody right now."

"But we aren't, are we?" said Honey. Standing, she gave a lithe stretch, reaching both arms overhead. "So you can waste your time all you want threatening us, but I am going to go comfort my poor, bereft children."

She cast one tremulous look at the wrecked beehives, then lifted her chin and began picking her way, barefoot, through the broken bottles and toppled provisions.

She had not taken two steps when the Sentinel leaped, landing directly in front of her. Honey reeled back, her breath hitching, her head tilting back to stare into the visor of the daunting figure.

Honey's flash of surprise disappeared and she set her jaw, planting her hands on her hips. The look was a reminder why she called herself the Queen Bee. Even in a negligee and curlers, even with her venomous insects having been sent away, she maintained a regal spirit. At least, in the face of opposition, she did. Nova couldn't help but notice how very different she looked now from her utter hopelessness mere hours before. Perhaps Honey only thrived when she had something to fight against.

Perhaps they all did.

"One more thing before you go," said the Sentinel, his voice a thunderous rumble from inside the helmet.

Nova tensed, gripping the gun at her side as she waited for him to reach out and wrap his fingers around Honey's throat or jaw, as he had done to her and Leroy. Nova began running through her options again. The dart wouldn't do anything against that armor, but perhaps she could use it to create some sort of diversion . . .

She was not the only one who was preparing for an attack. Leroy had pulled a capsule from his robe pocket, one she knew contained a powerful acid. Ingrid opened her palms, forming a new sphere of crackling blue energy between them. Phobia's entire form started to grow, his body stretching upward, wrapping himself in shadows so thick it was hard to tell where he ended and the darkness began. Even the buzz of bees had returned, growing louder as they spilled back out from the tunnel, a writhing, furious swarm that hovered ominously overhead.

The world stilled, but for those bees. The Sentinel seemed to hesitate, the blank facade of his visor making him seem more like a statue than a human being. More like a robot than a hero.

His fingers twitched and Nova wondered if he really thought that suit could protect him from all of them at once. She doubted that armor would withstand even one of the Detonator's bombs.

Part of her hoped they were about to find out.

But rather than grab Honey or lash out with another pillar of flame, the Sentinel stooped and grabbed hold of one of the metal shelving units. He heaved it upward, slamming it back into place against the wall. Turning, he grabbed the second unit and, with one hand, set it to right as well.

Nova's brow furrowed.

"No matter what any of you have done with your lives since the Day of Triumph," he said, "you are all enemies of the Council and the Renegades. But right now, the only enemy I care about is Nightmare."

He turned and faced the train car Nova was lying on. She ducked down against the roof as the Sentinel sauntered in her direction and jumped onto the tracks. He passed by Ingrid without glancing at her or her sizzling bomb.

"When you see Nightmare," he said, grabbing the remains of the concrete bridge that Aftershock had brought crashing to the ground, "tell her that the next time she goes after the Council, I'll be there, waiting to destroy her. And I won't wait for the Council's permission to do it."

He heaved the bridge against the side of the platform, clearing the tracks. He did not turn back to see how his message had been received, just continued on, stomping into the black opening of the tunnel. Soon the darkness swallowed him, and the steady ringing of his footsteps faded into silence.

It took a long time for the tension to disperse. Eventually, Honey sent the bees buzzing back toward their solitary alcove. Eventually, Ingrid released the crackling energy and Leroy tucked the acid bomb back into his pocket and Phobia sank back to his normal stature.

Then Ingrid lifted her hands to either side of her head and made a face at the tunnel where the Sentinel had gone.

"To be weak," Phobia rasped. "To be helpless."

Ingrid cast him a sideways look. "Excuse me?"

"That is his deepest fear," said Phobia, idly twirling the scythe blade overhead. "To be, in essence, without power."

Honey huffed. "How fitting for a self-righteous Renegade."

"Perhaps," said Phobia, the hood of his cloak swaying with a slow nod. "And yet, a difficult fear to exploit against one who has been given so very much of it."

"Are his abilities products of the armor?" Leroy mused, taking out a handkerchief that had been tucked against his chest and dabbing his slick face with it. "It would be beneficial to know if he represents a new evolution in prodigy strengths, or if his powers are the result of experimentation or engineering."

"And whether or not they can be replicated," said Ingrid, suspicion making her lip curl.

Phobia did not have an answer.

Releasing a slow breath, Nova rolled onto her back. Long ago, someone had spray-painted graffiti on the ceiling here and she found herself staring up into an ugly demonic face, its tongue lolling out.

They were right. If the Sentinel was a creation of the Council, who was to say there wouldn't be more coming? That thought led to a host of concerns. If they could give someone superstrength, super-agility, and even the ability to make and control fire . . . who knew what else they could do?

One Sentinel she could handle. But an entire army of them? It would leave the Anarchists, well . . . powerless.

She shifted and felt something crunch against her hip. Reaching into her pocket, she wrapped her hand around a piece of crumpled paper.

"We should have killed him," Ingrid said, and Nova heard the thuds and shuffles as they started to put their supplies back in order upon the shelves. "We should have killed them all."

"And live the rest of our lives behind bars?" Leroy clicked his tongue. "That would be a shortsighted attempt at vengeance."

"At least it would avenge my poor darlings," said Honey.

"Nothing has changed," said Phobia. "The Council is our enemy. The Renegades will fall easily once they are gone."

Nova unfolded the paper in her hands. It was the flyer she'd been handed at the parade, advertising the Renegade trials. At the top was scrawled, in bold letters: DO YOU HAVE WHAT IT TAKES?

Jaw twitching, she started to shred the paper to pieces.

Phobia was wrong. Things had changed that day. Thanks to Winston's attack and her own botched assassination attempt, the Renegades would be on higher alert than ever.

And now they had the Sentinel to contend with.

Where twenty-four hours ago she had felt optimistic about their chances, now it felt as though any hope of someday reclaiming a real life for themselves was evaporating before her eyes. The existence of the Sentinel was proof that they didn't know enough about their enemies, while the Renegades knew so much about *them*. Where they lived. The extent of their abilities.

But they didn't know about *her*.

And if that was the only advantage she had, then she was going to use it.

CHAPTER TEN

———◾◾◾◼◾◾◾———

O F THEIR GROUP, Leroy was the only one who had ever learned how to drive. It wasn't necessary for most people in the city, who could walk to just about anywhere they really needed to go, and plenty of people still made their living carting others from place to place, especially after the collapse of the public transportation system.

Still, though Leroy claimed to have gotten a legitimate driver's license before the Age of Anarchy started, Nova sometimes wondered if he just said that to imbue his passengers with a sense of confidence; in which case, it didn't really work. Perhaps it was partly due to the fact that he sat so low in the driver's seat she didn't think it was possible he could see clearly over the dashboard, or perhaps it was because Leroy's pleasant, toad-like smile never faded when he was driving, no matter how many people honked or cursed as they passed, no matter what mystery item thumped beneath the wheels, no matter how many pedestrians screamed and lurched out of their path.

132

"Where does this woman live, anyway?" she asked, glancing at Leroy from the passenger seat of his yellow sports car, a vehicle he claimed had been highly desirable back when he'd stolen it. (According to Leroy, it had belonged to a lawyer who had famously defended a man who had beaten a prodigy nearly to death. The lawyer had gotten the man off with nothing but a steep fine and some community service to answer for his crime. So stealing his car was as much a matter of justice as greed.)

Thirty years and exactly zero car washes later, the car more resembled an overripened banana than anything remotely desirable, at least to Nova's eye. Rust was creeping around all its edges, there were countless dents and paint scratches on the exterior doors, and the ripped upholstery carried the distinct aroma of mildew.

"By the marina," said Leroy, drumming his fingers on the steering wheel.

Nova scanned the buildings they passed. They'd left downtown and were making their way through the industrial district, where warehouses and storage yards had once been full of shipping crates ready to be loaded onto cargo ships or distributed to the rest of the country by endless trains and semitrucks. Though international trade was gradually returning to the city, most of these buildings were still deserted, home only to rats and squatters who, for whatever reason, weren't eligible for Council-sanctioned housing. That, or they preferred to make their own choices about where and how to live their lives, whatever the cost.

Through gaps in the warehouses and defunct factories she caught glimpses of Harrow Bay, sparsely lit by a handful of boats on the water. Her eyes traveled to the horizon which blended almost seamlessly with the black sky. Though they were still in the city, the light pollution was dimmed out here enough that she could see a scattered sprinkling of stars and she found herself scanning for constellations she recognized. The Fallen Warrior. The Great Cypress. The Hunter and the Stag.

As a child, Nova had been fascinated by the stars. She would make up entire stories about the celestial beings represented in those constellations. Back then she'd even convinced herself that all prodigies, like herself and her dad and Uncle Ace, had in fact been born of the stars, and that's how they'd gotten their superpowers. She'd never figured out exactly how that had come to be, but it had seemed to make perfect sense in her youthful logic.

She wasn't sure what was more amazing—her childhood theory on how prodigies came to be, or the truth. That each of those stars was its own sun, thousands of light-years away. That to look at a star was to look back in time, to an age in which there were no prodigies at all.

Leroy turned a corner and the car passed over a series of train tracks before tipping down a long, steep hill toward the marina.

"How do you know this woman again?" asked Nova.

"Oh, I don't, not really. But then—how much do we really know anyone? Can we say with absolute certainty that we even truly know ourselves?"

Nova rolled her eyes. "And again. How do you know her?"

Leroy grinned and jerked the wheel to one side. Nova stiffened and glanced out the window, but couldn't see whatever it was he was swerving around. A second later, he had righted the car in his lane. "She was a member of the Ghouls," he said, citing one of the villain gangs who had risen to power during the Age of Anarchy, one that had formed an alliance of sorts with the Anarchists. "I used to trade her disappearing inks for false documentation. Still do, when it's needed."

"She's a prodigy, then."

Leroy hummed his confirmation.

"Any powers I should know about?" Even when meeting a supposed ally, Nova liked to be prepared.

"Psychometry. Nothing dangerous."

Psychometry. The ability to see into an object's past.

"Well," Leroy added with a chuckle, "nothing dangerous so long as you don't get crushed beneath all her stuff. You'll see when we get there. She told me once that it's difficult to give things up, once you know what they've been through."

"I'm not afraid of stuff," said Nova, "as long as we can trust her."

"Oh, I didn't say that," said Leroy. "But outside of family, she's as close to trustworthy as we're going to get. And"—he sighed—"I don't believe we have any other choice."

Nova settled deeper into the seat, staring at the weathered boathouses that blurred past.

Her mind settled on that one ephemeral word.

Family.

She had had a family once. Mom. Papà. Evie. When they were taken from her, she believed she'd lost everything. So much of her childhood was lost in a haze of pain and loss, mourning and anger, betrayal and a sadness so raw there were entire days in which she couldn't summon the energy to eat, or even cry. Entire nights in which shadows terrorized her, becoming murderers and monsters.

There had been but one source of light in those first months. The only real family she had left.

Uncle Ace.

He had held her close so she couldn't see the bodies of her family as he took her away from the apartment, stopping only to grab the unfinished bracelet her father had been working on. He hadn't let her go until they arrived at the cathedral, what he and the Anarchists had called home in those days. It was the largest church in the city, which Ace had claimed long before Nova was born. At first, she found it haunting and eerie, with the lofted ceilings that echoed every footstep, the bell tower that had long ago fallen to silence and cobwebs, the paintings of dead saints that watched her pass with condemning eyes.

But Ace had done his best to make it feel like a home to her. She did not recall him talking very much, but he always seemed to be near when she needed a stable presence. Sometimes he held her hand or rubbed her back while she sobbed into his shoulder. Sometimes he would use his powers to distract her from her sorrow, making playful puppets out of the figures and statues that lined the sanctuary and chapel walls. And when her curiosity overcame her misery, he showed her every hidden alcove of the cathedral. The tombs beneath its foundation, full of bones and history. The massive organ where she was free to pound at the keys to her heart's content, filling the vast space with chilling chords that perfectly fit her mood. He had taken her to the belfry and let her tug on the ropes to make the smaller bells chime, then showed her how he could move the massive central bell with his thoughts. Their music had pealed across the rooftops of the surrounding city blocks.

The pain did not go away, but when Ace was there, it seemed to lessen, little by little.

Then, one day, he told her the truth of what had happened to her family.

Nova had been inspecting some reliquaries she'd found in one of the smaller chapels when Ace found her and sat her down on a worn wooden bench. He told her that one of the villain gangs—the

Roaches—had demanded that her father craft them a collection of weapons using his gift. They had threatened David's wife and daughters if he didn't meet their expectations.

When her papà began to fall behind on their requests, he went to the Renegades and begged for protection. Captain Chromium himself had promised that no harm would come to him or his family, but only so long as he stopped making weapons for their enemies.

And so her dad did stop. And the Roaches, in retaliation, sent a hitman after him and his family.

Only, the Renegades hadn't kept their word. Captain Chromium hadn't kept his word. They were not there to protect David's family when they needed their protection the most.

When Ace finished telling this story, he handed Nova a cup of cold milk and two vanilla wafer cookies taken from plastic packaging that crinkled deafeningly loud. Nova, six years old and so small her feet didn't touch the stone floor as she sat on the bench, ate the cookies and drank the milk without comment. She remembered not crying. She remembered that in that moment, she had not felt sad.

She had felt only anger.

Blinding, breathless rage.

As he stood up to leave so she could come to terms with the truth of her family's deaths, Ace had said simply, practically—"The Roaches were forty-seven members strong. Last night, I killed them all."

That was the one and only time they spoke of her family's deaths. What was done was done. The gang had killed Nova's family. Ace had killed the gang. Justice was served.

Except for the Renegades, who had failed to keep their promise.

Two months after that, Nova's life was overturned again.

On the Day of Triumph, Nova had been told to stay in the tombs.

She sat in the darkness, listening to the screams and thunder of the battle, feeling the rumble and crash of the earth and walls around her. It went on for hours. *Ages.*

Honey found her first. Or her bees did, and they led Honey to her. They escaped into a secret passageway, small and damp, smelling of soil and musty air, lit only by the small flashlight Nova had brought with her into the tombs. Honey's distress kept Nova from talking for a long time, but when the passage finally spilled them into an abandoned subway station, Nova dared to ask what had happened.

She received only three words in reply.

The Renegades won.

"HERE WE ARE."

Nova jolted from her thoughts. Goose bumps had erupted across her skin as her memory repeated that day.

She sat up straighter and peered through the windshield. Leroy had parked on the shoulder of a quiet, narrow road just off the shore of Harrow Bay. Rocky outcroppings and foaming waves caught the light of a hesitant moon, and she could see a handful of docks stretching into the water. Most of them were bare, but a few had small fishing boats moored alongside them, their sides thunking hollowly against the pier.

She turned in her seat. To her right was a tall cliff studded with scraggly plants that clung desperately to its side and a burial ground of white driftwood at its base. Behind them, the dark road curved inland and disappeared.

No houses. No apartments. No warehouses. No buildings at all.

"Charming," she said.

Leroy killed the engine. He was turned away from her, gazing out toward the water. "I don't much care for the ocean," he said solemnly. "Seeing it always fills me with regret."

"Regret?" Nova studied the choppy waves. "Why?"

"Because if I had learned to sail, then I could leave this place. In a boat, one could go anywhere."

"You have a car," said Nova, glancing sideways at him. "You could drive away if you wanted to."

"It's not the same." Leroy turned—not to face her, but to stare at his own crooked fingers on the steering wheel. "There's not a civilized place in this whole world where I wouldn't be recognized, and the others too. Our reputations would precede us wherever we went. So long as anarchy is synonymous with chaos and despair, the Anarchists will always be synonymous with villains." He cocked his head to the side and this time he did look at her, though it was so dark in the car she could only catch faint spots of moonlight reflected in his eyes. "But not you, Nightmare. No one knows who you are. You could leave us, you know. You could go anywhere."

She scoffed. "Where would I go?"

"Anywhere you like. That's the beauty of freedom."

He smiled, but it was a sad look, one full of that regret he'd mentioned.

Nova swallowed. *Freedom.*

She knew he was right. The thought had, in fact, crossed her mind a thousand times. No one knew what Nova Artino looked like, or even that she was still alive. No one knew that she had been raised by the Anarchists. No one knew that she was Nightmare.

"What are you saying?"

"We are here because you say you want to infiltrate the Renegades, so someday we might destroy them," said Leroy. "And no one would be happier than I to see that come to fruition. But

I cannot in good conscience go through with this without giving you an alternative. After tonight, you will have a new name, a new identity. You could leave Gatlon City. Or . . . you could stay. Get a job and an apartment. Start a real life, like everyone else is trying to do. You would have plenty of company if you made that choice."

Nova shifted in the seat, crossing her arms over her chest. "And what? Leave you guys to defeat the Renegades without me? In your dreams."

Leroy shook his head. "There will be no defeating them without you and what you might be able to learn. What you might be able to change." His voice quieted. "I have little hope of ever seeing the freedom we once fought for. *Killed* for. But you did not choose this life, Nova. Not like we did. You could still choose differently."

Jaw clenching, Nova stared at one of the boats. Swaying back and forth, a ceaseless, steady rocking.

"The Anarchists are my family," she said. "The only family I have left. I won't be free until you are. I won't rest until the Renegades are punished. For how they treat you. For how they betrayed my family. For what they did to Ace."

Leroy fixed her with a studious look. "And if revenge does not bring you joy?"

"It's not joy I'm looking for."

Reaching around the steering column, Leroy switched off the headlights and pulled the key from the ignition. "Then let's see if we can't find what you *are* looking for."

CHAPTER ELEVEN

ER THOUGHTS SPUN as she followed Leroy along the dark road's narrow shoulder. Their conversation in the car was still tumbling through her thoughts. Was she doing this for them? For Ace or Evie or herself?

Or was she doing it for all of humanity? All the people who were too blind to see how they would be better off without the Council. Without the Renegades.

Maybe, she told herself, it can be both.

She wasn't sure when she'd started to think of the Anarchists as her family. Certainly not during those initial months when she had loved only Ace, and thought only of her parents and her sister and herself. Though they had all occupied the same spaces within the cathedral, she had seen the Anarchists more like phantoms passing her in the nave or arguing in the cloister. There had been more of them then. Many died during the battle, some that she never even knew the names of. And by and large, they all ignored the foundling child Ace had dragged back with him. They were not *mean* to her—Ace would not have tolerated that—but they didn't go out of their way to be kind, either.

Once they were relocated to the tunnels, though, that began to change. There were so few of them left, all suffering the same defeat. It bonded them tighter than they had been before, even to little Nova. Suddenly, the remaining Anarchists took an interest in her.

Leroy learned about her interest in science and started to teach her chemistry, allowing her to play with his lab equipment and test out different concoctions. Ingrid trained her how to fight, with bare hands and whatever weaponry they could scrounge or barter for. Honey, afraid they were going to end up raising another savage like Winston, made it her purpose to guide Nova into being a *lady* . . . or at least the sort of lady who knew how to mix a proper martini and apply eyeliner without stabbing herself with the pencil. As for Winston, for a while he became Nova's only playmate, telling her fairy tales with shadow puppets and teaching her the fine art of hide-and-seek, where their new home offered endless hiding places.

And Phobia was . . . well. Phobia was Phobia.

He had never warmed to her, but then, he never seemed to warm to anyone else, either, so Nova learned even at a young age not to take his indifference personally.

Leroy approached a small, weary-looking dock. Nova could see the water foaming beneath them as they made their way over the rickety boards, damp with ocean spray. The air smelled of salt and seaweed and dead creatures washed up on the shore.

A single boat was moored at the end of the dock—twenty feet long, with nearly the full length of it taken up by an enclosed cabin. Its sides were speckled with barnacles and its flat roof was loaded with wooden travel trunks and a single rusty bicycle. A plastic chair sat on the small deck at its bow beside an empty wine bottle and a withered tomato plant sticking up from a repurposed milk jug.

There was no light coming from inside the boat and Nova wondered if they were expected.

Leroy reached over the edge of the dock and knocked on one of the dark windows.

From inside the boat, Nova heard the sounds of footsteps and the creak of old timbers. The same window that Leroy had knocked at thunked open a few inches, letting a warm yellow glow spill out onto the dock, and Nova realized that no light had gotten through before because the windows were all painted opaque black.

A pistol jutted out from the open window. "Who's out there?"

"It's only me, Millie," said Leroy. "We've come for those papers."

The gun shifted to the side and a woman's eye peered out through the opening, small and surrounded by wrinkles. She scrutinized them both. "Where was I the first time I ever met Leroy Flinn?" she said, her voice dripping with suspicion.

Leroy did not hesitate. "Rummaging through the supplies in the art department at the university. Searching for precision knives and laminate, if I'm not mistaken."

The woman grumbled under her breath and slammed the window shut.

Nova glanced at Leroy from the corner of her eye.

"She had a run-in with a face-changer a while back," he whispered. "Almost put her out of business. She's been a bit paranoid about it ever since."

The door at the end of the cabin swung open and the light from inside cut across the water. "Come in, then," the woman said. "Quick now, before anyone sees you."

Nova glanced around. There was nothing but cliffs and empty

road and the ocean in every direction. Leroy's lone yellow car was the only sign of civilization in sight.

Leroy stepped over the rail onto the deck and slipped into the cabin of the houseboat. Nova followed, shutting the door behind her as she looked around.

The cabin was narrow and crammed so full of stuff that Leroy had to turn sideways to fit down the aisle, following the woman as she made her way to the back of the boat. Open shelving covered the walls, sporting everything from cleaning supplies to cans of food to more wine. A wood stove in the far corner was the source of the light and an encompassing warmth that tipped just slightly toward oppressive. To her left, the wall was lined with more shelving units and storage crates of all shapes and sizes, many stacked with dishes, pottery, and piles of neatly folded towels. To her right, an assembly of old printers and computer monitors, scanners and an office copy machine, a laminator, boxes of blue latex gloves, and stacks and stacks and stacks of paper of all different colors and thicknesses. A maze of string crisscrossed overhead, down the full length of the cabin, hung with drying laundry and a variety of paper documents.

"Millie," said Leroy, pausing behind the woman as she set the gun down on top of a filing cabinet and started to remove a few sheets of paper from one of the lines, "I'd like you to meet Nova. Ace's niece."

"I know who she is," said Millie, thunking the edges of the papers together to level them, then pulling an empty folder from a desk drawer and sliding them inside. "Welcome aboard, Nova McLain."

"Um. Artino, actually."

Millie peered around Leroy and held the packet toward her. "Not anymore."

Taking the packet, Nova flipped open the folder and looked at the top sheet. It was a birth certificate, as simple and unembellished as those created during the Age of Anarchy tended to be. With few doctors' offices left to perform deliveries, many women gave birth at home with the help of a midwife, who may or may not have had professional training, who may or may not have cared to complete any sort of paperwork afterward, especially when there were no governmental departments expecting such paperwork to be submitted. Nova knew that both she and Evie had been delivered at home, but as far as she knew, her parents had never gotten a certificate for either of them.

This document, though, looked as professional as the ones that came from the era, stamped and signed by a one *Janice Kendall, midwife.* It included signatures from her imaginary parents, *Robert and Joy McLain.* It included her birthday, and it actually *was* her birthday—May 27—perhaps so Nova would be less likely to give the false date should anyone ask for it.

And, printed in neat handwriting in the center of the page, was her name.

Almost.

Nova Jean McLain

"Do I look Scottish?"

"Your father was Scottish," said Millie, opening the bed of a scanner and pulling out a sheet of paper. "You take after your mother."

Nova opened her mouth to refute—her dad was Italian, her mom Filipino, and she liked to think she was a strong mix of them both—but she stopped herself. What did it matter what the world thought her name was, or where she got her blue eyes or her black hair? What did it matter if anyone thought her parents were Robert and Joy . . . whoever they were.

She couldn't walk into the Renegades trials with the name

Artino, and Nova Jean McLain was as good a secret identity as any.

She lifted the birth certificate. The next page was the required application to participate in the Renegade trials. It had been filled out using an old typewriter.

Name: Nova Jean McLain

Alias: Insomnia

Prodigious Ability (Superpower): Requires no sleep or rest; maintains full wakefulness at all times without any decline in aptitude from sleep deprivation.

"Insomnia," Nova muttered. It wasn't exactly the sort of name that would strike fear in the hearts of her enemies, but it wasn't bad, either. She wondered if Leroy had come up with it, or Millie.

"There's a spot on the last page for your signature," said Millie, holding out a ballpoint pen. "Don't sign the wrong name, now."

Nova took the pen without looking up. Outside, the waves drummed a steady, crashing melody against the side of the boat. "I live on East Ninety-Fourth and Wallowridge?" She frowned. "Are there even habitable homes in that area?"

"Would you rather I put 'subway tunnel off the defunct Mission Street station'?" said Millie.

Nova glanced up. "I just don't want anyone to come investigating me and find out the residence in my paperwork is actually some convenience store that burned down twenty years ago or something."

Millie cast an annoyed look at Leroy, who returned a placating smile.

"I am not an amateur," she spat. Bending over a nearby desk, she started to sort the scattered pens, sticky notes, and razor blades into a collection of tin cans. "Should anyone come looking for you, they will find a two-bedroom row house that has been owned outright by

Peter McLain for more than forty years."

"Who's Peter McLain?"

"Your uncle," she said. "On page three, you'll find a two-hundred-word personal essay on how grateful you are that he took you in after your parents' untimely deaths."

"Okay, but who is he really?"

"No one. A figment of my imagination. A phantom, existing only in paperwork. Don't worry—all the paperwork will match up. As far as anyone knows, the house really is owned and occupied by Mr. McLain, and now his niece."

Nova glanced at Leroy, but he was watching Millie. "The application required personal references, I believe? What did you find for those?"

"A grade-school teacher who thought Nova was a delightful student to have in her class," said Millie, "and an old boss who saw it as a horrible loss when Nova chose to leave his employment, but who is thrilled to see her pursuing her dream of becoming a Renegade."

"An old boss?" Nova flipped to the next page, where she saw that Nova Jean McLain had been working at Cosmopolis Amusement Park up until a month ago. "I'm a ride operator? Come on. A chipmunk could do that job."

"Both references," continued Millie, as if Nova hadn't spoken, "are legitimate sources. True working civilians in this community who have graciously agreed to praise Miss McLain quite highly should they receive further inquiry about her." Her gaze slipped toward Leroy. "Of course, you'll be paying them for the honor."

"Naturally," said Leroy, looking down at the application. "Winston used to operate a side business out of Cosmopolis Park. I think he might have known this gentleman."

Millie nodded. "His personal dealings fared much better under anarchy than the Council. It was not difficult to persuade him to this cause."

Nova's gut tightened as she read through the application, and she didn't think it was from the constant swaying of the houseboat. It felt like there were too many holes in this hastily constructed life. An uncle she'd never met. Parents she felt no connection to. A teacher and an employer, a house and a job, and any one of them could be proved false if someone only bothered to dig a little deeper.

She had to remind herself that everyone born in the Age of Anarchy had holes missing in their records. All those things that had kept society organized before had been stripped away—from medical records to school enrollment, tax forms to bank statements. There was none of that. Only people trying to survive. To go on with life as best they could.

No one would think twice about where she lived or who she lived with or whether or not her old teacher was lying when she called Nova a delight.

The Renegades cared about finding the best prodigies to make their organization stronger, smarter, better. If she got in, all she would have to do was persuade them that she was worth keeping, and no one would care about her past or her connections.

They wouldn't think to dig any deeper until it was too late.

"I trust it's all to your satisfaction?" said Millie, looking not at Nova, but Leroy.

He nodded and pulled a roll of cash from an inside pocket. Millie took it and undid the rubber band, counting it out before rolling it back up. Nova watched it disappear in her fist with a new weight settling on her shoulders. She had not considered payment, or where that money would come from, but of course Millie would want something for her services. Seeing the transaction made this whole scheme seem suddenly very real. That was money Leroy had worked for—whether by selling legal substances for killing off vermin and pests, or less legal drugs and poisons distributed into the underground markets. Either way, it was his toil and hardship, and she felt a twinge of responsibility to see how very little all that money had gotten them.

One false identity. A name, an address, a past.

A single chance for Nova to enter the Renegade trials and become their spy.

"Don't forget to sign the application," said Millie.

Turning to the last page, Nova pressed the application against the top of the copy machine and clicked the ballpoint pen.

"McLain," Millie reminded her.

Inhaling deeply, she scrawled a signature across the bottom line. *Nova Jean McLain.*

She held the pen back to her, but instead of taking it, Millie grasped Nova's forearm and yanked her closer. Nova's body tensed, readying for a fight, but the woman merely bent over her wrist, inspecting the bracelet.

"David Artino's work?" she murmured, her voice tinged with awe. She traced one finger along the chain of the bracelet. Her lashes fluttered, her brow knitting as if in deep concentration. "He was indeed a master." She flipped Nova's arm over and shot her a sly look, tapping her pinkie nail against the bracelet's clasp. "And *he* certainly was a handsome young man, wasn't he?"

"Excuse me?" Nova stammered.

Leroy turned a mildly interested look toward Nova. "What handsome young man?"

"I don't . . ." Nova hesitated, picturing a relaxed smile and warm fingers wrapped softly around her wrist. She scowled and ripped her arm away from Millie. "No one. He was no one. Just some guy."

Tittering, Millie took the pen from her. "That's all, then. Good luck, *Insomnia*."

Still frowning, Nova snapped the folder closed. "Yeah, thanks."

She turned, winding her way back through the cabin. Leroy shuffled after her, moving slow as not to knock over any of the teetering piles.

"Out of curiosity," said Millie, when they were nearly to the door, "what will you do about the fingerprints?"

Nova glanced back. "Fingerprints?"

"We'll take care of it," said Leroy. Reaching past Nova, he shoved open the door, letting in a surge of salted air.

"They need fingerprints?" said Nova, stepping back onto the dock. The boathouse door slammed shut behind them, and a second later, she heard the click of a lock.

Leroy scuttled past her, his head ducked against the spray coming off the water. "They will run a fingerprint scan at the trials, yes."

Nova followed after him. "But . . . the gun. They have the gun I used at the parade. They must have tested it for prints and entered them into their database by now. If they scan me at the trials, they'll know."

"If the prints match."

"Of course they'll match!" She paused. "Wait. Why wouldn't they match?"

Leroy's footsteps quickened as he made his way up the dock, back to the shore and the road, eager to get out of the blustering wind. Nova kept pace, waiting, but he still had said nothing by the time they reached the car and slipped inside.

"Leroy," said Nova, shutting her door. "Why wouldn't the prints match?"

He did not look at her as he said, "Because we are going to alter yours."

Her fingertips tingled with subtle apprehension. "How?"

Leroy turned to her with a hesitant look, like he knew he should have brought this up before. But before he could respond, Nova figured out precisely how he meant to alter her fingerprints.

Her gaze dropped down to the hand he had settled compulsively on the car's stick shift. "Oh."

"The pain will be tolerable," he said, in what was perhaps meant to be comforting.

But it wasn't the pain that worried her. "Won't it be suspicious? To go in there with mutilated fingerprints?"

"Not as suspicious as a perfect match to the prints on that gun would be."

She gave him a wry look.

Leroy sighed. "We will make sure you have a plausible explanation," he said. "But . . . if you don't want to do it . . ."

"Of course I'll do it," she said, more angrily than she'd intended. "It will hardly be the worst thing that's ever happened to me."

Leroy gave her a look that bordered on pity, then he lifted his hand, like he intended to give her a high five. The dome light inside the car hadn't clicked off yet, and under its sickly yellow glow, Nova could see the poison start to leach out of his skin. First beading up in tiny pinpricks, then oozing together until his fingertips were coated in a blackish film. Nova didn't know if it was some sort of poison or acid that his body discharged, or some chemical entirely unique to his own physiology.

It didn't much matter.

She inhaled, bracing herself. Then she lifted her own hand and pressed her fingers into his.

CHAPTER TWELVE

THE ARENA WAS ALREADY THUNDERING with chants and stomping feet, and the trials hadn't even started yet. Adrian stood leaning against the wall just inside the opening that led out onto the field, looking around as the bleachers filled with people. The crowd was full of bright red signs handed out at the entrance, one side printed with HERO, the other—ZERO.

That was part of the fun, he supposed, for the non-prodigies who came to watch the trials. Though the decision of who was accepted into the Renegades was ultimately up to the teams themselves, the crowd could pretend to have a say by holding up their signs when each contestant went onto the field.

He had never liked trial days. This was the fourth annual and it still gave him a sense of unease in his stomach. There was just something so ridiculous about it all—that the future of a prodigy could be decided based on a few questions and a thirty-second demonstration of their power. Could that really be all it took to decide whether or not someone was fit to be a hero? Capable of fighting for justice, defending the weak, protecting the city? He seriously doubted it, and what's more, he suspected that if he'd been forced to enter through the trials, he might not have made it.

Adrian had become a Renegade practically by default. He was the son of Lady Indomitable, and since her death he'd been raised by Captain Chromium and the Dread Warden. No one would have dared object to him being given a uniform, and because of that, he was given plenty of opportunities to prove himself and his abilities. Bringing his artwork to life had turned out to be damned useful time and again.

But *useful* wasn't always what mattered at the trials. Not to the spectators, at least. They wanted to be dazzled and bewildered and maybe even a little frightened. They wanted explosions and earthquakes, and Adrian's power would have left the crowd unsatisfied.

Unless he'd drawn a hand grenade.

Actually, a hand grenade would have been kind of awesome.

Nevertheless, he hadn't been made to compete for a place in the Renegades, so he would never know whether he would have been chosen or not.

These days, it didn't really matter what anyone thought of his powers, not since he'd altered his own ability by giving himself the tattoos. He was no longer just Sketch, a Renegade and an artist.

He was the Sentinel, with more powers than had ever resided in one being before, at least as far as he knew. He was like no prodigy anyone had ever encountered. He had been transformed.

It felt strange to be wearing his Renegade uniform again after being in the Sentinel's armored suit—the form-fitting fabric suddenly made him feel vulnerable. He kept sliding his finger between the shirt collar and his throat, trying to give himself more space to breathe.

"Happy trial day, *woo-woo!*"

Adrian turned to see Oscar ambling down the cinder-block corridor. He punched his cane a few times in the air before propping it against the floor again. "Bring on the newbies, for I am ready to *pass judgment.*"

Ruby wasn't far behind him, bouncing on the balls of her feet. "How's it looking out there?" she asked, coming to stand beside Adrian. Her eyes widened. "Great skies, that's a lot of people." Her bloodstone dangled from her wrist, resting against her thigh as she surveyed the jam-packed arena. Then her attention moved down to the tables stationed around the field. There were close to forty of them, each draped with a red cloth. All patrol units were expected to attend the trials—at least, those who weren't on active duty that night—where they would sit at the tables and watch hopeful prodigies try to impress them and ultimately decide their fate. "Are there really that many patrol teams these days?" Ruby added. "There weren't half this many when I tried out. It doesn't feel this crowded when we're at headquarters."

"Not often they get us all in one room together," said Adrian. "I'm not sure how many are actively looking for new members, though." His eyes traveled up to the platform that hung over the far end of the field. The Council members, including his dads, were already seated, chatting amicably and occasionally pausing to smile for a camera. Even Thunderbird was there. The healers had given her permission to come, so long as she didn't do anything stupid, like try to fly. "I know the Council is hoping to bring on some new talent today, too, so we'll see how many they pick out."

Ruby shook her head, looking a little dazed by all the commotion.

"Can you imagine trying out under these conditions? It's so much pressure."

"You both got picked from trials," said Adrian. "It wasn't a lot of pressure then?"

"Oh, it was," said Ruby, with a nervous laugh. "I was terrified."

"Not me." Oscar grinned. "But I knew I'd get picked up. Who wouldn't want this on their team?" He lifted a palm and a puff of bluish smoke morphed into a vicious dragon. It flew off into the bleachers to a bout of squeals from the audience. "Seriously? There are endless practical uses for that trick."

"Seriously," said Ruby, with a sage nod. "*Endless.*"

"That's funny," said Adrian. "I seem to recall you being challenged by . . . what? Nine different teams, all at once?"

"Yes!" said Oscar, beaming with the memory. "And did they come to regret that or what? That was a shining moment for me. Come to think of it, I may actually have peaked on that day. I think my life has been downhill ever since."

Ruby laughed. "Do you remember the look on Mia Hagner's face when you defeated Steamroller? That was the best."

Oscar leaned his head against Ruby's shoulder, his eyes sparkling. "Please go on. Tell me everything you remember, in complete, excruciating detail."

Ruby rested her head against his. "I would, except you covered the whole field with fog so none of us actually got to see anything."

Oscar's squinted one eye. "Oh yeah. But trust me—it was a sound whupping."

Adrian shook his head, watching as the stands filled with onlookers, some of whom had started doing the wave. He clearly remembered the trials of all three of his teammates, though he hadn't been a team leader at the time. Danna had been accepted without question during her trial—being able to disperse into a swarm of butterflies made her quick, conveniently camouflaged, and a star when it came to hiding and sneaking into places where others couldn't easily get to.

But Oscar and Ruby had both been challenged, which meant that while one team had seen their potential, other teams had questioned if they deserved a place among the Renegades. They'd each had to prove themselves in one-on-one combat against a member of a challenging team.

Oscar could have wowed the audience with an entire flock of smoke dragons and an army of vapor knights to destroy them, and someone still would have questioned if a kid with a bone disease that kept him tethered to a cane could possibly become a hero in Gatlon City. But he had surprised everyone by taking out Steamroller, a prodigy known for mowing down anyone and anything in his path. Oscar had cast a thick fog over the field, blinding Steamroller, then tricked him into chasing after him until he was only a couple of feet inside the ring. Finally, he had barraged him with a series of darts made of thick black smoke. Steamroller had choked and gagged and stumbled out of the ring—and Smokescreen joined the Renegades.

Ruby, too, had been underestimated. Though she'd been practicing martial arts for years before then, her actual ability—that when she bled, her blood crystallized into ruby-like gems—was seen as belonging more on the black market than in a life of law enforcement. She'd faced off against Guillotine, who thought she'd been handed an easy victory when she slashed open Ruby's forearm during her first attack. Less than a minute later, though, Ruby responded in force, her arm and hand suddenly covered in red stalagmites as sharp as daggers. Guillotine suffered more than a few wounds of her own before conceding the battle.

"I'm going up for some food," said Oscar. "What do you guys want? Pretzels? Hot dog?"

"Cotton candy," said Ruby. "The one with both the blue and the pink mixed together."

"On it. Sketch?"

"I'm good," said Adrian.

"I'll bring you some popcorn. Don't let anything exciting happen without me." He winked and retreated into the corridor.

"No promises," Ruby sang after him. Then her eyes brightened as she pointed up to the stands. "Oh, look! Someone made you a sign!"

Startled, Adrian followed her gesture and spotted a woman holding up a handmade sign that read EVERHART = MY HERO 4-EVER!

"I'm pretty sure that's referring to my dad."

Ruby deflated. "You don't know that." She cocked her head to the side, as if seeing the sign from a different angle might change it. "Yeah, you're probably right. But we can pretend someone made you a sign?"

"I'm really okay with it," said Adrian, frowning at the crowd. He couldn't wait for this to be over. He wasn't nervous, exactly. More . . . embarrassed, in a way. To be participating in a tradition he wasn't sure he approved of.

They were supposed to encourage every prodigy . . . no, every *human* to be as heroic as possible. How was publicly rejecting anyone going to further that goal?

Besides, it wasn't just the contestants who were being judged today, it was the Renegades too. The public wanted to see the prodigy crusaders who were charged with protecting their city, with protecting *them*. They wanted to know they were in good hands.

And, okay, they also wanted an afternoon of free entertainment.

It all felt like an absurd way to handle their recruitment. Didn't anyone have better things to be doing?

"How's Danna?" Adrian asked, his eyes catching on another homemade sign in the bleachers that read, YOU LIGHT ME UP, BLACKLIGHT!!!

"Sad she can't be here," said Ruby. "She hates being cooped up."

"So would I," said Adrian.

Ruby suddenly tensed beside him. Adrian followed her glower. Genissa Clark, aka Frostbite, was making her way down the tunnel, surrounded by the rest of her team. They didn't cast Adrian or Ruby a single glance as they headed onto the field, even though the teams were supposed to wait to be announced before heading to their tables.

"I hope our table is far away from hers," Ruby muttered, crossing her arms.

Adrian's lip twitched, remembering now that Genissa was the one who had challenged Ruby's acceptance into the Renegades two years ago. He could understand her resentment.

Not that he cared much for Genissa or any of her teammates. He hadn't before, and seeing how they behaved toward the Anarchists hadn't sparked any great affection, either. Not that he held much sympathy for the Anarchists, but for Frostbite and the others to act like such power-drunk bullies was unacceptable under the code that Renegades were sworn to live by. Plus, seeing those destroyed beehives, even if they did belong to an enemy, had made Adrian's nose curl in disgust.

The villains' poor life choices weren't exactly the *bees'* fault, after all.

Even though he hadn't learned anything about Nightmare or found any evidence he could use to incriminate the rest of the

Anarchists, he was glad he'd decided to go into the tunnels that night. Word had quickly spread throughout headquarters that the Sentinel had made a reappearance, claiming to have been sent by the Council themselves. When the Council adamantly refused the claim, and it became clear that the Sentinel had been lying, the humiliation heaped on Genissa and her team was almost palpable.

Adrian had tricked them into abandoning their mission. He had made them look like fools, and he couldn't help but feel a tinge of smugness every time he thought of it.

The downside, however, was that the mystery of the Sentinel was growing daily. Who was he? Where did he come from? Could he actually be a secret project undertaken by research and development, or was he somehow involved with Nightmare or the Anarchists—an enemy meant to confuse them all?

What had started out as an investigation into Nightmare was quickly becoming an investigation into *him,* and that made him uneasy.

The other teams began dispersing across the field, too, some looking up questioningly at the Council, unsure if they were supposed to wait or not, but the Council was busy talking to one another and not paying the field much attention. The circle of tables started to fill up. The onlookers in the stands squealed, excited fans trying to catch the attention of their favorite heroes.

"Here we go!" called Oscar, appearing from the crowd in the corridor. His free hand was carrying a tray loaded with food and drinks waiter-style over his head. "Two-tone cotton candy for the lady, popcorn for my man, please help yourselves to some garlic fries or choco-crunchies, but do not touch my smoothie or I won't hesitate to kill you and everyone you've ever loved."

Ruby snagged the bag of cotton candy from the top of the pile.

"Oscar, can I have a sip of your smoothie?"

Oscar fixed a cold look on her for three, four seconds, then wilted. "Yeah, all right."

Jigging in place, Ruby took the smoothie from the tray. Oscar's eyes followed the straw into her mouth, his Adam's apple bobbing.

Adrian rolled his eyes, sneaking a handful of popcorn.

On the Council's platform, Blacklight approached the microphone and held his arms open to the crowd. "Welcome to the fourth annual Renegade trials!"

The crowd cheered. The stands were full of fluttering signs, screaming fans, stomping feet.

Adrian suspected this had not been the intention when the Renegades had first risen up all those years ago. Back then, anyone who was willing to stand up and fight against the villain gangs was a hero. You didn't need a special pin or a title to do it. You didn't need anyone's approval.

Now, they weren't so much vigilantes as celebrities. Celebrities who had an important job to do, but celebrities nonetheless. And they were becoming so political, influenced not by the needs of the people, but by what would garner the most public support. What would make them more interesting.

He knew the Council was only trying to hold the city together, still trying to solidify their tenuous control. He knew it hadn't been easy for them. They had all been in their twenties when they defeated Ace Anarchy—except Blacklight, who had been barely nineteen at the time. They had been heroes and crime fighters for years, but none of them had planned on becoming leaders and lawmakers.

They had done their best. They had built a new city on the bones of an old one, working tirelessly to heal the wounds the villain gangs had left on their society. Order and justice had come first—some sort of legal system, with the Renegades themselves both the creators and defenders of the new order. But that had been only the beginning.

The people told them they needed food, so the Renegades cleared away entire city blocks of rubble and debris to make room for community gardens and agriculture.

The people needed shelter, so they repaired countless abandoned buildings to make them habitable and safe.

The people needed education for their children, so they allocated funding for teachers and supplies and selected community centers where regular classes could take place.

The people needed security and representation, so they set up the Renegade call center and weekly appointments with the Council for citizens who wished to share their grievances.

The people needed livelihoods, so the Council fought to bring manufacturing and construction work into the city, establishing new trade deals with countries that had been cut off for decades.

When there was no funding to keep society moving forward, the Council exchanged the one resource they did have—superheroes and superpowers. In some ways, Renegades had become a commodity, one of the most valuable commodities the world over. Though prodigies came from all over the world to be trained and indoctrinated in Gatlon City, once they were a part of the ever-growing syndicate, they might be sent overseas to assist with hurricanes and floods, fight wars, vanquish crime rings, or help with extracting natural resources from the earth. Foreign governments, many of which had suffered themselves from the rise of villains and Anarchist copycat gangs, were willing to pay handsomely for the Renegades' services, and that wealth had trickled back into the city, just enough to keep them moving forward.

The relationships had come with a side benefit too. In a short time, the Renegades had become a multinational corporation, with embassies scattered across the globe. The result was that more and more young prodigies aspired to become one of the world's greatest heroes and would make the pilgrimage to the annual trials in hopes of being accepted into their fold.

So the Renegades grew stronger, and so did the city, and so did the Council. They had accomplished much in a decade. They had much to be proud of.

And yet, with all this fanfare, all the hoopla and ceremony, Adrian couldn't help feeling like they'd lost sight of the entire point. They were forgetting what they were.

Not celebrities. Not politicians.

Heroes.

"Would all patrol units please come onto the field," said Blacklight.

The teams who had opted to stay in the corridor filed forward. Adrian found their table almost directly across from the gate where prodigy contestants would enter the field. He sat in the middle, with Ruby and Oscar on either side of him. Oscar scattered his array of snacks before them, and if he or Ruby cared that they were the only team snacking on fries and candy, they didn't show it.

Ruby grabbed the small tablet that sat on the table and began reading through the instructions on how to accept or reject a contestant, and the important responsibility each team carried to make choices that would strengthen the Renegades as a whole.

After the initial burst of enthusiasm from the crowd had quieted, Blacklight explained the rules. Each contestant would be called out, one at a time, to answer questions from the team captains and perform a demonstration of their powers. Team captains could accept or reject the candidate, and the Council would have an opportunity to accept anyone who was not claimed by a team. If two or more teams wanted the same prodigy hopeful, that prodigy could choose which team to join.

"And at any time," Blacklight went on, "should a team disagree with the selection from one of their contemporaries, they may challenge an acceptance. In this event, the prodigy hopeful must go head-to-head against a member of the challenging team, and must win their duel in order to join the Renegades."

The crowd hollered. This was what they were hoping for. Not an easy selection process, but one full of twists and challenges and duels.

It wasn't about finding new heroes to protect the people, Adrian thought. It was about the spectacle.

But the rules weren't up to him.

"And now," said Blacklight, lifting a fist into the air, "let the trials begin!"

Jets of light exploded from his hand—beams of red and gray bursting into fireworks over the arena.

The crowd roared.

Adrian took out his marker and doodled a miniature cannon onto the tablecloth, its fuse already lit. It was no bigger than his hand, but let off a startling *bang* as it released a torrent of confetti and smoke. The recoil pushed the cannon back on its wheel carriage and Adrian barely caught it as it rolled off the table's edge. Ruby and Oscar clapped, but some of the Renegades at the next table cast them annoyed looks.

"A kazoo," whispered Oscar. "Make me a kazoo."

"Oh—I want cymbals," said Ruby. "The cute little finger ones?"

Adrian set the cannon down and kept doodling as Blacklight went on, "Please welcome our first contestant of the evening, trying out for his third year in a row . . . Dan Reynolds, aka . . . *The Crane!*"

"I think I remember this guy," said Ruby. "The origami one, right?"

It was indeed the origami one. A college-aged guy who could fold paper into intricately shaped creatures, and then make them move or flutter under his command. Unfortunately, the creatures weren't sentient, which severely limited their usefulness.

The crowd booed and held up almost exclusively the ZERO sides of their cards. Soon, Dan Reynolds was rejected for the third time.

"Poor guy," said Ruby. "That's rough."

"He should go into street performance," said Oscar. "Tourists would pay mad money for those little turtles." He gestured at a handful of colorful paper turtles that Dan had made, currently making their way slowly, slowly across the field. He blew his kazoo in sympathy.

The next contestant, who called herself Babble, could speak any language instantaneously.

"*Cool,*" whispered Ruby. "I wish I could do that."

Oscar leaned forward. "You bleed weaponized crystals."

"Yeah, but speaking all languages, without having to study them? Think how useful that would be."

None of the teams took Babble, but after a short discussion, the Council decided to bring her into the Renegade family anyway.

The crowd seemed neither excited nor disappointed. Perhaps they understood the practicality of the decision.

"Okay," said Oscar, rubbing his hands together, "a good one's coming up. I can feel it." He paused, before adding, "By the way, are we hoping to find someone today?"

"No," Ruby said quickly. "We're a great team just as we are. Right, Sketch?"

Adrian blinked, his fingers stalling on the illustration of a small gong. "Absolutely," he said. "We're a great team just as we are. But . . . who knows? Maybe someone will surprise us."

CHAPTER THIRTEEN

"NAME?"

"Nova McLain."

The man seated at the registration table entered something on his tablet. Without looking up again, he held out his hand.

Nova stared down at it. Was he asking for money? Did you have to pay to become a Renegade? She didn't recall seeing anything about that. She didn't have any money. Would they really exclude a prodigy just because—

The man glanced up. "Application?" he said slowly.

Nova flushed and cleared her throat. "Right," she stammered, pulling the application from her bag and slapping it onto his open palm.

The corner of the man's mouth drooped as he laid the papers down on the desk and smoothed out the wrinkles.

"Your alias will be announced when you're called onto the field," he said. "Are you sure you're happy with . . ." He scanned the document. "'Insomnia'? It can be hard to change after the fact."

Nova tipped forward, scanning the application upside down, though she knew it all by heart. Was he trying to tell her she *should* change it? Was Insomnia a poor choice? She liked it, actually, but now she was having doubts. It wasn't *Nightmare*, but it wasn't bad, either. Was it?

"Um . . . yes?"

The man, expression indifferent, entered the alias into the register.

"Right hand," he said, setting down the pen and picking a cotton ball from a canister. He dipped it into a shallow bowl half filled with clear liquid, then looked again at Nova, who had not moved. "*Right hand*," he said again.

She swallowed and gave him her hand. He rubbed the tip of each finger with the cotton ball and the distinct scent of rubbing alcohol wafted toward her. The cotton ball was cold and his hands were thick and clammy and Nova's skin crawled the whole time. Though it only took a moment, she couldn't help but let out a relieved breath when he finished.

The man tapped the top of a small machine. A screen showed a diagram of a hand, the precise spaces where she should place her fingertips indicated with blue ovals.

"Go ahead," he said. "You'll have to press and hold for a few seconds."

Bracing herself, Nova pressed her fingers against the screen. Her hand was trembling, but she did her best to hold steady as a ticker at the top of the screen indicated its progress through scanning her prints.

By the time it finished and Nova eagerly folded her arms again, the man was frowning. He met her gaze again, newly suspicious.

The prints on the screen were obviously mutilated—entire

patches of the whorls in her skin cut through with flat, empty planes.

"I burned them when I was a kid," she said, the rehearsed lie tumbling out of her before he could ask. "You'll see on my application that I'm really into science—chemistry and engineering, and . . . um. Anyway, I was doing an experiment. With acid. And . . . that happened." She gestured to the screen.

The man's lips pursed. "Well," he said, glancing at a second monitor, "they're not pulling up any matches in our system. So." He jerked his thumb over a shoulder. "Head on back through those doors and wait to be called."

Her body stilled. "Really?"

"Really, what?"

"Really, I can just . . . I can try out?"

"That's what you're here for, isn't it?" He peered around her. "Next?"

"Oh. Okay. Thanks."

Nova ducked away from the table and scurried through the swinging double doors.

The room he sent her to must have been a locker room at one point—dank, cold, full of concrete and poor lighting, with the faint aroma of old sweat permeating the walls. The actual lockers had been removed, leaving faded impressions on the walls where they had been, and an alcove in the corner still had drains in the tile floor, though only holes where plumbing and shower heads had once been installed.

Now the room was full of uncomfortable benches and a lot of nervous prodigies giving themselves quiet pep talks. A tinted picture window on one side looked out onto the field, where they could watch the ongoing trials. A current Renegade hopeful was making his way out into the center ring. Tables hosting the teams were set all around the field, and a giant paper banner had been strung between two pillars over the middle: DO YOU HAVE WHAT IT TAKES?

To her right, a platform jutted out over the field, where all five Council members sat watching the proceedings. Even from down here she could see bandages wrapped around Thunderbird's wing and she felt a spark of pride at the sight.

Last year, Detonator had suggested they stage an attack at the trials, but Cyanide talked her out of it, believing there would be too strong a concentration of prodigies and Renegade supporters for them to be effective.

Seeing it for herself, Nova knew he was right. There were prodigies everywhere. Renegades *everywhere*. It felt a bit like being surrounded by Queen Bee's hives, if one happened to be allergic to bee stings.

She focused on the field, where the contestant had just revealed that he had four extra arms emerging from his rib cage. The crowd came alive with red signs, the vast majority proclaiming— HERO!

Nova scoffed. Did they really think that extra limbs made you a hero? Or being able to shoot fireworks from your hands? Or even having a layer of chromium beneath your skin?

Heroism wasn't about what you could do, it was about what you did.

It was about who you saved when they needed saving.

She crossed her arms, tapping her fingers against her elbows while the trials went on. Prodigies had come from all corners of the city, some from the far reaches of the world, even, in hopes of being accepted among the elite.

Many were accepted, but those who weren't . . . the looks of devastation on their faces almost, *almost* made Nova feel bad for them. That's what they got, though, for putting so much faith into the Renegades.

She shut her eyes and exhaled. The bitterness was pooling on her tongue, filling her mouth with a sour taste. The smell of sweat and nerves clogged her throat.

She did not belong here. She didn't even *want* to be here. If Cyanide hadn't put the idea in her head, she doubted it ever would have crossed her mind.

But if she made it—if she became a Renegade—she could make a difference. What could she learn from the inside, about their headquarters, the Council, their plans for the city?

Not to mention her new enemy.

The Sentinel.

Even thinking the name made her stomach tighten, and she thought again of the smug righteousness he'd had on the rooftop when he'd said it. *I am the Sentinel.*

Gag. Ew. Bleh.

He was nothing but a fancy science experiment, but the nature of the experiment eluded her the more she thought of it. He had too many powers, too many abilities for one prodigy. She'd never seen anything like it. And if the Renegades had somehow contrived a way to bestow multiple superpowers on one individual, what would stop them from making an entire army of them?

It was already hard enough to fight against them. For ten years the Anarchists had clung to the last shreds of livelihood and freedom. Nova feared the Sentinel could be the end of life as they knew it.

But not if she could learn more, and find out some way to fight against him, or to destroy him entirely, and anyone else they made in his image.

Knowledge is power.

One of Ace's favorite phrases, drilled deep into her head over the years. To overthrow the Renegades, they needed knowledge. They needed to know their enemy's weaknesses and vulnerabilities.

And if they succeeded . . . if *she* succeeded . . .

To no longer be seen as a parasite in society. To be feared would be so much better than this—the sneering, the mocking, the small-minded insults from people who would rather be kept under the thumbs of their idols than be allowed to live free, by their own will and choices.

She opened her eyes again. Could she really pull it off? She would have to spend days or weeks or even months pretending to be one of them. How long would she be able to maintain such an act? How long before they, too, realized she did not belong?

Out in the arena, the crowd went into fits of laughter as a prodigy demonstrated her power—expanding her head like a helium balloon, then floating a few feet above the ground until it deflated again.

The laughter that filled the stands was amused at first, but soon turned toward cruel. It disgusted Nova. Sure, the girl might have looked silly, but could any of *them* do what she was doing? Did they really believe they were better than her?

The Renegade teams input their responses and the word REJECTED flashed across the scoreboard. The girl was sent off the field to a chorus of boos.

Nova felt sick with abhorrence when she heard her name blaring over the loud speakers.

"Next up—Nova McLain! Alias: *Insomnia!*"

She cast her gaze toward the ceiling. She didn't have to do this. She could still leave.

Or she could stay and try to do something worthwhile. She

could make her family proud.

She squared her shoulders and marched onto the field.

■ ■ ■

ADRIAN STRAIGHTENED IN HIS SEAT as a new prodigy stalked into the center of the ring. There was something familiar about her. She stopped beneath the banner and the blinding lights, looking not at the teams surrounding her, but up. At the Council.

It was the stance that struck him first—the way she held herself, like she was preparing for an attack from all sides. Like she welcomed it. The jut of her chin, the set of her shoulders, feet firmly planted on the ground. Relaxed enough, but ready for a fight.

His eyes widened. It was the girl from the parade. The one with the bracelet.

She was a *prodigy*?

Well. That could explain why she was so unimpressed by what he do could.

Pushing up the bridge of his glasses, he leaned toward Ruby. "What did they say her name was?"

"Uh . . ." Ruby looked down at the tablet. "Nova. Nova McLain."

"Insomnia," came Blacklight's booming voice. "You may proceed with a demonstration of your superpower."

Adrian scooted his chair forward, leaning his elbows on the table. His gaze kept darting between the girl on the field and the big screens above the stands that showed a close-up of her face. Wisps of wavy black hair cut just above her shoulders. A sharp nose and a sharp chin and sharp cheekbones, her determined frown making them all seem much too severe. Rich blue eyes, every bit as wary now as they had been when he'd offered to help fix the broken clasp of her bracelet.

The overhead microphone carried her voice as she responded,

172

"I'm afraid my superpower isn't one that can be demonstrated on a field in thirty seconds or less."

A quiet titter moved through the crowd. There was something defiant in her voice, so unlike the other contestants who had been enthusiastic, and sometimes desperate, to show what they could do.

"Then please describe it," said Blacklight. "Succinctly, if possible."

She answered, simply, "I don't sleep."

Adrian's brow twitched. The crowd, too, seemed to find this explanation baffling, though after a hesitant moment, there were a few sporadic boos from the seats, and a number of ZERO cards lifted into the air.

Blacklight asked, "Would you care to elaborate?"

One side of Nova McLain's mouth lifted, just a hair. "Certainly." She cleared her throat. "I don't sleep . . . *ever*."

There was some laughter from the audience. Two team leaders tapped *reject* into their tablet screens, including Genissa Clark.

Adrian felt Ruby and Oscar looking at him, but he kept his eyes on Nova McLain.

Insomnia.

"Now," Nova continued, "if you would like to know what useful non-*super* abilities I have, I can tell you that I'm adept at hand-to-hand combat and a multitude of weaponry. I can run a seven-minute mile, long-jump an expanse of eighteen feet with a running start, and I know an awful lot about physics, electronics, and renewable energy sources, among other things."

Oscar let out a low whistle.

"I can't tell if that was arrogant," Ruby muttered, "or just . . . you know, honest."

"The two aren't mutually exclusive," said Oscar.

"She doesn't sleep," said Adrian, tapping his marker against the table. "Could be good for surveillance, don't you think? We might be able to use her, especially while Danna's recovering."

Ruby leaned forward. "But why does she look like she has something to prove?"

Adrian smiled wryly. "This is Renegade trials. Everyone has something to prove."

And with a power that couldn't be demonstrated, that had no flash to it whatsoever, he could understand why she was acting defensive.

Realizing the crowd had gotten louder, Adrian looked up into the stands. There was a bigger mix of ZERO and HERO signs than there had been for any of the previous contestants—a divided audience, which surprised him. It seemed her cavalier attitude was winning her support, despite her lackluster ability.

But then he looked up at the scoreboard and realized that his was the only team who hadn't yet responded. All the others had already put in their rejections.

Nova McLain, too, was looking up at the scoreboard, and if she was hurt, it didn't show. Her face became determined as she looked at their table. Their eyes locked and the expression was replaced with surprise and recognition. She straightened.

Then, again, that slight narrowing of the eyes. That same wariness he remembered from the parade. And even though she was too far away for him to see them clearly, he realized with a start that he could recall the exact shade of her eyes. A deep cobalt, pierced through with the occasional shard of heather gray.

He swallowed.

"Sketch," said Blacklight, calling Adrian by his alias and making him jump, "do you or your team have any follow-up questions before making your decision?"

Pushing aside the bag of popcorn, Adrian pulled the table mic closer. Nova fixed him with a challenging look.

"So," he started, drawing out the word as he formulated his thoughts, "when you say you *never* sleep . . . you do mean never, ever, *ever*?"

A few snickers passed through the audience. Beside him, Oscar muttered, "Well said, Shakespeare."

Nova McLain looked uncertain, like she thought maybe he was mocking her. When the audience had quieted again, she leaned forward and repeated, "Never ever, ever . . . *ever*."

Adrian leaned back in his chair. He stared at her across the field and she stared back, unflinching. A volley of justifications were storming through his head, each more logical than the last.

A prodigy who never slept could be valuable—for surveillance, for security, for the simple mathematics of added work hours on the force. And they were without Danna right now. They were down a hand. They could use someone skilled in combat. She did say she was skilled in combat, right?

Plus, she was interested in science and electronics, and their research and development division was always looking for assistance, always starting new projects and running new studies. Surely they could use someone like this. Surely the Renegades could use her.

But all the logic in the world couldn't smother the truth that Adrian felt in his drumming heartbeat.

There had been something about her at the parade. He'd been watching her when Magpie had taken the bracelet—that was the only reason he'd seen it happen. Because he'd been drawn to her, even then. Not because she was pretty, though he'd definitely noticed that too. But because there was a fierceness in the set of her jaw that intrigued him. A resolve in her eyes that made him curious.

"Uh, Sketch?" Oscar whispered. "If this is a blinking contest, you lost, like, eight minutes ago."

Without looking at his teammates, Adrian grabbed the tablet. It was instinct, not logic, that forced his hand. The inexplicable certainty that she was meant to be there. With him.

Well—no, not with *him*. But with his team. And with the Renegades.

A bell chimed. His response popped up on the scoreboard—ACCEPTED.

Nova turned and stared at the board, as if in disbelief, and there was that suspicion again when she looked back at Adrian.

"Oookay," said Oscar. "You go ahead with that. Not like we should discuss this as a team or anything."

"Trust me," whispered Adrian. "I have a feeling about her."

On his other side, Ruby snickered. "Yeah, I can tell exactly what kind of feeling you have about her."

Adrian turned toward her, annoyed. "Not like *that*."

She raised a suggestive eyebrow.

An ear-splitting horn blared over the noise of the audience. Adrian jumped and glanced around, bewildered. It took him a long moment to understand what the horn meant.

Their decision was being challenged.

A few tables down, Genissa Clark stood, hands on her hips.

Adrian groaned and leaned back in his chair, dragging his palm over the top of his close-shaved hair. "Seriously, Clark?"

"The acceptance of Insomnia has been challenged!" said Black-light, to a roar of glee from the audience. Adrian glanced at Nova, but she was so lacking in expression he wondered whether she knew what that meant.

"Oh, come *on*," Ruby yelled. She pushed back her chair and

stood, craning her head to look at Genissa. "You're only objecting because it's *us*."

Genissa sneered. "Don't flatter yourself," she yelled back. She pulled the microphone closer, allowing her voice to be amplified to the stands. "We challenge the acceptance of Nova McLain on the grounds that there is no way for us to validate the truth of anything she's said. We can't prove whether or not she sleeps, nor have we seen any evidence that she knows about electronics or physics or . . . any of that other stuff she said. We object to this acceptance on the basis that, from what we've seen from Nova McLain today—which is precisely *nothing*—we cannot determine that she is worthy of the title of Renegade."

It was everything the crowd had come for. Drama. Doubt. A potential duel.

Adrian sighed and tried to catch Nova's eyes, apologetically, perhaps, though he wasn't sure what he had to apologize for. But her attention stayed fixed on Genissa. She didn't look upset. If anything, a spark of excitement had entered her gaze that Adrian was sure hadn't been there before.

"There has been a challenge!" Blacklight repeated, for anyone who wasn't paying attention. "Insomnia, in order to take your place among the Renegades, you must defeat one member of the challenging team in a one-on-one duel. You may choose your opponent. Do you accept this challenge?"

"Wait," said Adrian—so loud that his own voice booming back at him made him jump. "Frostbite, listen." Genissa turned a haughty gaze on him, one eyebrow lifted. "I know we can use skills like hers, both on my team and in the broader Renegades organization. I respectfully ask that you retract your challenge."

Genissa laughed. "News flash, Everhart. The rest of us don't sleep for sixteen hours of the day, either. It's not exactly a *super*power, and besides, how can any of us be sure she's telling the truth?"

"Why would she lie?" he said, the question echoing through the stadium.

"Because she wants to be one of us," responded Genissa. "Because they *all* want to be one of us."

"Then why wouldn't she make up a more . . ." Adrian flipped his fingers in the air. ". . . *super* superpower? Why not—"

"I accept the challenge."

Adrian's attention darted back to the field. Nova was standing with her hands clasped behind her back, chin lifted as she stared at Frostbite. "I accept the duel."

Smirking, Genissa Clark pushed her chair back from the table, ice crystals already forming along the knuckles of her hands.

"Not with you."

Genissa paused.

Nova pointed a finger at the enormous figure lurking behind Genissa's table—too big to sit with his teammates, his body too heavy for the collapsible chairs. He lumbered forward and the bright lights of the arena reflected off the rough stones implanted along his gargantuan arms.

Adrian's jaw dropped.

Beside him, Oscar started to choke on his drink. "Is she nuts?"

On the field, Nova turned her hand over and curled her finger, gesturing for the beast to come closer. "I'll fight the Gargoyle."

CHAPTER FOURTEEN

E VERHART.

Frostbite had called him Everhart, and in the span of a single heartbeat Nova realized why he had seemed so familiar to her at the parade.

He was Adrian Everhart. Son of Lady Indomitable, one of the original Renegades, and adopted son of none other than Captain Chromium and the Dread Warden. She felt like an idiot for not having realized it sooner. She had certainly seen his face on a fair number of tabloid covers, splattered across newsstands throughout the city, and even though she would sooner burn those periodicals than read one, she should have known. Even if she'd been too young to care when the adoption had made front-page news. Even if she believed that the public's ongoing idolization of their family was one of the major problems facing society that day, and she outright refused to partake in the media's obsession with them.

He was the son of her sworn enemies, and she should have known.

She would make up for her ignorance now, though. She had been accepted by a Renegade team. By *his* team, and if there were ever an opportunity for her to infiltrate their ranks and learn more about the Council and their weaknesses, surely this was it.

But . . . first things first.

The audience was in hysterics as Gargoyle lumbered onto the field, but they were muffled in Nova's ears. In her head, she could still hear Honey's screams as the Gargoyle tore apart her hives. She could still see the way he smiled as he did it.

Gargoyle was systematically flexing his biceps as he approached, each one thicker than Nova's head. The patches of stone on his exposed skin shifted and undulated, moving along with his flexing muscles.

A hint of a smile twitched at the corners of her lips.

She was going to enjoy this.

The rules were explained over the loud speakers. Nova did not have to knock him down or leave him unconscious, which was good, as there was no way she'd be revealing her true power and linking herself to Nightmare while in Renegade territory. Luckily, she didn't need skin-to-skin contact to defeat him. All she had to do was get him to touch the ground outside of the ring.

And try not to get crushed by the behemoth in the meantime.

"Do the contestants understand their objectives?" Blacklight asked, though the screaming from the stands was so deafening Nova almost couldn't hear him.

She lifted a hand into the air. "Can I have a weapon?"

The question echoed through the arena, momentarily quieting the crowd. She dropped her hand again. "We weren't allowed to bring non-prodigy weaponry with us today, but as my claim of being skilled with a multitude of weaponry is a part of what's being challenged, it seems fair that I have something to defend myself with."

Blacklight glanced back at the rest of the Council. This must not have been a question that had come up before. Turning back to the microphone, he cleared his throat. "Gargoyle, as her opponent, you may choose to accept or deny this request."

Gargoyle held his hands wide. His arm span was as long as a car. "Why not? It ain't gonna make a difference."

"What do you want?" yelled Frostbite. "I'll make it myself."

Nova rolled her shoulders, then her wrists, working out the pops in her joints. "A knife."

Frostbite smirked. "That's it?"

"That's it."

Pinching her fingers in the air, Frostbite drew them downward. A crystal-clear dagger appeared, eight inches long, handle and blade cut from glistening ice. She laughed as she tossed it at Nova, who caught it without flinching. The ice was so cold it burned. Nova tossed it from hand to hand, giving her skin time to adjust.

"That was a poor choice," said Frostbite, lowering herself into her seat between her teammates and throwing her feet up onto the table. "It won't even penetrate his skin."

Nova returned the smile and twirled the blade in her fingers as she went to take her place. Opposite her, Gargoyle was intimidating as hell, muscles continuously turning into rock and rock turning back into muscles. Even his teeth, when he grinned, seemed to be cut from jagged gray stone.

The horn blared, thundering over the din of the crowd.

Gargoyle charged forward. The ground beneath him split and cracked from the pressure of his steps and clouds of dust stirred in his wake. He pulled one arm back and Nova watched as his elbow down to his fat knuckles hardened into black-speckled stone.

Nova feigned left. He took the bait and swung, while she turned and dived into a roll beneath his other arm. She sprang back to her feet and was turning back to face him when a battering ram crashed into the side of her skull.

She was momentarily weightless.

Her body struck the solid dirt with a reverberation that jolted her entire skeleton. Stars flecked before her eyes. Groaning, Nova blinked up at the paper banner fluttering overhead and listened to the cheers of the crowd and the thuds of Gargoyle's footsteps ambling toward her.

"Okay," she muttered, once her head stopped ringing like a bronze bell. "Won't make that mistake again."

A shadow eclipsed the blazing lights of the arena. She smiled sweetly up at Gargoyle and lifted a hand. "Help a lady up?"

Snarling, Gargoyle bent and gathered the front of her shirt in his stone fist, hauling her off the ground.

"Every superhero wishes they could fly, right?" he said, lips peeling back to reveal a series of chipped teeth. "Well, darling, you're about to have the pleasure." He pulled his arm back, preparing to hurl her body out of the ring.

Before he had the chance, Nova swung her feet up, wrapping her ankles tightly around his bicep and locking her legs in place. When Gargoyle tried to throw her off, she clung tight. He growled and started to shake his arm, like attempting to knock off a stubborn spider.

The audience exploded in laughter.

He reached his other hand over to pry her legs away, and Nova swung forward, driving the tip of the ice blade into his palm.

The ice shattered, leaving a hilt with a short, broken shard.

He smirked. "Did you really think—"

Nova released her ankles, dropped to the ground, and sliced the uneven edge of the blade deep across his leg—a patch of skin that hadn't yet been transformed into stone.

Gargoyle bellowed and kicked out on instinct, clobbering Nova in the chest. She landed on her back, just inside the edge of the ring.

Rubbing her chest with her free hand, she rolled onto her side and climbed back to her feet. She took stock of her options as Gargoyle, huffing with renewed anger, and maybe embarrassment, prepared to charge again.

She licked her lips. Flexed her fingers once around the knife handle, then tucked it into her waistband, ignoring how the ice burned against her skin.

She braced herself—again.

The Gargoyle stampeded.

Nova stampeded back. Racing headlong, straight for her opponent.

A moment before they collided, Nova sprang upward. She landed with both feet on Gargoyle's shoulders and used the momentum to launch herself at one of the pillars that stood just within the circle. Her arms and legs locked around the pole and she started to shimmy upward.

Below, she heard Gargoyle's taunting, thick voice, saying something about the little girl running away, but she didn't much care what he thought she was doing.

Reaching the top of the pillar, she took the frozen knife handle from against her back and swung it at the strings that held the long paper banner over the field. The edge was still sharp, and the strings snapped with one clean cut. Her end of the banner fluttered to the ground.

Something splintered beneath her. The column shuddered. Nova glanced down as Gargoyle aimed a second punch at the column, driving a deep crack along the wooden beam.

The column started to creak and tip toward the center of the ring.

Nova dived off, rolling as she hit the ground. She snatched up the end of the banner and bounded back to her feet. Spinning to face her opponent, she lifted the blade and threw it end over end. It spun through the air in a perfect arc, right for Gargoyle's chest.

He blocked it with his forearm. What was left of the knife shattered into a hundred tiny shards of ice.

His laugh boomed through the arena, mimicked by the thousands of strangers in the stands.

"What's your plan now?" Gargoyle said. "Strangle me with a strip of butcher paper?"

Nova scowled. She wanted him enraged, not amused. She needed him to charge at her—with feeling, this time. Instead, Gargoyle turned back to the crowd and started riling them up some more, barking jokes about the wittle girl who lost her wittle knife.

Nova glanced around, searching for something else she could use.

Her eye caught on Adrian Everhart.

He was standing behind his team's table, both hands planted on the tablecloth, his fingers drumming anxiously as he watched the duel. He met her gaze with an intensity that had been lacking at the parade.

Her pulse skipped.

Licking her lips, she scanned the random assortment of objects scattered across his table.

She pointed. "That."

Adrian glanced down, lifting his hands as if he thought they might be concealing something.

"The cannon!"

Uncertain, Adrian picked up the small cannon figurine.

Wrapping her forearm up in the banner and hoping with everything inside her it would be strong enough to hold her weight, Nova started to run.

Gargoyle turned back, curious, as Nova made a full turn around the ring, then kicked off and pulled herself a few feet higher on the banner. The Gargoyle ducked as she neared him, but she wasn't going for an attack. Instead, Nova stomped both feet down hard on his shoulder and used the leverage to swing herself outward from the ring. "Now!"

Adrian lobbed the miniature cannon at her as Nova swung past their table. She caught it in her free hand, then slid down the banner and somersaulted back into the ring.

Gargoyle's laughter boomed through the arena. "What does that thing shoot—marbles? Oh, I'm terrified! Please don't hurt me!"

The crowd hollered in response.

Crouching near the center of the ring, the banner clutched in one fist and the cannon in the other, Nova grinned. "If you're so brave, why don't you come a little closer and find out?"

Gargoyle shook his head, smirking. "Careful what you ask for."

Then he was running at her again.

Nova jogged backward on the balls of her feet, the banner fluttering at her side.

At the last moment, she tossed the cannon between them. It rolled into Gargoyle's path, directly beneath one of his large feet. He stepped on it and the wheels shot out from beneath him, sending him off-balance. He yelped. One hand swiped toward Nova as he stumbled and she darted out of his reach. Spinning to the side, she lifted the banner overhead.

Gargoyle struck the paper like a flailing bull and Nova leaped up onto his back, wrapping the paper around his head to blind him. The other half of the banner was torn from the second column and Gargoyle tripped and fell, the momentum from his own charge sending him rolling onto his side. He landed in a heap, inches from the edge of the ring while his massive hands pawed at the paper blindfold.

Nova sprang up onto the mountain of his chest and grabbed one of his hands. It came away from his face holding a ball of scrunched paper. Confused and disoriented, his one revealed eye glared up at her as she used all her body weight to force his hand down onto the fake grass at his side.

The horn blared.

Gargoyle jerked his hand away as if the grass had burned him. He sat up, throwing Nova off him. She landed with a grunt on her side, well outside of the ring, but she didn't care. She was already laughing as she peered up at the giant who was staring in dismay at the implant of his own hand in the grass.

"Rock paper scissors," she said, hauling herself to her feet and brushing off her pants. "Paper beats rock."

She strolled past him, ignoring Frostbite and her team and instead focusing on Adrian Everhart. The boy from the parade. The one who had fixed her bracelet.

He held her eyes as she approached and the way he looked at her made her victory feel newly, inexplicably real. It wasn't entirely a look of shock, though there was a bit of that. But there was something dumbfounded and impressed and proud there, too, and it made her heart swell.

She'd been challenged by a Renegade—at *trials*—and she'd won. But before she reached the table, she was attacked from both sides. Two sets of arms wrapped around her and someone squealed in her ear.

Instinctively, Nova dropped to the ground, grabbed their ankles, and yanked upward.

The two Renegades hit the ground hard. The boy groaned pitifully. The girl gaped up at the arena ceiling, mouth shuddering open and closed as she struggled to find her breath again.

Nova snarled, recognizing Smokescreen and Red Assassin. She didn't have any weaponry to defend herself against them, but she spotted the ruby gem attached to Red Assassin's wrist and reached for it, considering a dozen different ways she could use it to her advantage—

"Whoa, whoa, whoa!"

Nova's hand stilled. She lifted her head. Adrian Everhart leaped over the table and approached her with hands raised, a fine-tipped marker tucked between his fingers.

"They're with me—us," he said, even as his concern was giving way again to that slightly baffled, slightly endearing grin. "They're on your team."

Blinking, Nova glanced down again. Red Assassin managed to sit up, while Smokescreen grunted, "Pleased to meet you."

"I think," gasped Red Assassin, eyeing Nova in wonder, "we'll get along just fine."

Nova gulped.

"See? They're fine. You're fine. Everybody's fine," said Adrian.

"Gargoyle is not fine," said Smokescreen, rubbing his hip.

"Not concerned about Gargoyle." Uncapping his marker, Adrian crouched down so he was eye level with Nova and, without bothering to ask permission, started to draw something onto her shirt, right over her racing heart. She flinched at the unexpected touch, but if he noticed, he pretended not to.

When he had finished, he capped the marker and stood.

Nova peered down at the gleaming red pin on her chest. That familiar, iconic, hateful *R*.

"I'm Adrian," he said, holding out a hand. A Renegade. Holding out a hand—*to her.*

Bracing herself, Nova took it and allowed him to pull her to her feet. His grip was firm, but his expression was warm and kind, his dark eyes focused on her from behind those thick-framed glasses. The chaos of the arena grew dim and distant. The whole world seemed to shrink to this tiny pocket of space, where Nova could feel only the press of his palm, unafraid of the touch of her skin. Where she could see only that friendly, unreserved grin. Where she could hear, not the chants and cheers of the crowd, but only his voice, his words.

"Welcome to the Renegades."

CHAPTER FIFTEEN

DRIAN AWOKE EARLY, all sense of tiredness wiped away the moment he opened his eyes. He didn't normally consider himself a morning person, but as he sat up in bed he felt charged with energy. Like the day ahead was brimming with potential.

Not just because of the trials. Not just because they had a new teammate starting today—someone who he was pretty sure every other team on that field had regretted rejecting the moment she defeated Gargoyle.

But more than that, they had a new lead in the Nightmare case.

The night before he'd overheard his dads talking about the gun that Ruby had taken during the rooftop fight. Their investigations department had traced it to a guns dealer who had bought and sold a lot of weaponry during the Age of Anarchy, a man named Gene Cronin who went by the alias the Librarian. Not a particularly original name, as he had, in fact, operated a public library during the Age of Anarchy, and still did.

Adrian was sure they'd be assigning someone to investigate

Cronin soon, maybe even today, and he was determined that he and his team get the mission. After all, they had a new team member. A prodigy who never slept. It was a surveillance dream come true.

In some uncanny way, it felt almost foreordained.

On top of that, he'd finally perfected the concept for his new tattoo and the Sentinel's new power, and—Adrian checked the communicator band on his wrist and saw that it wasn't even five o'clock yet—with more than three hours still before he had to leave for headquarters, he even had time to give himself the tattoo that morning.

He headed upstairs to make a pot of coffee, even though he didn't feel that he really needed it, and to check that his dads were still sleeping. He paused in the foyer, listening to the creaks of the house. Everything was still and dark.

They weren't exactly morning people, either.

Ten minutes later, he returned to his converted basement, coffee mug in hand. The basement was divided into two rooms—the first housed his bed, a sofa, a bookshelf overflowing with old sketchbooks and comics, and a small TV with an assortment of video games. The second room he considered his art studio, even though calling it that made it seem much cooler than it really was. Mostly it was just an easel, a cheap plywood desk, and a floor covered in drop cloths splattered with years-old paint.

Everything he needed was already in the bottom drawer of the desk. He sat down in the rolling office chair and began arranging his supplies.

Rubbing alcohol and cotton balls. Bandages. The jar of tattoo ink he'd purchased from an incense-filled shop on the edges of the Henbane District, where it had been shelved between a potted money tree and a hookah pipe.

He laid his right arm across the desk, palm up, and used his opposite fingers to measure how long he would make the cylinder. Three inches, maybe four, midway between his wrist and elbow. At one end he would include a scope symbol, for targeting. Clean, simple, effective.

It was all in the intention, anyway. He had gotten the zipper to work, so this one should be easy. He had been extremely intentional with the zipper, making sure that he had sketched out the exact armored suit he wanted, down to every tiny detail, never allowing his focus to waver as he inked the tattoo into his skin.

Intention. He'd learned at a young age that it mattered far more than anything else where his ability was concerned. Not skill. Not execution. Intention.

If the zipper could hide away an entire armored bodysuit, then surely this cylinder could produce a steady stream of percussive energy beams.

Easy.

Adrian dipped a cotton ball in the rubbing alcohol and cleansed the skin over his forearm. After it had dried, he drew the symbol with a blue ink pen. It was a slower process than the first tattoos had been, having to sketch it out with his nondominant hand this time; but once he was finished, it still looked precisely how he wanted it to.

He had been so nervous that first time, that first tattoo. His brain had constantly supplied him with any number of practical warnings about needle-transmitted diseases, not to mention the pain that he knew would come with self-tattooing. Despite all the wounds and injuries that came as a result of being a Renegade, he still wasn't on board for pain when it was, strictly speaking, unnecessary.

But he'd worked up the courage, first testing out his tattooing skills on the skin of a grapefruit before working up the nerve to do it on himself.

The flame had been first. Though it was small, it had taken more than an hour to complete.

Next had been the springs on the soles of his feet, and *those* had hurt. But he gritted his teeth and bore it, and the first time he'd launched himself two stories into the air, he knew it had been worthwhile.

It wasn't until after the success of the springs that he'd had the idea for the Sentinel. It was inspired by a fictional character he'd created when he was eleven, back when he'd had the dream of someday drawing comics for a living, which at the time was somehow more interesting to him than being a Renegade. He'd completed three full issues of a comic that he titled *Rebel Z*, one he'd never shown to anyone else. In the story, twenty-six homeless street kids were kidnapped and forced to become science experiments for a madman. The first twenty-five all died as a result of the experiments, but the last boy, known only as Z, became a superhero newly imbued with a number of awe-inspiring superpowers. In the second issue, he obtained an armored suit. In the third issue, he started calling himself the Sentinel, and he became a vigilante set on destroying the madman and anyone who had helped him take advantage of so many innocent kids.

After that, Adrian got bored with the story and stopped making the comics. He never did get to watch Z exact his revenge, but he did find himself thinking about the character again and again, even as the years passed. A vigilante with a mission, an alter ego, and unstoppable power. A superhero in every sense of the word.

When he'd had the idea for the zipper tattoo, the temptation had been impossible to resist. He hadn't considered straying from the Renegades' codes at the time. If anything, he'd been excited to tell his dads and his friends about the Sentinel, once he knew it worked. He had intended to reveal himself after the parade.

But then the parade happened. Danna got hurt. Nightmare got away. And suddenly he could see the appeal of keeping a secret identity, well . . . secret.

It wouldn't be forever. Once he was sure he could control all the Sentinel's powers, then he would reveal himself. Or, perhaps he would wait until after he'd found and arrested Nightmare. Or until he uncovered her connection to his mother's killer and brought *them* to justice too.

Just like Rebel Z—once his mission was complete, he would reveal himself. Until then, the Sentinel had work to do.

Adrian laid out his tools, filling a shallow dish with black ink and lighting a candle. He swiped a new alcohol-dipped cotton ball over his skin one more time, fading the blue ink slightly, then dabbed it dry with a clean towel.

Finally he sterilized the needle—an everyday needle he'd found in a forgotten sewing box in a cabinet in the laundry room—running the point back and forth through the flame.

Adrian flexed his forearm, dipped the needle into the ink, and set to work.

The first stick was always the worst. That moment when he wondered, yet again, if it was a really bad idea to be doing this.

But the doubts faded faster every time.

He soon fell into a steady rhythm. Hunkered over the desk, watching his fingers progress along the blue lines. Needle in, needle out. Pausing only occasionally to wipe away tiny beads of blood with a clean rag. A thousand tiny punctures into his flesh as seconds and minutes ticked into hours. At one point he heard the telltale creaks of the overhead floorboards announcing that someone was moving around the kitchen upstairs, but he ignored it. His dads always left him alone when he was down in his room and, besides, they probably thought he was still sleeping.

When he was done, Adrian set down the needle, stretched out his neck with a few satisfying pops, then held out his arm to admire his work. Sore and shining and permanent.

He stashed the implements back in the drawer, then headed up to the bathroom on the main floor to wash and bandage the skin. He had just finished the wrapping and pulled on a long-sleeve shirt when he heard Simon calling him.

"Yeah?" he asked, walking into the kitchen.

Simon was standing over a skillet that hissed with bacon, while Hugh leaned over the bar sorting through a large stack of mail.

"I thought I heard you awake," said Simon, nodding toward a plate overflowing with cantaloupe, strawberries, and scones. "Have some breakfast."

Adrian stared at it. "Really?"

"Really," said Simon, giving him a stern look, though Adrian knew it was just because he felt guilty that the idea of a homemade breakfast was worthy of suspicion. "We're starting a new family tradition. Breakfast together once a week. Now get some bacon and sit down."

Adrian suppressed a smile and did as he was told. Hugh and Simon liked to start new family traditions every few months, and over the years had cycled through everything from Friday board-game nights to summer picnics at the park to a short stint in which they agreed to all go jogging together at six a.m. every morning, which had lasted exactly one day. Adrian knew it was their way of *trying*, as though after all these years his dads still weren't convinced that the three of them really were a family.

So Adrian, who loved his dads, the men who had taken him in without a second thought after his mother died, accepted four slices of bacon and sat down at the bar. "Does this new family tradition come with fresh-squeezed orange juice?"

"Don't press your luck," said Simon, making up a plate for himself.

"So," said Hugh, dumping a stack of junk mail into the garbage bin. The Council kept saying they were going to start up a citywide recycling program one of these days, but it, like so many of their aspirations, had yet to become a reality. "Are you looking forward to having a new teammate starting today?"

Adrian blinked. He'd been so focused on the tattoo he'd nearly forgotten about Nova McLain.

Nearly.

"Yeah," he said, breaking open his scone and slathering it with butter. "I think we're all really excited to have her."

Simon shook his head. "When she opted to go against Gargoyle, I thought she was out of her mind. But I was impressed with how she handled it. We need people who can be resourceful like that, who can think fast during an altercation."

Adrian smiled wryly at the term *altercation*. At some point his dads had gone from talking like superheroes to talking like police chiefs, and he wasn't entirely sure when it had happened.

"I just hope you all work well together," said Hugh, shredding open an envelope. "Chemistry is important on a team. And you all seem to have a good thing going so far. Hopefully she's a good fit."

"But if not," said Simon, "we'll be able to find a place for her. She was a good choice, Adrian. I'm not sure what made you accept her, but I don't think anyone will be questioning whether or not she deserves to be a Renegade after that showing." Reaching across the counter, he nudged the pile of mail aside and replaced it with a plate of food. "Hugh. Eat."

Hugh glanced down, momentarily surprised, then picked up a strip of bacon and chomped it in half.

"Out of curiosity," said Simon, buttering his own scone, "what made you pick her? I didn't think you were looking to add to the team."

Adrian took a big bite and realized after the fact that it might have been a subconscious attempt to give himself a bit of time before responding. He took a swig of his long-cold coffee and shrugged. "Intuition, I guess."

"Intuition," parroted Hugh, nodding, as if Adrian had just spoken with great wisdom. "It's important to listen to those feelings when you have them. Strong intuition can save lives, especially in our line of work."

Adrian set down his mug. "Right. On that note . . . how's the Nightmare investigation going?"

Simon picked up his plate and came around the bar, claiming the stool beside Adrian. "You're still concerned about her?"

"Concerned that there's a would-be assassin on the loose in our city and we have no idea what she's capable of or what sorts of connections she might have? A little, yeah."

Simon cast him a vexed look. "We might have received a promising new lead yesterday, as a matter of fact. We'll be looking into it more this afternoon."

"The gun?" said Adrian, attempting nonchalance. "The one that's been linked to Gene Cronin?"

Hugh glanced up. "You were eavesdropping."

"I was getting a snack. If it was top secret, you shouldn't have been talking about it in the dining room."

Hugh and Simon exchanged glances.

"Yes," said Simon. "We can't say for sure if the Librarian sold her that gun, but we'll be looking into it."

"You're going to question him?"

"Not immediately," said Hugh. "If he's still involved in illegal weapons dealing, then to approach him too soon, without sufficient evidence, could put him on the alert. Could make him halt whatever dealings he's involved with."

"That gun isn't considered sufficient evidence?"

Simon shook his head. "It could have been making its way through criminal rings for the last ten years. Until this gun came into our possession, we had no reason to believe that Gene Cronin was still in the trade. As far as we can tell, the Vandal Cartel disbanded after most of their members were killed in the Battle for Gatlon, and Gene Cronin hasn't shown any sign of participating in illegal activity since. That gun could have passed through countless hands before making its way to Nightmare."

"But you don't think that's the case," said Adrian. "You do think he's still trading, right?"

Hugh smiled wanly. "We think it warrants looking into."

"We'll probably start with surveillance on his library," said Simon. "He's a recluse, so if he is still working on the black market, chances are good that any business happenings are taking place there. We'll scout out the place for a while, watch for any indications of illegal activity."

"But that could take days . . . weeks, even. Why not just go in and search the place?"

"Without significant evidence that he's committed a crime?" said Simon, sounding offended at the idea.

"Oh, come on," said Adrian. "He's a gun dealer. He's a criminal. Why defend him?"

"He *was* a criminal," said Hugh, "in a different time, a different society. If we started punishing everyone for crimes committed a decade ago, we'd have no one left in this city *to* defend."

"We're still recovering from the Age of Anarchy," added Simon. "The code authority protects the rights and privacies of everyone, even those who were once involved with the villain gangs. Because how can we expect people to change if we don't give them the chance to?"

Adrian glowered, unconvinced. It seemed to him that having a gun that could be traced back to Gene Cronin was plenty reason to search his library, but he could see he wouldn't be making headway in this argument anytime soon. "Have you picked a team for the surveillance yet?"

"No, but we'll probably use—"

"We volunteer."

Simon hesitated, his fork halfway to his mouth with a strawberry speared on its tines. "What?"

"Adrian—" started Hugh.

"Don't say no," he insisted, his gaze swiveling between them. "Just listen. We want to be involved with the Nightmare investigation, and this would be an easy way for us to do that. Nobody else is going to want to sit outside a public library all night, waiting for something exciting to happen. And we'll have the new girl—Nova. She doesn't even need to sleep."

Simon's brow furrowed thoughtfully and Adrian could see that this, at least, seemed to carry some merit with him.

"Why are you so interested in the Nightmare case?" said Hugh, throwing another batch of mail into the garbage bin.

"My team has faced off against her twice now," said Adrian. "It's starting to feel a little personal. Besides . . . she attacked *you*."

Hugh snorted dismissively, and Adrian couldn't tell if it was a show, or if he really didn't feel that Nightmare's attack warranted concern.

"I'm serious, Dad. If you hadn't noticed, she almost killed you."

A muscle flexed in Hugh's jaw.

"And she took down Tamaya with . . . with a fishing net," Adrian went on. "Not to mention being partially responsible for Monarch's injuries, and managing to evade Oscar and Ruby and"—he inhaled sharply, rolling one hand through the air in a gesture that he hoped showed some amount of indifference—"that Sentinel guy too. Her power might not seem like much, but she is a threat. We can't underestimate her again."

"We're not underestimating her," said Simon. "We are taking the attempted assassination very seriously. So seriously, in fact, that it would be irresponsible to send an inexperienced street patrol unit to do an investigative job."

Adrian tensed, heat rising into his cheeks. "Over the last year I think our team has more than proved our ability to handle any assignment sent our way."

"Except for the two times Nightmare got away?" said Simon.

Adrian scowled. "Low blow, Pops."

Simon's expression softened. "Look, we're not saying that we don't think you could handle this. If anything, we'd rather keep you out on patrol duty, where your skills are truly used to everyone's advantage. Did you know crime rates went up eight percent last quarter? We need every unit on the streets we can get."

"And how much could a guy like Gene Cronin be playing into those rates?" Adrian said, forcing himself to speak slowly. To sound rational. "If he really is selling illegal weaponry to criminals, how much good could be done just by capturing this one guy?"

"And for that," said Hugh, "we'll be sending an investigative unit."

Adrian sighed in frustration. "Come on, give it to us. Please."

"Adrian, what does it matter?" said Simon. "You said yourself, no one wants to be staring at a library all night when they could be out helping people."

"Because I want to be a part of this," said Adrian, losing the battle to keep his voice even. "Because I want to find Nightmare."

Simon drew back, his head tilting to one side, and Adrian noticed for the first time just how unruly his beard had gotten. He glanced at Hugh and saw that his own hair was in need of a cut, his face in need of a shave.

When was the last time either of them had taken a day to just relax? To just *be*? It was always the Council, the city, the Renegades. Adrian could only imagine the pressure they were under, along with the rest of the Council. The whole world was looking to them for guidance and protection, for security and stability and justice.

He sighed, dragging his fork through the crumbs that had fallen from the scone. "Oscar heard her say something during their fight on the rooftop," he said, hoping beyond hope that they would never bother to confirm this lie. "She said . . . *one cannot be brave who has no fear.*"

He didn't need to look up at his dads to feel the shift in the air. Hugh inhaled sharply. Simon sank away from the bar, leaning against the back of his stool.

Hugh drummed his fingers against the countertop. "You don't think Nightmare was connected to her death, do you? From what I can tell, she's much too young to have been involved."

"No, I know she is," said Adrian. "But what if she knows who did it? What if they're still alive?"

"It could be a coincidence," said Simon.

"Or it might not," countered Adrian.

Simon massaged the spot between his thick eyebrows, where he always rubbed when he was deep in thought. "Cards like the one found on Georgia were also found on countless bodies during the Age of Anarchy. Maybe Nightmare read about them somewhere and is . . . adopting the phrase for herself."

Adrian looked away. There was a logic to this suggestion, and it probably should have occurred to him as a possibility much sooner. But . . . somehow, it didn't feel right. When Nightmare had said it, she hadn't been using it as a catchphrase, something she hoped would be quoted in the newspapers the next day. Rather, it had seemed so flippant, so unplanned. Words that came naturally, in the way that things heard repetitively over time often did.

"It would be out of character," said Hugh, "for a villain to stop leaving their mark like that, if they were still around."

"I know," said Adrian. "But not impossible."

It was the reason everyone had been so quick to assume that Lady Indomitable's murderer had been killed in the Battle for Gatlon. After that, those mysterious notes had stopped showing up on bodies. Overnight, those dreadful clues vanished. It made sense that whoever had been leaving them was gone.

But Adrian was no longer sure.

"Please," he said. "I just want to find her. I need to know where she heard those words. I need to know what they mean to her. And you're sending a team to investigate anyway, right? Give us a chance. That's all I'm asking."

Hugh picked up his still-steaming coffee and drank it all in three large gulps, which was how Adrian knew he was considering his request, though the action itself made Adrian flinch. Like so many things, Hugh was invincible to something as simple as burning his tongue on a scorching cup of coffee.

When he set the cup back down, Hugh looked across at Simon.

And that look, blank as it was, told Adrian all he needed to know. It was a struggle to bite back the smile that threatened to emerge.

Simon wilted. "Your team may be excused from street patrol for two weeks in order to assist with the Nightmare investigation. We'll have surveillance protocols sent to you by noon, and we expect regular reports on any findings, no matter how trivial they may seem. After two weeks, we'll determine if you can continue this investigation or be returned to your city patrol."

Adrian started to smile, but Simon held up a hand, halting it halfway up his face.

"But I mean this, Adrian. At the very first indication that Gene Cronin is involved in any sort of illegal activity, or should you find any evidence suggesting a connection to Nightmare or any other villain, you are to request backup from an experienced investigative team. You are not to engage Cronin on your own. Understand?"

"Yes, absolutely," said Adrian, allowing that grin to shine through. "We will. Thank you."

"Don't thank us yet," said Hugh. "You haven't yet learned just how painfully tedious this sort of work can be."

Adrian shrugged. "Oscar will be there. How boring can it possibly be?"

Hugh smirked. "Good point."

"We need to get going," said Simon. "A full roster of Council petitions today, and countless meetings with research and development, and working out details on next month's gala . . ." He groaned. "Sometimes I think it will never end."

"It's not easy, leading the world into a new age," said Hugh. He shoveled the rest of his food into his mouth, then dumped his empty plate into the sink.

Adrian watched his dads gather up their things, donning black blazers and scarves over their uniforms in a way that seemed laughable—like kids putting winter jackets on over their Halloween costumes.

They were about to leave when Simon paused and glanced back, his eyes speculative. "Adrian . . ."

Adrian sat up straighter, preparing himself as he watched Simon wrestling with whatever it was he wanted to say.

"I want you to tread carefully with this, all right?"

Adrian's brow knit. "What do you mean?"

"No matter what happens, no matter what you find, nothing is going to bring your mom back. I know you want answers. We all do. But it won't change the fact that she's gone."

"This isn't about wanting her back," said Adrian. "It's not really about wanting answers, either. If anything, I just want the same thing every Renegade does." Adrian allowed a faint smile. "Justice."

CHAPTER SIXTEEN

———■■—■—■—■—■———

NOVA STOOD ON THE SIDEWALK outside Renegade Headquarters for longer than she probably should have, ignoring the people that moved around her, grumbling at the girl in their way or the tourists who clustered beside the bus stops to take pictures of the red letters hung over the massive glass doors.

Even tilting her head back she could only barely see the top of the building. It was practically a haze, so far up in the sky, towering over the rest of the cityscape. She had seen the building from afar a thousand times, stared at it from rooftops across the city and imagined how she could scale the walls, slip inside, take revenge against the Council and so-called heroes who treated it like their palace. But she had never pictured herself entering through the revolving main entrance. Never once thought she would be welcome there.

Those revolving doors had been spinning incessantly since she'd arrived. She didn't think everyone who worked in the building was a prodigy, but there were certainly plenty of people coming and going who wore the signature gray uniforms, though just as many in suits and casual business clothes. Some of the Renegades stopped to smile and wave at the tourists, and were always greeted with a flurry of squeals and camera flashes. All the worshipers come to gawk.

Nova's brow tightened as she glanced around, realizing that *she* was among the awestruck gawkers. Huffing, she tore her feet from the sidewalk and forced them to move forward. Her palms were sweating as she neared the doors. A woman emerged in a sleek pantsuit. She didn't even glance at Nova as she took off down the sidewalk, speaking into a device around her wrist and leaving the door to spin leisurely behind her. The gap between the glass barricades yawned open in admittance.

Nova swallowed and stepped inside.

Her heartbeat was a rapid staccato as the doors enclosed around her, then circled open on the other side.

Just like that, she was inside Renegade Headquarters. She dodged out from the revolving door and froze, every muscle braced, but not a single alarm sounded.

She was on a landing that overlooked a bright and sprawling lobby, where the Renegade *R* greeted her, inset into the glossy white floor. A staircase led down to the lobby on her left, a curving ramp to her right, both dropping toward a half-moon desk with the word INFORMATION bolted to the front in large steel letters.

The Anarchists had contemplated an attack on Renegade HQ a thousand times, but they had always known it would be too much risk to try to infiltrate it. There would never be a time when they weren't vastly outnumbered, as hundreds of prodigies worked and trained inside the building on any given day. Nova could see now that what they'd assumed was true—the Renegades had not left themselves vulnerable to attack. After a quick scan of the lobby she had already pinpointed more than a dozen cameras and sensors and alarms, along with, of course, the armed and uniformed Renegades posted at practical intervals around the space, including one on either side of the landing where she stood. She wondered if guard duty was a full-time gig around here, or if it was a role they rotated people in and out of. She would have to find out. That was precisely the type of information Leroy had meant when he suggested she could make a good spy for them.

Everyone else seemed to be ignoring the guards, so she did, too, though her nerves twitched as she passed one on her way toward the staircase. An ominous chill went down her spine as she had the premonition that she was about to be tackled from behind. That she would be arrested, bound, made to answer for her crimes against the Council. That maybe her acceptance into the Renegades had been nothing but a ploy to lure her here.

But no. Nothing happened. She passed by the guard without looking into his face, and so far as she could tell, he didn't look at her, either, though he might have glanced disinterestedly at the *R* pinned to her shirt, the one that felt like it was burning a hole into her skin. That was her pass, after all. That was the secret code to enter this place.

This pin was proof that she belonged there.

As she made her way down the stairs, the vast lobby seemed to transform around her. No longer flanked by security guards, she began to take in other details about the space. There were seating areas with sleek leather couches and coffee tables littered with newspapers and magazines. A small café stood in the distant corner, surrounded by little round tables where people were bent over paperwork as they sipped from paper cups. On the far side of the lobby were stairs curving up toward a wide sky bridge and a glass overlook—a large, circular room encased in glass. She could see some sort of glass sculpture taking up the floor of the enclosure, but couldn't tell from this distance what it was.

Her attention turned up to the television screens that were scattered around the room, hanging from the ceiling or attached to pillars. Most were tuned to a variety of news stations, both local and international, but some offered internal messaging. ANNUAL RENEGADE POTLUCK THIS SUNDAY, BRING THE WHOLE FAMILY! Or, NEW ENFORCER NEEDED FOR NIGHT PATROL TEAM—APPLY AT SECURITY DESK. Or—

Nova's feet stalled on the last step as one of the messages on the screens was replaced with something new. A hazy photo of *her*.

WANTED: "NIGHTMARE"—REPORT ANY INFORMATION TO THE COUNCIL.

Her back went rigid and she felt that sickening swirl of anxiety in her stomach again, the same sensation she'd had all night and all morning. What was she *doing*?

She would be found out. Surely someone would recognize her.

Except—two of the Renegades who should have recognized her already had seemed oblivious. Surely, if she could fool Red Assassin and Smokescreen, she could fool anyone.

She looked hard at the image on the screen. Costumed as Nightmare, there was nothing to give her away. You couldn't even see her eyes in the photo, just the glint of her mask beneath the overhang of her black hood. No one would recognize her, not by looks at least. It was her mannerisms that threatened to give her away, those little things that one did subconsciously. The way she walked, or where she put her hands when she was standing still, or even how she fought in hand-to-hand combat. And, perhaps more than anything, the way she despised the Renegades and the Council, and the way that hatred could overflow from her mouth at any moment.

She would have to take care to smother those instincts. To play the game. To be one of them.

She reached for the pin attached to her T-shirt, the one Adrian Everhart had drawn at the trials. Her fingers ran over the sharp corners of the *R*, traced along the letter's curve.

Today she was a Renegade, so that someday she would be their downfall.

She approached the information desk, where a portly man with impressive sideburns was typing at a computer. He smiled when he looked up at her, but Nova couldn't quite bring herself to return it.

"Hi," she started. "I was recruited at the trials. I'm supposed to—"

"Insomnia," he said brightly, launching to his feet and holding a hand toward her. She stared at it for a long time—pinkish-red skin and neat fingernails and a braided leather bracelet around his thick wrist. Though it was an innocent gesture, a *normal* gesture, everything about it felt uncanny.

Here was a Renegade, maybe a prodigy, maybe not, but either way, he was offering his hand to her. Contact. *Skin.*

Even the Anarchists didn't like to touch her. Not because being put to sleep was such a great tragedy, but because sleep left you vulnerable. *She* made people vulnerable.

She waited too long.

The man—Sampson Cartwright, according to the tag on the desk—awkwardly closed his hand into a fist and reeled it back. "I saw you at the trials," he said, snapping his fingers as though this could make up for the awkward moment. "You were great. The look on Gargoyle's face . . ." His eyes glinted, almost merrily, or perhaps with mocking, and it was a strange realization for Nova to think that not every Renegade got along with one another.

Sampson cleared his throat. "Anyway, you're on Sketch's team, right? I don't think he's come in yet, but I can check and see if . . ."

Nova's heart lunged into her throat. Sampson kept talking, but the words dulled to an annoying hum in her head.

The Council had just emerged from one of the elevators behind the information desk.

No—not the whole Council. Just Captain Chromium and Tsunami.

Nova's mouth went dry at the sight of them. They were talking to each other, easy, carefree. Tsunami was laughing, politely covering her mouth with her fingers as she did. The Captain's eyes were twinkling, with a hint of something like mischief. Unlike the rest of the Renegades, they did not wear the typical gray-and-red uniforms, but their own iconic costumes—the Captain's shoulder pads and leggings, Tsunami's billowy skirt.

They strolled across the lobby. Not toward Nova, exactly, but not away from her, either. Neither looked at her. Neither noticed that a villain was in their midst. Neither could have any idea that her hand had traveled to her belt at their arrival, fitting her fingers deftly around the pen she'd picked out from among her trove of weapons that morning. The one with the secret compartment behind the ink refills. She had one poisonous dart already loaded.

Her pulse stammered. She was *there*. She was inside Renegade Headquarters, mere steps away from two members of the Council, and no one had any idea that she was a threat.

This was a new taste of power. Not just to be Nightmare, and all the secrecy and anonymity that afforded her. But now, to be Insomnia.

To be *one of them*. To travel in their midst, to come this close, and to have no one even cast her a wary glance.

The weapon pressed into her palm.

Could she take one of them out, right now, at this very moment?

It would be her end, without a doubt. If she wasn't killed instantly, she would be captured and imprisoned for life.

But still—the possibility was there. The *potential.*

If not now, if not today, then soon. An opportunity would arise, and she would be ready for it.

With a painful swallow, she forced her hand to release its grip on the pen, just as the two Council members turned into a hallway and disappeared.

"I know exactly what you're thinking."

Disoriented, Nova spun back to Sampson Cartwright, who was watching her with a knowing, serious look. Her heart stuttered and that sense of vulnerability returned. Was her hatred written so plainly on her face? Were her thoughts so easily deciphered?

Or . . . worse . . .

Her breaths stuttered as she leaned toward Sampson. "Are you a telepath?"

Sampson stared at her, speechless for a moment, then released a hearty laugh. "I wish! I'm not even a prodigy. But, come on . . . everyone gets a little star struck the first time they see the Council up close." He gestured at the pen clipped to her belt. "You can ask for an autograph next time. Don't worry. They get it all the time, and they're actually really nice about it."

Nova sank back, relieved that this stranger hadn't been reading her mind while she stood there plotting against his precious Council, but also dismayed that he had so utterly misinterpreted her expression.

She was saved from the ireful response that rose up within her by her name echoing across the lobby.

"Nova!"

She turned. Smokescreen and Red Assassin were striding toward her. That same flash of adrenaline she'd felt at the arena coursed through her system at the sight of them, but it was quelled by their open smiles. For once, there was no grayish haze drifting around Smokescreen's ankles, and Red Assassin's gem hung innocently from the wire around her wrist. She was also carrying a bundle of gray cloth.

"Nova McLain," said Smokescreen, planting his cane on the tile while he gestured around at the massive lobby with his free arm. "Welcome to HQ. You find the place all right?"

Nova blinked. "It's the tallest building in the city."

"He's being witty," said Red Assassin. She shifted the bundle of cloth to one arm and held out her hand. Ungloved. "I'm Ruby, by the way. This is Oscar."

Ruby. Oscar.

Normal names. Normal *people*.

This time, Nova took the offered hand. Her power sparked inside her at the touch, but she smothered it with what she hoped was a friendly smile. "Nova."

Rather than shaking her hand, Oscar threw an arm around her shoulders and started leading her across the lobby. Nova tensed at the contact, but he either didn't notice or ignored it. "We are overjoyed to have you," he said. "Come on, Adrian's on his way in now. He said he'd meet us in the lounge."

"Uh—hold on, one second," said Nova as something startling occurred to her. She ducked out from beneath Oscar's arm. He and Ruby stared after Nova as she darted back to the information desk. Leaning over the counter toward Sampson, she whispered,

"Hey, could you tell me if there *are* any mind readers in the Renegades?"

Sampson's eyes darted once toward Ruby and Oscar, then back to Nova. "Um. No? Not currently. We had one a few years back but she was transferred to one of our foreign embassies."

Nova beamed. "Okay, great. Thanks. I was just curious."

Waving, she jogged back to the others.

"Everything all right?" asked Ruby.

"Excellent," said Nova, drawing on every reserve of enthusiasm she could find. "That guy was really helpful."

"Sampson is good people," said Oscar, nodding toward a bank of elevators. "Come on, let's get you changed."

"Changed?"

Trekking beside her, Ruby waggled the cloth bundle. "Say hello to your new uniform! I grabbed the size I thought would fit, but the pants might be a little long on you." She glanced at Nova's feet. "We have an alterations team on staff. They'll want to fit you for a pair of boots before you leave today. You can keep your own shoes for now, but hopefully you'll have official footwear in the next day or so. They're sticklers for proper attire around here."

"A few years ago a recruit was chasing after a purse snatcher and sprained his ankle," said Oscar. "So now the uniform comes with boots that have ankle braces, supreme slip-resistant soles, and every other feature they could think to put into them. Great cushion too. You'll love them."

Nova forced a wan smile.

"Either way," said Ruby, "this uniform will be worlds better than what you're used to wearing, right?"

Nova stumbled over her own feet, picturing Nightmare's hooded jacket and metal face mask. "Excuse me?"

"I've been to Cosmopolis Park," said Ruby, who was practically skipping beside Nova. "Those awful uniforms, with the striped pants and those hats . . ." She gestured down the length of her body, and though it had been years since Nova had been to the amusement park, she could easily picture the outfit Ruby was describing, with its red-and-white-striped trousers, yellow bow tie, and straw porkpie hat.

She shuddered to imagine herself wearing it. "You read my application?"

"We wanted to get to know you a little better before you got here," said Oscar, grinning. "Don't worry. Your talents were completely wasted as a ride operator. You'll be much happier here."

They reached the elevators and Oscar jabbed the *up* button with the butt of his cane. As they stepped inside, Ruby handed the bundle to Nova, then stepped back to inspect Nova's belt. "Are these some of your inventions?"

"Just a few," Nova said. It had been difficult to decide what to bring that morning. She couldn't bring any of her favorite weapons or gadgets, as they would all be recognized as tools Nightmare had been seen with over the past year. But she'd been asked her to bring examples of her work, so she had to pick something.

In the end, she'd chosen the blow-dart ink pen, a shock-wave gun that could temporarily stun an opponent up to thirty feet away, and a set of exothermic micro-flares.

"Cool!" said Ruby, with more fervor than Nova thought the inventions warranted. "When we're done giving you the tour today, you should go show these down at R and D. They live for stuff like this."

"Don't tell her that!" said Oscar, as if aghast. "They'll want to take her away from us."

Ruby feigned a gasp. "Good point. Nova, you should definitely not go talk to the folks in R and D. Ever."

"They're killjoys down there, anyway," added Oscar. "The ones that always bring the vegetable trays to the party, you know what I mean?" He gave her a knowing look.

"That Nightmare had better look out now that we have you on the team," Ruby added.

Panic raced down Nova's spine. "Nightmare?" she said, her voice strained. "What do you mean?"

"You've heard of her, right?" said Smokescreen. "She's been all over the news lately."

Without waiting for Nova's answer, Ruby said, "That's kind of her thing too. I mean, her superpower is putting people to sleep by touching them, but she also has access to some really neat weapons. There's footage of her from a few months back scaling a building like a spider, not using any handholds. They say it has something to do with the gloves she was wearing." She shrugged. "R and D is trying to replicate them, but I don't think they've had much success so far. Still"—she tapped the shock-wave gun on Nova's hip—"if we'd had this at the parade, she'd be history."

Nova attempted an encouraging smile, not bothering to tell them that the shock-wave gun fired at a much slower velocity than a regular gun with real ammunition. She was *fairly certain* that Nightmare could dodge the blast just fine.

The elevator doors opened, and somewhat relieved to be out of the confined metal box with two of her enemies-turned-allies, Nova exhaled and followed them. They led Nova into another open space, though this one was significantly more relaxed than the lobby. More couches and TV screens, though just as many had video games being played on them as were showing the news. Vending machines lined one wall, and a number of long tables stood in front of the windows, where men and women in gray uniforms were laughing over bags of trail mix and candy clusters.

Nova scanned the occupants of the table, searching for hints of their abilities and weaknesses, but there was little she could discern when they were just sitting around chatting. A man with wavy black hair had a ukulele strapped to his back. A young girl had a birthmark the shape of a skeleton key along one side of her face. A woman had a small cloud of purple dust erupt from her fingers every time she snapped, evidently trying to think of a specific word that was eluding her.

"This is the lounge," said Ruby. "Open access for anyone on the patrol task forces or who works in enforcement. Mostly we come here to unwind when we're waiting for a shift to start, or if it's been a slow night for crime."

"Not that there have been many of those lately," said Oscar. "Or . . . ever." He gestured toward a hallway. "There are private rooms down here if you ever need to take a power nap." He paused. "Or, I guess, not a power nap, but . . . something equally restorative and . . . restful . . . like, meditation. Or something." Ears turning pink, he glanced at Ruby for help.

"*Or*," said Ruby loudly, finding a door with a vacant tab by the doorknob, "if you need to get changed." She pushed the door open. "Keep your belt on over the uniform. It'll be part of your signature."

"We'll wait out here," said Oscar. "Want something from the vending machines?"

"No, thank you," said Nova, stepping into the room and letting the door shut behind her. After ensuring she was alone in the room, she reached back and turned the bolt on the lock. The room looked how she imagined a college dormitory would look, but with better quality furniture. A narrow sleeping cot, the blankets neatly tucked around the corners. A glass-topped desk containing today's edition of the *Gatlon Gazette* and a sleek table lamp. A small counter in the corner with a built-in sink. A full-length mirror hung on the back of a closet door.

The only decoration was a large framed poster over the bed—a vintage print showing a spread taken from some comic book Nova didn't recognize. In the vibrant color panels, a masked superhero was scooping a red-haired woman into his arms and flying her to safety above a jutting city skyline. The woman's eyes were shining deliriously as she cried out in bold Comic Sans—"I knew you'd come! You *always* come!"

With a disparaging laugh, Nova turned away from the print.

The room was nice. Far nicer than what she was accustomed to. But there was something faintly unnerving about the place. It was too clean, too neat, too *perfect*.

Too full of false promises.

She would not be lured into security by simple comforts like a noticeable lack of vermin skittering across the floor.

She unrolled the gray bundle and held the uniform up by the shoulders. It was a simple bodysuit that would cover her from throat to wrist to ankle, with red detailing along the limbs and a red *R* emblazoned on the chest.

She shook her head at it and sighed. "All right, Insomnia," she said, dropping the uniform onto the bed and peeling off her shirt. "It's too late to change your mind now."

CHAPTER SEVENTEEN

———■————

ADRIAN WAS BEAMING when he entered the lounge. In the hours since he'd gotten permission from his dads for his team to handle the library surveillance mission, he'd already been to visit the location of their first non-patrol task. He hadn't gone inside the library, but he'd staked out an abandoned office building just across the street that would provide them with a perfect place to set up, and a particular corner office with a window looking straight into the alleyway around the library's east side, where a back door struck him as the perfect entrance for shady people coming to do shady dealings. He'd made a list of supplies, from binoculars to snack foods to a deck of cards, because a bored Oscar was a dangerous thing. Mostly, though, his head had been full all morning of fantasies in which his team not only uncovered a ring of black-market weapon dealings and put Gene Cronin behind bars, but where they easily tracked down and arrested Nightmare too.

He spotted Oscar and Ruby playing Battle to the Death, one of two standing arcade games in the lounge, there to keep the patrol units entertained when they waited for an assignment. The game was a classic two-person combat challenge, and Oscar and Ruby developed an instantaneous rivalry when it had been brought in the year before. As far as Adrian could tell, their skills continued to be neck and neck, to each of their continued frustrations.

He came to stand behind them as Ruby's avatar did a roundhouse kick that sent Oscar's flying offscreen. Ruby whooped and flung her hands outward in celebration, smacking Adrian in the nose. He cried out and pulled back, adjusting his glasses with one hand and pressing the other over his nose.

Ruby recoiled. "Sorry!" she squeaked, though her look of remorse quickly turned into a suspicious scowl. "Except, not really, creepy stalker guy. How long were you standing there?"

"About two seconds," said Adrian, scrunching his nose a couple times to clear the painful tingling that was running through the cartilage.

"Oh," said Ruby. "In that case . . . sorry!" She paused. "Except, still not really, because I *totally just beat Oscar's high score!*" She pumped her fist into the air.

"This battle is far from over," said Oscar, leaning against the machine. "I demand a rematch."

Ruby popped her knuckles. "You can have as many rematches as you'd like. I am never giving up this lead."

"Hey, guys," said Adrian, "where's the new girl? You didn't scare her off already, did you?"

"Changing," said Oscar, jerking a thumb over his shoulder while Ruby deposited a new coin into the machine's slot.

"Oh," said Adrian, glancing toward the private rooms, just as a figure emerged from the hall. He straightened. "Oh."

Nova caught his eye and seemed to falter midstep.

Breaking away from the others, Adrian approached her, tucking his hands into his pockets. He was still in jeans and a jacket himself, figuring there wasn't much point in putting on his uniform if they wouldn't be doing any patrol duty.

"How does it feel?" he said.

She glanced down. Holding her bundled street clothes in one arm, she ran her other hand self-consciously down the side of the uniform. "Long."

Adrian followed the look and saw that the legs of the uniform were puddled on top of her sneakers.

"But I can sew," she said. "I'll fix them when I get home."

"Naw, don't worry about it. I'll have the alterations department pull another uniform and amend it. You'll have it tomorrow, or maybe the next day. They can get backed up right after the trials."

Nova opened her mouth and he could sense an argument building there, so he quickly added, "We didn't bring you on to be a seamstress."

She hesitated, then closed her mouth again, and in that moment Adrian realized what made her look so different when she'd first emerged from the hallway. At first, he'd thought it was just seeing her in uniform, a uniform that stood for bravery and strength, traits she'd displayed at the trials but that were now exaggerated by the bold red R.

But no, it wasn't that at all.

She looked different because she seemed, in that moment, laughably, almost hysterically uncomfortable. Nervous and maybe even a little awkward, rather like she had when he'd drawn the bracelet clasp onto her wrist. It almost didn't seem possible that this could be the same girl who had challenged the Gargoyle with unwavering courage. Who had emanated nothing but fierce determination while surrounded by an entire arena of screaming spectators.

"Here," said Adrian, pulling out his marker. "You need a bag." He moved toward the nearest table and sketched out a large tote bag. Lifting it from the acrylic surface, he took the handles and gave it a shake, holding it open for Nova to drop her clothes into.

"Thanks," she murmured, shoving the clothes inside. She wrapped her hands around the base of the bag's handles, almost as if she were avoiding touching Adrian's hands as she took it from him. "You sure do enjoy showing off with that trick, don't you?"

Heat warmed the back of his neck. Had he been showing off?

"Well, it can be pretty convenient . . . sometimes."

Nova looked briefly like she would smile, and he started to wonder if she was teasing him.

"Anyway," he said, gesturing toward the corner of the lounge, "you can put it in the lockers over there while we give you the grand tour."

A rage-filled scream pulled their attention toward the arcade game, where Oscar was laughing maniacally while Ruby pounded at the buttons. "My controls froze up! That so doesn't count!"

"Please direct all complaints to the great scorekeeper in the sky," said Oscar, popping his knuckles in mockery of how Ruby had done so before.

Adrian capped his marker and tucked it away. "Believe it or not, they're actually really great superheroes."

Nova met his gaze, and he could tell she was unconvinced. "Did you mention something about a grand tour?"

———✳✳✳———

ADRIAN HAD PLANNED ON only taking Nova around to the areas of headquarters they used frequently as a team. The lounge she'd already seen, so he thought they would stop by the cafeteria and the training hall, then do a quick team-simulation on the virtual reality floor and call it a day. But the second the four of them stepped into the elevators, Nova's curiosity surprised him. She wanted to know about the armory and how they distinguished what weapons were housed there versus those that were stored in the vaults specifically intended for powerful prodigy artifacts. She wanted to see the laboratories in research and development, and though they didn't have clearance to go inside, Adrian caught her craning her head to see through an open door as one of the technicians passed by. She was curious about their forensics work, the investigations departments, Council Hall, and the state-of-the-art prison cells—though here again, Adrian could only describe them to her as best he could; he had never actually been inside to see them himself.

To his surprise, she even wanted to see the call center, located far up on the seventy-fifth floor of the building. Ruby and Oscar gave halfhearted attempts to talk her out of it, explaining that it really wasn't all that interesting, but Nova's enthusiasm for the various aspects of the organization, even the dull aspects, was becoming contagious. He and his team spent so much time on the streets, communicating with headquarters through hasty messages transmitted into their communication bands, it was easy to forget just how complex their whole system was. Seeing Nova's wide-eyed intrigue and trying to answer her emphatic questions reminded him that the Renegades had become so much more than the group of vigilantes seeking to defend the people of the world. They were still protectors, but they were now inventors, lawmakers, and activists. They were working to improve society in a hundred different ways at any given time, and seeing how interested in it all Nova was served to make him more interested in it, too.

Arriving on the seventy-fifth floor, they stepped out of the elevator onto a circular platform that looked over row upon row of computer desks. The surrounding walls were taken up by satellite imagery projected in real time onto massive screens, some showing Gatlon City, others the nearby suburbs or other parts of the country. Green lines, red markers, and digital notes were being constantly added and removed from the screens, and the room buzzed with activity. Phones ringing. Staff barking into their headsets and clacking at their keyboards. People shouting orders or demanding to know the status of various ongoing situations.

A home invasion is being reported in C14—how fast can a patrol team get over there?

That landlord on East Bracken is complaining about the graffiti again—do we have a clean-up crew available?

I need a squad to check out this bomb threat outside the arena. What's Metalocks's status?

Metalock is still dealing with that explosion in Murkwater, but we can send Dead Drop.

He says this is the fourth time his store has been vandalized in the past two months. I swear, didn't we already catch these guys?

We have a situation at the B-Mart on Sixty-Second. . . . Sounds like a man is getting aggressive over receiving incorrect change?

Adrian leaned his elbows on the rail that rimmed the platform. "We think of this as the nervous system of the city," he said. "Distress calls come here, the situation is assessed, and a patrol team or sometimes a solo Renegade is assigned to deal with it."

"Much more efficient than prowling the streets at night, searching for crime," said Ruby, "which is what they did in the old days."

"More efficient," said Oscar, heaving a dramatic sigh, "but not nearly as glamorous."

"It's amazing how they could pull this together in such a short period of time," said Nova. "The laboratories, the virtual-reality simulators, *this*. How did they build this in just ten years?"

"Nine years," said Ruby.

"Eight," corrected Adrian. "They took over this building eight years ago. It was home to squatters during the Age of Anarchy but was abandoned by the time the Council decided to make it their headquarters. As for turning it into *this*"—he gestured around the bustling call center—"when you have a team full of metalworkers and earth elementals, prodigies who have basic telekinesis skills and superstrength, not to mention one really helpful cyberlinguist, it tends to come together pretty fast."

"Cyberlinguist?"

"A prodigy who can communicate with cybernetic technology," he explained. "He's our tech guy."

Nova hummed and he couldn't quite read her reaction. Her gaze returned to a map of Gatlon City, her eyes tracking a yellow dot as it blinked its way down Drury Avenue. "You seem shorthanded."

Adrian nodded. "It is a problem these days."

"Then why turn so many prodigies away at the trials?"

"We're only shorthanded when it comes to patrols. The rest of the system is fine, but we need more people who can be out on the streets, handling criminals and enforcing the laws. So these days we only take on recruits we think will be suited to that." He frowned. "Though I'll be the first to admit that the trials probably aren't the best way for us to be finding new talent, but it isn't up to me."

"Who is it up to? The Council?"

"Everything," Ruby said with a cheerful laugh. "Everything is up to the Council."

"Pretty much. What we do here, it isn't just fighting crime anymore, or even helping people. It's about keeping the city from falling apart again, and for that, we need unity. And . . . well, as obnoxious as the trials might get, they do bring people together."

Nova's gaze continued to dart around the room. "So why do you keep dealing with things like painting over graffiti, or stepping in on behalf of a clerk who can't figure out the correct change? Why not set up a non-prodigy police force to deal with situations that don't need a . . . you know. A superhero."

"A non-prodigy police force?" said Oscar, amused. "No one would apply."

"Why not?" said Nova. "That's what they had before the Age of Anarchy."

"Because now they have superheroes to handle these things for them," Oscar said with a mild shrug.

"But it's their city too," Nova insisted. "Their lives, their livelihoods? They can't expect prodigies to do everything for them all the time."

Her attention switched to Adrian, but he wasn't sure how to respond. It was true that it would help them a lot to be able to hand over some of the lower-priority assignments to a civilian police force, but he couldn't help feeling like Oscar was right. With the Renegades willing to shoulder all the responsibility, why would anyone apply for such a force?

Nova's shoulders sank a little. "Or not?"

"We could suggest it to the Council?" chirped Ruby. "Maybe start inviting people who were police officers before the Age of Anarchy to apply for a special task force?"

Adrian nodded. "I could mention it to my dads when I see them later."

Beside him, Nova seemed to tense, and a moment later she shifted her weight, pulling a few inches away from him. He hadn't even realized just how close they'd been standing. He scanned her face, but it had gone unreadable as she scrutinized a map of the Wallowridge neighborhood.

He cleared his throat. "Ready to go see the training hall?"

Nova's face cleared as she spun back to him, and whatever discomfort he'd sensed vanished so quick he wondered if he'd only imagined it. Her smile was sudden and eager. "Absolutely."

CHAPTER EIGHTEEN

—▪—▪—■—▪—▪—

THE TRAINING HALL was the only part of headquarters that was kept in the building's sublevels. When the skyscraper was first built, its foundation had encompassed a massive parking garage. After the Renegades took over, they demolished floor after floor of concrete, leaving only the foundational walls and pillars to protect the integrity of the building overhead. What was left was a vast open space beneath the vaulted ceilings for them to exercise their powers.

Like the lobby and the call center, the training hall was a hub of activity, but all the chatter of the upper levels was replaced down here with movement and action. Renegades launching themselves over platforms, scaling walls, shooting at targets, facing off in large netted-off rings, swinging across an obstacle course of ropes and bars, and—more than anything—showing off their vast array of abilities.

Adrian headed the group as they left the elevator bank, heading down the walkway that passed over the training facilities. He soon realized that Nova's pace had begun to slow, until she stopped altogether. Adrian glanced back to see her face awash in speechless awe.

He followed her gaze around the room, trying to imagine this was the first time he'd ever seen it. To their right, twin brothers were sparring with quarterstaffs, but one turned into orange liquid and the other into orange vapor each time they were struck. Next to them was a blindfolded boy firing a bow and arrow at a series of moving targets and hitting them dead-center every time. On Adrian's left, an earth elemental turned the contents of a sandbox into a two-level sand castle without touching a grain. Ahead, there was a woman who transformed into a grizzly bear in the blink of an eye, then charged at a man with great bull horns erupting from his skull. In the distance, a girl had created a vortex above her head and was sucking her opponent toward it, while said opponent used his own barbed hands and toes to grip the floor and fight against the vacuum.

"Sweet rot," Nova whispered.

"It is a little overwhelming the first time you see it," said Adrian.

Nova stepped forward, wrapping her hands around the railing. "I had no idea there were . . . so many of you."

"The numbers vary," he said. "Our permanent staff is around four hundred, but we get prodigies from all over the world who come here to be trained for a few months, then leave. We have the best facilities for it, and the best reputation."

"Trained for what, exactly?"

"To be superheroes," said Ruby, fidgeting with the wire around her wrist. "What else?"

"And when they're ready," continued Adrian, "they go back home and take up the cause of the Renegades wherever they're from. There are Renegade chapters all over the world now. People who have dedicated themselves to the defense of justice. And it all started right here. Well, not right *here*." He cast his eyes toward the tall ceilings. "The Renegades technically started in the Dread Warden's basement, but that was a long time ago."

He led them down the narrow walkway that extended across the length of the training hall, two stories over the grounds below. Adrian pointed out different areas Nova might want to check out when she had the chance, from obstacle courses and target practice to sparring rings and a climbing wall outfitted with various materials to mimic different climbing surfaces to an enclosed saltwater pool to row after row of barbells and free weights.

"Just say the word if you ever want a spotting partner," said Oscar. "Ruby and I come down here all the time."

"Not Adrian?" said Nova, glancing at him.

Adrian cast Oscar a wry look. "I like the climbing wall and the obstacle courses, but free weights bore me out of my mind."

"He's intimidated by me," said Oscar. "He doesn't like being reminded that I can bench-press way more than he can."

"That's true," said Adrian, shrugging.

They continued on, Adrian doing his best to point out any resources that might be of interest to Nova, except *everything* seemed to be of interest to her. They had just passed the equipment rentals counter, where a vast wall held everything from nunchakus to snowshoes, when Nova gasped and grabbed Adrian's elbow. He startled and turned to her. Nova retracted her hand just as quickly, fisting it against her stomach instead.

"It's that girl," she said, nodding toward the floor. "The one from the parade."

He followed the look. "Oh yeah. That's Maggie. Alias Magpie, because of her, um . . . appreciation of small, shiny objects."

Nova drew herself up, cheeks flushing. "She's a thief! The Renegades tolerate that?"

"Who are we talking about?" said Ruby, craning her head. On a mat below, Magpie was standing on a plank over an enormous tank full of dirt, using her power to excavate increasingly large and heavy metallic items from the ground, as if her small hand held the power of an industrial magnet. "Oh, her. She's mostly a scavenger, I think."

Adrian nodded. "There are lots of abandoned places in this city, and she's helped us find a lot of useful stuff. Silverware, batteries . . . things like that. It comes in handy, especially while we try to get trade and manufacturing up and running again."

Nova scowled. "Taking my bracelet wasn't scavenging."

"I know," said Adrian. "You're right. Obviously, theft is against the code. But a lot of the kids who come here, Magpie included, had pretty rough childhoods. Sure, there are some parents who think it's great when their kid turns out to be a prodigy, but there are also lots of people who are still afraid of what we can do. Who don't trust us. And for them, to have a kid with superpowers is"—he frowned, his heart twisting as he thought of countless stories he had heard of young prodigies being neglected, abused, even abandoned—"not ideal," he finished lamely, returning his gaze to Nova. "Anyway, when they get here, we try to teach them right from wrong, but it can be hard to overcome some of the survival instincts they've developed up to this point. We're working on it, though."

Nova was still watching Maggie down below, her lips pinched. Then she glanced down to where her fingers were spinning her delicate bracelet around the wrist of her gray uniform. Clamping her hand over the bracelet, she sighed. "Don't tell me the Renegades have set up a children's home for wayward prodigies, on top of everything else."

"Nothing that official," said Adrian, smiling faintly. "But when kids come to us without any families of their own, we do try to find a Renegade family for them to live with."

Nova glanced up at him, and he could see a question lingering behind her eyes. Maybe she was wondering about his own family, his own past. The adoptive celebrity dads everyone wanted to know about.

She turned away without mentioning them, though, lifting her chin as she scanned the busy hall. "Where does the Sentinel train?"

Adrian tensed. "What?"

Her expression was thoughtful as she peered around. "The Sentinel," she repeated. "That Renegade that showed up at the parade? Does he train here with everyone else, or is there a special area for him? Or . . . Renegades like him. Are there more than one?"

Her tone was light, innocent, but Adrian couldn't stop gaping at her, unable to tell if the question was really as innocuous as it sounded, or if there was something more to it than appeared on the surface. If there was an accusation hidden beneath her words.

When Nova faced him, curiosity was etched into her features.

It was Ruby who responded first. "He's an impostor," she said, with enough spite to make Adrian flinch.

Nova turned to her. "The Sentinel?"

"He's pretending to be a Renegade," said Ruby, "but he's not. He's a fake."

Nova's gaze shifted between the three of them, a small wrinkle forming between her brows. "You all really believe that?"

Her focus landed on Adrian and he managed to gather himself, shaking off the bout of paranoia. "No one had ever heard of him before that day. Whoever he is, he hasn't revealed his identity to anyone here."

"But he's a prodigy, and a powerful one," said Nova, and somehow, that small, offhanded compliment sent a faint surge of pride through Adrian's chest. "And who other than the Renegades would have the resources to make a suit like the one he wears? Or find a way to combine multiple superpowers into one human being?" She glanced at Ruby and Oscar, but somehow her attention always seemed to return to Adrian. Searching and quizzical, as though she could tell how hard he was trying to act oblivious. "If you guys don't know who he is, then . . . maybe he's a classified project that hasn't been revealed to everyone yet. Right?"

"That's what I thought at first too," said Oscar. "But when the Council heard that he'd been acting on their behalf, claiming to have acted on their orders and whatnot, they seemed livid."

Adrian lowered his gaze.

"And I'm not sure you can fake that sort of thing," Oscar added. "At least, not all of them. Not like that."

"Huh," said Nova, and it was clear she remained skeptical. "I guess we'll find out eventually."

Adrian scratched his right forearm, where his new tattoo was still sore beneath the bandage.

"Oh, look!" said Ruby, pointing down to the training floor. "There's Danna."

Glad for the diversion, Adrian followed the gesture and spotted Danna on one of the training mats below, bracing herself against a padded bench. On the other side of the mat, one of their trainers was holding, of all things, a slingshot.

As they watched, Ballistic, the trainer, aimed straight up and fired, sending a high-drag projectile flapping toward the ceiling.

Danna crouched, flipping her long dreadlocks over one shoulder as she focused on the target. Then she leaped and her body dispersed into a cyclone of butterflies soaring upward. The creatures surrounded the projectile and Danna reformed, grabbing it with one hand and dropping back down to the ground. It was nearly a perfect catch, but as her feet touched the ground again, she let out a pained grunt and collapsed to one knee.

Adrian grimaced.

"Monarch?" said Nova.

"You've done your research," said Oscar. "She's on our team, too, but she got injured at the parade so she couldn't come to the trials."

"Come on," said Ruby, latching on to Nova's arm. "We'll introduce you."

They made their way to the next staircase. As they approached Danna's mat, Adrian could hear Ballistic reminding her to stay in swarm formation as she descended, as her body wasn't ready for such a fall. Danna fisted her hands as she rebuked, "It's not that easy! Twenty-nine butterflies were burned off. It'd be like you trying to catch the thing with three missing fingers!"

She spotted their group and straightened, swiping her forearm across her damp brow. Her attention turned to Nova.

"They let you out of the med wing!" cried Ruby. Releasing Nova, she swung her arms wide in celebration. Adrian barely recoiled fast enough to avoid another hit to his nose. "That's faster than they thought, right?"

Danna heaved a sigh, casting a sour look at the trainer. "They said I could start retraining myself to use the swarm. You'd be amazed what a difference it makes when I lose a bunch like that. It's like learning to control them all over again."

Adrian's shoulders knotted. *Twenty-nine butterflies were burned off.*

"But I need to make it through the obstacle course before they send me out on patrol again," Danna continued. "It'll be at least another couple of weeks."

"After those burns?" said Oscar, nodding at the small lump where there must have been bandages beneath her uniform. "Lucky it wasn't worse."

"And that the healers are so great," added Ruby. Beaming, she gestured at Nova. "You haven't met our new girl yet."

Danna faced Nova. "Insomnia, right?" she said, holding out a hand. "I saw the trial. Impressive."

Nova accepted the handshake, though as soon as Danna released her she quickly pulled her hand back against her side. "Gargoyle's not as scary as he thinks."

Danna chuckled. "I won't lie. It was refreshing to see someone put Frostbite's team in their place." She slumped onto the padded bench. "Five-minute break?" she called over to Ballistic, but he had already turned and started working with Flashbolt, a boy who had what looked like glass marbles embedded in his palms.

Danna turned her gaze back up to Nova. "I heard Sketch thinks you'll be a decent surveillance asset."

Nova's eyebrows lifted and she glanced at Adrian.

He scratched the back of his neck. "We haven't really started to discuss—"

"But there's a lot more to being a good spy than people think," Danna interrupted.

Nova's gaze sharpened. "You don't say."

"You were great at the trials, but they don't really prepare you for reality, you know. In a real situation, especially a surveillance mission, you have to pay attention to the details. And remember them. Put the smallest clues together to make a whole. You never know what's going to be important, so you can't discount anything."

Adrian cleared his throat. "Danna is sort of the team surveillance expert. But obviously, what she can do is a different skill set than what you can do. We don't expect . . . we're grateful to have you both."

Nova's lips formed a thin smile. "Thanks for the tip, Monarch. Truly, I think I can handle it."

"I'm sure you can," said Danna. "I just want you to stay on your toes. I need to make sure these slackers are in good hands when you're out there without me."

"Test me, if you want," said Nova, with a casual shrug. "See if I pass inspection."

Adrian glanced at Oscar, and seeing the awkwardness written plain on his face was glad he wasn't the only one sensing the tension. "This isn't—"

"No, really," said Nova. "I don't mind. It wasn't fair that she wasn't at the trials, and I want Danna to feel confident in your choice. Eventually, she and I will be on the team together too, right? So, go ahead. Let's see how good I am at this surveillance stuff."

Danna leaned back on her palms, eyes narrowing thoughtfully. "Okay. Without looking . . . how many exits are there out of this hall?"

"Oh, come on," said Ruby. "This is her first day."

"Seven," said Nova, holding Danna's gaze.

A second passed, before Oscar turned in a circle, counting exits under his breath. When he finished, he gave a mild *huh*.

Adrian, too, found himself scanning the hall.

"Though one could argue," Nova added, "that with this many prodigies around, able to manipulate metal or blow their way through concrete, there is potential for countless more exits if needed."

Danna's face softened. She was beginning to smile when Nova continued, "There are also ten security cameras, two fire extinguishers, and five vending machines—one of which sells nothing but candy, which seriously has me questioning the Renegades' commitment to adequate nutrition."

Oscar laughed. "She's already got our number there. Wait until you see the cafeteria. They have a mac-and-cheese bar!"

Danna's lips turned upward. "How many occupants?"

Nova lifted an eyebrow. "Do *you* know how many people are in here?"

"Nope," said Danna. "Just checking that you're not actually better at this than I am."

Nova rocked back on her heels. "Well, I don't have an exact count. Fifty-ish, I'd guess. And so far, I've only discerned the abilities of sixteen of them."

On the mat beside them, the trainer threw a disc and Flashbolt lifted his hands, shooting a series of colored lightning bolts out of his marbled palms, striking the disc as it arced through the hall.

"Seventeen," Nova amended.

Adrian grinned. "Now who's showing off?"

Nova turned a startled look on him, and there was a moment in which the confident, bold contestant from the trials stood beside him. But a second later, her cheeks flushed and she shrank back slightly, bashful or disoriented. He couldn't quite tell which.

Danna nodded appreciatively. "It sounds like you'll be fine. Just try to keep them out of trouble, won't you?"

"Is that in my job description?" Nova asked.

"Not at all," said Danna, pulling her dreadlocks back and securing them in a low tail. "But I'll feel better if I know you're spending half as much energy watching over these guys as you apparently spend watching everyone else."

Nova grinned brightly and stuck up her thumbs, in what Adrian was absolutely sure was mock positivity. "You can count on me."

"Well," said Adrian, clapping his hands together. "We better let you get back to it. Don't let Ballistic push you around too much, okay?"

Danna grunted, waving halfheartedly after them as they made their way back toward the stairs.

"That just leaves one more stop on this tour," said Adrian.

"The cafeteria?" said Nova, not very enthusiastically.

"Don't knock the cafeteria," said Oscar. "It is free and it is awesome."

Adrian shook his head. "Not the cafeteria, though I'm sure Oscar will gladly show you around there later if you ask. Actually, I have someone special I want you to meet. We call him the Bandit."

"The Bandit?" she said, with a mild laugh.

"Yep. He has, in fact, requested a special audience with you."

"The *Bandit*," she drawled again. "What is this, the Wild West?"

Adrian grinned back at her. "Some days I wonder."

CHAPTER NINETEEN

———▪▪■▪▪———

THEY TOOK THE ELEVATOR back up to the main lobby, then climbed a spiraling staircase, through a short corridor, and out onto the sky bridge Nova had noticed when she first entered the building. She spotted the glass room again, a circular enclosure full of small sculptures that had glistened like crystal stalagmites from down below.

As they got closer, the view through the windows became clear and she saw that it wasn't random sculptures at all, but a model of Gatlon City, constructed in jaw-dropping detail. It was made entirely of clear, sparkling glass.

"What is this, an art installation?" she said as her eyes traced the skyline to the edge of City Park, up to the top of Renegade Headquarters and across to Merchant Tower, then down to the docks on the marina and the bridges that spanned Snakeweed River.

"Not exactly," said Adrian, rapping his knuckles on the window. "It's more like . . . a model playset. It's sort of the Bandit's pastime."

"And who is the Bandit?"

"His real name is Max." He knocked on the glass. "Hey, Max—you have a guest."

Nova spotted a figure emerging on the other side of the cityscape. He was a kid, maybe ten years old, with sand-blond hair that curled messily around his ears and thick eyebrows. He picked his way through the glass city, his bare feet making their way along Broad Street, stepping carefully over taxicabs and trees in miniature planter boxes and the occasional glass pedestrian. He was so intent at first on watching his footing that he was halfway across the city before he noticed Nova.

He froze, his eyes widening. "Insomnia!"

"Bandit?" she guessed.

He jogged the rest of the way to the window that divided them. On this side of the model city, the skyscrapers dropped off into warehouses and shipyards. A wide expanse of what would have been the beach surrounding Harrow Bay offered him a convenient place to stand. "That fight at the trials—that was the best thing I've ever seen. I can't *stand* Gargoyle. And wow, look, you're even shorter than I thought!"

Oscar leaned against the glass wall. "Have you ever even talked to Gargoyle?"

Max cast his gaze upward in disgust. "Please. I've seen enough interviews with Frostbite and her team to know his brain is two-thirds sedimentary."

Nova's mouth stretched into what might have been the first real smile she'd had all day. "Did you just make a geology joke?"

Max ignored the question, turning instead to Adrian. "Can you draw her?"

Nova's eyes widened. "Draw . . . who? Me?"

"Uh, sure," said Adrian, his gaze darting in her direction. "If she doesn't mind."

"You have to say yes," said Max, digging into his back pocket and pulling out a six-inch-tall glass figurine of Gargoyle. "Look. I'm setting up the trials." He pointed in the direction he'd come from. "The arena's back there. I wanted to stage it at the part where you won and joined our team."

Nova looked past the skyscrapers, and though she couldn't see the arena from where she stood, she could easily imagine it on the other side of the downtown district, mirroring its location in the real world.

"*Our* team?" She looked at Adrian, who had already crouched down and started drawing on the glass wall.

It was Oscar who responded. "Max can't do patrols, so we made him an honorary member of the group. That way he at least gets a uniform."

Nova looked back at the boy, who was currently wearing flannel plaid pajamas.

"How's this?" said Adrian.

She took a step back so she could see his drawing—a simple, yet remarkably accurate portrait of herself on the glass. The drawing was not wearing the Renegade uniform like she wore now, but the simple ribbed shirt and sport leggings she'd had on at the trials. He'd even drawn the tiny cannon in her hand.

"Perfect," said Max.

Adrian pressed his palm against the drawing, and Nova watched as the ink seeped right through the window, emerging on the other side as a three-dimensional figurine.

"Wow," she mused. "My first day on the job and I'm already an action figure."

Adrian lifted his head and grinned.

Max took the figure and scampered back through the city. He paused when he was turning the corner onto Raikes Avenue. "Thanks, Adrian. It was a pleasure to meet you, Insomnia. I'm a really huge fan."

Adrian saluted him, and Nova, not knowing quite how to react to this odd encounter, saluted too.

"Thanks?" she started, though Max had turned his back on them. She took in the city again, inspecting it more closely than before. "Did you make all this?"

"It's been a pet project for years." Adrian stood again and put away the marker. "A labor of love. Keeps Max occupied, at least."

She scanned the inside of the room, or what she could see of it. There was a path that led around the sky bridge and a closed door on the other side of the enclosure. "He's not locked up in there, is he?"

When no one answered, she glanced around to see that a shadow had passed over Adrian's face, and both Ruby and Oscar were frowning. Not so much angry or sad as . . . resigned.

"It's not a prison," said Adrian. "He could leave if he wanted to, or needed to. But he knows . . ." He hesitated. "He never tries. To leave."

"Why not?"

He met her eyes. "We call it the quarantine. He has to stay in there for his own good. And ours too." He shrugged. "It's as comfortable as they can make it."

"So he's sick."

"Not exactly," Adrian said, drawing out his words. "He's . . ."

"Dangerous," said Ruby, at the same time Oscar supplied, "Valuable."

Nova cocked her head in confusion, but before anyone could elaborate, she heard a large clunk and hiss from the door into Max's quarantine. It opened to reveal another enclosed chamber beyond it. A woman entered the circular room wearing a cumbersome suit, complete with a full-face shield and self-contained breathing apparatus. Though most of the suit was pristine and white, it was embellished with metallic cuffs around the wrists, ankles, and throat. It looked like the sort of uniform one would wear to scour a nuclear wasteland.

The woman carried a white medical box.

Beyond the skyline, Max stood up, looking mildly annoyed at the interruption.

The woman didn't have to say anything for Max to set down the Insomnia and Gargoyle figurines and start picking his way toward her.

"What's going on?" said Nova.

"They have to take regular samples from him," said Adrian. "Blood, saliva . . ." He shrugged. "I'm honestly not sure what they're doing with most of it."

"Trying to cure him?" she said, thinking it should have been obvious.

But Adrian shook his head. "I don't think so. It's not really like that. They're working on something down in research and development, I think." Adrian sighed and turned his back. "Come on, let's give the kid some privacy."

Nova followed the group across the sky bridge, glancing back once to see Max rolling up his sleeve as the woman in the suit prepared a syringe.

"You still haven't told me what's wrong with him," she said. "Or why he's dangerous, or valuable, or all of the above."

The others exchanged glances, and Nova bristled.

"It's sort of classified," said Adrian, looking apologetic.

That word sent a shiver along Nova's spine. *Classified.*

Classified was exactly what she was there for.

"But I'm one of you now, aren't I?" she pressed. "Why can't I know too?"

Adrian shrugged. "We're not even supposed to know. It's just . . . I have the luxury of getting to hear a lot of things that I'm not technically supposed to hear."

"So you overheard classified information and you told them," she said, gesturing at Ruby and Oscar.

"It's your first day, Nova," said Ruby. "We're not trying to exclude you, it's just . . . it's your *first day.* And what's going on with Max doesn't have anything to do with us."

"Besides," said Oscar, "we have more pressing things to deal with right now, don't we?"

Nova frowned, recognizing the change in topic. She couldn't help but feel irked. Though to be fair, she knew *she* wouldn't have trusted herself with classified information, either, no matter how well she'd done at the trials.

She filed away a mental note for later—*Find out what's up with the Bandit and the quarantine, and what are they doing with his blood samples?*

"—with this."

Nova gave herself a shake and looked down. Adrian was holding a narrow strip of thin plastic, about the length of a ruler, but she hadn't heard what he'd been saying about it.

"What is it?" she asked, taking it between her fingers and holding it up to eye level, peering at Adrian on the other side.

"Renegade communicator," he said.

"Pretty much a fancy phone," said Ruby.

"And a hip accessory," added Oscar. He rolled back the sleeve of his uniform, revealing a similar strip of glass wound around his wrist. "High-end designers are already trying to copy it. They'll be all the rage this time next year."

"Fashion aside, R and D is very proud of these. Here." Adrian took Nova's left forearm, but hesitated when he saw the delicate bracelet. He took the other arm instead. Taking the device back from her, he started to bend it, curving it until it fit snugly around her wrist, an elegant spiral against her skin. It was so light she could barely feel it—or perhaps she was simply too in tune with the warmth coming off Adrian's fingers to pay much attention to the communicator.

"This part will light up and sound an alarm when there's an emergency," he said, pointing to one end of the device. "If the call center has already designated a location for us to report to, a city map will show up along the middle here, indicating where to go. Down here," he tapped the other end of the strip, resting near Nova's thumb, "is how you communicate with one of us. Just press your finger here and say the name of the person you want to contact."

"Or you can hold it up in front of your face," said Oscar, mimicking the action, "and it will automatically start to record a video message. Very nifty."

Nova turned her wrist from side to side, feeling the start of a grin. New tech, a new gadget. Finally, they were speaking her language.

But then a thought occurred to her that smothered that first twinge of excitement. Technology like that had to include a tracking device. Which meant, so long as she wore it, the Renegades would know just where to find her.

She had no idea whether or not they would bother to use it that way, but regardless, it made her feel like they'd just wrapped a venomous snake around her wrist.

"Thanks," she said, trying to look appreciative. "It still hardly feels real. You know . . . being a *Renegade*." She made mild jazz hands beside her face.

"You get used to it," said Adrian, with an understanding smile.

"Do you?" chirped Ruby, beaming. "I haven't yet. It's still pretty much the most awesome thing ever."

"Try to keep the communicator on you at all times," said Adrian. "You probably already have a message on there with our instructions for tomorrow night."

"Tomorrow night?"

"Our first assignment." Adrian's expression brightened. "We're running surveillance on Cloven Cross Library."

Nova stilled.

"It's run by a guy named Gene Cronin," he continued. "He used to be a member of a villain gang called the Vandal Cartel, and we have reason to believe he might still be dealing in illegal weaponry, including, perhaps, the gun that Nightmare used to try to assassinate Captain Chromium at the parade."

Nova stared at him, her body tense as she waited for Adrian's composed act to drop away, for him, to say that he knew her secret identity after all and this had all been a ruse to trap her here inside their headquarters.

Instead, he gestured at the elevator bank. "We'll take you back up to the lounge so you can get your things. You have the rest of the day off to rest. Or . . . whatever it is you do." His lips quirked, but Nova hadn't been ready for a joke and any humor was lost among her scattered thoughts. "Anyway," said Adrian, his smile fading. "We'll meet you outside the library, tomorrow night at eleven. You can wear street clothes. We'll probably want to stay incognito."

"Wait," said Nova, following him blindly into the elevator.

"That's it? Surveillance? We're not . . . I don't know, tracking down a mass murderer or something?"

"Huge letdown, right?" said Oscar.

Adrian shot him an ireful look. "We like to ease recruits into the mass murderer hunts. But this mission is really important. If we can find evidence that Cronin is still trading on the black market, it could open a lot of doors into criminal rings throughout the city. Crime rates have been going up for the last four years, and if Cronin is out there supplying criminals with weapons, stopping him could be a huge victory for us."

Nova tried to listen, nodding when it seemed appropriate, though her mind was spinning. She knew full well that Gene Cronin, who she knew mostly as the Librarian, was very much selling on the black market and had very much supplied the gun that she'd tried to use against the Council.

"But before we can do anything else," Adrian continued, ignorant to how this conversation had unnerved her, striking far too close to her own secrets, "the Council requires evidence that Cronin is breaking the law. They won't allow a raid or even a permit to search the library until we have something concrete."

"Seriously?" said Nova, unable to keep the disbelief from her tone. "The Council won't allow an unsanctioned raid?"

They'd allowed plenty on the subway tunnels. . . .

Adrian's face turned mildly annoyed, though she could tell it wasn't at her. "The Council is really strict when it comes to following the new codes. You know, back during the Age of Anarchy, they would do anything they had to do to try to clean up all the violence and theft that was going on. But now they're trying to reestablish a justice system, like we used to have. I think they're afraid that if we start bending the rules, other people will get the impression that it's okay for them to do it too."

"You mean people don't like to see hypocrisy in their leadership? Shocking."

"I know," said Adrian, casting his eyes toward the ceiling, his quick smile making a return. "Their reasons make sense. But it does mean our hands are tied in situations like this. But who knows? Maybe we'll find something tonight that will provide enough evidence to really start investigating Cronin."

"During our surveillance," clarified Nova. "On a public library."

"Right." Adrian nodded. The elevator doors opened and he led her back to the bank of lockers where she'd stashed her clothes. "Lucky for us, we have the Renegade who doesn't need to sleep."

"Yeah, lucky you," she said, grabbing the bag that Adrian had sketched that morning and slinging it over her shoulder.

His expression fell a little. "I know it's not exciting, and your skills obviously lend you to much more hands-on missions—"

Nova laughed. "It's okay. I'm not disappointed. If anything, I'm a little relieved."

And it was true, though she'd let him assume his own reasons for it.

This was a mission she could work with. She could easily play the role of dutiful Renegade, while not doing or saying anything to incriminate Cronin, who had always been an ally of the Anarchists. If anything, she might even be able to find a way to lead the Renegades off his trail . . . and hers.

"Good," Adrian said. "Then we'll see you tomorrow."

She pressed her lips together and nodded. "Great. Right. I'll . . . uh, see you then." She turned and started back for the elevator. "Thanks for the tour."

She had just stepped inside when she heard her name.

"Nova?"

She glanced back.

"How's the bracelet holding up?"

She held Adrian's gaze, feeling once again the way he'd gripped her hand, the gentle trace of the marker's tip on her skin, the flutter of her pulse beneath it.

She shook her wrist slightly, feeling the brush of metal against her skin, right at the edge of the uniform's sleeve. "Hasn't broken again."

He nudged up his glasses and for just a moment, he looked almost shy. "Just let me know if you ever need anything, um, drawn. Okay?"

The elevator doors closed before Nova could think how to respond to this. As the car started to sink, she held up her arm, inspecting the bracelet's clasp for what must have been the hundredth time. The mirroring details, the subtle difference in color. When he had drawn it, he had made the clasp functional, so that it could be unclasped and taken off if she wanted to, though she never did.

She spun the bracelet around and peered at the socket where a gem would have been placed if her father had finished it, but she wasn't really seeing the bracelet or the chain or the empty prongs.

Her mind raced over the past few hours, struggling to sort through everything she'd learned, trying to discern how much of it was valuable and what she would need to gather more information on in the coming weeks. The elevator reached the ground floor. As she crossed the lobby of Renegade Headquarters and headed back onto the streets of Gatlon, she traced over her memories of the day.

She saw an underground training room full of powerful enemies.

She saw a woman in some sort of specialty hazard suit coming to collect samples from a boy they called dangerous and valuable.

She saw two Council members making their way through the

lobby, laughing as if they hadn't a care in the world.

She saw Adrian and that subtle shift of confidence, that hint of awkwardness as he watched the elevator doors close.

As she put more distance between herself and the headquarters, she began to feel the pressure of eyes following her. It was rare enough to spot a Renegade in the city that people stopped to gawk at her as she passed, and a few tourists even snapped her photo. Then there were the opposite reactions—the prodigy haters who sneered, or the ones who wouldn't make eye contact out of fear or disgust.

Either way, admired or loathed, Nova became more eager with every step she took to get home and get out of her uniform as fast as possible.

She wasn't a Renegade.

She was Nightmare.

And she did not like to be seen.

CHAPTER TWENTY

AST NINETY-FOURTH AND WALLOWRIDGE was an even crummier neighborhood than Nova had envisioned. It wasn't that she was too proud, exactly, to have the Renegades thinking she lived there. It was just—if she was going to be given a fake home, couldn't Millie have picked something a bit nicer? Maybe one of those abandoned mansions in the suburbs or a condo with a water view or, at the very least, a place that didn't look borderline condemned?

The home that Nova McLain apparently shared with her uncle was a row house with a brick facade sandwiched between more row houses, each with peeling paint on their window trim and tiny yards overgrown with grasses and weeds. There was trash in the street gutters, empty beer bottles on her front step, and an old tire leaning against the wall. One of the upstairs windows appeared to have a bullet hole through it, and a couple of their neighbors had their doors and windows completely boarded up.

Standing on the sidewalk, she let her gaze travel up and down the street, taking in the graffiti on the walls, the cars on blocks. It was so still and quiet that she couldn't be sure if anyone lived there at all. If they did, they were awful caretakers.

At least they live somewhere with daylight, a voice whispered in the back of her thoughts.

Nova frowned at her brain's intrusion into her critique of the neighborhood, but then she thought about it, and her face softened.

Actually, sunlight was a definite plus.

And at night, there would be stars.

She climbed the short stairs and stepped over the beer bottles. A brass mail slot in the door had long ago been engraved with the single word: MCLAIN.

It was the first indication Nova had seen that her fake identity might actually be tethered to someone in the real world, contrary to what Millie had told them. It made her wonder what had become of the real McLains.

Nova tested the doorknob and found it unlocked. She shoved the door open, revealing a narrow sitting room and a collection of cobwebs. She was surprised to see furniture—two dated armchairs and an entertainment console, though whatever TV or radio had been there before was long gone, replaced with a thick layer of dust. The room had once been done up in a garish paisley wallpaper, though strips of it were starting to peel.

What gave her the most pause, though, were recent footprints left across the dusty hardwood floors, making a series of back-and-forth paths between the front door and the staircase that lay straight ahead.

Settling a hand on her belt, which still held the instruments she had brought with her to Renegade HQ that morning, she stepped inside. She passed a collection of framed photographs on the wall— the McLain family, perhaps—but did not bother to inspect their faces as she headed up the staircase. The wood groaned beneath her, shattering the still silence of the house. She froze and listened. When only the sound of her own breath could be heard, she turned the corner and proceeded up the rest of the staircase. On the second floor, there was a door to her left, barely cracked open, and an open living area to her right, with a bedroom beyond it.

Nova reached out her hand and nudged open the first door the rest of the way. Inside was a bed frame with no mattress and yellowed curtain panels hung over two tall windows, one of which was fluttering around the bullet hole.

Turning, she made her way to the second bedroom—the master, judging by the small tiled bathroom attached to the closet. There was no furniture in this room, though. Only a backpack, a paper grocery bag, and a green sleeping bag in the corner with a large form curled up inside it.

Nova paused in the doorway, staring at the form and hoping it wasn't dead. A stranger's dead body wasn't exactly the sort of housewarming gift she'd been hoping for. After watching for a moment, she detected a subtle rising and falling of breath.

Sighing, Nova crossed the room. She spotted a handgun lying not far from the figure and, pressing her foot onto it, dragged it back out of reach. Then she cleared her throat.

The figure didn't move.

"Hey."

A quiet snuffle.

Scowling, Nova crouched down and nudged the figure through the sleeping bag. The figure yelped and rolled over, then shot upward. The man had a beard of thick whiskers and ears that stuck out too far from his head. Despite the gray sprouting in his hair and the wrinkles cut through his brow, Nova had the impression he was younger than he looked, but had been aged prematurely by too many unkind years. His hand went for the spot where the gun had been, but when it landed on only the floorboards, he glanced down and spotted it tucked behind Nova.

His bewilderment turned to a sneer. "Who're you?" he barked.

"The new tenant," she said. "Sorry, but you're going to have to find somewhere else to crash."

His eyes swooped over her Renegade uniform and she could see indecision warring behind his groggy eyes. It was clear he wanted to tell her to get lost and let him go back to sleep, but most people these days opted to treat any Renegade with respect, regardless of whether or not they actually supported their rule over the city.

"What?" he said. "You people claiming this block for another one of your social projects or something?"

"Or something." Grabbing the gun, she stepped over the man's sleeping bag and threw open the sash of the nearest window. She tossed the gun outside. It landed with a soft thud in a patch of weeds in the back alleyway.

"Hey!" the man yelled.

Nova headed back toward the staircase. "You've got two minutes," she called over her shoulder. "If you're not gone by then, you'll be the next thing I throw out the window."

She was halfway through the next room when he yelled back, "You think you can throw me out a window? I've had mutts that were bigger than you!"

Nova paused and turned back, peering at him through the doorway. "Now you have one minute."

She went back downstairs to finish her tour of the house, which was composed of a powder room and a small kitchen-dining-room combo in the back of the ground floor. A sliding glass door led out onto a tiny square yard, which was mostly weeds, including a particularly monstrous blackberry bush that was in the process of devouring a child's tricycle.

Thirty-four seconds later, she heard the stairs creek and the front door slam shut.

Nova exhaled. "Home, sweet home."

She returned to the kitchen and started digging through the cabinets. She found a box of black trash bags tucked into one corner and started filling it with bottle caps and crushed soda cans and the occasional dead cockroach that littered the floors. She hadn't planned to stay there when she first decided to come check the place out. Rather, she'd been thinking strategically. She figured that if the Renegades *were* tracking her movements through the communicator band, they would expect her to return home at some point, so she might as well get it out of the way. Her plan had been to hide the bracelet here, then return to the subway tunnels to tell the others what she'd learned during her first day at HQ.

But now that she was here, it occurred to her that, if they *were* tracking her, it wouldn't be enough to just stop by from time to time. She would be spending time here, like it or not, and she might as well make it . . . well, not comfortable. But somewhat tolerable.

She had finished her preliminary trash collection when she heard the front door squeal open again.

Groaning, she dropped the trash bag and stormed back toward the front room. "I'm telling you, this place is no longer—"

She drew up short.

Ingrid stood in the doorway, lip curled in disgust as she scanned the entryway. "Well," she said, stepping over the threshold, "I was going to congratulate you on your improved lot in life, but I'm no longer sure this is an improvement."

Leroy and Honey filed in behind her. Honey turned around to shut the door, but hesitated and used her toe to nudge it shut instead. She was clutching her hands at her chest, as if afraid they might inadvertently touch something and end up with tetanus.

Nova rolled her eyes. Almost a decade spent in a dank, gloomy tunnel and Honey Harper still managed to be an elitist.

"What, no Phobia?" Nova said dryly.

"He wasn't interested in joining us," said Ingrid. "His lack of curiosity is inhuman."

"That," said Honey, sneering, "or he happens to have a deep-seated fear of paisley wallpaper. No, wait, that's me."

Nova's cheek twitched. "What are you doing here?"

"We were curious how your first day went," said Leroy. He fluffed a dingy floral throw pillow and plopped into one of the armchairs. Honey gawped at him, horrified.

"I was going to come back to the tunnels after I"—she glanced around—"scouted out the place."

"We figured." Ingrid made a slow pass around the perimeter of the room, inspecting the drab furnishings and wallpaper. "But we didn't think that would be such a great idea, in case you're being followed."

Nova frowned. "And if I am being followed, you don't think it's a problem that whoever's following me would have just seen three Anarchists letting themselves in to my house?"

"Well, you're not being followed, obviously," said Ingrid. "Except by us. We've been tailing you since you left Renegade Headquarters. We would have noticed if someone else was too."

"But you didn't know that," said Honey, daring to take another step into the room. "And it still seems risky for you to be coming into the tunnels so long as you're . . . that." Her eyes swept over Nova's uniform. "We don't want to draw any unnecessary attention to ourselves."

"So, what?" said Nova, crossing her arms. "Am I banished from going home so long as this charade continues?"

"Come on, Nova," said Ingrid. "It's hardly a loss. You're getting a whole house out of the deal." She opened her arms, gesturing at the room around them.

"All my stuff is there," said Nova. "My weapons, my inventions, my clothes . . ."

"You're not being banished," said Leroy. "You are always welcome to return, of course. But let's give it a day or two, just to make sure the Renegades aren't keeping tabs on your whereabouts. Besides . . ." He shrugged. "You always spent as much time above ground as possible. I don't see this being much of an inconvenience for you."

Nova pinched her lips together, unable to argue that point. "Fine. It's not like I plan on spending a whole lot of time here, either. As soon as I make it past my first official mission, I'll be spending any free time at headquarters, learning whatever I can."

"That's the spirit," said Ingrid. She had completed her lap around the room and now stopped in front of the wall with the framed photographs. She took one down from the wall, revealing a bright square of wallpaper where it had hung, indicating just how much the rest of the walls had faded with time.

"Did you learn anything of interest today?" said Leroy, shifting his weight to try to get more comfortable on the lumpy cushions.

Nova tossed the trash bag onto the floor and did her best to recount the day she'd spent touring headquarters. Though she had learned very little about the experiments happening in research and development or anything at all about the Sentinel, she had at least begun to develop a tentative grasp of how the organization functioned. The hierarchy. The structure. The scope of what they were hoping to accomplish.

And it went so far beyond what she'd expected.

Sure, she knew their stance on crime and law enforcement and even on social programs. She knew the Council saw themselves as benevolent leaders attempting to solve all the problems of humanity, without any apparent grasp of how their involvement was only dooming society to helplessness and desperation.

But she had rarely stopped to think of the Renegades as a global organization, with their power continuing to grow with every prodigy who came here to be trained. Were cities around the world becoming as dependent on the rule and protection of prodigies as Gatlon was? How long before all of humanity gave up on personal freedom and responsibility? How long before they forgot what that felt like at all?

She had now seen the proof of their power with her own eyes. Not only in their technology and weapons development, but in sheer numbers as well. She knew that only a fraction of their workforce had been in the training halls when she'd toured them, and she could still feel the way her lungs hitched when she saw them.

So many prodigies, all dressed in those gray uniforms, all sporting those red *R*s. Having never seen so many Renegades together at one time, it had been easy to underestimate them as a whole. But there she had witnessed a cacophony of flashes and explosions, natural elements wielded like weapons, prodigies defying gravity and physics, their bodies transforming and flying and brawling and training and on and on and on.

So much power enclosed in one space made her nerves vibrate. So much.

The Renegades had so much. And what did the Anarchists have? A bomb maker, a beekeeper, a poison distiller . . . and her.

It sounded like the start of a bad joke.

But she refused to be swayed from her cause. Seeing the inner workings of the Renegades had changed nothing, other than, for the first time in years, the Anarchists had an advantage. She would learn what secrets were being developed behind closed laboratory doors. She would learn how to undermine their systems and protocols, one way or another. She would learn who the Sentinel was and whatever the Council intended to use him for, and she would stop him before he ever had a chance.

The Sentinel.

That had been something. She was sure she had detected nervousness in Adrian when she'd brought up the soldier. She was sure he had been feigning ignorance, but she didn't think it was just from her. She had gotten the impression that, whatever he knew, he was keeping it from Ruby and Oscar too.

Which made sense.

Surely, if any of them knew about the Council's top-secret ventures, it would be him.

"It's a start," said Leroy, when she had finished accounting all she had seen and heard during her first day as a Renegade. "Have you determined your primary objectives going forward?"

"Research and development," said Nova. "They're very secretive there. I want to know what they're working on, and what consequences it might have for us, and the city. Also, the Sentinel. I want proof he's a Renegade tool, and I want to know who he is and what they plan to use him for. From there . . ." She shook her head. "I'm not sure. I want to know their weakest links. Maybe a direct attack on the Council was premature. Maybe there are other ways to bring the organization collapsing in on itself. Sneakier ways."

Ingrid nodded. "If you want to blow up a building," she said, "take out the support beams."

Nova met her gaze. "Unfortunately, I won't be blowing up anything for a few days, at least. The team that picked me at the trials has been assigned a specific mission. This will interest you, though."

Ingrid raised an eyebrow.

"Starting tomorrow night, we're running surveillance on Cloven Cross Library."

"What?" yelped Ingrid, tossing the framed photo into a corner. Nova scowled at where it crashed against the floorboards, feeling a peculiar sense of ownership—over the house and everything in it, even over the family that was, in some alternate universe, *her* family. "What did they find on Cronin?"

"Nothing," said Nova. "Yet. But they somehow traced the gun that I used at the parade back to him." She glanced from Ingrid to Leroy. "You *did* get it from him at some point, didn't you?"

"Years ago," said Leroy, rubbing his cheek so hard the scarred flesh wrinkled and bulged around his fingers. "He used to stock that particular model a lot. I should have realized they would draw a connection back to him. That was sloppy of me."

"They don't have any proof of his involvement yet," Nova insisted. "They're just suspicious. As long as the Librarian can refrain from buying or selling anything illegal for a while, they shouldn't be able to pin anything on him."

"Unless they search the library," mused Honey, toeing at a mysterious stain in the area rug. "If they find his inventory, well . . . that will be that."

"They can't search it," said Nova. "Not without evidence of illegal activity. It's part of their *code*." She couldn't avoid the sarcasm, even though, in this case, the Renegade code was proving to be a good thing. For them, at least. And the Librarian.

"I don't like it," said Ingrid, starting to pace. "If we lose access to Cronin's network . . ." Her gaze smoldered. "We're already outgunned enough."

"Again," said Nova. "They can't search—"

"Oh please." Ingrid snorted. "If they suspect he's dealing again, they'll find a reason to search the library, even if they have to plant the evidence themselves."

Nova's shoulders dropped, and she wondered whether that was true. Adrian had seemed adamant about this surveillance mission, and the importance of finding evidence that would allow the Renegades to legally search the library. Was that just a ploy? A show of goodwill to the community, a demonstration of their own due diligence, before they planted the evidence that would get them the results they wanted?

"Then . . . we have to warn him," said Nova. "I can go right now. The surveillance is set to begin tomorrow night. That gives him more than twenty-four hours to clear out any weapon stock or documentation that would incriminate him. Should be plenty of time."

"You can't go," said Ingrid, tapping her fingers against her hips. "It would be far too suspicious if anyone recognized you."

"But you said—"

"I will talk to Cronin," Ingrid continued. "I've worked with him more than anyone. I can't exactly say we trust each other, but he'll be more likely to listen to me than anyone else here. Besides, the man's a coward. If he thinks the Renegades are on to him, his instinct will be to run and save his own skin." She inhaled sharply. "Like he did at the Battle for Gatlon."

Nova glanced at Leroy, who shrugged. "There is a reason he's one of the few villains who survived that slaughter, and it certainly isn't because of his strength or bravery."

"But if he runs again," said Ingrid, "I bet you anything he'll skip town for good, and that won't leave us any better off than if the Renegades arrested him. So I'll make sure to motivate him in a way that helps our cause, more than hinders it." She turned her focus back to Nova, her expression calculating. "How many Renegades are going to be involved in this surveillance mission?"

"Just four, I think. Me and the three other members of my team."

Ingrid held her gaze for a long time before asking, "Including the Everhart boy?"

The way she said it made the hair prickle on Nova's scalp and she found her fingers wrapping idly, almost protectively, around her filigree bracelet. "Yes," she said. "He's the team leader. But . . . from what I can tell, he's never done any surveillance like this before. I don't think any of the team has."

"Of course," said Ingrid. "But he's the perfect candidate to conjure up a piece of incriminating evidence, isn't he?"

Nova swallowed, wondering why that thought hadn't occurred to her.

Leroy stood and brushed the dust from his backside. "Nova will keep a close eye on him during their mission. If he does try to plant any evidence against Cronin, she can deter him."

"Don't bother," said Ingrid. "It will be better if they search the place and get it over with."

"What?" said Nova.

"I'll make sure there's nothing there for them to find," said Ingrid. "*You* make sure that team of yours conducts that search, say . . . early morning, right after the library opens. The sooner they can cross the library off their watch list, the sooner we can go about business as usual."

"And," added Honey, "the sooner Nova can focus on investigating all those other things at headquarters."

Nova opened her mouth to argue, not entirely sure she would be able to persuade Adrian to search the library in the event they hadn't seen anything suspicious. But she hesitated. This was what she was doing with the Renegades, wasn't it? Throwing them off course. Weakening them in any way she could.

"Fine," she said. "You give me something to work with—something suspicious that I can use to get them inside the library, just in case Adrian isn't planning to fake the evidence himself. And I'll make sure they search the place. But if they find anything, even one cartridge, one *bullet*—"

"Relax, Nightmare," said Ingrid, grinning. "I'll take care of everything."

CHAPTER TWENTY-ONE

THEY SET UP inside an abandoned fourth-floor office across the street from Cloven Cross Library. The space held remnants of squatters coming and going over the past decades—layers of graffiti and drifts of garbage in the corners. Scavengers had picked every ounce of scrap metal clean, including the doorknobs and the wires in the walls. An old makeshift desk of plywood sat in one corner beneath a layer of dust, and some of the cubicle walls still stood, smelling like mildew and punctured with staples and nail holes and scraps of posters long ago ripped away. On one of the walls Nova noticed a thirty-year-old calendar, still stuck on July, showing a faded photo of some far-off coastal town, where all the sun-bleached buildings were painted in shades of coral and peach. Nova could imagine some bored office drone dreaming about traveling there someday, a place as different from Gatlon City as they could possibly get.

The Renegades had prepared for the evening by bringing a large soft blanket that Adrian spread out over the filthy carpet as soon as they settled into the space. Ruby laid down some pillows for comfort before promptly throwing herself down on top of them. Oscar opened a cooler and offered everyone a soda and some pretzels, which Nova declined.

She paced to the windows and looked out onto the library across the street. It was just past eleven o'clock and the library had been closed for hours, indicated by a plain sign hanging from a string on the front doors. The entire two-story building was pitch-black inside, and though there were old light sconces hung beside the entryway, they seemed to have burned out long ago, leaving only a solitary street lamp by the sidewalk to cast a dreary amber glow over the front facade.

It was a dignified building. The exterior was all massive brownstone, and the windows were framed in dark oak and accented with prominent keystones. The doors in the entryway were flanked by double entasis columns supporting a bold triangular pediment, the words PUBLIC LIBRARY long ago engraved into the stone.

Despite how its imposing facade had weathered over the years, there were clear signs that it was not strictly maintained, from a rash of invasive ivy taking over the west wall to great patches of shingles missing from the roof. Cracked windows left unfixed and garden beds around its foundation that had once been home to tidy boxwoods now gone wild with weeds.

From their lookout, Nova could see partway down the alley that separated the library from a discount-ticket movie theater, where a row of dumpsters and trash cans disappeared into shadows. There were two small doors along that wall of the library, neither as formal as the main entryway, but both still trimmed in ornate stone moldings. The effect was lessened, though, by the iron bars that someone had outfitted over both doors at some point in the last hundred and fifty years. One door could have been an emergency exit, Nova guessed. The other, perhaps, a back entryway for staff or a place for deliveries.

There was no activity in the alley. There was no activity anywhere. Even the ticket booth of the movie theater was dark.

Ingrid and the Librarian had had more than twenty-four hours to prepare for the Renegades' visit. That should have been plenty of time for him to cancel any illegitimate business dealings and make sure nothing incriminating was left lying around.

"What do you think?" said Adrian, appearing at her side.

Nova kept her attention on the street below. "What exactly are we looking for?"

"Villains," Oscar said. "Doing villainous things."

Nova sent him an unimpressed look.

"Anything that could be qualified as suspicious activity," said Adrian, pulling her gaze toward him. He returned the look with a shrug. "I figured, if this is a cover for illegal weapon sales, or anything else, then all of that activity would happen through the back doors, right? And it probably wouldn't happen during normal business hours." His frown deepened. "I don't think, anyway." He nodded toward the alley. "If we see someone coming or going, especially if we recognize them, or if they leave with something that looks like it could be weapons, then we'll tail them and see what we can find out."

Nova smothered the start of a smile. Twice she had come here with Ingrid to offer trades for equipment they needed, and both times it had been in the middle of the day and they had entered through the front doors, like any other patron. Gene Cronin had a system set up for his *side* business—a handful of specific books tucked in among the stacks that acted as a code word to the receptionist when brought up to the desk together. It was a discreet way to indicate they weren't there for reading material.

But if the Renegades wanted to believe that all illicit activity happened through back doors under the cover of nightfall, so be it.

"So we're just going to watch those doors all night?" she asked.

"Pretty much." He grimaced. "I figured we'd go in shifts. I thought you could go last, since you'll be the least likely to fall asleep."

Least likely. Like it still might be a possibility.

Nova stepped away from the window. Adrian nodded at Oscar, who took his place as the first lookout.

"Is the Librarian a villain?" asked Oscar, staring across the street. "I mean, like, with superpowers? Or is he just a bad guy?"

"He's a prodigy," said Adrian, "but I'm not sure exactly what he does. Nothing violent, I don't think."

"Knowledge retention," said Nova. The others turned to look at her and she started. "Is . . . what I've heard," she added lamely. "I think that's why they call him the Librarian. Not just because he, you know, runs a library, but supposedly he remembers everything he reads, word for word. Forever."

"Makes sense," said Ruby, opening a bag of candy.

Allowing herself to relax once the attention of the group moved away from her, Nova sat cross-legged and stared at the pile of snacks they'd brought. Red licorice ropes, jelly beans, peanut butter cookies, and an assortment of canned energy shots.

"This is the first time you've all done this, isn't it?"

"What do you mean?" said Ruby, grabbing a handful of jelly beans, picking out the purple ones and dumping them back in the bag, before throwing the rest into her mouth at once.

Nova gestured at the spread. "This is a sugar crash waiting to happen. Didn't anyone think to bring . . . I don't know, carrots? Or some nuts or beef jerky . . . or you know, something with nutrients?"

Ruby blinked at her, then looked blankly at Oscar. Neither spoke.

"I could run to the store," said Adrian. "There's a corner store three blocks away. If you need something . . ."

Realizing that he was looking at her, Nova shook her head. "It won't matter to me, but . . ." She waved her hand through the air. "Never mind. Don't worry about it. I'll take over whenever the rest of you pass out, which I'm betting will be sooner than later."

"Shows what you know," said Oscar. He was leaning against the window frame, tapping the end of his cane against the floor. "I've got the stamina of a triathlete."

Nova's eyebrow lifted.

"He didn't mean it *that* way," muttered Adrian.

"Didn't I?" said Oscar, with a suggestive glance in his direction.

Adrian snapped his fingers at him. "Eyes on the window."

Nova glanced from Oscar to Ruby. It was the first time she'd seen them in civilian clothing—he in a checkered-blue dress shirt, the sleeves rolled to his elbows, and she in a T-shirt with the SUPER SCOUTS logo scrolled across the chest, a fan-comic from overseas that was immensely popular, but that Nova had never actually read. As Red Assassin, her black-and-white hair was always pulled back high on her head, but tonight it was down in loose pigtails that made her look adorably harmless. What was most striking, though, was the thick white bandage wrapped around her upper arm, disappearing beneath her sleeve. Nova wondered if Ruby had been injured during their fight at the parade, though Nova was sure *she* hadn't wounded her.

Adrian, too, was dressed casually, almost exactly as he had been at the parade. Red sneakers. Blue jeans. A dark long-sleeved T-shirt. There was nothing particularly fashionable about the outfit, but it fit him well, hanging in just the right way to suggest toned muscles underneath.

She looked away quickly, annoyed that the thought had occurred to her.

"We brought games," said Ruby, when the silence tipped toward uncomfortable. She riffled through a backpack and pulled out a deck of cards and a box of dominoes. The tiles inside clacked noisily as she set it down on the blanket. "Anyone?"

When a quiet lack of enthusiasm greeted her, she shrugged and grabbed the deck of cards instead. "Fine. I'll play solitaire."

Nova watched her lay out a row of cards. "So. This is the life of a superhero." She glanced up at Adrian. "No wonder everyone wants to be one of you."

He met her look with a smile and lowered himself onto the other corner of the blanket. "Everyone wants to be one of *us*," he corrected. "And yes. We are living the dream."

"Okay," said Oscar, propping one foot up on the windowsill. Without looking back, he lifted his hand in the shape of a pistol and shot an arrow of white smoke in Nova's direction. It struck her chest and dispersed. "Origin story. Go."

"Excuse me?" she said, waving away the remnants of odorless smoke that wafted toward the ceiling.

"You know," he said, glancing back. "When someone decides to write the highly dramatized comic-book version of the story of Insomnia, where will it start?"

"He wants to know where you got your power," said Ruby, slapping down a new card.

"Was it the result of some personal trauma?" said Oscar. "Or human experimentation or alien abduction?"

"Oscar," said Adrian, warning, and Oscar turned his

attention back to the window.

"Just making small talk," he said. "We should know more about her than just her ability to turn an ink pen into a receptacle for blow darts."

"We know she can clean the floor with the likes of Gargoyle," said Ruby.

"And that she can give sass to Blacklight in the middle of an arena full of screaming fans," added Adrian. He grinned at Nova, who looked away.

"Fine, I'll go first," said Oscar, and though she couldn't see his face, Nova had the impression that this was where he'd wanted to take the conversation from the start.

"By all means," she said, leaning back on her palms. "Origin story. Go."

Oscar inhaled a long breath before proclaiming, quite dramatically, "I died in a fire when I was five years old."

When he said nothing else, Nova glanced at Adrian to see if there was a joke she'd missed, but Adrian merely nodded.

"So . . . ," started Nova, "you're a smoke-controlling zombie?"

She saw Oscar's grin in the reflection of the window. "That would be *awesome*. But no. I'm not dead anymore, obviously."

"Obviously," agreed Nova.

"As the story goes," he said, "my mom was down in the basement of our apartment building doing laundry when one of our neighbors fell asleep and her cat knocked over a candle she'd left burning. The whole place went up in flames in—I don't know—*minutes*. I was in my bedroom and I heard people screaming, and then I saw the smoke, but I was petrified, and besides, I'm not exactly fast, right?" He shook his cane. "So by the time I got the courage to try to get out of the apartment, the fire was coming up the stairs and I didn't know what to do. So I just froze in the hallway, watching the smoke until it was so thick I could hardly see, and couldn't breathe. I passed out, and that's how the Renegades found me."

"The Renegades?" said Nova.

"Who else? Tsunami, to be specific. She's the one who put out the fire, then she handed me off to Thunderbird who flew me over to the hospital, but they didn't have much hope I'd make it. I didn't have a pulse by that point. But while they were all mourning the death of this kid, I was having a dream." His voice darkened, taking on an air of importance. "I dreamed that I was standing on top of our apartment building and I was breathing in——this long, long breath that went on and on. It was such a deep breath that it pulled all the smoke right out of the air and into my lungs. Finally, I stopped breathing in, looked up at the sky, and exhaled. And that's when I woke up."

"In the hospital?" said Nova. "Or the morgue?"

"The hospital. It had only been about ten minutes since they'd brought me there—plenty of time to declare me legally dead, but still. My mom was there, too, and she saw me exhale, and this big cloud of smoke came out of my mouth." Oscar puckered his lips and blew. A gray cloud burst across the surface of the window. "And here we are."

Nova cocked her head. "So . . . your power. It doesn't have anything to do with . . ." She gestured at the cane, and though Oscar wasn't looking at her, he tapped the cane against the floor a few times in acknowledgment.

"Nope," he said. "*This* I was born with. I mean, not the cane. But my bones don't grow like a normal person's. Some rare bone disease." He grinned back at Nova. "Probably the best thing that ever happened to me, though, right? Just think——if I'd been faster,

I might have gotten out of that apartment building just fine, and I'd be stuck with all the other spry, non-prodigy suckers out there."

"Right," said Nova. "Not dying of carbon monoxide poisoning when you were five years old would have been *awful*."

"See?" Oscar looked pointedly at Adrian. "She gets it."

Adrian rolled his eyes.

"And when you tried out for the Renegades . . . ," started Nova, leaning forward. "Nobody thought this was . . . a problem?" She nodded to the cane.

Oscar snorted with pride. "Sure they did. To date, I hold the record for most challenged contestant at the trials. And yet, here I am." He gestured at Ruby. "She was challenged during her tryout too. In fact, it's sort of becoming a theme around here."

"Let me guess," said Nova, cupping her chin in her palm and inspecting the top of Ruby's bleached hair as she bent over her cards. "Your origin is that . . . you stumbled across a cache of ancient magical artifacts in a dusty antique shop somewhere, including a ruby hook and dagger, which imparted you with mystical fighting abilities from some long-forgotten culture."

Ruby laughed. "Um, no, but that might be what I start telling people. It's certainly less traumatic than the truth."

"Oh?"

Ruby turned over the last card, checked that she had nowhere to place it, and started gathering them all back up into her palm. "Before society collapsed, my grandmother was a well-respected jeweler. She'd been running this shop in Queen's Row for forty years when the Anarchists took over, and it was one of the first places that got raided after all the credit cards stopped working and everyone was panicking and thought we'd go back to bartering for gold and jewels. You know, before they realized that food, water, and guns were the actual valuables in a world like that. After a few days of looting, everything was gone, except what my grandma had stashed in her safe. So she took out every gem and diamond she had left and started hiding them where she didn't think they'd be found, including a bunch in secret places around our house."

"You lived together?" asked Nova.

"Oh yeah, she's lived with us since before I was born. Grandma, me, my parents, and my brothers."

"You have brothers?" said Nova.

"Two of them," said Ruby, fixing a look on her. "But it's not really relevant to this story."

"Sorry."

"So anyway, she hid these priceless gems all over the house—in little holes in the walls, secret compartments in our dressers, things like that. And they all sat there for twenty-plus years while my family tried to figure out how to survive, and eventually my brothers and I were born, and side note—yes, we all have really annoying gem-themed names, *thanks* Grandma. Well, one night we were playing hide-and-seek and I hid behind the grate on our fireplace and happened to find this little bag full of rubies that had been tucked up inside the chimney. I'd heard about the jewelry store and the raids and everything and didn't really know what to do with them, so I just put them back. Until a few months later . . . Do you know how, not long before the Day of Triumph, some of the villain gangs started figuring out how to make trades internationally and that's when gold started to become valuable again? Well, my grandma was one of the first people they turned to. One night our house got raided by villains looking for anything that might have been missed before."

"Which villains?" said Nova, having asked the question before she realized she was about to. "What gang?"

"The Jackals," said Ruby, shuddering. "I'll never forget those creepy masks."

Nova pressed her lips together. She'd seen photos of the Jackals taken before the Day of Triumph. They had been one of the few villain gangs to wear a cohesive uniform—all black clothes with signature masks painted to look like the animals they'd been named for.

She wasn't sure why she felt disappointed, but Nova realized that a part of her had been expecting Ruby to say that her family had been assaulted by the Roaches, the same gang that had sent the hitman after Nova's family. The gang Ace had slaughtered in retaliation. They had been one of the largest and most powerful gangs in Gatlon City, so it wouldn't have surprised her if they'd been the tormenters of Ruby's family. Some said they even got their name from the Renegades themselves, when one of the early vigilantes complained that no matter how many of those villains they stamped out, they could never seem to get rid of them all.

There had been a tiny, faint wish that she and Ruby might share this mutual, long-dead enemy.

She curled her knees against her chest, digging her fingertips into her legs.

What a stupid thing to wish for.

"We didn't have much by that point, as most everything valuable had been bartered off," said Ruby, "but they started tearing the house apart anyway. While they were busy threatening my dad, I ran upstairs to the fireplace and took out the rubies—which in hindsight is probably the stupidest thing I could have done, because they might not have even found them up there, but I was four, so what did I know? And then . . ." She inhaled, as if this were the painful part to talk about it. "I dumped them into my mouth and I swallowed them."

"Of course you did," said Nova.

"In one fell swoop." Ruby cupped one hand and mimed throwing a handful of rubies into her mouth and swallowing, not unlike how she'd gobbled down the jelly beans earlier. "I'm not really sure what possessed me to do it, other than how I just couldn't stomach the idea of the Jackals walking away with anything more than they'd already taken. The trouble was, one of the Jackals saw me do it. He grabbed me and started demanding that I cough them up. Or, vomit them up, I guess. But I wouldn't do it. So . . ." For the first time since the start of her story, Ruby's face darkened with anger. "He stabbed me."

Nova's eyes widened.

"Once in my arm," said Ruby, glancing down at her bandaged arm. "Twice in my chest. Once right here." She pointed at a spot near her stomach. "I knew he was going to kill me. But then . . . well, here." She unclipped the end of the bandage and began to unwrap it from her arm, uncovering her flesh just enough that Nova could see a deep and, apparently, very recent wound. It began to bleed as soon as the bandage was removed, the red blood dripping down into the crease of her elbow, trickling toward her fingers.

Until . . .

Nova's lips parted and she leaned closer, mesmerized, as the blood began to harden into sharp, symmetrical formations that jutted upward from the wound.

"I didn't know what was happening," said Ruby, "but I started to fight back. I ripped off the Jackal's mask and stabbed him in the eye."

Nova's jaw dropped even more.

"Which sounds really brave in hindsight," added Ruby, "but all I remember is how terrified I was. It was more instinct than anything else. But it worked—the Jackals ran off after that and they never came back."

Ruby swiped her other hand across the gash, snapping the crystals off at their base with a quiet *crack*. She tossed them into the corner, where they shattered amid the piles of paper and debris.

"I've bled rubies ever since. They'll form on new wounds for a little while, but those tend to heal pretty fast. Whereas the places where he stabbed me . . ." She started to wrap the bandage around her arm again, securing it tight. "They never stop bleeding. They never healed."

Nova stared at the glistening gems on the floor, then back at Ruby. "What about the alias?" she asked. "Smokescreen and Sketch make perfect sense, and I get the Red part, but . . . Assassin?"

Ruby's whole face brightened. "Actually, my brothers came up with it. It was kind of an inside joke. We used to pretend we were superheroes when we were kids—like everyone does, right?"

Nova didn't answer.

"So they made up names for all of us. Jade was the Green Machine, Sterling was the Silver Snake, and I became Red Assassin."

Nova looked at the stone dangling from Ruby's wrist. She could still distinctly recall the feel of her ruby dagger pressed against her throat. "So . . . you've never . . . ?"

"What? Killed someone?" Ruby guffawed. "Not so far." Then she grew suddenly serious. "I mean, I *would* kill someone. If I had to."

"But it's always a last resort," added Adrian.

"Correct me if I'm wrong," said Nova, knowing she wasn't, "but didn't Renegades used to kill people all the time? Back during the Age of Anarchy, there were always stories about them taking out members of the villain gangs."

"New rules," said Adrian, "new regulations. We're always supposed to bring them in to custody as peacefully as we can, and avoid unnecessary violence whenever possible."

Nova gaped at him. It felt so . . . so silly, in comparison to what she had been taught all her life. The strong over the weak. An eye for an eye. If someone wronged you or yours, then you did what you had to do to ensure it didn't happen again.

Which often meant killing the one who had wronged you.

Every one of the Anarchists had countless deaths on their hands. She could remember nights when they sat around talking about their most brutal kills. Bragging about them. Laughing about them. When they'd developed the plan for Nova to take out Captain Chromium, Leroy had joked about throwing her a party afterward, to commemorate her first kill.

Her first.

Because they all assumed there would be more to follow. Even Nova had assumed it.

So why did the thought suddenly make her uneasy? Because she'd failed the mission? Or was it something else?

"Hey, guys," said Oscar, pressing a hand against the window. "The back door's open."

They all sprang to their feet—even Nova, and for a moment she forgot that the last thing she wanted them to witness was suspicious activity happening in that alleyway. But when they'd all clustered around Oscar, they saw that it was only a girl taking out a garbage sack and throwing it onto a pile beside the nearest dumpster.

Nova recognized Narcissa, Gene Cronin's granddaughter, but none of the others seemed to know who she was.

Narcissa let the dumpster lid slam shut and brushed her hands off on her pants before retreating back into the library.

Oscar grumbled. "False alarm."

"Should we go through their garbage?" said Ruby. "Do you think they're throwing away any incriminating evidence?"

Adrian frowned thoughtfully. "Maybe, but let's see what tonight turns up first."

Nova peered at him from the corner of her eye. Is that where he would place the false evidence?

"My turn," said Ruby, nudging Oscar on the shoulder while Nova and Adrian returned to the blanket. "I'm bored."

"Oh yeah, because this is exciting stuff," he said, but relinquished his place at the window without argument. Lying down, he stretched out onto the pillows.

"How about you?" said Nova, turning to Adrian. "Were you challenged at the trials?"

"Nope."

"Adrian didn't have to try out," said Oscar, kicking Adrian in the shin. "Cheater."

"Oh right," said Nova. "Because of . . ." She hesitated over the right words. His family? His dads? His adoptive relations, who just happened to be the most influential prodigies in the city, perhaps the whole world?

"It's not like they bent any rules for me or anything," said Adrian. At some point he had pulled out his fine-tip marker and he was fidgeting with it now, twisting the cap back and forth. "But I was hanging out around headquarters since they first started renovations. By the time someone thought to start hosting trials to bring in new talent, I was already . . . you know. A part of the team. Obviously, I would have tried out, if anyone had asked me to."

He scowled at Oscar, and something about his defensiveness made Nova relax.

"I know you would have," said Oscar. "And you would have kicked ass."

"Thank you," said Adrian, scratching his temple with the pen. "I mean, I could have drawn a hand grenade. Come on."

"No one's doubting you," Oscar insisted.

"And what's your origin story?" said Nova. "I'm guessing that marker doesn't contain magical ink?"

Adrian's quiet smile returned as he glanced down at the marker. "No magic. Sadly, no thrilling near-death experiences or villainous jewelry heists, either." He sighed heavily, as though he'd been dreading this moment, though a hint of a smile remained. "Like twenty-eight percent of today's prodigies, I was born with my power. At least, I think I was. It manifested pretty much the first time I was handed a crayon."

"Manifested how?" said Nova.

He shrugged. "I started to scribble, and those scribbles started to come to life and squiggle around the apartment like little primary-colored worms that my mom was always trying to sweep up. Now, things got really interesting when I was . . . maybe two or three? My power works by intention more than anything, so back then, I was still just scribbling random lines, but in my head I was drawing dinosaurs and aliens. So then the house became overrun with tiny little squiggle lines that believed they were dinosaurs and aliens and were always trying to chomp down on people's toes when they were walking around. Which is about the time Mom thought it would be a good idea to hire an ex–art teacher who lived a couple streets away to start giving me drawing lessons."

Oscar snorted loudly. "Notice how he complained about the lack of excitement in his story, but then it turns out there were actual meat-eating dinosaurs in it? You're such a one-upper, Sketch."

"It was a harrowing tale," agreed Nova. She was grinning, though her thoughts were roiling in the back of her head. Adrian had mentioned his mom, and now she found herself comparing his face to pictures she'd seen of Lady Indomitable—the sixth and final of the original Renegades. The resemblance was clear. Nova could picture her effervescent smile easily, a smile that rivaled the Captain's in brightness and charm, and one Adrian had clearly inherited.

His mother had been a Renegade, too. Would probably be on the Council today, if she were—

Nova's heart squeezed.

If she were still alive.

She racked her brain, trying to recall what had happened to the superhero, but all she knew was that she had died a long time ago. Nova had never really cared that much. One less Renegade to worry about. But now she found herself succumbing to curiosity, wanting to know what had happened to her, but not knowing how to ask.

"No more stalling, Insomnia," said Adrian, yanking her attention back. "It's your turn."

"Oh." Shaking her head, Nova flipped her hand through the air, like the story was so dull it was hardly worth mentioning. In fact, she had been born with her power—what she thought of as her *real* power, the ability to put people to sleep. She had a vague memory of her mom once joking about how hard it had been to breastfeed Nova as a baby because she kept dozing off every time Nova nursed.

But the power *they* knew about, the fact that Nova never slept . . . that had come later. When, for weeks, every time she shut her eyes, gunshots rang in her ears.

Bang.

Bang.

Bang.

"It happened when I was six," she said, picking at bits of fuzz on the blanket. "I just . . . stopped sleeping."

"But you could sleep before then?" said Ruby, her gaze on the library.

"Sure. Not as much as most kids. But . . . some."

"Could you still, though? If you wanted to?" said Oscar. "Or is it impossible for you to sleep anymore?"

Nova shook her head. "I don't know. It's been a long time since I wanted to."

"What happened when you were six?" asked Adrian.

She met his gaze, and the memory was right there. The dark closet. Evie's crying. The man's remorseless stare.

"I had a dream," she said. "I dreamed there were these tiny little squiggly dinosaurs that kept trying to bite my toes and when I woke up, I thought, that's it. Never again."

Oscar and Ruby laughed, but Adrian's gaze only softened. "What a nightmare."

She shivered.

"Your parents must be saints," said Oscar, pulling her attention toward him. "To put up with a kid that never slept? I hope you were good at entertaining yourself."

His words struck her in the chest. She flinched, and Oscar blanched, his eyes widening in horror. "I'm sorry. I forgot."

The unexpected apology caught Nova off guard, and the sting of his words was quickly replaced with suspicion. Did they know? How did they know?

"Your papers mentioned, um . . ." Oscar rubbed the back of his neck.

Adrian cleared his throat. "You live with your uncle now, right?"

Nova's gut clenched again, even though she knew Adrian's

question had been well intentioned. An attempt to draw all their thoughts away from the single explanatory line they must have read when they reviewed her fake papers. *Both parents were killed by an unknown villain gang during the Age of Anarchy. Currently resides with Peter McLain, paternal uncle.*

"Uh, yeah," she stammered. "He took me in after . . ." She swallowed. "They died a long time ago."

"How old were you?" Ruby asked, her voice soft, though her attempts to be calming only made Nova's hackles rise.

She fixed her gaze on Ruby. "Six."

From the corner of her eye she saw Adrian tilt his head curiously.

Six when her parents died. Six when she stopped sleeping.

How had this edged so treacherously close to the truth?

Without looking at him, Nova pulled herself to her feet. "I'm going to go scout out the roof. We might have a better view of the alley from up there."

Ruby and Oscar traded looks and she could tell they wanted to stop her. Or maybe apologize, though the words didn't come, and Nova was glad for it.

She didn't want an apology, or pity, or sympathy, or even kindness. She didn't need those things from anyone, least of all a bunch of Renegades.

CHAPTER TWENTY-TWO

———————————

NOVA STAYED ON THE ROOF for more than an hour, longer than she'd meant to, but when she realized she was expecting one of the Renegades—no, expecting *Adrian*—to come check on her, it sparked a sense of stubbornness that refused to ebb long after she knew she should have gone back down to their makeshift surveillance room.

She wasn't waiting for him. Why would she?

Even as she stood on the roof, watching the silent stone facade of the library, the stillness of its black windows, the occasional car that breezed past on the street, she could feel the words heavy on her tongue, waiting for their chance to come out.

Why did you stop sleeping? he would ask.

And against every ounce of logic inside her, she would answer.

I fell asleep—the very last time I ever slept. And when I woke up, there was a man with a gun. He killed them both. He killed my sister. He tried to kill me. And the Renegades didn't come . . .

After that, every time I tried to sleep I would hear it happening all over again, until, eventually, I stopped trying.

That was her origin story. The whole of it.

And it was none of Adrian's business, or anyone else's for that matter.

She couldn't understand why talking about it had made her so defensive or given her such a strong compulsion to tell them the truth of her power and where it had come from. She'd never told anyone, not in so many words, though she thought Ace understood the gist of it, and of course all the Anarchists had figured out that she wasn't one for sleeping not long after she'd moved into the cathedral. But she'd never had any cause to actually *tell* someone the story. She'd never really wanted to.

Why would she now?

Instead, she paced. Back and forth across the rooftop, enjoying the fresh air on her skin. Though she'd worn leggings and a simple T-shirt, civilian clothing, as instructed, she'd opted to wear the uniform boots she'd picked up at headquarters earlier that day. She figured she might as well use this reconnaissance mission to start breaking them in, though now she could tell it wasn't necessary. They were, in fact, ridiculously comfortable, and a part of her hated the Renegades for winning even at this.

Finally, when she felt sure that any compulsion to give out unnecessary information was gone, Nova made her way back down to the fourth floor.

Ruby and Oscar had fallen asleep. Oscar had not moved from his spot on the pillows, and Ruby was now lying with her head beside his, but her body perpendicular, so they made a kind of right angle on the floor with nothing but their heads nearly touching. It seemed almost as though Ruby had gone out of her way to place herself in a position that wouldn't suggest anything beyond the fact that she was tired and Oscar was hogging the pillows.

Though she could have moved her pillow to the other side of the blanket. If she'd wanted to.

Stepping over Ruby's legs, Nova approached Adrian. He had pulled the desk in front of the window and now sat with his feet dangling over the side, with a sketchpad on his lap. He was drawing the library with quick, hasty lines, focusing mostly on the dark shadows that spilled from the alley.

Nova climbed up onto the desk and sat beside him, her toes tapping against the glass.

"You all right?" Adrian asked, without looking up.

"Fine," said Nova. "The view from the roof looks pretty much the same as the view from here."

"I know. I scouted it out yesterday morning."

Her lip twitched and again she wasn't sure what was more annoying—that he hadn't followed her to ask about her parents, or that she still sort of wished he had.

"So, other than squiggly dinosaurs and bracelet clasps"—she glanced at the sketchpad—"what sort of things do you like to draw?"

He hummed in thought, sketching in a blur of shrubbery around the library's foundation. "I draw a lot of tools and weaponry for the Renegades. Armor pieces. Handcuffs. Things that might come in handy when we're out patrolling. Not just for our team, but for everyone. It's really made a big difference in the things we can accomplish."

"I bet it has," said Nova, trying to keep any resentment out of her tone.

"But when I'm left to my own devices," said Adrian, "I like to draw the city."

"The city?"

He set down the pen and turned back the pages of his notebook.

A number of them were blank and she wondered if there had been drawings there before—drawings that had since been brought into reality—until he arrived at a series of dark, detailed images. Unlike all the marker drawings she'd seen, these were done in charcoal. He handed Nova the sketchbook and she took it delicately, feeling her breath hitch.

The first image was of the beach at Harrow Bay, shadowed by the monumental Sentry Bridge. A couple was seated on the rocky shore, sharing a newspaper as they huddled beneath a single raincoat.

She turned the page and saw Ashing Hill—a neighborhood of cobbled-together shacks and ruddy houses that had been a hot spot for drugs and crime during the Age of Anarchy. Probably still was, for all Nova knew, but in this picture Adrian had captured three children harvesting bouquets of dandelions and clovers from the edges of the overgrown sidewalk.

She flipped on, seeing a street musician strumming a guitar on the corner of Broad Street, two huge dogs curled around his ankles. Then a sketch of the ticket booth outside the old Sedgwick Theater, most of the lightbulbs burned out on the sign and the posters on the wall still promoting a musical act from years ago. Then a view of the crowded flea market on North Oldham Road, where people came from all over the city to sell everything from hand-crocheted baby mittens to broken clocks to garden-grown zucchini.

Nova turned another page and paused.

She was staring at a scene of a shadowed glen surrounded by a low stone wall and thick, crowded trees. In the center of the glen stood a single statue, half covered in moss. It was an elegant figure, covered head to toe in a long cloak, with a hood that fell so far forward as to completely cover its face. All that could be seen of the person within the cloak was their hands, which were held just slightly apart in front of the figure's stomach, as if they were holding an invisible gift.

Nova exhaled and flipped past the drawing. She reached the end of the notebook and started to turn back through the pages again. "These are extraordinary."

"Thank you," Adrian murmured, and though he must have known they were extraordinary, she still detected a hint of self-consciousness in his voice.

"Could you bring these to life?" she asked. "If you wanted to?"

He shook his head. "I have to intend to bring it to life as I'm drawing it. Otherwise it's just a drawing. Besides, even if I could, they wouldn't be any bigger than the page they're on. It would be sort of like making a super-ornate pop-up book." He paused, and added, "Though someday I would like to try making a life-size mural—a landscape that I could make real. It's been something I've been thinking about for a while."

Nova flipped back to the drawing of the statue. She traced her thumb beside the hooded figure, careful to keep it hovering above the page so she wouldn't smudge the lines. "This is at City Park, isn't it?"

"You've been there?"

"My parents used to take me to the playground when I was little. One time I wandered off without them realizing it, and I ended up here." She tapped her finger against the page, where the hooded figure stood serene but imposing. "My parents were in such a panic when they finally found me, but . . . I loved it. I felt like I'd just stumbled onto something no one else knew about. I even remember . . ." She hesitated as filaments of memories spun through her thoughts. She frowned and glanced down at the drawing, then shook her head. "You're really good."

"I've had a lot of practice," said Adrian, taking the sketch pad as she handed it to him. He fidgeted with the pencil, but didn't turn the page. "But enough about me and my extraordinary artwork. What sort of hobbies do you have to occupy your extra fifty-six hours per week?"

Nova looked across at the library. It was far past midnight and the building was dark as a tomb, its single lamppost by the sidewalk dim and flickering. Seeing it this way, the place might have been abandoned these past ten years, just as it might have been if Cronin hadn't chosen to keep it operating even during the Age of Anarchy. Even if that philanthropic cause had been a cover for his black-market dealing . . . it had to count for something, right?

"Mostly I train. And study. And . . . tinker." She cast him a sideways smile. "Some of us can't just draw up a tool and get to use it. We have to actually *invent* it."

"I invent things," he said, tapping the eraser side of his pencil against his temple. "In my mind."

"It's really not the same thing."

He grinned.

"But I guess I've taken up lots of hobbies over the years. Not many stick, but I'm always trying to find new ways to keep busy."

"Like what sorts of hobbies?"

"I don't know. I took up knitting for a while, but never progressed beyond really ragged scarves. Then there was bird-watching, juggling, embroidery, astronomy—"

"Whoa, whoa, whoa," said Adrian, laughing. "Start over. Knitting? Seriously?"

"It's an undervalued art," said Nova, managing to keep a straight face. It had, in fact, been a four-month preoccupation when she was twelve or so, but she'd been less interested in making winter accessories and more interested in the idea of being able to tote around weapons as vicious as ten-inch-long needles and no one batting an eye about it.

"And bird-watching?" said Adrian.

"Bird-watching, yep." That hobby had been Leroy's idea, who had insisted that it would help develop her patience, stealth, and observation skills. "Mostly around the bay. Did you know this area is home to over forty species of waterfowl?"

"In fact," said Adrian, "I was not aware of our waterfowl population, but that does seem like good information to have."

"You never know when it might come up in conversation."

He grinned again and Nova saw that his cheeks dimpled, just a tiny bit, once his smile got broad enough.

She swallowed.

"Okay, what else did you say? Juggling?"

She could still hear Ingrid waxing on about the many physical benefits juggling offered—from dexterity to balance to hand-eye coordination.

"I got pretty good at it, actually," she said.

"If I draw you some bowling pins, will you give me a demonstration?"

"Nope."

"How about some scarves? Softballs? Flaming torches?"

She turned her head away, in part to hide the smile she was having trouble keeping back. "We're supposed to be on a very important mission, you know. I'd hate to be a distraction."

"Fine. I'll let it go . . . for now. What was the other thing you mentioned?"

"Astronomy."

"Right. Now, that one, I get. Being up all night, you've probably spent a lot of time looking at the stars."

Nova looked up, to the few bright stars that could be seen dotting the sky between the buildings. There had been no ulterior motive for learning about the night sky, only that she found it fascinating. She could remember the sky being full of stars when she was a child. They were more difficult to see these days, now that so much of the city's power grid had been fixed.

She liked electricity, but some nights, she would have given almost anything to see the Milky Way again.

Nova was still staring at the stars when, behind her, Ruby started to mutter in her sleep—Nova heard only *show you a zero . . .* and then what might have been *casserole*. She looked back as Ruby rolled onto her side and curled into a fetal position, her head sliding off the pillow and onto Oscar's outstretched arm.

"Are they . . . ?" she asked, gesturing between their sleeping forms.

"No," said Adrian, who was turning pages in his sketchbook again.

"But they like each other?"

"Hard to say." He found the sketch of the library and glanced back once, his eyes softening a bit as he looked at his friends. "I'm almost positive Oscar likes her, but I think he's too afraid to do anything about it. And Ruby . . . she pretends to be oblivious, but I wonder." He thumped his pen against the paper. "So, what are you training for?"

"Hm?"

"You said you spend a lot of your time training. For what?"

She leaned back on her hands. What did she train for? To destroy the Renegades. To avenge her family's deaths. To someday see Ace's vision realized—a world in which all people could be free. Where the people would not be heralded over by villain gangs *or* the Council. Where prodigies would not be subjected to constant injustices and cruelty, as they had been before the Age of Anarchy.

A world in which the Anarchists could return to sunlight and not fear persecution for even the slightest misstep.

"For this, I guess," she whispered, tracing the filigree of her bracelet. "To be a Renegade."

Adrian nodded, as if this were a perfectly reasonable thing to train for. "And is it everything you hoped for and more?"

Smirking, Nova looked back at Oscar and Ruby again and saw that Ruby was drooling a tiny bit. "So far, I can honestly say that it is surpassing every expectation."

Turning back to the window, she saw that a slivered moon had risen over the library. It must have been going on two o'clock in the morning.

"What's the significance of the bracelet?"

Nova looked down. She hadn't realized she'd been fidgeting with it again. "Oh. It . . . was my mom's." She cleared her throat. "Thank you, by the way. For fixing it."

"My pleasure," he murmured. Reaching over, he took hold of the filigree between two fingers and twisted it around so he could see the empty setting. "What happened to the stone?"

She pulled her hand away, settling it on her lap. "This is how it was when I got it," she said, picturing the bracelet abandoned on their tiny kitchen table. Ace had grabbed it as he carried her from the apartment, refusing to let another piece of David's work fall into the hands of the gangs.

Her stomach tightened. "Aren't you tired?" she asked.

Adrian blinked at the change of topic, but his surprise quickly turned to sheepishness. "Not too bad. I've worked night patrols before, plus I had one of those energy shots right before you came back down."

"Go rest for a while." Nova brought her legs up onto the table, sitting cross-legged and watching the street and the alley and the pitch-black windows as nothing, nothing, nothing happened. "This is what I'm here for, right?"

"I know, but . . . I don't want to miss anything."

"Miss anything of what?" said Nova, gesturing toward the library. He frowned.

"Adrian," she said, more firmly now. "I can handle this. If you don't get some sleep, you're going to be useless, so . . ." She gestured to the blanket.

He sighed and lifted his hands in resignation. "Fine. But you'll wake me up the moment you see anything suspicious, right?"

She sighed, feigning exasperation. "What do you think I am, an amateur?"

Adrian stretched out on the blanket, pillowing his hands beneath his head. "Watch it, Insomnia. You haven't even been a Renegade for three whole days yet."

She turned back to the window. In the glass, she could see her own reflection, and she was caught off guard by the faint smile still playing around her lips. She settled her focus on the library, and said the words she thought Adrian would believe without question— what any Renegade would hear as the absolute truth.

"Yeah, but some days I feel like I've been a Renegade my whole life."

Nova shut her eyes to hide the laughter in them. It sounded so painfully ludicrous, but she was proud of her delivery. She'd almost convinced even herself.

She waited for some smart comment to be shot back her way, but none came.

She frowned. Waited some more.

And heard only heavy breathing.

Nova glanced back over her shoulder. Her jaw fell.

He was *already asleep.*

"Ugh. You would be one of those." Sighing, she wrapped her arms around her legs, settled her chin on her knee, and stared out into the dark world beyond this abandoned office. She had always been astonished by people who could fall asleep fast, like there was nothing to it. Like their spirits weren't burdened with suffering and resentment. Like their hearts and minds could so easily be at peace.

After a while, she dared to look back at Adrian—just to make sure he really was asleep. She frowned as her gaze alighted first on the steady rise and fall of his chest. Her attention swept down his lean body to casually crossed ankles, then back up to his face. He had removed his glasses and set them, neatly folded, beside the wall. His face was different without them. More open and tranquil, though that could have been as much because of the sleep.

She knew it was a stereotype, but the glasses really did give him an air of studiousness. Of artistry. Without them, he looked like . . . well, like a superhero.

A really good-looking superhero.

Nova flushed, suddenly mortified at the direction of those thoughts, and hastily turned back to the window, vowing not to stare at him for another second.

The vow was harder to keep than she ever would have admitted, but keep it she did. Listening to the sounds of deep breathing. The occasional rustle of fabric and peaceful sigh as her companions slept and shifted and slept some more. In the city, a distant siren. A motorcycle roaring to life a few blocks away.

It wasn't the shortest night of her life, but it wasn't the longest, either.

She searched for any sign of activity inside the library, but there was nothing but stillness and darkened windows. Which was good. Ingrid and the Librarian would have had all the previous day to clear the library of incriminating evidence. There was nothing to do now but wait until morning, when Nova could encourage the Renegades to go inside and the Librarian could prove that he had nothing to hide, thereby putting an end to this investigation.

Nova was getting anxious to get it over with. She had other things to be doing than sitting with a patrol unit on a hopeless surveillance assignment. She had things to investigate at headquarters—secrets to uncover, weaknesses to ascertain, and she wasn't going to get any of that done here.

Eventually, the sky overhead began to shift from black to navy to sapphire, a progression she was intimately familiar with. The window was facing north, so she had no hope of seeing the sunrise, but she sensed it in the gradual lightening of the clouds and the way shadows began to stretch long down the street, and how all at once the windows of the library began to glimmer with morning light.

At eight o'clock sharp, the CLOSED sign in the window was flipped over to OPEN. Nova couldn't see who had turned it—Narcissa, or Gene Cronin himself?

Nine minutes later, the first patron arrived, an elderly woman carrying a basket full of thick paperbacks, her head tucked beneath a plastic hood, even though there were no rainclouds in the sky.

Nova climbed down from the desk and nudged Adrian with her toe. "Hey, Sketch."

It was Ruby who woke first, startling when she found herself restrained by Oscar's arm across her waist. She moved it off of her and sat up, brushing her black-and-white hair aside. Oscar and Adrian woke up moments later—Adrian jolting upward the moment he spotted Nova and remembered where they were.

"Did something happen?" he said, his hand fumbling across the floor until it landed on his glasses. He unfolded them and slipped them back onto his face, blinking up at Nova. "Did you see something?"

"Yeah," she said, leaning against the desk. "The library opened. An old woman just went in carrying a bunch of books, but . . . I have a feeling she might have been hiding a machine gun under her jacket."

Adrian blinked up at her and she noticed he had a speck of white caught in the lashes of his left eye—what her mother had used to refer to as "sleep dust." Nova had the most peculiar urge to lift up his glasses and run her thumb across the lashes to clear it away.

"She's being sarcastic, right?" said Oscar, rolling a kink from his shoulder.

Nova glanced at him. "Yes."

A cacophony of giggles from outside drew them all to the window. On the street below a crowd of young children had just arrived via three minivans and were being paraded into the library. Perhaps a day-care retreat or a school field trip.

They stared until the last of the children and their teachers had disappeared through the large main doors.

"Well," said Ruby, slapping her hands together. "We didn't really expect to catch anything on our first night, did we? I mean, who knows how often his illegal dealings go down."

Nova shifted her attention between the three Renegades. "Is this really our plan? To stake this place out every night for all eternity? What if we never catch anyone? What if his black-market clients don't use the alleyway, but go in through some other entrance? He could have a secret underground tunnel for all we know. Or—just a thought—what if he's not actually dealing in black-market guns and this is a waste of time?"

"It's too early to determine any of that," said Adrian.

"So how long do we keep doing this before we try something else?" Nova pressed.

Adrian opened his mouth, but hesitated.

"Well," started Ruby, "longer than one night, at least."

Nova gestured at the window. "Look, I know I'm the new guy here, and maybe I don't have all the information to be making this call, but I really don't think we're going to learn anything from an abandoned office building, staring at a closed public library every night. I think the only way we'll know if illegal activity is happening in there is to actually go inside."

Adrian shook his head. "The Council was very specific. We can't do a search without first having some evidence of criminal activity."

"So let's go inside and get some evidence. It's a library. It's open to the public. It's not breaking any rules if we go . . ."

She trailed off, her eye catching on a lone figure on the street below. Her breath hitched.

She quickly pulled her attention away, but it was too late. Adrian followed the look, his lips parting in surprise.

"Jackpot," he whispered.

"What? What is it?" said Ruby as she and Oscar pressed closer to see.

"See that woman down there?" said Adrian, his eyes tracking her as she crossed the street and ducked into the shadow of the library. "I'm almost positive that's Ingrid Thompson. The Detonator."

Nova swallowed, staring at Ingrid as she paused on the front stoop of the library and looked back, in what was probably intended to give the Renegades a good look at her, but that also served to make her look extra suspicious as she slipped inside.

Adrian lifted his communicator band to his mouth. "Sketch to the Council. We've just witnessed an Anarchist, the Detonator, entering the Cloven Cross Library. There are civilians inside. An extraction team is requested. We'll hold the area."

"An extraction team?" said Nova, gaping at him as she tried to muddle through what Ingrid could be thinking. The last thing she was supposed to do was give *actual* evidence that Gene Cronin was dealing on the black market—and seeing an Anarchist enter the library may not be evidence, but it wasn't going to help the case for his innocence, either.

But Ingrid must have a plan. She knew Nova was up here. Did she still want Nova to bring the team inside?

"The extraction team will go in after the Detonator, and maybe the Librarian too," said Adrian. "They'll probably bring backup. The Detonator hasn't been active in almost ten years, but she had a reputation for being pretty volatile back in the day."

Inhaling sharply through her nostrils, Nova looked down at the closed library doors. Whatever Ingrid was thinking, she would have planned on there being only three Renegades on this mission. Whatever she was planning, an extraction team probably wasn't on the agenda.

"We should go in," she said.

Ruby looked at her. "What?"

"The Detonator makes bombs, right? She could blow up that whole place in seconds. What if . . . what if she gets into a fight with Cronin or something else sets her off? There are children in there. We can't risk anyone getting hurt!"

The others exchanged looks, significantly more anxious now than they had been even seconds ago.

"We're supposed to call for backup," said Adrian, but his words carried little conviction. "We're not supposed to engage."

"That was when it was just us and the Librarian," said Nova. "But things have changed. Now there's an Anarchist involved. What if this is our only chance to catch them both, red-handed?"

Adrian looked at each of them in turn, his brow setting in determination. "Making sure the civilians are safe *is* our top priority . . ."

"But if we go in there and start ordering people outside," said Oscar, "that'll just tip the Librarian off that we're on to him."

"And probably scare off the Detonator too," said Ruby.

Adrian peered down at the library for an agonizingly long minute, as if mesmerized by the sunlight glinting off its windows. "The civilians are our top priority," he repeated. "We'll find the Detonator and the Librarian and hold them until help arrives. No violence if we can help it, and no need to cause a panic." He looked up, his jaw set.

"Now we're talking," said Oscar, a wisp of gray smoke curling around his fingers as he grabbed the head of his cane. "Let's go be superheroes!"

CHAPTER TWENTY-THREE

———■—■—■—■—■———

THE OAK DOORS SLAMMED SHUT behind them and Adrian found himself engulfed by stale air and the aroma of leather and brittle pages. He paused in the vestibule, taking in the entryway and the lobby beyond. He had never been to this library before, and now he was wishing he would have come inside when he'd scouted out the area before. He wouldn't have felt quite so vulnerable now, to be going into a place completely blind, having very little knowledge of its floor plan or exits. He could have come inside during business hours, attempted to be discreet . . .

The problem with that was, thanks to his dads, it was too likely he would be recognized.

So, he took the time now to observe what he could. Inside the entrance hall, two alcoves stood to either side, each containing a marble statue. To his left, a noble scholar held an open book in one hand, the other raised up in a gesture of brilliance, as if the book had just revealed to him the secrets of the universe. In the other alcove, a scribe noted his thoughts into a journal with a long, feathered pen.

Worn wooden floorboards stretched ahead into a central lobby, where a silhouette on the floor indicated where the old administration desk had once been bolted down. A cheap banquet table stood off in one corner, framed by dark wainscoting on the wall and a large antique mirror that reflected what little daylight reached this central room. The beams of light that did enter through a couple of smartly placed upper windows illuminated drifts of thick dust circulating through the space.

Adrian moved forward, one hand taking the marker from his back pocket and clutching it instinctively. Beside him, Nova gave his hand a curious look, before meeting his gaze with something almost like teasing.

He looked away. It may not be a gun or a knife, but it was still the most effective weapon he had.

Tattoos notwithstanding.

His jaw tensed as he approached the table, where the lobby's only occupant sat on a stool entranced by what appeared to be a romance novel. The girl was perhaps a year or two younger than him, with ginger hair braided thickly over one shoulder.

"Excuse me," Adrian said, sounding ridiculously polite even in his own head.

The girl, though, did not even look up. Just reached across the desk and slid a clipboard toward him—a form for checking out books.

He cleared his throat and, this time, tried to sound not like a concerned citizen, but like a Renegade. A superhero. "We're here for the Detonator."

The girl's head shot upward. She blinked at Adrian, then took in the others, her gaze lingering longest on Nova, long pale eyelashes fluttering over grayish eyes. Her lips parted as she turned back to

Adrian and squeaked, "I beg your pardon?"

"The Detonator," Adrian said again. "We saw her come in here, not ten minutes ago. Where is she?"

The girl's mouth opened. Closed. Her eyes darted once more to Nova, then back. "You . . . Aren't you . . ." She looked at Nova again, dumbfounded. "Are they Renegades?"

It wasn't really a question. Adrian wasn't sure how she could tell without the uniforms—maybe she recognized some of them from the media. Maybe they simply had a *look* to them. He liked to think so.

What was odd, though, was the way she was staring at Nova, almost like she recognized her.

"We sure are," said Nova, her voice run through with assertive pride. "Renegades. All of us. Bold, valiant, and . . . um . . ."

"Just," whispered Ruby.

Nova nodded. "That's the one. Now tell us where—"

"Are we in trouble?" the girl said, slamming shut her book and clutching it against her stomach, mostly covering the depiction of a shirtless swashbuckler on the cover. "We haven't done anything, I swear. Is this because we've been stocking that cookbook again? Because we were told it was within our rights to—"

"The Detonator," Adrian said, more forcefully now. "Stop stalling and tell us where she is."

The girl hesitated. Looked once more at Nova, and this time Adrian frowned and followed the look. Nova turned to him and shrugged, apparently as baffled as he was.

"I . . . I don't know who that is," the girl stammered. Her face was red as a cherry now, and Adrian doubted it had much to do with her reading material. "I'm sorry. I can't help you."

"A woman, about this tall," Adrian deadpanned, indicating her height. "Wears lots of armbands and can make explosives appear out of thin air. Sound familiar?"

The girl gave a weak, apologetic smile. "Not really?"

"How about the Librarian," said Oscar, stepping closer to the desk. "Where's he?"

"He's in the . . . uh . . . the back," the girl said, her attention darting over all four of them again. "Cataloging new . . . reference . . . materials."

"Take us to him," said Adrian. "Now."

"Oh, you can't go back there," the girl said. "He doesn't like to be disturbed."

Adrian's teeth gritted. He could feel the ticking of time, like the steady drum of his own heart. Every second a chance for the Detonator to get away, for Gene Cronin to hide whatever had brought the villain here in the first place. "Disturb him anyway."

The girl opened her mouth, poised to refuse, then looked at Nova again and hesitated.

She cleared her throat and nodded. "Right away."

Slipping off the stool, she turned and walked—not around the table or toward one of the doors or even the staircase that stood a few feet away—but to the large mirror hung on the wall behind her. She pressed her fingers against the surface and the glass rippled outward as if she had just touched a vertical pond. Then, without fanfare, she stepped into the mirror and was gone.

They all stood there, staring at their own mystified reflections for a long moment.

Oscar, of course, was the first to break the silence. "That," he said, pointing, "is a cool trick." He walked around the desk and rapped his knuckles against the mirror, then pulled it away from the wall and looked behind it to ensure there wasn't a secret passageway of sorts. "Neat."

"I remember hearing about her once," said Ruby. "A girl who can travel through mirrors. I remember wondering why she wouldn't apply to be a Renegade, and eventually I figured it was probably just a rumor."

"The problem," Adrian said, tapping the end of his marker against the table, "is now we have no idea where she went, or if she's really going to get the Librarian, or if they're both about to make a run for it." Frowning, he looked around.

From the main lobby, he could see a reading room to his right, the tables interspersed with short bookshelves and magazine racks. More bookshelves stretched the full length of the wall, broken up by the occasional rolling ladder or broad, dirt-covered window. To his left were the stacks—row upon row of tall, slender shelves. From that direction he could hear the occasional giggles of children.

"Ruby, Nova, let's start staking out the exits," he said, turning to inspect the staircase that led up to the second floor. Though the stairs were carpeted, in places that carpet had been worn through nearly to the wood steps beneath. "The Librarian or the Detonator might be trying to escape right now."

"Escape?" came a wary, broguish voice. "Have I been witlessly drawn into a trap that must be escaped from?"

Adrian turned to see a stooped man standing in the doorway to the reading room. He had a pointed white beard and scraggly white hair, he wore socks with holes in them and no shoes, his trousers and cardigan were wrinkled and baggy on his slim frame, and his skin was so pale it looked as though he had never met the sun.

Adrian stood straighter. "Are you the Librarian?"

"I am . . . *a* librarian."

"Are you Gene Cronin?"

The man peered at him, uncertainty making the corners of his lips twitch, as if he wasn't sure if he was supposed to smile or not. "My granddaughter said there were Renegades who wanted a word with me." He laughed, but it was an uncomfortable sound. "I thought she must be playing a practical joke. But here you are. I should have known better. Narcissa likes jokes about as much as I do." His lips gave up the fight and settled downward in a concerned frown. "To what do I owe the pleasure?"

"Minutes ago we witnessed the Detonator, a known Anarchist, entering this library," said Adrian, "and we have reason to believe your dealings with her aren't of an entirely lawful nature."

"The Detonator!" barked the Librarian, his eyes darting away from Adrian to scan the others. "The Anarchists? I haven't had anything to do with them for . . . well, close to ten years now, isn't it?" He reached up and spent a moment smoothing down a patch of unruly hair, though it popped right back up as soon as he let his hand fall to his side again. It hung awkwardly at his side before he reached out and pressed his palm against the doorway, knuckles turning white against the wood. "It pains me to think that, even now, the Renegades refuse to trust me. I pay the Council's taxes. I follow the Council's rules. And on top of all that, I provide a great service to this community." He gestured around the lobby. "Do you know there are only nine functioning public libraries currently open within Gatlon city limits? There used to be well over a hundred. And all nine of those are thanks to the selfless efforts of people like me, who have made it our lives' work to continue the free distribution and sharing of knowledge and wisdom. To make sure that the people have access to this . . . to *books*. Meanwhile, what has your beloved Council done to respect the work of scholars of years past? To further the enlightenment of society?"

Adrian furrowed his brow, not sure at first that the Librarian wanted an answer. "They reopened schools," he supplied, thinking that should have been obvious. "Whereas you spent decades selling guns to villains who would just as soon keep the people ignorant and helpless."

Beside him, Nova stiffened. He glanced at her and saw a flash of something cross her features—annoyance, or denial. But it was gone as fast as it had come.

"Insomnia?" he asked.

She kept her gaze trained to the Librarian as she said darkly, "Are you telling us you have *nothing* to hide?"

Gene Cronin pursed his lips until they started to turn as white as his beard. Then he huffed. "Of course I have nothing to hide. During the Age of Anarchy, I did what I had to do in order to survive. Now, I am content to make my living through more peaceful means."

"And that includes hosting private meetings with villains like the Detonator?" said Adrian.

"You are mistaken," said Cronin. "I have not seen the Detonator, or any Anarchist . . ." His gaze swiveled back to Nova. ". . . in a long, long time."

"Then you won't mind if we look around?" said Adrian.

"This is a public library," said Cronin. "Browsing is always encouraged."

Adrian's fingers tightened around the marker. "Maybe you'd be willing to give us a tour of the areas that aren't open the public. If you really don't have anything to hide, like you say."

Cronin inclined his head. "It would be my pleasure." He crossed the lobby to the staircase and had gone up three steps when Adrian stopped him.

"Not that way," he said.

Cronin glanced back.

"This building has a basement, right? Let's start there."

The Librarian's face went blank. "There is nothing in the basement but the furnace and outdated stacks."

"Then it will be a quick tour," said Adrian.

Nostrils flaring around his mustache, Cronin abandoned the staircase and headed toward the east room. They followed him through a pair of tall bookcases and down an aisle of desks. In the far corner, Adrian spotted a stone fireplace, though there was no fire currently lit. A young man was seated cross-legged on the floor, reading a picture book to the children scattered around him.

The sight made Adrian's blood cool. He glanced at the others, and saw the same apprehension mirrored on Ruby's and Oscar's faces, though Nova had her gaze intently latched to the Librarian's back.

There was no reason yet to alarm anyone, he told himself. But still . . .

"Smokescreen," he whispered, "you stay up here. Clear the library at the first sign of trouble."

Oscar glanced at him, and if he was annoyed to be excluded, it didn't show. Nodding, he stepped back into one of the rows of bookshelves, disappearing from view.

Cronin led them to a door labeled STAFF ONLY and spent a moment fishing around in his pockets for a key. Once he had opened the door, they descended a narrow staircase into the basement, where the air was mustier and thicker, permeated with the stench of molding paper.

Cronin cleared his throat and stepped aside when he reached the bottom of the staircase, allowing them to spill into the room and look around. More bookshelves took up the space, though they were spaced more tightly together than those above, some allowing barely enough room to pass between them. Every spare inch was taken up with books. When a shelf could hold no more, the books were piled up on top of the books that were already there, causing some of the shelves to sag under their weight. There were books piled up in corners like snowdrifts. Books stacked under and over desks. Books with broken spines and bent pages tossed haphazardly into a pile that overflowed into the walkway.

A single desk had been shoved against the far wall, its surface littered with takeout boxes and paper files. On the floor beside it stood a plain full-length mirror, like something that would be found in the dressing room of a cheap department store. Though the mirror walker—Narcissa, he'd said—was nowhere in sight.

Not far away, a short concrete stairwell led up to a door marked with an EXIT sign—probably, Adrian thought, the side door that led to the alley they'd been watching all night.

"And there you have it," said the Librarian, picking a book off the discarded pile and lovingly unfolding its bent pages. "Anything else I can do for you? Perhaps you'd care to take back a book on political science for the Council to peruse in their spare time? I think it might benefit them." He placed the book onto a shelf, tenderly stroking its spine like a pet.

Ruby groaned. "Do you think we're idiots? We *saw* the Detonator come in here. Just tell us where she is, and things will go a lot easier for you!"

Cronin drew himself upward, uncurling the slump of his spine. "I am sorry, but you seem to be suffering from an overactive imagination."

Ruby cast Adrian a frustrated look. He knew the feeling. This had all taken up so much more time than he'd expected it to, and he found himself regretting his decision to enter the library, rather than wait for backup like they were supposed to. Already he could see the error of his decision. If his team had merely blocked out the library's exits, they would have known if the Detonator had tried to leave. They would have been able to stop her. Instead, she could have gone out through the back door ages ago.

He felt like an idiot. He felt like his dads had been right to doubt his ability to handle this, and that angered him as much as anything.

But it was too late now to change direction. What would an experienced team do in this situation, to make up for the mistakes he'd already made? Should they threaten Cronin if he didn't give up the Detonator's location? Arrest him? Start punching holes in the walls, looking for secret alcoves that held illegal contraband?

"So," said the Librarian, heading back toward the stairwell, "if you'd like, we can continue the tour upstairs. We have a marvelous collection of rare books and first editions on the second floor—"

A loud *clunk* made him freeze.

Adrian spun, glancing at the wall the sound had come from. It was yet another wall sporting floor-to-ceiling bookshelves, no different from the others. But as he stared, the books began to tremble, and the wall began to move outward, scraping loudly against the floor.

"No . . . ," Cronin murmured. "What is she . . . *no!*"

Adrian took a step toward the bookshelf. Ruby twisted her wrist, unraveling the wire that held her bloodstone. Nova settled a hand on her belt.

The wall of books swung outward, though what lay beyond was too dark for Adrian to see. Then there was a quiet click, and a single desk lamp flooded the space with dim, green-tinted light.

They were staring into a room not much bigger than the office cubicle they had spent the night in. There was a single desk in the room's center, holding nothing on it but the lamp. A woman sat in the rolling chair behind the desk, her boots kicked up on its surface as she tipped back in the seat.

Ingrid Thompson. The Detonator.

But this was not an office.

This was an armory.

The three surrounding walls were lined with shelves and display cases and neatly labeled cabinets, only this room was not full of books, but weapons. Boxes of bullets and cartridges. Rifles, shotguns, handguns, pistols, bandoliers stocked with ammunition, lethal-looking darts, crossbows, hunting knives, and what he suspected was a box of hand grenades.

"Oh, for all the diabolical schemes," Nova murmured from behind him. "This is why we can never win."

The Detonator smirked. "Took you long enough, Renegades. I was beginning to think I'd have to come find you myself."

CHAPTER TWENTY-FOUR

NGRID SHOULDN'T HAVE BEEN THERE.

The *guns* shouldn't have been there.

Nova took in Ingrid's haughty expression, her mind buzzing with disbelief, with irritation, with . . . *betrayal*. They'd had a plan. They'd had a good plan. What was Ingrid doing?

"Adrian Everhart," said Ingrid. She pulled one hand out from beneath the desk, gripping a handgun. She tapped the handle against the desk. "What a sweet surprise."

"That girl told you we were here," said Adrian, his expression oddly neutral for having a gun aimed at him. "The mirror walker."

Nova swallowed. It was as good a guess as any, and Ingrid didn't seem inclined to correct him as her lips drew into a haughty smile.

"The best part of all this," she said, "is that I'm going to kill you, and no one will know it was me, because no one will be alive to tell them. Except"—her eyes narrowed as she scanned Adrian and Ruby, the Librarian, and finally Nova—"you're missing one."

"And you're missing some brain cells!" yelled Ruby. She threw her bloodstone at one of the tall shelving units beside Ingrid. The wire spun around a shelf bracket, hooking tight, and Ruby yanked back, bringing the enormous structure toppling down. Ingrid screamed as a shower of guns and ammunition crashed onto her head. The heavy shelves landed on her shoulders. The desk chair rolled out from beneath her and Ingrid collapsed onto the floor—the descent of the shelves caught by the top of the desk.

Growling, Ingrid crawled beneath the desk and lifted the gun.

Adrian turned and threw himself at Ruby in the same moment Ingrid pulled the trigger. The gunshot was deafening in the enclosed space, the bullet lodging itself in a thick encyclopedia as Adrian and Ruby tumbled to the ground. They rolled behind a bookshelf.

With a terrified cry, Gene Cronin turned and started for the stairs, but Nova reached out and grabbed the back of his shirt. She slammed him into a corner behind another teetering shelf. "This wasn't the plan," she whispered. "What's going on?"

"You tell me!" he spat back, his eyes wide with horror. "Ingrid said she was here for new bombshells, but I have the distinct impression I've been set up!"

Nova frowned. "What did she tell you yesterday?"

"Yesterday? I didn't see her yesterday!"

A crash came from the artillery room. Releasing Cronin, Nova peered through a gap in the bookshelf as Ingrid cleared a path through the weaponry that had fallen from the shelves.

Nova searched for Adrian and Ruby, but could see no sign of them in the labyrinth of shelving.

"Here's what's going to happen," said Ingrid. "I'm going to kill you, then I'm going to go find your friend and kill him too. The smoky one, right? I'm sure he hasn't gone far." She cocked the gun again. "Then, while Captain Chromium is reeling from the death of his only son, I am going to burn down Renegade Headquarters and everything they've built. I will show them what it's like to work so hard for something, only to have it destroyed in *minutes*."

As Nova watched Ingrid pick her way through the mess, a movement near the floor caught her eye. She stood on her tiptoes, straining to see over a pile of books, and spotted Adrian. Or, his hand, as he sketched hasty lines onto the floor.

"We could run for it now," whispered Cronin. "The stairs are right there. We could—"

"Shut up," said Nova, snarling.

Ingrid rounded a shelf, the gun at the ready as she searched for Adrian and Ruby. She took another step and suddenly the lines drawn onto the floor jerked upward—a rope cutting across the aisle at her ankles. Ingrid tripped. She yelped, crashing to her knees. The gun flew from her hand.

Stepping out from behind a shelf, Adrian stopped the skidding gun with his foot. "You were saying?"

Ruby let out a battle cry and dropped down from the shelf beside Ingrid, landing on her back and wrapping her wire in front of Ingrid's throat, pulling her head back.

Adrian grabbed the gun and aimed at Ingrid, but in the same moment Ingrid flung herself at the shelf, throwing Ruby's back against it. Ruby cried out in pain, and her surprise allowed Ingrid to launch Ruby over her shoulders, sending her sprawling onto the floor.

The shelf they had struck wobbled, books sliding and tumbling over the sides. With a roar, Ingrid hooked her elbow around the side of the shelf and tipped backward, pulling it toward her. The shelf fell, toppling over into the next shelf, which smashed into the next, like a row of precarious dominoes, until the room was full of collapsing shelves and falling books.

Cronin shoved Nova aside, ducking past her before she could think to grab him. She snatched the shock-wave gun from her belt and pointed it at him, but hesitated, watching as he bolted up the stairs.

He was gone before the last encyclopedia had dropped onto the growing piles.

"Ruby!" Adrian yelled. Nova crept forward, but couldn't spot him in the chaos and dust. "Are you okay?"

"Not Ruby," came a groaning reply. "Red. Assassin."

"Right. Sorry."

Nova spotted him crawling out from the pocket of space left by one of the fallen shelves.

Then a flash of royal blue caught her attention. A glowing sphere was anchored to the back wall, the energy inside it beginning to crackle.

One of Ingrid's bombs, preparing to detonate.

She saw Ingrid standing a dozen feet away from Adrian. Her face was cruel as she stared at him.

Nova's heart jumped. She lifted the stun gun, but . . . who was she supposed to aim at? Was she a Renegade today, or an Anarchist? Who was she supposed to be protecting? Who was she supposed to stop?

Ingrid raised her hand, her fingers poised to snap.

Nova screamed, "Adrian, get down!"

Without hesitation, he fell to the ground.

Ingrid snapped.

The explosion shook the building, blowing chunks of the foundation outward. The blow knocked Nova off her feet. She flew backward, crashing into a wall of shelves. A flare of almost unbearable heat surged over her skin and she turned her face away, throwing her arm protectively over her head, at the same moment an avalanche of books tumbled around her shoulders.

It was a mere two seconds of pandemonium, and then it was over. Nova's ears were ringing and when she dared to lift her head, the air was full of scattered papers and debris and smoke.

Smoke.

"Sweet rot," she muttered, though she couldn't hear her own voice inside her head. "Please let that be coming from Smokescreen."

She grasped a shelf and used it to pull herself from the pile of books. Blinking rapidly to clear the dust from her eyes, she spotted Ruby first, pushing a fallen chair off her legs. Then Adrian, rising to his hands and knees and shaking away the debris that covered him.

The relief that washed over her was unexpected, a little disorienting, and completely overshadowed by the sight of Ingrid storming through the mess. She was holding a gun again—Nova didn't know if she'd managed to retrieve the one Adrian had taken from her, or if this one was new. But she recognized the fury on Ingrid's face. The enraged eyes. The roar coming from her twisted mouth, even if Nova couldn't hear it.

Adrian looked up.

Ingrid lowered the gun, aiming for his head.

Still clutching her own weapon, Nova targeted Ingrid and fired.

It was an invisible force that knocked Ingrid off her feet, sending her sprawling over one of the toppled shelves.

Adrian's head swiveled toward Nova.

"Fire!" she screamed, though it sounded like she was yelling into a pillow.

Though she hadn't yet seen the flames, black smoke was billowing up from the pile of books closest to the gaping hole in the foundation. The heat from the blast was smoldering inside those pages, waiting to combust, ready to burn through all the flammable material it could devour.

Adrian scrambled to his feet and shoved his hands into his pocket. His determined expression faltered, replaced with a frown. Pulling out his hands, he patted down his pockets, then his sleeves. Panic rising in his expression, he looked down at the floor, turning in a complete circle, before looking up at Nova and Ruby. He said something.

Nova shook her head, gesturing to her ear.

He said it again and this time she could make out the shapes of his lips—*My pen.*

She gawked in dismay. What was he going to draw, a fire extinguisher?

Wait—actually, that might work.

Feeling around her own belt, she pulled out the ink pen with the hidden projectile dart and tossed it to Adrian.

He caught it at the same moment another explosion blew back the stack of books. They went up in a bonfire of flames. Nova stumbled away, pressing back against the wall.

On the other side of the room, Adrian stooped and grabbed Ingrid, heaving her unconscious body over his shoulder, then yelling at Ruby. *Go! Go! Go!*

They bolted for the stairwell before the flames could cut off their path. Nova joined them, launching herself over fallen shelves, clambering over the desk, and flinging herself up the stairs. It didn't take long for the flames to spread, surging from one stack of books to the next, black smoke permeating the air and clouding the staircase as they climbed.

They burst through the door onto the ground floor of the library, which seemed astonishingly bright and airy in contrast to the dim, smoke-filled basement.

A terrified voice broke through her disoriented thoughts, and she saw Oscar charging toward them, arms flailing. "We're missing one!"

Adrian drew up short. "What?"

"There were thirty-one patrons," Oscar said. Nova tipped forward, straining to understand him. "I counted, and as soon as I heard that first gunshot I started getting them out of here, but I only got thirty! There was one more—a kid, I'm pretty sure. Maybe he got out already on his own, I don't know, but—"

"Split up," Adrian yelled, and though his voice still sounded distant, Nova realized the ringing in her ears was beginning to subside. "Find the kid first. Then if you can, try to find Cronin and Narcissa too. But first, find that kid!"

Ruby and Oscar both spun away, dashing through the stacks.

"What are you going to do with her?" Nova asked, staring at Ingrid's limp body and having the sickening vision of Adrian tossing her back down into the burning basement.

"Arrest her," he said. "I'll secure her outside and do another headcount of the civilians, just to make sure the kid didn't slip by unnoticed, then I'll come back to help."

Nova stuffed the stun gun back into its holster and held out her hands. "I'll take her."

"What?"

"I'll take her outside and secure her."

Adrian's gaze darted down her body and she knew what he was thinking.

"I'm strong enough," she insisted. "If you find that kid, you'll be able to get them out faster than I could. Come on, you're wasting time. Hand her over."

Adrian frowned for a second longer, then shifted his hold

on Ingrid and draped her around Nova's shoulders, so she could carry her like sack of grain. Not that she had ever carried a sack of grain.

She'd never carried an explosion-happy prodigy before, either.

She gritted her teeth, adjusting her grip on the leg and arm that dangled over her shoulders. Truth be told, she didn't think Ingrid was that much heavier than her duffel bag when it was full.

"Got her?" said Adrian.

"Fine. Go."

Nova stumbled toward the lobby. The entire place seemed abandoned, with no sign of anyone—not Cronin and his granddaughter, not Ruby or Oscar. Just her and Ingrid and billows of smoke creeping along the rafters. She stared down at her own plodding feet, wondering if she was just imagining the heat rising up from the floor, into the soles of her fancy new boots.

The wooden floorboards, nailed to wooden beams. The exterior walls might be stone, but everything inside—all the framework, all the furniture, *all those books*—it was an inferno waiting to happen.

And that didn't even take into account the room full of ammunition and explosives in the basement, any of which could start detonating once the fire's heat got to them.

Ingrid's weight dragged on her as she crossed the vestibule and pushed her way through the main doors.

A crowd of terrified civilians was clustered on the sidewalk in front of the steps. Not just the patrons from the library, but a growing collection of neighbors and onlookers too. Soon there would be media. Soon there would be more Renegades.

Nova ignored them all as she shouldered her way through. The crowd parted, gasps and whispers replacing the fuzzy noises in her skull.

"Official . . . Renegade . . . business . . . ," she grunted, trudging into the street. A man stepped forward, hands extended as if to relieve her of the burden, but Nova snapped at him. "Don't touch. She's dangerous."

He recoiled.

No one followed her as she crossed the street, into the shade of the office building. The dead weight of Ingrid's body was just becoming unbearable when Nova reached the corner and dropped to one knee, rolling Ingrid off of her. Ingrid landed with a thud and a groan.

Nova sat back on her heels, gasping, and did her best to work out the muscles of her neck and shoulders. "Next time," she said, "I'm going to let you burn."

Ingrid groaned again.

Grabbing her elbow, Nova pulled Ingrid up to sitting, then leaned her against the building. She unhooked the handcuffs the Renegades had assigned to her from the back of her belt. Evidently they were handed out to every patrol unit, even though, in this case, Adrian and his team weren't supposed to be *patrolling*.

"You shot me," Ingrid mumbled, her words slurring as she fought to recover from the effects of the shock wave.

"Did not," said Nova. "I stunned you. There's a difference." She slapped one side of the cuff to Ingrid's wrist.

Ingrid started, her expression starting to clear. "What—"

"I'm only doing one hand," said Nova. Yanking Ingrid's arm upward, she attached the other cuff to the bars across the first-floor window. "You'll be able to free yourself easy, and I'll chalk it up to a beginner's mistake."

Ingrid craned her head, staring blearily at her trapped wrist. "You were supposed to help me," she said. "They'd be dead by now."

Releasing a hasty breath, Nova crouched closer to her. "You didn't warn him at all, did you? You set this all up. You set *me* up."

Ingrid coughed. "If I'd told you, you would have gotten trigger shy, and you know it. Just like at the parade. But you're a smart girl. You should have figured it out." She scooted herself closer to the wall. "A Renegade team walking right into our hands. The Captain's son, no less. Finally, our chance to show them the pain and loss we've had to suffer. And you ruined it!"

Nova's body began to shake with restrained anger. She stood and took a step back from Ingrid. "My goals are a bit more comprehensive than taking out *one* patrol unit. I thought we were together on that." She shook her head, blinded by frustration. "We'll talk about it later. Right now, I have to go do damage control, because *someone* completely ignored my plan. The plan that would have protected the Librarian and hidden our connection to him, I'll remind you."

"They would have charged him with something," Ingrid grumbled. "They would have found a reason to arrest him. It was only a matter of time."

Nova pursed her lips. Yesterday she believed that was true. Now, she was no longer sure. All night long, Adrian and the others had done exactly what they'd said they would do. Watch and wait. They only decided to enter the library after Ingrid revealed herself. If Adrian had intended to plant incriminating evidence, she'd seen no sign of it.

"Maybe, maybe not," she said. "All we know now is that we've lost the Librarian and access to everything that was in that storeroom. The Renegades won. Again."

CHAPTER TWENTY-FIVE

———————■————————

NOVA STOMPED BACK across the street, her thoughts reeling. She was in this for the long haul. She was acting the part of the Renegade not so she could teach them a lesson today or tomorrow. Not so she could undermine a single mission or take out a single team.

She would bring about the end of the Renegades. She would take down the Council. She would avenge the family they had sworn, and failed, to protect. *Her* family.

Ingrid was an idiot for being so shortsighted, for trying to take the easy road to revenge. But then . . . Nova had been an idiot too. She should have known something was wrong from the moment they stepped inside the library and she saw that speechless, terrified look on Narcissa's face. She should have reacted faster, before everything got so out of control.

But she'd been so focused on completing the mission. She'd put too much faith in Ingrid, convinced there would no longer be any incriminating evidence left behind. The Renegades would search the place and, when they came up empty-handed, this investigation would be over.

Instead, Ingrid had duped Nova, and now everything was in ruins.

Or at least, the library was in ruins. Smoke was streaming out through the lower windows. Nova could see the massive hole in the foundation where the bomb had hit. The cloud of smoke spilling out from that crater was black as pitch.

The crowd was watching her as she approached, their attention shifting from her to Ingrid to the library.

"What's happening?" a woman demanded. "You're a Renegade, aren't you? Aren't they going to do anything about this?"

Nova stopped and turned to face the woman, annoyance growing fast inside her. "Do something," she said. "Like . . . catch the bad guy?" She gestured back at Ingrid.

The woman peered down her nose at Nova. "Like put out the fire."

"Where's Tsunami?" said a kid.

"Yeah!" another spouted. "Or someone else with water power! That's what you need."

Nova opened her mouth, preparing to tell them that right now, they were doing the best they could with the powers they had, but then she hesitated, remembering that the public's favorable—or unfavorable—opinion of the Renegades wasn't her problem.

"Whatever," she muttered, shoving through the crowd and facing the library. She peered up through the windows. There was no sign of Adrian or the others. Had they found the missing kid? Were they still in there looking?

They must have. They were professionals. They were *actual* superheroes. If they hadn't found the kid yet, they would, any minute now.

But . . . what about the Librarian?

Nova exhaled, struggling to retain focus in the upheaval. To not lose sight of her priorities.

The Librarian was found out. He would be arrested the moment they found him again, charged with illegal weapons dealing and conspiracy and who knew what else. Any hope of the Anarchists maintaining their connection to his distributors was gone.

Unless she could find him first. Unless she could somehow get him to safety. Maybe, just maybe, she could still right this sinking ship.

Gene Cronin was a coward. That's what Ingrid had told her a dozen times. He would have run. He would be long gone by now, probably halfway to the city limits.

Wouldn't he?

She massaged the back of her neck, uncertainty crowding her thoughts, when a series of explosions rumbled the foundation of the library. They were followed by the deafening creak of wood caving in on itself. The crowd pushed back as a cloud of black smoke spewed out from the windows and the massive hole in the lower wall.

Nova knew the explosions were from the stockpile of explosives in the basement, though she couldn't be sure if there were more detonations still to come.

Then she heard the screams.

At first, she thought she was imagining it. A terrified echo coming from her still-scattered mind.

Someone shoved her from behind. The woman from before, crying, "Someone's still in there! I heard them! *Do* something!"

And though it took all of Nova's willpower not to turn around and yell at the woman to *do something* herself, she ignored the instinct and took off running—not into the library, but around the corner, sure the screams had come from the back.

No sooner had she rounded the far corner than she saw him. A kid, six or seven years old, hanging out of the second-story window.

He had the collar of his shirt pulled up over his nose and even from down below she could see his panicked, bloodshot eyes.

Nova glanced in each direction, but there was nothing she could use to climb. No random ladder lying around, no convenient overgrown tree. She inspected the side of the building and, without giving herself a chance to overthink it, dug her fingers into the mortar of the stones and hauled herself upward.

She got only a few feet up the side of the building before her foot slipped and she crashed back to the ground, landing hard on her back. Overhead, the boy sobbed, his fingers clutching the sill of the window.

Nova got back to her feet, but another explosion rocked the ground, nearly knocking her over again. A window on the first floor had exploded outward, succumbing to the heat and pressure building up inside the library. Blinding orange flames roared inside, licking at the stone walls.

Nova shut her eyes, calculating the risks. Though it took only seconds to make the decision, it felt like an eternity.

Opening her eyes again, she reached into the compartment on her belt that held her handmade exothermic micro-flares. And, buried deep beneath them, her gloves.

Nightmare's gloves.

She shoved her fingers into the black leather and strapped down the buckles, then pressed the switch that engaged the pressurized suction cups. Stomping forward, she leaped for the building, pressing her palms into the facade.

The suction held.

Nova started to climb. Press, stretch, release. Her toes grappling for purchase in the mortar. Her arms burning with exertion as she hauled herself higher and higher. Billows of smoke streamed up from the windows below, filling the air around her.

By the time she reached the window on the second story, her arms were ready to detach from her shoulders. But she made it inside, hauling herself in through the window and collapsing on the floor beside the child.

He stared down at her, lip trembling. "Help?" he said meekly.

She nodded. "Give me a second."

One breath in. One breath out.

She sat up and staggered to her feet. This floor, too, was filling with smoke, though it wasn't yet too thick to see. "Come on," she said, wrapping an arm around the kid's shoulders. He followed her without resistance through a series of archive rooms, until they reached the main staircase.

Nova drew up short, staring down toward the lobby. What had been the main lobby was now a sea of smoke and flames. The floor itself was smoldering and, even as she stared, the floor beneath the scholar statue in the vestibule gave out from the weight, collapsing in on itself.

Nova backed away, nudging the kid toward the wall.

"Okay," she said slowly. "Won't be going that way."

She ushered him back the way they had come, to the open window she had climbed through. She stuck her head out and analyzed the fall. It wasn't too bad . . . for her.

"Do you know how to tuck and roll?"

The kid whimpered. "Can't you . . . can't you *fly*?"

She stared at him. "If I could fly, why would I—" She lifted her hands, still cloaked by the gloves, then groaned. "Never mind. Listen. You're going to climb onto my back and I'll scale the wall back down. You're going to have to trust me, okay?"

Though the kid's face was full of fear, it was overshadowed by pure, inexplicable hope. "You're a Renegade," he said. "Of course I trust you."

Nova's gut clenched and every instinct wanted to argue that point. *Don't. Don't trust them. They don't deserve it.*

But she bit back the reply and had started to crouch down so he could climb onto her back when she heard yelling.

Wrapping a hand around the kid's wrist, Nova peered out the window again and spotted Ruby and Oscar running through the overgrown ivy below.

"Nova!" Oscar yelled, then flinched. "By which I mean, Insomnia! You need to get out of there!"

Relief pulsed through Nova's veins. She cupped her hands around her mouth and yelled back, "I found the kid! Look!" Turning, she scooped the kid beneath his armpits and held him up in the window for them to see.

Ruby clasped a hand over her mouth. She and Oscar traded looks, but it was a short-lived silent discussion.

"Hold on," said Ruby, unwinding the wire from her wrist. She stepped away from Oscar and started to twirl it like a lasso in the air. "Stand back!"

Nova jumped away from the window, pulling the kid with her. A second later, Ruby's bloodstone flew over the sill. As soon as it jolted backward, the points of the gem peeled open, transforming it into a grappling hook that snagged tight to the windowsill.

"Cool," the kid murmured.

"Have you ever done a zip line?" said Nova, peeling off her gloves and stuffing them back into her satchel.

"A what?"

"Nothing. Come on, it's just like playing on the monkey bars. Hand over hand. If you fall, that guy with the cane will catch you, okay?"

The kid peered at the thin wire, then down at Oscar, his brow creased with uncertainty.

"He's a Renegade too," said Nova. "He can bench-press, like . . ." She considered. "I don't know. A lot. More than you weigh, for sure."

Seemingly comforted, the boy swung one leg over the sill. Nova helped him get started, showing him how to reach out with his hands while keeping his ankles locked around the rope.

He was halfway down and she was just beginning to relax, debating whether she would traverse the rope, too, or take the faster route of jumping, when Oscar yelled up to her, "Where's Adrian?"

She tensed. "He's not with you?"

Oscar shook his head. "We haven't seen him since you came out of the basement."

Nova leaned back from the window and glanced around. The air inside the library made her feel like she was inside a sauna. A smoky, stifling sauna.

Adrian wouldn't still be in here, would he?

Unless the smoke had gotten to him. Unless he was unconscious somewhere, dying of smoke inhalation, or trapped beneath a burning bookcase, or—

A scream cut over the roar of the fire. Nova stilled. It wasn't Adrian.

But that only meant that someone else was still in the library.

She followed the screaming to the far corner of the third floor, where a walled-off room stood off from the main stacks, its contents visible through a glass window in the shut door. A sign beside the door read RARE BOOKS AND FIRST EDITIONS. Nova threw it open and found a room mostly clear of the smoky haze that had filled up the rest of the building, though it immediately began to spill in through the open doorway.

Gene Cronin and Narcissa stood before an open window. Narcissa spun toward Nova and shrieked, "Shut the door!"

Nova did, slamming it with a defiant shove.

The Librarian did not even glance over at her. He was too busy pulling books out of glass cases and hastily wrapping them up in paper towels, before throwing them out the window in great armfuls. "Help me!" he cried. "Narcissa—quick! The manuscripts case. We have to save the manuscripts!"

"They're just books!" Narcissa yelled back. "We have to save ourselves!"

"*Just books?*" Cronin roared. "My life's work! Some of these are the only known copies left in the entire world! First editions . . . signed copies . . ."

"Narcissa is right," said Nova, stepping farther into the room. She scanned the space again, thinking Adrian would appear from behind one of the cases, but it was only the Librarian and his granddaughter. Adrian wasn't there. She gulped, and tried not to picture him trapped in the fire below. "The ground floor is compromised. The whole building is going to collapse in on itself any minute. You have to get out of here." She scanned the room. Two walls held double-hung windows, all of which had already been opened, perhaps in an effort to let out what smoke seeped through the cracks in the door. A brick fireplace stood on the western wall, looking ironically as though it hadn't seen fire in decades, with an ornate mirror hung over the mantel. Nova guessed this decorative element was intended more for Narcissa's convenience than an attempt at decorative elegance.

Otherwise, there were four glass cases displaying ancient books, scrolls, journals, and manuscripts, and even an assortment of antique scribing and printing tools, from ink wells to lead type.

More bookcases along the walls, crammed full of works that weren't quite as rare or valuable as those in the cases. There was the door Nova had entered through, and . . . that was it. No other escape routes. They would have to go through the window.

"Why did you bring them here?" Narcissa wailed, furious.

Nova spun to face her. "What?"

"You did this! You and the Detonator—you tricked us. Why?" Frightened tears were pooling in Narcissa's eyes and her fists were clenched so tight they were shaking. It occurred to Nova that she, at least, was not trapped here. There was a mirror. She could leave anytime.

But she hadn't left yet. She was still trying to save her grandfather.

Nova bit the inside of her cheek, trying to think clearly, while Narcissa's hateful look cut into her. She'd always liked the Librarian's granddaughter. She didn't know her well, but she'd always seemed nice enough when Nova had come with Ingrid to conduct their business. Though she was the Librarian's granddaughter and obviously knew about his activities, she'd never struck Nova as particularly . . . villainous.

For the first time, she started to wonder what Narcissa thought about *her*. In their few interactions she'd seemed quiet, even meek. Nova had assumed that was just her personality, but now she questioned if Narcissa might be afraid of her.

Because she was Nightmare?

Or because she was Ace's niece?

"You need to leave," Nova said, pacing to the nearest window. "Can you take your grandfather through the mirror?"

"It doesn't work like that," Narcissa snapped.

"Well then, you get out through the mirror while you can. Gene and I will go out through the window." She looked down at the two-story drop. "I think."

This side of the room looked out onto the street in front of the library, where the crowd of civilians had continued to grow.

A quick glance to the office building showed her that Ingrid was gone. The handcuffs lay on the sidewalk beneath the small smoldering crater where Ingrid had set off an explosion between the wall and barred window.

The other two windows opened toward the side alley and the theater. If they jumped, they could aim for the nearest dumpster, which would take the blow easier than concrete would. But Nova doubted Gene Cronin could handle that fall, even if she did instruct him in the basics of tuck and roll.

"He's seventy-four years old!" cried Narcissa. "You really think he's going to jump out a window?"

Nova sighed. Where were Winston and his hot-air balloon when she needed them?

A crash resounded behind her and Nova spun around, worried that the building was starting to collapse on them. But no—a window had broken. Shards of glass were flying through the air, scattering across the floor, following the trajectory of the figure that had just launched through the window.

Nova's jaw dropped as she watched the figure pull off a perfect tuck and roll before bounding effortlessly back to his feet. He spun around, armored body braced for an attack and daylight glinting off the blank visor.

"Seriously?" Nova drawled. She'd known it was only a matter of time before more Renegades started to show up, but she hadn't expected their secret warrior. Like those onlookers outside had said—a water elemental would have been nice.

But maybe it made sense. The Council knew about this mission, and had a vested interest in Adrian's well-being. Maybe they'd sent the Sentinel to observe their progress. In which case, the question wasn't, what was he doing here? But more, what had taken him so long?

The Sentinel's head swiveled toward her and he said in a deeply concerned voice, "Is everyone all right?"

Nova spread her arms wide. "We're trapped in burning building. What do you think?"

"I'll get you to safety," he said. "All of you. On one condition." He turned his focus toward the Librarian, who had stopped tossing books out the window to gape at the newcomer. "I want to offer you a trade, Gene Cronin."

Cronin's mouth worked in silence. He held a leather-bound book to his chest, squeezing it like a life preserver. "I . . . who are you?"

"I am the Sentinel."

It was said in that same righteous tone Nova remembered, and she couldn't help rolling her eyes.

"Answer me quickly," said the Sentinel. "We don't have much time."

"I . . . a trade? Yes. Yes, all right. I am a fair businessman. But . . . everything's been destroyed. If you're here for guns or explosives, it will have to wait until I can reestablish connection with my—"

"That doesn't interest me," said the Sentinel. "I'm here for information."

Nova frowned, her suspicions growing. Outside, she heard someone calling her name and she turned to see Ruby and Oscar racing through the alley, each carrying one end of a long aluminum ladder. Relief swelled through her chest. She wondered where they had gotten it from, though at the moment it didn't much matter.

"Information?" said Cronin. "Well, that I have in spades."

"I'm looking for Nightmare."

Her heart jolted and she spun back to face the Sentinel. He wasn't facing her and she could see the visor only in profile. But Cronin—she could see him just fine, and the way his stunned eyes shifted toward her made her pulse thunder beneath her skin. She gave a quick, desperate shake of her head.

"Tell me where I can find her," said the Sentinel, "and I'll not only get you safely out of this building, but I'll take you somewhere that will give you a significant head start when the Renegades come looking. You and your granddaughter can leave this city and never come back."

Narcissa's gaze swiveled from the Sentinel to Nova, her eyes wide. It was impossible to tell if the Sentinel meant what he was saying, or if the offer was merely a ploy to get the Librarian to talk. Perhaps the Sentinel would betray their deal as soon as he had the information he wanted. That's what a villain would have done. But a Renegade? Who were all about honesty and integrity?

But if he did mean to follow through with such an offer, he'd be letting the Librarian go free, a man who had put hundreds of illegal weapons out into the streets. What would the Council say about that? Had they already approved this deal, all in an attempt to find Nightmare? To find *her*?

Nova swallowed, debating whether or not she should be flattered.

"Nightmare?" Cronin said. His eyes stayed focused on the Sentinel now and Nova could almost see his thoughts grinding inside his head as he tried to work out his best chance for long-term survival . . . and freedom.

"She's wanted for an attempted assassination on the Council, though I suspect I don't need to tell you that. You supplied the gun she used, didn't you?" The Sentinel took a few steps closer, his feet clopping against the floorboards. "I want to know where she is and who she's working for. Answer that and you'll have the rest of this day to find yourself accommodations other than a prison cell."

"Where she is," Cronin squeaked. "Who she's working for?"

His focus slipped off the Sentinel and settled on Nova. Her hand dropped to her belt and the stun gun holstered there.

Cronin's Adam's apple bobbed sharply. "Well," he gasped. "That's a . . . a complicated matter." He cleared his throat. "You see, the girl who . . . who goes by Nightmare, as . . . as some know her . . . by that name . . . well, she—"

A flaming blue sphere soared in through the broken window. It landed on the wooden floor, bounced once—

Nova dived for cover behind a display case, throwing her arms around her head, while the Sentinel launched himself for Cronin and Narcissa, shielding them both.

The detonation blew the corner off the library, tore a hole through the floor, and heaved the walls outward. Plaster and glass and roof shingles cascaded onto Nova's back. The floor beneath her tilted sharply toward the epicenter of the explosion. She grabbed for one of the built-in shelves, holding tight to the molding as the floor dropped out from under her feet. Books rained down around her but she swung her knee upward for purchase and held on.

The rumbling of the walls had not yet stopped when she felt a surge of heat and all the smoke released from the floor below, searing and thick. Nova coughed and looked around, trying to see through the haze. Flames were surging down below. The wall to her right was gone and she could see the theater across the alley, but at least the opening allowed for the smoke to billow outward. She coughed. Her eyes stung. There was no sign of the Sentinel or

Cronin or Narcissa. Had they fallen through to the floor below? There was no sign of them down there, either.

The bookshelf she was clinging to began to cave inward, the exterior walls weakened by the explosion. She gritted her teeth and searched for a way to get out, but there was nothing else to grab on to. She sensed that to take a single step onto the splintered floorboards would send them crashing down.

Her gaze snagged on a light sconce overhead. If she could get to it, she might be able to grab on and swing her body toward the opening . . .

Though her palms were slick with sweat, she curled her fingers around the shelving and reached, scrambling upward, even as the shelves groaned and tipped toward the broken floor. Gravity tugged at her. She stretched, her arm reaching toward the sconce. Inches away . . . what might have been a mile away . . .

Her fingers slipped.

Nova screamed as she fell into the fire.

CHAPTER TWENTY-SIX

S OMETHING GRABBED HER IN MIDAIR.

Nova felt her body being crushed against a hard, unforgiving shell, and she was soaring upward again. She sucked in a shocked breath and stared up at the Sentinel's visor. The feeling of weightlessness was brief. He thudded down on the second-story floor, which cracked and groaned under the force of his landing. He turned and launched them both back toward the destroyed wall. Wind and smoke blew into Nova's face and she turned away, shielding her eyes against the Sentinel's chest.

This time, the sense of flying led to a sense of falling, and soon he had landed with the impact of a bulldozer on the roof of the theater. He dropped to one knee, his arms cradling her. "Are you okay?"

Nova realized that she was shaking. All of her, shaking, as she lifted her head and saw only her own stunned expression reflected back on the surface of the visor.

He was holding her. Like she was . . . precious cargo. Or an innocent bystander. Or . . . or . . . a damsel in distress.

Clenching her jaw, Nova slammed both palms against his chest plate and forced herself out of his arms. He fell back in surprise, catching himself on one elbow as she leaped to her feet and backed away. She grabbed the shock-wave gun from her waistband.

The Sentinel held a hand toward her. "I'm here to help." He slowly got back to his feet. "You can trust me."

She laughed—a mad, disbelieving sound. "I highly doubt that."

Her eye caught on movement and she spotted Gene Cronin and Narcissa beside a large roof vent. Narcissa was clutching her grandfather's arm, but he was still holding one of the old, delicate books from the library. Narcissa's face was ashen, her braid mussed and her clothes streaked with soot. Cronin wasn't faring much better, though he had already been so disheveled it didn't make that much of a difference.

Another explosion roared from across the street and Nova spun around, imagining more bombs being lobbed at them. But this time, it wasn't the Detonator who had caused the noise. It was the library, succumbing to the fire. The remaining beams and rafters had caved in, sending a roar of sparks and flames that engulfed what remained of the roof. Soon, all that would be left would be a few exterior stone walls. A skeleton of the structure they had housed.

Her heart squeezed.

Was Adrian still . . . ?

No. No—he was strong and clever. He was a Renegade. Surely, he'd found a way out.

The Librarian let out a pained wail and fell to his knees. "My library . . . my *books* . . ."

Narcissa hovered over him, rubbing his back, but he did not seem to notice her beyond his devastation.

"Paper and ink," drawled an angry voice.

Nova grimaced.

Ingrid appeared, stepping out from behind an old, rusting searchlight—what might have been used to promote a new movie premiere, back in a far-gone time. She already had a smirk on her face and a new explosive crackling between her palms.

"You'll get over it," she said. "It's all those lost weapons that are the real tragedy."

Cronin smiled wistfully. "The weapons might have supplied my livelihood, but those books . . . those were my life."

Ingrid snorted. "Pathetic," she said, turning her attention toward the Sentinel. She started to toss the sphere of energy up, catching it in one hand, before tossing it up again. "Well, well. If it isn't the Renegades' shiny new toy. Who would have thought you'd be involved in this little raid too?"

"Stand down, Detonator. You've caused enough damage today." The Sentinel's right hand began to glow, the gray-tinged metal turning white-hot from wrist to fingertips.

Nova stared in disbelief.

That was new.

Surely he didn't have even more abilities that she hadn't seen yet. How could it be possible?

"I know I have," Ingrid said with a cheerful laugh. "And it feels *so good*. After nine years of smothering my power, feigning obedience to the Council's demands . . . to finally remind the world what I can do. Great powers, it feels good!" She let out a hoot toward the sky, then started to laugh. "You know, my focus had been to take out that Everhart boy, but *you* . . . you might be even better. To take out the Council's own lackey. Do you think your armor can withstand a direct hit? I have my doubts . . ."

"Council's lackey?" said the Sentinel. "I think you have me

mistaken for someone else."

"Oh, I don't," Ingrid countered.

The Sentinel extended his glowing gauntlet in front of him, fisted tight. "I'm not here on the Council's orders. I'm not here for anyone's business but my own."

Ingrid sighed. "Do you really—"

A narrow beam of white energy launched from a cylinder on the Sentinel's forearm and slammed into Ingrid's chest. She stumbled and fell back, gasping for breath.

Nova's jaw was hanging open now, her mind momentarily shocked into silence.

The suit, the fire, the long-distance jumping, and now . . . what was that? Some sort of concussive energy beam?

How many abilities did this guy have?

The Sentinel lowered his arm. "Why is it that some villains get so obnoxiously chatty?"

"Is she dead?" said Nova.

The Sentinel turned to her. "Stunned." He hesitated, glancing down at his arm, which had returned to the same dark gray color as the rest of the armor. "I think. I've never actually used that one before."

Nova gaped at him. "What do you mean, you've never used it before?"

They were interrupted by Gene Cronin's faintly dazed voice. "*She* did this." He had made his way to the edge of the roof and was watching the library burn, its flames dancing in his sorrowful eyes. "She set up this trap. She threw those bombs. She destroyed everything." He let out a small, humorless laugh. "What can one expect, from a woman who calls herself *the Detonator*? I should have known better . . . I should never have trusted an Anarchist . . ."

He unfolded his arms and Nova saw that he was still clutching the leather book he'd had inside the rare books room. "But I remember everything," he whispered. "Every single word. This knowledge. It will not be lost." He shut his eyes and his face took on a look of exultation. Of deep, driven purpose. "This is why I was bestowed this gift. To preserve all those words, those stories and ideas. To rescue them from extinction. If it takes the rest of my years on this earth, I will record them all. It will be the great pride of my life."

"Do you plan on doing that while you're in a jail cell?" said the Sentinel. Cronin turned to him, as if surprised anyone else was still standing there. "Because the Renegades may or may not be willing to supply you with enough paper to replace"—he gestured at the library—"all of that."

Cronin swallowed.

The Sentinel stepped closer, his voice lowering. "But my offer stands. I can get you and your granddaughter away from here. Just tell me what you know about Nightmare."

"Sweet rot," Nova muttered. "Is that all you care about?"

The Sentinel did not look at her . . . but the Librarian did.

Nova drew herself up, fixing him with the most threatening look she could manage.

"Nightmare," said Cronin, and, suddenly, he started to laugh, as if it had just occurred to him what a hysterical situation this was. "Oh, Nightmare. Yes. I might know where you can find—"

A gunshot ricocheted through Nova's ears. Gene Cronin's head snapped back, an arc of blood spraying across the rooftop. His body seemed to sway, momentarily suspended, before he collapsed backward. The book he'd been holding tumbled opened beside him, its crisp yellow pages fluttering.

Narcissa screamed.

The world paused. Nova stared at the blood sprayed across the wall, and though she knew it was red, everything seemed suddenly awash in gray. Her lips were parted, but she might have stopped breathing. Her wide, disbelieving eyes swept toward Ingrid, landing on the gun in her hands.

Ingrid raised her chin. There was little to read on her face. Anger. Perhaps pride. But no remorse, so far as Nova could see.

In her bleary thoughts, Nova pictured them sitting around the subway platform later that night, listening to Ingrid tell of how she had taken out the Librarian moments before he could betray Nova's identity. She imagined Ingrid laughing about it, and the others joining her.

But it didn't seem so funny at the moment.

Nova knew Gene Cronin would have given up her secret. Whether now, to the Sentinel, or later to the Council. If he survived this night he would have eventually talked, even if merely to spite her and the Anarchists who had caused the destruction of his library. He had to die if she was to go on with this mission. If she was to have any hope of staying in the Renegades and working to remove them from power once and for all. He had to die. It was the only way.

Sometimes the weak must be sacrificed so that the strong may flourish.

But those thoughts seemed very far away and, she realized, she was hearing them not in her own voice, but in Ace's.

As she watched Narcissa fall, sobbing, over her grandfather's body, Nova knew that she could not have killed him. Not even to protect herself.

What sort of villain did that make her?

Lips pulling into a sneer, Ingrid raised the gun toward Narcissa. The second liability.

A bolt of blinding energy struck Ingrid in her side, knocking her off her feet again. The gun flew out of her hand. A second blast followed almost immediately, sending her rolling a few times until her shoulder struck the rusted spotlight.

The Sentinel stormed toward her, his arm glowing, preparing to fire again—when a flash of blue struck the rooftop at his feet. The explosion sent him soaring through the air and over the rooftop's ledge and left a crater of cracked concrete where he had stood.

"Stop it!" Nova yelled. "Stop blowing things up! Just stop!"

Ingrid sat up, gripping the side of the spotlight with one hand and preparing another bomb in the other. "We can't let her go," she said. "You know that."

Nova stared at her, the words swimming meaninglessly in her head for a long time before she realized Ingrid was talking about Narcissa.

Setting her jaw, Nova marched forward and picked up the fallen gun.

"Go ahead," said Ingrid, letting the blue sphere extinguish, evaporating back into the air. "It *should* be you. Why should I do all the heavy-lifting when it comes to protecting your identity?"

Nova cocked the gun and slipped her finger over the trigger.

It should be her. She needed to be concerned with her own self-preservation. The sanctity of her own secrets. Killing Narcissa is what any Anarchist would do. What Ace would have wanted her to do, and almost certainly what he would have done himself.

Nova let out a shuddering breath, turned, and took aim.

Ingrid stilled, eyeing the barrel that was suddenly targeting her own chest. "Don't be a fool."

"Run," Nova said.

Ingrid glared. Nova glared back, a drop of sweat falling into her eye.

Slowly Ingrid pulled herself to her feet. She eyed Nova warily as she took a step backward toward the fire escape, then two. "You're making a mistake."

"Can't be as big as the mistakes you made today."

With her brow beginning to twitch, Ingrid turned and started to run. Nova waited until she was launching herself over the edge of the roof before she squeezed the trigger.

The bullet hit Ingrid in the back of the arm. She cried out as she fell and Nova heard the clang of her body hitting the metal landing of the fire escape. Then the structure shook and thumped as she staggered her way down, jumping from landing to landing. Below, Nova heard someone yell—Ruby?—and soon, another cacophony of explosions rocked the building. Cursing, she ran to the ledge and peered down to the street, where a new patch of stones was missing from the wall of the theater and now scattered across the road. Ruby was on her back, coughing, with Oscar kneeling at her side. And Ingrid—

Nova scanned the street, only spotting Ingrid's tall boots as she disappeared around a corner.

She slumped forward, unable to tell if she was relieved or not to see Ingrid get away.

Her legs were shaking as she pushed herself off the side of the roof and turned around.

Only for her heart to lodge into her throat again.

Narcissa was no longer kneeling over the Librarian's body. Instead, a series of bloody footprints tracked across the roof, to the ledge facing the destroyed library. Narcissa had climbed up onto the low parapet, carrying the book her grandfather had managed to save.

"Narcissa, no!"

Ignoring her, Narcissa lifted her arms in a graceful arc over her head, then tipped forward over the edge. Nova screamed and ran toward her, though she knew she was far too late. She grabbed the ledge and leaned over, just in time to see the glinting surface of a broken mirror on the concrete below, as Narcissa swan-dived into it and disappeared.

The air squeezed from Nova's lungs as she watched the reflection of blue sky and smoking flames shudder in the glass, before turning still once more. She recognized the mirror as the one that had been above the mantel in the rare books room. Bricks from the fireplace were scattered throughout the alley, blown there from the explosion.

Nova groaned, exhausted to her core, and sank down to her knees, her arms dangling limply over the wall. Her head fell forward, pressing into the cool stone, and she had the distant thought that she would be perfectly content to sit there, unmoving, for a month. Even if the air was full of smoke and debris. Even if there was a dead body and a pool of blood mere steps away from her. She did not want to move. She didn't know if she could.

She felt heavy and drained. Her thoughts jumbled together as she tried to cope with what her expectations had been for the day, and what had become reality.

As she tried to determine what to do next.

Narcissa had gotten away. Nova knew that Ingrid had been right—the girl was a liability. She knew too much. And though Nova didn't regret her decision not to kill her, or to let Ingrid kill her, she also wondered how long she would be haunted by the fear that Narcissa would turn up at any time and give up her secrets out of revenge . . . or, perhaps even more likely, use those secrets as blackmail.

The Librarian was dead. Good—because he couldn't betray her. Bad—because he had been one of the Anarchists' few reliable resources.

Bad—all those guns were destroyed. At least, she assumed most of them were destroyed, and any that weren't would no doubt be in the hands of the Renegades by the day's end. Double bad.

But, good—they had not learned anything about Nightmare. Not who she was or where to find her. Not even definitive proof that the Librarian had supplied her the gun she used at the parade.

Although, the Sentinel surely would have deduced that there was a connection between Cronin and Nightmare, based on how Cronin was so close to responding to his questions, but Nova couldn't think clearly enough yet to determine how much danger that really put her in. After all, a lot of criminals came to Cronin for supplies. It didn't exactly narrow down the search.

A clang reverberated across the rooftop, the sound conjuring the memory of metal armor and cold arms tightening protectively around her as they flew through the air.

Nova inhaled sharply.

"Are you okay?" said the Sentinel, sounding more gentle than he ever had before.

Nova swallowed. She didn't respond and didn't turn to look at him, even as his footsteps thumped closer. He stopped, not beside her, but beside the Librarian's body.

Nova turned her head enough so she could glimpse him from the corner of her eye. He stood just outside the pool of dark blood. She inspected his profile, his suit, the arms that she had seen burn with flame and glow with energy, but that were now dull, metallic gray. There were signs of stress from the battle—singe marks on his side, dents on his back. But for the most part, he looked little worse for wear.

She had all but forgotten about the gun, which she had dropped in her rush to stop Narcissa. Now she found it beside her knee, the handle cool in her palm as she picked it up.

"Would you really have let him go?" she said, sitting back on her heels. "If he'd given you the information you wanted?"

The Sentinel said nothing for a long time, before finally admitting, "I hadn't decided yet."

"You mean the offer wasn't sanctioned by the Council?"

His head turned toward her. Instead of answering her question, though, he asked again, "Are you okay? Do you need . . . help? Getting down?"

"I'm fine," said Nova, running her thumb down the gun's handle. "What do you want with Nightmare, anyway?"

The Sentinel cocked his head and she could imagine him watching her. She wished she knew what he looked like. The blank canvas of his face had become deeply unnerving.

"She and I have unfinished business."

She raised an eyebrow. "And the Council, too, no doubt?"

"They don't dictate everything I do," he said, a little stubbornly. "Nightmare is a threat to all Renegades, but . . . I have my own reasons for wanting to find her."

"Okay, Mr. Alter Ego," said Nova, attempting to infuse some lightness into her voice, "my curiosity is piqued. Who are you, really?"

He turned to face her more fully and she was sure, at first, that he would tell her. He certainly seemed to consider her question long enough.

Finally, he said, "I'm not your enemy."

Her cheek twitched. "Prove it. Lots of people think you're an impostor, trying to discredit the Renegades. If that's not the case, then take off the helmet and show yourself. No secrets between allies, right?"

Again he stood unmoving for a long, still moment, before he shook his head. "Not yet."

"*Insomnia!*"

Nova swallowed. Lifting her head, she could barely see Ruby and Oscar on the street below, staring up to the top of the theater with worry scrawled on both their features. Spotting her, Oscar pointed, then cried out, "Are you okay?"

Nova didn't respond. She was looking past them, around them, scanning the ground below in all directions . . .

Ruby and Oscar were alone. Adrian was not with them.

Her gaze darted to the library, but the fire had gotten so bright and the air so hazy with smoke she almost couldn't stand to look at it.

"Where's Adrian?" she yelled down to them, and watched as both of their faces fell.

Nova shuddered. Adrian wouldn't have just disappeared. He must have been trapped inside. Dread clawed at her, even as she told herself it was a good thing. One less Renegade in the world. One less superhero . . .

But she was seeing his notebook full of stunning, heartfelt drawings. She was hearing the way he laughed when she told him about juggling and bird-watching. She was seeing Max's face light up as Adrian drew the tiny glass figurine for his tiny glass city.

She was not convinced that his death—and such a horrible, horrible death—could possibly be a good thing.

"It's all right," said the Sentinel gently. "Here. Let me take you down to them."

"I'm fine."

"Are you sure?"

She glanced back and frowned, wondering if she was imagining the way his shoulders had curled inward, giving the strangest impression of . . . of *shyness*.

"I have to go soon," said the Sentinel. "But it would only take a second for me to—"

"No," said Nova, pushing herself up to standing, though her legs still felt weak. "You haven't answered any of my questions, *Sentinel*. Who are you? What do you want with Nightmare?" Her voice rose, scratched raw from the hazy air. "Are you working for the Council or not?"

"I can't tell you any of that. I'm sorry."

He did, in fact, sound apologetic, but that only served to stoke Nova's fury. Here he was, her enemy, the Renegade she most needed information about, and so far she felt like she'd learned nothing that she didn't already know yesterday. "All right, how about this question," she snapped. "Is that suit bulletproof?"

"What—?"

Nova revealed the gun and fired. The bullet hit him in the chest, squarely over his heart. The bullet did not penetrate the armor, but he still cried out and stumbled back—though whether in pain or surprise, Nova couldn't tell.

She frowned. "I guess it is."

The Sentinel touched a gloved finger to the bullet lodged into the chest plate. "What are you—?"

Nova fired again. And again. Each bullet pinging off the armor.

The Sentinel leaped upward, flipping over Nova's head and landing behind her. He tried to grab her arms but Nova dropped to the ground and rolled out of his reach. Leaping back to her feet, she pivoted and raised the gun again.

"Stop!" the Sentinel demanded, lifting both hands in supplication. "I'm not fighting you. I'm on your side."

"I just witnessed you trying to strike a deal with a villain!" Nova yelled. "You won't give up your identity, and you all but admitted that you don't follow the Council's laws. That makes you a criminal." She shot again, but this time the Sentinel dodged, throwing himself behind the spotlight. Nova marched after him. "So, you're either a villain who's pretending to be on the Renegades' side, or you're a brand-new class of Renegade, and for whatever reason, the Council doesn't want us to know about it. Which is it? And *why?*"

She rounded the spotlight, only to be knocked down as the Sentinel slammed into her. Nova fell hard on her back and felt the gun being ripped out of her hand. The Sentinel threw the gun over the side of the building. Then he reached for her waist and snatched the shock-wave gun from her belt too.

"Hey!" she yelled, grabbing for the gun.

The Sentinel's fingers wrapped around her wrist and pulled her back to her feet in one swift motion, yanking her so close her own breath fogged against his visor. "I'm not a villain, and I'm not your enemy," he said, "but I can't tell you or anyone else who I am, not until I've found Nightmare and gotten the answers I need."

He released her suddenly and Nova dropped back, rubbing her wrist—though more to clear off the sensation of his cold grip than because he'd actually hurt her.

Then he tossed her stun gun over the side of the building too.

"Hey!" Nova yelled again. "I made that one!"

The Sentinel didn't answer. Turning, he launched himself into the air. Nova watched as his body cleared the smoldering remains of the library and disappeared into the thick black smoke.

CHAPTER TWENTY-SEVEN

NOVA KNEW THAT HER DROP from the bottom platform of the theater's fire escape to the alleyway was terribly lacking in grace, but she was beyond caring. Her legs ached, her arms ached, and besides, no one was around to see her. The rooftop had carried the stench of smoke, but it was a hundred times stronger down here, thick and inescapable. She pressed her nose into her elbow and stayed as close to the theater wall as she could to avoid the heat emanating from the library as she picked her way past the debris.

The crowd had grown, though most people had moved away from the burning building. Someone cried out in hopeful surprise when they spotted Nova emerging from the smoke, but it was immediately followed by a groan of disappointment. She dropped her arm, scowling, at the same moment a kid squealed. A second later, a body crashed into her, small arms tying around her waist. She gasped and peered down at the kid's head. The child she had found on the top floor. The one she had rescued—with Ruby's and

Oscar's help. She had never seen him reach the bottom of Ruby's rope and she was surprised at the relief that washed over her at seeing him now.

"Thank you," he said, his words muffled against her rib cage. So simple. So complete.

With a weary smile, she patted him on the head.

In that moment, she could begin to see why any sane person might want to become a Renegade.

"Oscar, no!"

Nova lifted her gaze and saw Ruby and Oscar. They stood out from the crowd, daring to stand closer to the library than anyone else. And, perhaps also because their faces were not alight with awe and curiosity, but anguish.

Extricating herself from the boy, Nova made her way toward them. Ruby had tears shining in her eyes, though she wasn't yet crying. Actually, as Nova got closer, she realized they were both holding back tears, though Oscar was working hard to disguise them with a determined scowl. He was trying to pull away from Ruby, but she was clinging to his sleeve, refusing to let go.

"I survived one fire," he said. "I'll survive this one too!"

"You don't know that!"

"I'm not letting him die in there!"

"He might already be—"

"*Don't say that!*"

Ruby stepped back, her face pinched.

Nova stepped closer. "Adrian?"

Ruby's face scrunched up in agony. "Still no sign of him." The words were followed by a sob, but she clapped a hand over her mouth, the struggle to hold in her emotions apparent in the shaking of her shoulders. "Did he say anything to you?"

"He said . . ." Nova struggled to remember. It felt like ages ago since she'd offered to take Ingrid from him. "He was going to look for the lost kid." Her gaze slid back to the child, who had returned to the other children across the street.

"I'm going back in," said Oscar, tearing his arm from Ruby. His limp had become more pronounced as he started to make his way toward the library. Despite the flames and smoke ravishing the shattered windows, the front facade of the building was relatively unscathed compared with the rest of the structure. The exterior brownstone was standing strong, but Nova knew that inside it would be little more than a shell by this point. A smoldering, blackened shell.

"Oscar!"

Ruby's scream was punctuated by a loud crack within the library, followed by a *boom* and a spurt of new flames and sparks billowing up out of the open ceiling. Another part of the second-story floor had just caved in.

Nova shuddered and took a few steps closer, watching the building burn.

Surely, he would have gotten out before it was too late. Surely . . .

But not if he still believed there was a child needing to be rescued. Somehow, though she knew so little about Adrian, she knew this for sure. He would not have left so long as he believed someone needed his help.

She wrapped a hand around the bracelet on her wrist. The sickening thought came to her, unbidden. Ingrid had achieved her goal. She had killed Adrian Everhart.

Captain Chromium and the Dread Warden would be devastated.

Nova felt only hollow disbelief—none of the accomplishment, none of the joy she might otherwise have expected. He might have been her enemy, but . . . she did not think he deserved to die.

The sudden blow of an air horn screamed through the street. Nova tensed and looked around, unsure where the noise had come from.

It sounded again. A crude, distressed honking, over and over.

Brow knitting, Nova took a step closer to the library. Her heart had started to pound. With disbelief, but also . . . with hope?

She exchanged looks with Ruby and Oscar, then she took off running, sprinting around to the back of the library. This wall had mostly collapsed when Ingrid launched the bomb into the rare books room and great chunks of brownstone had blown halfway across the street, leaving behind a mountain of rubble where the wall had stood. Inside, the flames were dying down, but the collapsed floors were still smoldering and the air was alive with blackened book pages drifting into ashes.

The horn continued to blow, sounding from somewhere within the smoking ruins.

Oscar stamped past Nova and reached for a piece of splintered wood on top of the nearest pile of debris. With a grunt, he heaved it off the pile, then reached in for a destroyed bookcase. Nova could see he meant to clear a path to wherever that noise was coming from. But not seconds later, Oscar roared and stumbled back, staring at his burned hands. He let out a stream of curses and started using his cane like a crowbar to lift pieces of debris instead.

Ruby joined him a second later, flinging her bloodstone hook and dragging away chunks of stone and wood and plaster.

Nova gulped, her hand landing on the satchel on her belt. Her gloves were heat proof. *Nightmare's gloves* . . .

She shut her eyes and told herself that if anyone became suspicious she would be able to find a perfectly reasonable explanation for why she had gloves so similar to those Nightmare had been seen wearing.

She tried not to think of how the Anarchists would scream at her for doing something so stupid, something that risked giving her away, all to save one measly Renegade—

Exhaling, she opened the pouch and reached inside.

An enraged roar echoed in every direction. Nova looked up to see a massive, inexplicable tidal wave of water rolling toward them—towering over them, its crest foaming white. Yelping, Nova grabbed Ruby and Oscar by the backs of their shirts and hauled them away from the library. They all fell back onto a patch of ivy and watched, speechless, as the wall of water fell and gushed over the library. The fire hissed and a great cloud of steam rolled up over them. The water gushed outward, flooding the land around the library and soaking Nova's backside. No longer clean and clear, the water was muddled with ash and debris.

She spotted Tsunami, standing delicately in the center of the road, her palms open toward the sky and her face serene. The image she struck was so in contrast with the chaos of the past hour that Nova found she could only stare at her in wonder. Then Tsunami dropped her hands and turned her head just slightly. She gave a subtle, encouraging nod, and Nova noticed the other Council member who had arrived.

Captain Chromium barreled forward, and Nova had barely grasped these new arrivals before the Captain was tearing through the wreckage as if the fallen library were nothing more than a child's set of building blocks, tossing whole floor beams aside, crushing his fist into half-standing walls of stone. Steam continued to rise up from the ruins, and though the fire was extinguished, Nova knew all those materials must still be blistering hot. But what did he care? He was Captain Chromium.

Ruby climbed to her feet first, and Nova and Oscar followed, watching speechlessly as the superhero tore a path through the destruction. At some point, the blast of the horn started up again, and he changed his course, making his way through toppled, burned bookshelves and crumbled stone columns. From the corner of her eye, Nova saw Ruby slip her hand into Oscar's. Nova squeezed her own hands into fists.

Halfway into the wreckage, near to where the children's books had once been, the Captain grabbed a massive bookshelf and heaved it off into the rest of the remains. And there, underneath, was . . .

Nova stared, incredulous.

Ruby let out a strangled, confused noise.

Oscar started to laugh.

In the middle of the burned, smoldering building, Captain Chromium had found an igloo.

Or, the remains of an igloo. Much of it had melted away, and some chunks of ice had cracked and fallen in front of the igloo's arched entrance.

Seconds later, a figure emerged, crawling through the small opening.

Adrian was drenched. In one hand he held the horn, like something that would be strapped to a motorbike. In the other hand, he carried Nova's pen.

Before he could speak, the Captain pulled him into an embrace. Adrian grimaced slightly, but didn't pull away.

When the Captain had let go, they picked their way back to the others. Adrian spared a grateful smile for Tsunami, who smiled back, then disappeared around the front of the library, presumably to see if anyone else needed assistance.

"An igloo, Sketch?" said Oscar, shaking his head.

Adrian shrugged. He looked positively exhausted, but there was still a lightness in his eyes, a faint smile on his lips. The marked joy of one who had defied death. "Sometimes inspiration just strikes, man."

Finally allowing a sob to escape, Ruby ran forward and wrapped her arms around Adrian, giving him one tight squeeze, before pulling back and punching him in the shoulder. He flinched, more than Nova thought was warranted, given that it hadn't been that hard of a hit.

"Where *were* you?" Ruby cried.

Adrian blinked at her, then glanced back at the quickly melting igloo.

"I mean—why didn't you get out?"

"I was looking for that missing kid," he said, wrapping one arm around Ruby and giving her a friendly embrace. After he let go, she stepped back and crossed her arms, a sour scowl still drawn into her face, clear that she wouldn't forgive him that easily for the distress he'd caused. "I was in the stacks and the smoke got so thick I couldn't see anything. I got really disoriented and felt like I was just walking in circles. Once I realized I was trapped, I made the igloo to protect myself. Then the ceiling collapsed. The igloo protected me, but . . . at some point I passed out. Smoke inhalation, I think." He inhaled deeply, gratefully. "When I came to and realized I was still inside that igloo, I made the horn to call for help."

He turned to Nova and held out the pen she had given him, what felt like ages ago. "Thanks for this."

She took it numbly, holding his gaze and feeling like she should say something, but she couldn't think of any words that would convey what she was feeling. She wasn't even sure what those feelings were.

But she couldn't deny that she was glad Adrian Everhart was alive. She was glad that his smile was just as warm and relaxed now, after an extremely trying day, as it had been at the parade. She was glad . . .

Well. Maybe she was just glad.

Adrian looked like he wanted to say something to her, but couldn't quite find the words. He was staring at her, a question in his eyes, but he seemed to think better of it as he swallowed and looked away.

"We need to get you to headquarters," said the Captain. Nova started. Momentarily caught up in Adrian's dark brown eyes, she'd almost forgotten the Councilman was there. "The med staff will want to see you."

Adrian shook his head. "I'm fine. I feel fine."

"This isn't open for debate. That goes for the rest of you too." The Captain fixed each of them in turn with his icy blue stare, which could not have been more different from the celebrity smile he usually wore. "Go back to headquarters. Get checked out, then get some rest. We'll speak more about this tomorrow." He looked at Adrian again, and Nova could tell he was trying to use some sort of stern, fatherly expression, but it didn't quite reach his eyes. He was clearly too overwhelmed with relief that Adrian was okay, and something about that look made her feel like a screw was being turned in her stomach.

She'd once had a father to look at her like that too.

The Captain turned to go.

"Dad, wait."

He paused.

"The Detonator was here," said Adrian. "She's the one who set off the explosions. Cronin was still selling on the black market, just like we suspected."

"The Detonator? Ingrid Thompson?"

Adrian nodded.

The Captain pressed his lips. "And what about Gene Cronin? Where is he?"

"He's . . ." Adrian hesitated. He glanced once at Nova, then the others. He cleared his throat. "I think he might have gotten away."

"No," said Nova. "He's dead. Ingr—the Detonator killed him, up on the roof of that theater." She pointed. "Then she ran. I tried to stop her, but . . . she got away."

"We saw her too," added Oscar. "When she got down to the alley, Ruby and I tried to chase her, but she threw some of those bombs and we couldn't follow fast enough."

"What about the mirror walker?" said Ruby. "Does anyone know what happened to her?"

"She escaped through a mirror, after . . . after the Detonator killed Cronin," said Nova. "She could be anywhere."

The Captain sighed, massaging the bridge of his nose. "This proves your theory, Adrian. It seems the Anarchists haven't been quite as dormant as we thought. I don't think we can pretend any longer that they aren't still plotting to bring about a second Age of Anarchy. They will have to be dealt with."

Nova tensed. "When? What will you do?"

The Captain looked at her. "I'm not sure yet. But they'll be preparing for us to make a move after today. We'll have to act fast."

She gulped. What did that mean? They would retaliate in days? Hours?

The Captain frowned then, as if a thought had just occurred to him. He turned back to Adrian. "Did you find out anything about Nightmare?"

Adrian's mouth tightened. "Nothing."

The Captain nodded, and Nova did not think he seemed particularly surprised. "Go back to HQ. We'll discuss this more tomorrow."

"The Sentinel was here too," Nova said.

Captain Chromium drew up taller. "The Sentinel?"

She nodded, watching the Captain closely as she said, "I shot him."

Everyone stilled, eyes swiveling toward her in surprise.

"Multiple times," added Nova.

"Did he attack you?" asked the Captain, his expression darkening.

Nova blinked, finding it impossible to admit that, actually, he had saved her.

So why had she done it? She could hardly remember. She'd been livid at the time. Angry at Ingrid and her betrayal, angry that everything was falling apart around her, angry that Adrian might be dead and her first mission had gone so awry and that it all might have been worth it if she could have just learned who or what the Sentinel was, but he wasn't telling her anything.

Angry that he was pretending to be her ally, when she knew to her core that he was her enemy.

But she couldn't explain any of that to Captain Chromium.

"At first, I thought he was sent by you, the Council," she said. "But he said he wasn't. He said he's acting on his own objectives and, honestly, I couldn't tell if he was an enemy or not. When he refused to reveal his identity, I shot him. It hardly seemed to slow him down and he still got away, but . . . I thought maybe you should know. I thought . . ." She cleared her throat. "I thought maybe if he *is* working for the Council, you should tell us, so we can know how we're supposed to treat him, as an ally or not."

Her speech was followed by a long silence. From the corner of her eye, she could see Ruby and Oscar exchanging stunned looks, but she kept her gaze resolutely on the Captain. Waiting for any reaction that would give away the truth.

He rocked back on his heels, eyebrows shooting upward, and let out an astonished, "You don't pull your punches, do you?"

Her jaw twitched. "Is he a Renegade or not?"

Captain Chromium sighed. "Not," he said. "At least, as far as I know. Whoever he is, he isn't acting on our orders." He cocked his head, and Nova had the impression that he was watching her far more closely than he had been before now. "And while I appreciate your efforts to defend our reputation, this might be a good time to point out that, as part of the Renegade code, we generally frown on shooting people who haven't committed a crime."

He nodded at each of them in turn. "Tomorrow," he said again, then turned and went to join Tsunami.

Nova clenched her fists, watching him go. She still didn't know if he was telling the truth, and her own ignorance infuriated her.

"You really shot the Sentinel?"

She glanced at Oscar. "I did," she said. "He deserved it. I'm pretty sure."

Adrian coughed.

"But he's, like, twice as tall as you," said Oscar. "And probably weighs three times as much."

"He's not *that* tall," said Nova.

Oscar shrugged. "Just saying." He shook some chunks of white dust from his hair. "You know, I'm not sure you picked the right alias. Insomnia is too passive. I vote we change it to Velociraptor."

Ruby laughed. "Relatively small, but surprisingly ferocious?"

"Exactly. All in favor?"

"I like Insomnia," said Nova, pretending to be annoyed.

Only when it became too difficult did she realize she was smiling.

CHAPTER TWENTY-EIGHT

S HE DIDN'T WANT TO WASTE her time going all the way to the house on Wallowridge, so instead Nova buried her Renegade communicator band beneath a dead potted plant on the stoop of a small café, three blocks from the entrance to the subway tunnels. She was surprised at how easily she'd adapted to wearing it, and as she made her way through the abandoned subway station and down the dark stairs, she found herself continually checking her wrist, only to remember it wasn't there.

The moment she was close enough to the Anarchists' underground encampment, she knew things had changed. Clangs and thumps were echoing through the tunnels, and she passed hundreds of displaced bees, their fat bodies crawling aimlessly along the walls.

She found Honey haphazardly throwing anything within reach into her old wooden travel trunk, filling it with dresses, shoes, silk robes, cosmetics, and an assortment of dust-covered liqueur bottles.

"What's going on?"

Honey yelped and spun to face her. "That is *it*, Nova. The next time you sneak up on me, I am leaving a wasp in your bed linens." Huffing, she tucked a curl of hair behind her ear. "And we're leaving."

Nova gulped. "Leaving?"

"Leaving. Now, I have a lot of packing to do, so . . ." She flipped her fingers, shooing her away, but Nova didn't move.

"How are you going to get that trunk up the stairs? It'll weigh a hundred pounds by the time you get all this stuff in there."

Honey cast a pleading look toward the ceiling. "My problem, not yours. Skat!"

Frowning, Nova turned away. She moved faster now, passing Winston's abandoned platform without so much as a glance. When she arrived at Leroy's train car, she heard yelling coming from within. She went inside without bothering to knock. Ingrid and Leroy were both filling boxes and tote bags with as much of Leroy's lab equipment as would fit.

"Honey says we're leaving?"

They both glanced at her, and Ingrid's expression, which was already angry, now turned positively enraged. She didn't respond, just turned her back on Nova, giving her a good glimpse of the bloodied scarf tied around her upper arm, where Nova had shot her.

"We're leaving," confirmed Leroy. "Pack up what you truly need, leave the rest."

Nova shook her head, her heart beginning to thump painfully in her chest. "We can't leave."

"We must."

"What about—"

"The Renegades are coming, Nova." Leroy looked up from the box he was packing and fixed her with his black, penetrating gaze. "They could very well be on their way at this minute. I trust you know that better than anyone."

She shook her head. "We can fight. We'll have the advantage of a familiar field. Maybe . . . maybe this is our best chance to really strike out at them. We can lure them down here and then—"

"We have already considered this," said Leroy, with a heavy sigh. "We have plans to slow them down. Diversions that will help us get out safely, before they can follow us. But it will not be enough. There are too many of them. We cannot win. We must leave."

She stared at him, aghast. He made it sound so simple. They would just *leave*.

But it wasn't that simple, and they all knew it.

Leroy's stern face slipped into something almost sorrowful. "I know," he whispered. "It won't be forever." He pointed his chin toward the door. "Now go, gather your things."

Clenching her jaw, Nova turned and ran. She did as she was told, because that seemed easiest. She pulled her duffel bag from beneath the bed and took a moment to contemplate what she truly needed.

Nightmare's hooded jacket and face mask. Her throwing stars and the netting bazooka. A few changes of clothes.

She looked around, but found that she had little attachment to anything else in this abandoned train car. What really mattered to her?

The bracelet her father had made, and the safety of the Anarchists. *Her family.*

Slinging the duffel bag over one shoulder, she jumped down from the train car. Across the way, her eye landed on an old advertisement hung on the tunnel's wall. It was promoting a book—a thriller from some bestselling author Nova had never heard of—though the protective plastic over the poster had long ago been tagged with graffiti. The bright splotches of paint continued into the tunnel's shadows.

She let her bag fall with a loud thud onto the tracks. She stepped up to the poster, dug her fingers around the edges, and yanked.

A narrow, cobwebbed passage disappeared into blackness. The air inside was stale and damp, and that smell brought the memories surging back. The tunnel had seemed bigger then, when she and Honey had run from the cathedral tombs, eventually landing inside the subway tunnels. It was tall enough for even Ingrid to stand up in, but so skinny that the others had been forced to go sideways through parts of it.

Nova knew that Ingrid had set off a bomb on the other end, right beneath the cathedral's nave, preventing anyone else from finding the tunnel and following them.

This was not an escape.

But . . .

She had taken a single step inside when she heard an unfamiliar yell.

Her pulse skipped.

Nova pulled her foot out and slammed the poster shut, checking that all signs of the tunnel were disguised, before grabbing the bag again and running toward the screams.

She found the others gathered in front of the tiled mural for Blackmire Station, standing on the platform where Winston had set up his circus tents. Honey was giggling madly, her eyes glazed as she bent over the tracks, watching the tunnel. Leroy was crouched a few feet away, fidgeting with what looked like a hand grenade, while Ingrid and Phobia hovered near the staircase that led back toward the surface. It was an exit none of them ever used, given that the entrance at the top had long ago been enclosed with sheets of steel.

"They're here?" she asked.

"Oh yes, they're here," said Honey, tittering. "And they've just learned how very painful a sting from the red-jacketed needle wasp can be." She glanced at Nova, smirking. "Some say it feels like a molten hot knitting needle being plunged into your flesh." She laughed again. "And I just let loose the whole hive." She giddily clapped her hands. "Oh, it feels so good to be doing something, finally. Even if that something *is* running away."

"What's our plan, exactly?" said Nova.

"You and Honey should start heading up to the surface," said Leroy. "Ingrid will bring down this next section of tunnels, then come up and open a path out of Blackmire Station for us to get through. While she's doing that, I will be filling this chamber with a cocktail of poisonous vapors. And . . ." He glanced at Phobia's still, dark cloak. "Phobia will act as our last defense—ready to force back anyone who makes it to the stairs."

"What do you want me to do?"

Leroy glanced at her. "We want you to survive," he said slowly, "so you might someday destroy them."

Ingrid snorted.

Nova looked away.

"Here we go, Nova darling," said Honey, grabbing Nova's arm and dragging her toward the stairs. Though Nova's muscles were still sore from the exertion at the library that day, she was propelled forward with a mix of adrenaline and an instinct for survival, knowing that if the Renegades discovered her, she would see only the inside of a prison cell for the rest of her life.

"What happened to your trunk?" said Nova.

"We'll come back for it later," she said flippantly. "My babies will watch over it for now."

Nova frowned, not sure she wanted to know what that meant.

The stairs grew dark as they ascended away from the platform. Nova took the flashlight from her belt.

Honey grinned at her, seemingly unworried by all that was happening, which struck Nova as uncanny. She—who was always so ready to overdramatize everything.

"Ever so resourceful, you little nightmare," she sang.

Nova ground her teeth, but didn't bother to rebuke the nickname. They never listened to her anyway.

They had just reached the second landing when an explosion shook the dark walls. Honey tripped, grabbing for one of the rails. "Ow!" she yelped, rolling onto her hip to inspect her knee, which Nova could see was scraped and bleeding. Honey whimpered and dabbed at the wound with her fingertips.

Nova grabbed her elbow. "Come on, Queenie. You could have just been stabbed with a burning hot knitting needle, so let's keep things in perspective."

Honey started to glare at her as she got back to her feet, but then she was giggling again. "That was Ingrid, wasn't it? The Renegades are nearly to the platform."

"Which means Leroy is getting ready to set off those poisons, which means we need to get out of here."

Three staircases later, they made it to the top floor, where the thick metal sheeting enclosed the opening. Nova shone the flashlight around the edges, searching for some weakness in the wall.

The beam from her flashlight was joined by the flickers of blue light over the ceiling. Ingrid sprinted up to the landing, eyes flashing as she gripped her blue sphere. "Get back," she snapped, not looking at Nova or Honey as she stepped forward.

Nova darted back down to the next landing and crouched beside the stairs. She heard Leroy panting as he climbed the steps, and could make out the edges of Phobia's wisping cloak swooping behind him.

Far down below, she heard the echoes of distant coughing, choking, hacking. She swallowed and wondered how many Renegades would survive this night.

And how many Anarchists.

Her thoughts had just turned that direction when Ingrid's sphere exploded, thundering through the stairwell.

When the walls had stopped trembling, Nova lifted her head. Ingrid had detonated the bomb against the concrete side wall of the entrance, leaving a hole about three feet in diameter and a lot of broken rubble at her feet. Weak daylight spilled through as dusk crept over the city.

Nova clicked off the flashlight.

Ingrid looked back at the group and raised an eyebrow. "Well?"

Leroy stood first, still gasping from the climb, and went to join Ingrid. Honey dusted off her sequined dress, fluffed her hair, and strode up to the top floor as if she were arriving at a gala.

Footsteps pounded on the staircase, several stories below. Nova glanced back and saw Phobia on the next landing. His edges seemed to bleed into the darkness and it was as though he were expanding. Growing outward in all directions, until he was nothing but a swell of impenetrable blackness. The sound of thudding boots grew louder and Nova dared to peer over the rail. She did not recognize the figure below, but she did recognize the gray uniform.

Suddenly, Phobia disintegrated, his entire body morphing into millions of swarming black widow spiders. They skittered down the stairs, over the walls, dropped down from the ceiling toward their prey.

Nova wasn't sure what made her shudder—the sight of so many

spindly-legged spiders swarming into the shadows, or the blood-curdling shriek that cut through the air.

"Nightmare!" called Leroy.

She turned and ran, diving through the hole Ingrid had created. Leroy's yellow car was waiting for them, miraculously, and Nova wondered how long this escape plan had been put into place. Was it something they had drawn up ages ago—in case of emergency—and never bothered to tell her?

"Do we know where we're going?" said Nova.

"Your place," said Honey, sweeping around the car and dropping gracefully into the passenger seat. Nova stared. It was only a two-seater sports car, but she supposed this was not the time to worry about seat belts or comfort.

"*My* place?"

"Honey, scoot in to the middle," yelled Ingrid. "You can sit on the center console. Nova, get in the trunk."

"One moment, Detonator," said Leroy, putting himself between Ingrid and the car. "I think it will be best if you find other accommodations."

She recoiled. "Excuse me?"

"You acted rashly at the library today, and this is the result. You brought this on us, and the Renegades will focus their efforts now on finding you above all else. I'm afraid I cannot permit you to come with us."

Her nostrils flared and she turned to Nova. "None of this would have happened if *she* hadn't been confused about her loyalties."

"Me?" yelled Nova. "If you'd just warned Cronin like you were supposed to—"

"If you'd just killed those Renegades, like *you* were supposed to!"

"Well maybe," said Nova, her voice rising, "you should have

bothered to tell me your plan, rather than leading me right into your stupid trap!"

"You wouldn't have had the nerve to go through with it! You never follow through. You never pull the trigger when it counts, Nova. You might be Ace's niece, but you are not one of us!"

"Enough," Leroy growled, grabbing Ingrid's arm. She snarled and turned her hate-filled gaze toward him, energy sparking around her fingertips. "You lost us the Librarian. You brought the Renegades to our door. If anyone is no longer an Anarchist, it's you." Without taking his focus from Ingrid, he nodded toward the car. "Nova, get in."

"No."

Leroy turned to her, surprised.

Pacing to the car, Nova tossed the duffel bag into the trunk and slammed it shut. "As far as any of them know, I'm a Renegade. I don't need to run, or hide." She shot one last glare at Ingrid, then nodded at Leroy and Honey. "See you at home."

She walked away. It wasn't long before she heard the squeal of tires. She glanced back in time to see the car turning the corner. Ingrid was not inside, but even as Nova scanned the street, she could find no sign of her.

Dragging in a long breath, Nova made her way back to the café where she'd buried her communication band and strapped it back to her wrist. She did not linger long on the city streets, but headed into a nearby alley and up the rickety fire escape of an apartment building, one she'd climbed hundreds of times. When she reached the top, she crossed the roof to where she could see Renegade Headquarters in the distance, the tower lit up in white and red like a beacon. Enormous spotlights around its spire shone disks of white on the clouds overhead.

Nova swung one leg over the concrete parapet and laid down,

letting her foot dangle. She turned her face up to the sky and let herself breathe deeply for the first time in what seemed like weeks. Her hair and clothes stank of smoke. Her muscles were wound as tight as springs and she found it difficult to relax now that there was no one to fight, nowhere to run.

Dusk was turning fast to night. Though the sky was full of clouds, to the east those clouds were tinted deep purple and heather gray. Somewhere beyond the gloom, the sun was setting.

And she listened.

To a chorus of dogs barking at one another from building to building. To the screams of a couple who were arguing in the apartments below. To the sirens that echoed up from distant streets. Sirens meant Renegades, and she imagined some patrol unit, somewhere, rushing to help whoever needed it. Maybe even rushing to help their comrades trapped down in the subway tunnels.

She knew Adrian, Ruby, and Oscar wouldn't have been down there, otherwise she would have been called to action, too, as part of the team. But how many Renegades had been a part of the raid? How many were hurt? How many had died?

Ingrid had set off another war today, and the Anarchists had just won their first battle. Would they be celebrating tonight, without her? Or would they be mourning the loss of their home, the loss of that little bit of independence their arrangement with the Council had afforded them . . . even, perhaps, the loss of Ingrid?

Nova shut her eyes and thought, if she were a villain worthy of the name, she would be with them now. Celebrating, or mourning.

And if she were a hero, she would be hurrying to help any Renegades who might be trapped and hurt beneath the rubble.

Instead, she listened to the sounds of a city in distress, and did nothing.

CHAPTER TWENTY-NINE

—▪—▪—■—▪—▪—

T HE COUNCIL WILL SEE YOU NOW."

Adrian looked up. Prism stood before them, a woman whose body was made entirely of crystal that reflected a variety of rainbows when she moved. She had been on the administration staff since Adrian was a kid, and he had one fond memory of a potluck at Blacklight's apartment in which Prism had entertained Adrian for hours by making Blacklight's cat chase little dots of colored light around the floor.

Today, though, she was all professionalism as she led Adrian and the others toward the elevator. Once they had piled inside, he looked around at his team. Ruby was biting her lower lip, looking almost fearful. Oscar was leaning against the wall, inspecting his fingernails. And Nova was doing what she always did—observing. Her blue eyes scouring every inch of the elevator, darting from the security camera in the ceiling to the emergency call button on the wall to the series of numbers over the door.

The elevator shot upward so fast Adrian's stomach swooped. The back wall was made of glass and as they cleared the roof of the next building, the skyline presented itself, all the way to the Stockton Bridge. It was a clear day, and with the sun overhead the city looked almost iridescent, with golden light glinting off thousands of windows and wispy amethyst clouds gliding in from the south.

"You've been up here before, haven't you, Adrian?" asked Prism, light and jovial.

"Nope," he said.

"Really?" she said. "Not even just to visit?"

"I try not to bother them if it can be avoided."

"Oh, sweetie, you're never a bother." She grinned. The sunlight off her teeth made the wall glitter with pink and yellow spots.

The doors dinged and Prism exited first, her bare feet clipping on the floor.

Adrian took two steps out of the elevator and his breath hitched.

He had heard that Council Hall was a marvel, and he knew there were people who made up all sorts of petitions just for a chance to come and see it, but he still hadn't been fully prepared. A white-marble walkway stretched out before him, enclosed on either side by a wall of water that spanned from the floor to the high ceiling. The water was not solid like ice, nor was it moving like a waterfall, but rather seemed to just hang there, suspended in space, trembling from the air vibrations as Prism walked past. He wondered what would happen if he touched it. Would it be like bursting a bubble? Would the delicate equilibrium be broken and the wall come crashing down onto the floor? Or would his hand go right through, no different from submerging it in a pool?

He would have to ask one of his dads later.

And then there were the lights—tiny speckles of golden light drifting aimlessly over their heads, reminiscent of winking fireflies.

Though not one was any larger than a speck of dust, together they gave the impression of something serene and alive, like glowing algae drifting on a wave. They filled the space with a warm hue, and the reflection off the water made rhythms of light dance along the walkway. The effect was hypnotic and tranquil and Adrian felt more like he had just entered a supernatural day spa than the hall of their official governing body.

At the end of the walkway stood five chromium thrones. He knew he shouldn't think of them as thrones—the Council got defensive whenever anyone suggested they were trying to become *royalty*—but he didn't know how else one could describe the massive seats that sat in a semicircle around a slender podium.

Blacklight and Tsunami sat in the first two chairs on Adrian's left—no doubt they were responsible for the water and lighting effects in the hall, which only made him more curious. Did the water and floating lights stay when they weren't around, or did they send them away at night, transforming the hall into . . . well, just a hall?

Then there was Captain Chromium in the center seat, followed by the Dread Warden, both wearing their superhero faces—kind but stern.

The fifth and final seat was occupied by Thunderbird, her posture stiff and craned slightly forward to leave space for her wings, which were opened and curling around the back of the seat.

Perhaps the most unnerving part of seeing them there was that his dads, like the others, were wearing their iconic superhero uniforms—not the gray bodysuits the current Renegades wore, but the vigilante costumes they had long ago become famous for. The Dread Warden in his black cape and domino mask. The Captain in muscle-defining Lycra and shoulder armor.

Adrian had known their identities since he could remember, since years before he'd even become an official member of their family. Just like he'd known that his mom was the amazing and ferocious Lady Indomitable. They never tried to keep it a secret. But despite knowing the facts of their alter egos, there had always been a disconnect in his mind. A gap between the superheroes the world idolized and the adoptive dads who wore sweatpants and stained T-shirts and who had a monthly tradition of eating an entire tray of cinnamon rolls for dinner while watching cheesy sci-fi movies.

"Announcing to the Council," said Prism, "Mr. Adrian Everhart. Mr. Oscar Silva. Miss Ruby Tucker. And Miss Nova McLain." She stepped aside, motioning for them to approach the podium.

Adrian stepped in front of the others, though he could feel their presence as they filed in around him.

Kasumi was the first to speak. "Welcome, Renegades," she said—congenial enough, but *so formal*. It felt surreal to be standing there before them, in this magnificent hall. Kasumi, Evander, and Tamaya had all been to their house for a dozen dinner parties. He'd met their spouses at backyard barbecues. He'd babysat Tamaya's kids when he was younger.

But they weren't those same people here. They were Tsunami and Blacklight and Thunderbird. They were the Council. It almost made Adrian laugh, which is how he realized how nervous he really was.

"We are here," said Captain Chromium, "to discuss what happened at the Cloven Cross Library. I have already informed the Council of what you told me, but I think we all want to hear it again, from your perspective. I hope you all can recognize the tricky position you've put us in. On one hand, we are of course grateful that a major supplier of black-market weaponry has been shut down, and that your efforts revealed the active status of the

370

Detonator and the Anarchists."

"On the other hand," said the Dread Warden, "you were expressly ordered *not* to engage with the Librarian, and not to even enter the library without backup. You disobeyed a direct order, and as such, we feel some consequences are in order."

"First things first," said Kasumi. "We want to commend you for following the protocol of prioritizing the safety of civilians. We understand you all acted fast to clear the library of innocent bystanders, and we have heard how Miss McLain went back into the library to rescue a young boy from the fire. We praise you for your bravery and selflessness."

Adrian glanced sideways at Nova, sending her a small smile, but she kept her gaze straight ahead and her expression neutral.

"That said," continued Kasumi, "we cannot overlook the protocols that went ignored, or how the need for rescuing said civilians might have been avoided entirely had you acted more responsibly."

Adrian swallowed.

"It's important that we get all the facts straight," said Tamaya. "You aren't in trouble, necessarily." She paused, and Adrian had the distinct impression that she was glancing over the word *yet*. "But it is of utmost importance that we all abide by our own rules. Otherwise, we'd be no better than the Anarchists."

Beside him, Nova tensed, and he heard her mutter, "Because that would be terrible."

Tamaya's eyebrows lifted. "What was that, Miss McLain?"

"Nothing," said Nova. "Just agreeing with you. Rules, consequences, etcetera. All sounds very authoritarian."

"Mr. Everhart," said Tamaya, and it took Adrian a moment to realize she meant him, not the Captain. "Why don't you start from the beginning?"

Adrian inhaled deeply and told them—starting with their surveillance in the office building that turned up nothing all night. He mentioned the patrons they'd seen enter the library, including a group of children. Then they saw the Detonator.

"Did you recognize her?" interrupted Evander. "Had you ever seen Ingrid Thompson before?"

"Only in pictures," said Adrian, "but I knew it was her. Those armbands, you know."

"So you *suspected* it was the Detonator," clarified Evander.

"No," said Adrian slowly, "it *was* the Detonator."

Evander leaned against the back of his chair, scratching his red beard. Adrian went on, explaining their conversation, as well as he could remember, and their decision to enter the library.

"Why didn't you wait for backup?" said Simon. "That was all we asked of you, Adrian."

Adrian sank inward a bit. The question felt more personal than professional. A father disappointed that his son had broken a promise. And in this case, that broken promise might have gotten him killed.

"We were afraid the lives of those children were in danger," said Ruby. "We didn't know what the Detonator had gone there for. We didn't know if she would do something . . . rash."

"Like blow up the building," added Oscar. "Just as an example."

"We were also concerned that the Detonator would leave before backup arrived," said Adrian. "We didn't know how long she would be at the library and we were worried we would miss our chance to . . . to prove she was there. That she was dealing with the Librarian."

"But you were a *surveillance* team," said Tamaya. "You were intended only to conduct surveillance, not to engage."

"We were a patrol team before that," said Adrian. "And we've been taught that when we see someone conducting illegal or dangerous activity, we stop it."

Tamaya frowned but, after a second, she seemed to give credence to this point. "Go on, then. What happened after you entered the library?"

They told them. About Narcissa and Gene Cronin acting suspicious. About the basement and the room full of weapons and how the Detonator was waiting for them. About the explosions. The battle. Their attempts to clear the library of civilians. The lost child and how Nova and the others had managed to save him, and how Adrian had been trapped inside during the search.

This was, of course, not strictly true, but he stuck firm to his story, while Nova went on to tell them about the showdown between the Detonator and the Sentinel above the theater. Truly, he wasn't sure he ever wanted his dads to realize that he had gone back into the library even after it had collapsed. Even protected by the Sentinel's armor he knew it was a risk, but he also knew it was the only way to convince them he had been inside the library the whole time. He had stayed inside the suit while he drew the igloo, hoping he would be found before the ice melted away, but also knowing that, if worse came to worst, he could always transform back into the Sentinel again.

He hadn't needed to, though. They'd found him.

The Captain had found him, and Adrian still felt guilty for the worry he must have caused them all.

"What else did the Sentinel say?" asked the Dread Warden.

Adrian peered at Nova, watching for some sign of how she felt about his alter ego—beyond the fact that she'd shot him.

Multiple times.

But Nova was unreadable. "He mostly just wanted to know

about Nightmare. Who she is, where he can find her."

"Popular gal," muttered Oscar.

Nova's lips twitched. "He fought her at the parade, didn't he? I think maybe he's embarrassed that she beat him."

"She didn't—" started Adrian.

Nova glanced at him, but he pressed his lips into a firm line.

Clearing his throat, he started again, "I'm sure there's more to it than that."

Nova shrugged. "Either way, he didn't get anything useful out of Cronin. The Detonator shot the Librarian before he could say anything. Then she ran. I shot at her but only managed to get her in the arm, and Ruby and Oscar weren't able to stop her, either. Then Narcissa got away. Then . . ." She scowled. ". . . the Sentinel got away, too."

"And in your opinion," said Tamaya, folding her fingers together, "if you had waited and called for backup as you were intended to, would the Detonator and the Sentinel *and* the Librarian's granddaughter all have slipped through our fingers? Would the library be in ruins, along with what we can assume was volumes of evidence that might have led to the arrests, not only of Gene Cronin, but perhaps countless criminals and villains that have been trading with him all these years? To that effect, do you think Gene Cronin would be dead if you had assistance, or would he currently be in custody, where we could question him for further information?"

Adrian didn't answer. None of them did. He didn't really think they were expected to. His attention slid to his dads. Simon was rubbing his cheek. Hugh was tapping his fingers against the arm of his chair.

Finally, it was Simon who cleared his throat and sat up straighter.

"We will never know what different outcomes might have occurred had you acted differently. We *do* know that, because of you, Gene Cronin and all those weapons will never be a threat to the people of this city again."

Tamaya scoffed. "One positive in an otherwise egregious mess."

"What do you propose, Thunderbird?" said Hugh. "We all agree that they went against our orders and acted irresponsibly. At the same time, Adrian made a strong point—they were trained as a patrol unit first and foremost. They had reason to believe that illegal activity was happening inside that library, and they acted on it. It is difficult to fault that."

"Then perhaps," said Kasumi, "the solution here is not to punish them for their mistakes, but to encourage their strengths by returning them to their regular patrol duties. Perhaps we should not have transferred them to this case in the first place, and our error can be remedied by removing them from it."

"No," said Adrian, his shoulders tensing. "We want to see this through. We want to find Nightmare."

"We know you do," said Simon. "But if you cannot be trusted—"

"We can be trusted. Look, we acted prematurely, we get it. Message received. It won't happen again." He reached for the small podium, gripping its sides. "But I still believe we can find her."

"Adrian," said Hugh, his tone firm. "You were reckless, and I have to assume that is in part because of how . . . personal this assignment is becoming for you. Finding Nightmare is not worth risking your life."

"We'll be more careful next time. I promise."

Hugh frowned and exchanged looks with the others. It was, in the end, Blacklight who suggested three days of probation for the team from street work and patrol duty, though they could continue to use any resources at headquarters to further their investigation as needed. The ruling was agreed upon, and they were dismissed, but Adrian stayed at the podium.

"What about the Anarchists?" he said. "What about the Detonator?"

Hugh sighed. "We attempted to apprehend them last night, but they were expecting us. I'm afraid the Detonator got away, as did the rest. We will be releasing a report to all patrol units this morning, encouraging them to be on full alert so long as these villains are at large." A shadow passed over his face. "Unfortunately, many of our finest Renegades were injured in the altercation. We had become complacent with regards to the Anarchists, believing they could not be a great threat without Ace Anarchy at their helm. It's now clear how wrong we were."

Adrian clenched his fists. "Why weren't we there? We forced the Detonator to reveal herself. We should have had the chance to go after her—all of them."

"Well, thank the powers you weren't," snapped Simon, his eyes blazing with such intensity Adrian drew back a step. "Did you hear what Hugh just said? Renegades were injured last night—a *lot* of Renegades, some of them our best fighters and tacticians. You aren't—" He hesitated, a small grimace creasing the space between his dark brows. He was substantially calmer when he continued, "Each of you has the makings of a great superhero. I, for one, would like to see you survive long enough for that potential to be realized." Then he fixed his gaze on Adrian, fierce with worry. "We need you to be careful."

Adrian swallowed, and for the first time he started to give more consideration to the Detonator's ramblings at the library. She had wanted to hurt *him* more than any of them, knowing how it would hurt his fathers. He'd dismissed the threat outright—she was a villain, she wanted to kill all the Renegades—but now he wondered how much of a liability he posed. If something happened to him, could they go on being the superheroes the city needed?

Of course they would. They would have to.

But the look of horror that crossed, even briefly, over Simon's eyes gave Adrian pause. Before he knew it, all the irritation he'd felt for not having been included in the raid on the Anarchist's tunnels melted away.

"Will you let us know if you find anything about them?"

Simon glanced around at the others, before nodding.

"And . . ." Adrian wiped his palms down his sides. "And did they find anything that might have suggested a connection to Nightmare?"

It seemed, for a moment, that they were all hesitant to answer. Finally, it was Hugh who said, "There was a train car, one that was recently occupied and lived in. We dusted for fingerprints, and some matched the prints that were found on Nightmare's gun. But we did not find her uniform, or as yet, any clue as to where she or the others might have gone."

The knot in Adrian's stomach loosened. It was something. It was a start, and a confirmation.

She *was* an Anarchist.

Licking his lips, he met each of the Council member's eyes in turn. "Might I make one request?"

"A request, Mr. Everhart?" said Tamaya, her expression suggesting that she thought it was the height of insolence for him to be making requests after everything that had happened.

"I would like to question Winston Pratt."

Behind him, Nova inhaled sharply.

"We know now, or have plenty reason to believe, that Nightmare is an Anarchist. We have an Anarchist in custody. I would like to interrogate him myself." He hesitated, before adding, "It will be a good way for us to fill our time during the probation."

"Winston Pratt has already been questioned," said Evander.

"But not since we've had specific evidence connecting him to Nightmare, right?" said Adrian. "Other than her pushing him out of that balloon, at least."

"We'll consider it," said Hugh, and his tone gave nothing away—no promises, no hopes.

"Thank you," said Adrian, inclining his head.

They were dismissed.

Adrian ushered his team back through the hall. Oscar and Ruby both seemed to deflate the moment they stepped away from the podium, as if they'd been holding their breaths the whole time, and it occurred to Adrian that the Council might be really intimidating to them. He supposed *he* was intimidated a bit, too, but he knew it wasn't the same.

"Wait—Miss McLain?" called Kasumi.

Nova froze. Her back straightened like a pin and Adrian caught a flash of nervousness cross her features, before she quickly schooled them into her practiced nonchalance. Still, she couldn't fully hide the gulp as she turned back around.

"Yes?"

"We understand that you have an interest in weaponry," Kasumi said. "It so happens that our armory has become quite overwhelmed as they attempt to catalogue all the equipment that was saved from the fire. We thought you might be able to assist them. It could be a good opportunity for you to learn about some of the other operations we do here."

Frowning, Adrian stepped up beside Nova. "Hold on. Nova has demonstrated that she's more valuable to the Renegades than for basic data entry. Can't you get someone—"

"I'll do it," said Nova. He turned to her and saw that she was smiling, though it was the stretched-thin kind of smile that didn't quite seem to fit her. "I'd be happy to help." She looked at Adrian. "It will keep me busy during our probation. And, besides, I can always work nights."

CHAPTER THIRTY

NOVA FOLLOWED THE OTHERS into the elevator, still edgy over the whole experience before the Council. She was proud of herself for staying so calm during the proceedings, when every time she looked into their faces she thought of little Evie, she heard gunshots, she remembered all over again that these were the people who had promised to protect her family, and had failed.

"Well," Oscar said brightly as the elevator doors shut behind them, "that could have been worse. They say probation—I hear *vacation*."

"No kidding," said Ruby, slumping against the wall. "I was worried they'd take us off street duty forever and force us to do, I don't know, admin tasks or something." She grimaced at Nova. "Sorry about that assignment, by the way. It sounds awful."

Nova shrugged. "Boredom is my ultimate enemy. I like having something to keep busy with."

Truthfully, she couldn't imagine a better assignment. Entry into their arms database and computer systems? Irresistible. Anything that could speed up the process of uncovering new, useful information would be gratefully welcomed at this point.

Anything to get Leroy, Honey, and even on occasion Phobia out of "her" house. It hadn't even been a day yet and already she was rife with anxiety, sure that some Renegade would decide to check up on their new recruit, only to find her home overrun with Anarchists.

Besides, they couldn't avoid the tunnels forever, no matter how much they were enjoying daylight and plant life on their very own patch of land. Even if that patch of land was smaller than a sleeping bag and that plant life was nothing but nettles and dandelions.

Dandelions, she had heard Honey say that morning, were severely underrated.

The elevator plummeted back down to the ground floor and they spilled out into the lobby.

"Lunch, anyone?" said Oscar. "It's taco day in the cafeteria."

"I'm going to visit Max," said Adrian, glancing up toward the sky bridge. "I'm sure he's been watching news stories about the library all night."

Nova's pulse jumped. Though her focus had been caught up in the Sentinel lately, she remained intensely curious about Max. *The Bandit.* She still knew so little about him, his abilities, or why he was stuck in that quarantine. "Can I come too?"

Adrian looked at her, surprised—but, pleasantly, she thought. "Sure, if you want."

When they arrived outside the quarantine, Max was smashing a hammer into the rooftop of the Cloven Cross Library. Pieces of glass were scattering around his knees but if he was worried about cutting himself, it wasn't apparent. He was, at least, wearing protective goggles as he decimated the model.

Adrian knocked at the window.

When Max showed no sign of having heard him, he knocked louder.

Max startled and looked over his shoulder, pushing the goggles up on top of his moppy hair. He grinned, and there was something so bizarre about seeing that bright smile, coupled with the goggles, the hammer, and a demolished library that Nova couldn't keep back a laugh.

"That's looking really good," said Adrian, twirling one finger in the direction of the library. "But more destruction on the east side. That wall is pretty much gone."

"I wasn't done yet," said Max, a bit stubbornly. Standing, he crossed his arms and surveyed the city around him. "I was thinking, now that the Detonator's active again, I'm probably going to be doing a lot of restructuring in the next few weeks."

"Hopefully not," said Adrian, frowning. "We're aiming for less overall destruction, not more."

"Speaking of restructuring," said Nova, walking a few feet along the glass wall to get a better view of the Merchant district, "would you mind if I offered a few suggestions? You seem very concerned about accuracy."

Max straightened, almost giddily. "Yeah, anything."

She pressed her finger against the glass. "See that row of town houses you have on Mission Street? It's actually one block up, on Stockton."

Max stepped over a few blocks and pointed. "These ones?"

"Yep."

Adrian cocked his head. "Are you sure?"

"Positive. I've spent a lot of hours just . . . walking. I know the city pretty well."

"But then what goes on Mission?" asked Max.

"Two-story commercial buildings. There are stores on the ground floor, maybe offices on the second, although I guess some of them could be apartments. There used to be a boarded-up real estate office on the corner, and when I was a kid there was a pharmacy, but I don't know if it's still there."

"Hold on," said Max. "I'm going to get something to write this down."

He disappeared into his back rooms and Nova realized after a moment that Adrian was watching her.

"You used to live around there?" he asked.

"When I was really little. My family had an apartment a few blocks away. Why?"

He looked away, shrugging. "My mom used to patrol that area a lot. It was kind of her . . . route, I guess."

Nova started. "Your mom?"

Adrian gave her a look, at first surprised, then amused. Leaning toward her, he fake-whispered, "I'm not *actually* related to the Captain and the Dread Warden, you know."

She rolled her eyes. "Obviously. I know who Lady—"

"Okay, say that again," said Max, skipping past the marina. "Two-stories, real estate office, pharmacy questionable. Now, is that on this corner?"

Nova shook her jumbled thoughts away. "Um. Yeah. Wait—no, that one, across the street. Yeah, that one. If it's still there."

"Could you find out for me?" Max said.

His gaze was so hopeful that Nova had no choice but to shrug. "Sure?"

"Nova's really busy," Adrian interjected. "She was just given a new assignment from the armory."

Max scowled at him. "Then maybe you can find out. What are

you doing today that's so important?"

Adrian glared back.

"We'll find out," said Nova. "Just give us a few days. Also, our trip to Council Hall this morning gave me an idea." She jutted her chin toward the model of Renegades Headquarters, its surreal tower rising above the rest of the skyline. "How would you like to have functioning elevators on the headquarters tower?"

Max went still. "What do you mean?"

"It's simple. I made one for my dollhouse when I was a kid. I mean, this will require some more materials, but the principle is the same." She ticked off on her fingers. "We'll need some syringes and a long tube, and Adrian will have to redraw the elevators in a way I can connect them to the new hydraulic lift. I'll sketch up a plan to show you what I mean."

Max turned his excited attention toward Adrian. "You'll do it?"

"Sure, of course," said Adrian with a surprised laugh, and the smile he gave Nova—a little intrigued, a little grateful—brought unexpected warmth to her cheeks. "Am I drawing up the syringes and tubing, too, Miss Engineer?"

"Absolutely not," said Nova, feigning disgust. "The whole point of this experiment is to show how normal, everyday objects can, through the power of physics, be turned into something really cool. That point gets missed when you just"—she waved toward Adrian's hands—"*conjure* whatever you need."

He nodded seriously, though his eyes were still shining behind the thick frames of his glasses. "Right. Because I could, in theory, just redraw the elevators to make them functional. You know . . . by magic."

Nova pointed a finger toward his nose. "My science trumps your magic. You'll see."

"I can't wait," said Adrian.

"The technicians have syringes."

She glanced toward Max, who had made his way over so he was standing just on the other side of the glass.

"Lots of them," he added, and Nova couldn't keep her eyes from darting to the bruises on the inside of his arms.

"Right," she said. "That'll work. I bet they have rolls of tubing lying around somewhere too. Maybe Adrian and I can go in and . . . talk to them? See if they'll let us borrow some stuff?" *And look around while we're there . . .*

But Adrian shook his head. "Even I don't have clearance to go inside those labs. But I bet if Max made them a list, they'd bring it to him."

Nova's shoulders sank, but only briefly as she saw another opening. Her brow furrowed as she turned back to Max. "They try really hard to keep you happy in here, don't they?"

Just like that, she saw his enthusiasm deflate, and Nova had the distinct impression that he tried to forget that he was trapped in there as much as possible.

"Sorry," she said. "It's just . . . what are they doing to you? What are all the blood samples for?"

Max looked down at the needle wounds in his arm, stretching the skin to inspect them, as if this was the first time he'd paid them much attention. "Blood samples, tissue samples, bone-marrow samples . . ."

"Exactly," said Nova.

But when Max looked up, it wasn't at her, but at Adrian, his expression slightly pleading. For his part, Adrian's smile had disappeared, overshadowed by a furrowed brow and tight lips.

"Oh, right," said Nova. "I don't have the clearance for that information."

"It's really important, what they're doing," said Max, and Nova wondered if he was trying to convince her, or himself. "They think they're on the verge of a breakthrough, even. It's going to change prodigy relations forever."

"Prodigy relations?"

Max flushed. "That's what they keep saying."

"What does that mean?"

Adrian cleared his throat.

Nova glared at him. "Top secret?"

He opened his palms apologetically. "We don't make the rules."

No, she thought wryly. *Your family does.*

But she tried to smile as if she understood. "Am I allowed to ask where your parents are?"

"They're dead," said Max, without a beat of hesitation or an ounce of sorrow.

"Oh," stammered Nova. "I'm . . . I'm sorry."

"Don't be," said Max. "They threw me off Sentry Bridge when I was two weeks old."

Nova's heart jolted and she stared, speechless, as Max casually stooped and shuffled around a few of the glass boats tied to the docks at his feet.

"They were afraid of prodigies?" she breathed, thinking of what Adrian had said about the prodigy children who were so often abandoned by their superstitious parents.

But Max shook his head. "They *were* prodigies. Villains. Members of the Roaches."

The Roaches. The same gang that had ordered the death of her family.

"But then . . . why?"

Max glanced up at Adrian and again she could see the hesitation as the conversation crept too close to confidential territory. She followed the look and saw that Adrian's shoulders were tense, his jaw clenched, his anger toward two villains who would so heartlessly murder their own child quickly surfacing.

"I was dangerous to them," said Max, speaking slowly. "And the rest of the gang too. They knew they'd be better off without me."

"How did you survive?"

"Captain Chromium and the Dread Warden saw it happen. The Captain dived in and rescued me, while the Dread Warden went after them. They got away, but . . . I figure they probably died in the Battle for Gatlon."

Nova's fists clenched. "They would have been dead before then."

Max looked up, surprised, and she felt Adrian's head swivel toward her, too, and immediately her brain started scouring for truths and lies and she found herself picking through her words as tentatively as Max had been. Perhaps, she thought, it was unfair to begrudge him his secrets when she was constantly tiptoeing around her own.

"All the Roaches were killed a few months before the battle. The whole gang was slaughtered." She glanced at Adrian. "Didn't the Renegades know that?"

He frowned, shaking his head.

"Oh. Well . . . they say Ace . . ." She cleared her throat. "Ace Anarchy himself did it. Supposedly, there was a . . . a dispute of some sort. Between the two gangs."

A dispute. Like the Roaches murdering Ace's brother and his family.

"Huh," said Adrian, scratching behind his ear. "That explains why the Roaches were so quiet those last few months."

Nova glanced from Max to Adrian and back. "So, the Captain rescued you and, what, did they adopt you too? Are you two, like, brothers?"

Adrian's smile started to return, and the sight of it made something unwind in Nova's chest. "Something like that."

"I always had to be kept separate from the others, though," said Max. "Captain Chromium is the only one who's immune to me. When they started construction on headquarters, here, they designed these rooms for me, specifically. They wanted me to feel like I was still a part of the Renegades, still in the middle of everything, even if . . . you know. I'm not really."

"Captain Chromium," Nova mused, trying to keep the scorn from her tone. Always with the invincible Captain. "And the suits they have to wear to get close to you?" she said, nodding toward the chamber outside the quarantine.

"They were decontamination suits," said Adrian, "but they've been retrofitted with chromium in the lining and around the edges. It allows people to get close for a little while, but his power will still affect them eventually."

Nova's lip curled. It seemed that whatever Max could do wasn't fatal, otherwise his parents couldn't have transported him all the way to the bridge. But then, what was everyone so afraid of? "I really wish you could just tell me what it is you do."

"Someday," said Adrian. "It's not personal. Most people here don't know. Not that we don't think we can trust our own Renegades or anything, but the Council is afraid that if too many people knew, it could leak out, and . . . there are a lot of people who would want to kidnap Max."

"Or kill me," Max added, calmly as giving a weather report.

"Okay," said Nova, "I won't pry anymore."

She only sort of meant it. They had given her more information than they probably realized—at least enough to start formulating some theories, and she hoped that once she had access to the

Renegade databases she would be able to learn a lot more. "So now I know what became of *your* parents . . ." She glanced at Adrian. "What about your mom? Did Lady Indomitable die in the battle?"

He shook his head. "Before. They received a tip that one of the villains was planning a retaliation murder, because some guy had been selling out their secrets. Mom volunteered to go stop it. But the next day, she was found in an alley . . ." His jaw twitched. "She'd fallen from the rooftop. Or, maybe she was pushed. The thing is, falling off a building shouldn't have killed her, because . . ."

"She could fly," said Nova, thinking of those photographs she'd seen of the original six. Lady Indomitable had been beautiful and strong, twists of black hair framing her face and that smile like a constant toothpaste advertisement. She and the Dread Warden were the only members of the vigilante group to wear capes, and in every picture of her she seemed to be levitating a few feet off the ground while the golden material flapped behind her.

"No one saw it happen," said Adrian, "and no one knows which villain was responsible for killing her, or how they did it. How they could have disabled her long enough to . . ." He trailed off, and he didn't have to finish.

How does a prodigy who can fly fall off a building?

"What about your dad?" she said. "I mean, your biological dad. Don't tell me he was a superhero too."

He chuckled. "I don't think so. She told me he was some guy she rescued when a shoe factory collapsed. She flew him to safety, they were both pumped up on adrenaline, one thing led to another . . . honestly, at that point I told her to skip to the end of the story, 'cause I was five, and ew." He shuddered and Nova couldn't help but laugh. "Anyway, they tried going on a few dates after that but he couldn't handle the pressure of dating a superhero, so it ended before she even realized she was pregnant."

Nova leaned her shoulder against the glass wall. Inside the quarantine, Max had seemingly grown bored of the conversation and was rearranging the buildings she'd pointed out to him earlier.

"Do you think you'll ever try to find him?"

"Naw. If he couldn't handle a superhero girlfriend, I doubt he could handle a superhero son. Besides, it was big news when my mom had me. I'm sure he would have heard about it, and later when the adoption happened. If he'd had any interest in being a parent, he had plenty of opportunities to introduce himself." He was frowning sardonically as he said it, but the look was short-lived as he turned his attention back to her. "What did your uncle think when you got home last night?"

The hair prickled on the back of her neck.

"My uncle?" she squeaked.

He nodded. "We get a lot of pushback from family members, especially during a recruit's first few weeks in the field, once they start to realize what a dangerous job it is. And yesterday was even more dangerous than usual." He seemed to be looking right into her and Nova felt all her old paranoia rearing back to the surface of her thoughts. "But we have a really great outreach team that's always happy to get involved, if you need their help. Someone could give your uncle a call, or he's welcome to come into headquarters and get a better sense of what we do. Sometimes that goes a long way in helping them feel more secure."

"An outreach team," said Nova. "To talk to my uncle."

"Only if you want them to." That little wrinkle formed over his nose again. "Did he say anything to you? Try to talk you out of coming back? We hear that a lot."

He seemed truly, legitimately concerned, and Nova felt a laugh burble up and catch in her throat. That hysterical, disbelieving guffaw soon turned to actual choking.

Nova turned away, coughing and pressing a hand to her chest, squeezing her eyes shut as they started to water. She felt a hand on her back, placed gently between her shoulder blades, and she shivered so hard at the touch that Adrian pulled his hand away. Even as she cleared her throat and tried to bring her breaths back to normal, she felt the sting of disappointment that the touch, concerned and innocent as it might have been, hadn't lasted just a little bit longer.

Swallowing around her scratchy throat, she looked back at Adrian, still smiling with faint amusement.

"Um, no," she finally said. "My uncle really isn't that worried about me. But again . . ." She gestured vaguely at herself. "I've been training for this my whole life, so I think he knows there's no talking me out of it."

Adrian nodded in understanding. "Well, if he does start to have concerns, just let me know. We don't ever want anyone to feel like they're torn between the Renegades and their family."

Her lips stretched out again, and she knew he must think she was crazy, but she couldn't disguise how hilarious she found this entire conversation. "No," she said. "That would be awful."

"Hey, Sketch."

They turned and the sight of Magpie, the young thief from the parade, was fast to douse Nova's grin. The girl was stomping across the sky bridge, a deep scowl on her face making her look far older than she probably was. Or at least like a kid who wanted people to think she was older, but couldn't quite pull it off.

"Magpie!" said Adrian, and Nova could tell he was intentionally effusing his voice with joy and brightness, perhaps in an effort to balance out the cloud of pessimism that hung over the girl. "Been making good choices lately?"

She ignored the question, coming to a stop a few feet away and holding an official-looking manila folder out to him. "Council's got me on messenger duty this week," she said, sounding like this was an unspeakable punishment.

"Oh, good," said Adrian. "That'll keep you out of trouble for a while." He held up the envelope. "Excellent delivery. I'll be sure to let them know you are surpassing all expectations. Keep up the good work."

She let out a dismayed groan, shot one bitter glance at Nova, then turned and stalked back toward the elevators. Nova couldn't help checking the security of her bracelet as she walked away.

"She'd make a decent villain," she murmured.

"Let's not mention it," said Adrian, ripping into the envelope. "Just in case it hasn't occurred to her yet, I don't want to be the one to put the idea in her head."

Nova watched his hands as he tugged out a single sheet of white paper. At the top was printed a large *R* in red foil. "Does the Council not believe in sending messages through the communicator bands like the normal folk?"

Adrian shook his head, eyes scanning the letter. "Everything that goes over the system is subject to review and inspection. Evidently"—the corner of his mouth lifted as he met her gaze—"they don't want the whole organization to know they've approved our request to talk to the Puppeteer."

CHAPTER THIRTY-ONE

"I DON'T THINK I SHOULD GO," said Nova, trailing behind Adrian as he barreled through the tables in the cafeteria.

"What are you talking about?" he said, without looking back at her. "Of course you should go."

"You don't need me," she insisted. "I don't know anything about interrogating people. And . . . and I could get started on that cataloging job, right? Really, I'll just be in the way."

Adrian stopped and spun toward her. Nova drew up short, shrinking beneath his concerned gaze.

"Are you afraid of the Puppeteer?" he asked, astonished.

Her face scrunched. "*No*," she said, before she realized that saying yes would have gotten her closer to her goal of not being in that room with the one person in headquarters who knew exactly who she was . . . and who had no idea that she was impersonating a Renegade. "I mean, he is totally creepy. And I don't like . . . puppets. Or marionettes. Even sock puppets freaked me out when I was a kid, so I guess, yeah. Yeah, I might be afraid of him after all.

Can I sit this one out?"

Adrian's face took on that calm, understanding look that Nova was developing a love-hate relationship with. "They'll have him restrained. We'll be perfectly safe. Besides, his powers only work on kids."

"I don't want to go. Please."

Adrian blinked and finally, she sensed his resolve crumbling. Hope surged through her veins.

"Nova . . . ," he said finally, gently, "you were the only one on that rooftop with the Detonator and the Librarian. You might have insights into the Anarchists and their connections that would be lost on the rest of us. And let's face it, you're really observant. You might pick up on something that we would miss. So . . . I'm sorry, but I think we need you there." He smiled hesitantly, as if to soften the denial of her request. "I promise, he isn't a danger to us. Nothing is going to happen to you."

She swallowed, wishing she could believe that was true.

He turned away, heading toward Ruby and Oscar, who were seated at a small table near the corner. Ruby's plate was empty but for a few leftover shreds of lettuce, and Oscar was protecting his own plate from her as she attempted to stab one of his black olives with her fork.

"They have an entire bin full of olives!" Oscar shouted. He lifted his plate off the table, holding it as far out of her reach as possible. "Go get your own!"

"You don't even like olives," Ruby shot back, nearly falling into his lap as she leaned across him, fork jabbing at the air. "You only got them to taunt me!"

"Okay, lovebirds," said Adrian, dropping the envelope onto the table.

Ruby immediately fell back into her chair, face reddening,

whereas Oscar grinned, looking supremely pleased with the label.

"Our request has been granted. We have thirty minutes to prepare our questions."

They both stared at him, confused.

"Request for what?" said Oscar, at the same time Ruby asked, "What questions?"

Adrian looked between them and sighed.

———※—※—※———

THIRTY MINUTES LATER, Nova found herself trapped inside a metal room, sandwiched between Ruby and Adrian as they listened to the door locks clunking behind them. A second door stood opposite them—through which they would bring in the prisoner. A single table was bolted to the center of the floor, along with two chairs, one on each side. On the far side of the table were shackles, the thick wrist cuffs attached to metal domes that would fully enclose the hands, crafted especially for prodigies who needed use of their hands and fingers to manifest their abilities.

Had they suspected they would be facing the Detonator when they set up their surveillance on the library, Nova guessed the team would have been outfitted with similar handcuffs too, rather than the standard cuffs they'd been given.

"So . . . ," said Oscar, nodding at the nearest chair, "are you going to take that?"

Adrian shook his head. "Go for it."

"I don't need it," said Oscar, with a casual, one-shouldered shrug. "You're the head honcho here. If you want it—"

"Sit down, Oscar."

Oscar scowled, and Nova could feel him bristling at Adrian's abruptness. It was unlike Adrian, and suggested that he, too, was more nervous than he was trying to let show.

With a sigh, Adrian gestured at the chair. "I need you to play bad cop. The bad cop would take the chair, right?"

Nova smothered a smile. He made it seem so easy, diffusing the tension. Respecting their weaknesses—in this case, they all knew that Oscar's body was still recovering from the exertion of the day before, even if he would never admit to how much he was hurting. But with this simple compromise, Adrian was also valuing the many ways Oscar contributed to the team, even if that contribution was simply Oscar's talent for the dramatic. There had been times when Nova wondered if Adrian became a team leader because of his family name, but she was becoming more and more certain that he'd earned it.

Either way, his suggestion worked. With a proud tilt of his chin, Oscar settled himself into the chair, leaning the cane against the table. He crossed his arms stiffly over his chest. "Oh yeah," he said, with a pleased nod. "Bad cop is ready."

"Which of us is good cop?" said Ruby, glancing at Adrian and Nova in turn.

Nova couldn't answer. Her mouth was so dry she was afraid trying to speak would only lead to the words gumming up on her tongue.

"I'm good cop," said Adrian. He glanced at Nova. "You're the observer. If you have something to say or add, jump in, but otherwise, I want you focused on any signs he might be lying . . . or telling the truth."

"So who am I?" said Ruby.

Adrian grinned. "You're the muscle."

Ruby beamed, hopping excitedly from foot to foot as she loosened the wire on her wrist.

"Hold on," said Oscar, glancing over his shoulder. "Maybe I wanted to be the muscle."

Nova stared at Ruby's bloodstone, glinting in the room's dim lighting. "We're not going to *torture* him, are we?"

They turned to her as one, each of their faces equally appalled.

"Great skies, Nova," said Adrian. "We're the good guys, remember?"

She sank back, not sure if she should be embarrassed by the question or not. It hadn't seemed ridiculous when she'd asked it.

Across the room, they heard the clunking of more locking mechanisms. Nova's body went rigid. She rubbed her damp palms down the sides of her uniform.

The door opened and two guards entered, leading Winston Pratt by his elbows. He was dressed in the black-and-white stripes of a prison jumpsuit. His wrists and ankles were both bound with chains and his usually jaunty step was weighed down, his shoulders tight, his arms squeezed in beside his body as if he were attempting to avoid the guards' grip.

Nova was surprised to see that his makeup remained—or what she had always assumed was makeup, though she'd never seen him without it. The black paint around his eyes, the rosy circles on the apples of his cheeks, and the sharp lines drawn from the corners of his crimson mouth down his jaw, giving the effect of a wooden marionette. The lines were not even smudged.

For the first time, in all the years she'd known him, she wondered whether it was makeup at all or if his power really had transformed his face into that of a puppet.

Or a puppet master.

His eyes darted around the room, skipping from the chairs to the walls, the lightbulb in the ceiling, to the shackles on the table, to Oscar, to Adrian, to Nova, to Ruby.

Back to Nova.

He blinked furiously, as if trying to clear away a pestering eyelash. His brow squeezed tight.

Pressing her lips, Nova did her best to convey secrecy to him, subtly shaking her head and hoping that he caught the desperate intensity of her gaze.

But Winston Pratt had never been adept at the art of subtlety.

He continued to stare, his lips parted, his head cocking curiously to one side as he was pressed down into the chair. He put up no resistance as his chained hands were settled into the shackles and the domes clamped securely around them.

"You have fifteen minutes," one of the guards said to Adrian. "This interrogation is being recorded"—he gestured toward a small camera on the ceiling—"for future review at the Council's discretion. If you want to end your session early, just knock on the door and we'll be back."

They left.

Winston was still gaping dumbly at Nova, and the others were starting to notice. Adrian and Ruby each glanced at her, to which she attempted an uncomfortable, confused shrug.

"Okay, Mr. Pratt," said Oscar, leaning forward and folding his hands on top of the table, "or should I call you . . . the *Puppeteer*?"

This, at least, managed to pull Winston's gaze away from Nova.

"We're going to ask you a few questions," said Oscar, "and I strongly suggest you answer them." He popped his knuckles, then leaned back again and curled a finger over his shoulder. "Go ahead, Sketch. He's all yours."

Eyebrows rising in what might have been amusement, or embarrassment, Adrian moved forward to stand beside Oscar. "I understand you've already been questioned a number of times," said Adrian, "but we have one specific topic we want to discuss with you."

Though Winston was looking at Adrian now, his jaw was still slack with befuddlement, and Nova felt like her insides were being wrung through a washing machine. She found herself imagining a situation in which her identity would be revealed—here, now—and wondering if she had any hope of getting out of there with two locked doors and three Renegades that she knew would turn on her the second they realized who she was.

"First," continued Adrian, "you should know that the Detonator attacked a library yesterday. She set off multiple bombs in public spaces. As a result, the Renegades went to the subway tunnels where you and your companions have been living in an attempt to arrest her. However, those Renegades were attacked and the Anarchists have since disappeared, abandoning the subway tunnels."

Winston's brow drew together. He started to shake his head, dazed. "They wouldn't leave . . ." He looked again at Nova.

She tried to remain expressionless, while also maintaining the mantra in her head—*silence, secrecy*—as if she might suddenly develop telepathy.

"One thing they found in the tunnels, of particular interest," said Adrian, "was a recently inhabited train car. We have reason to believe this car belonged to the villain who calls herself Nightmare. We now know that Nightmare is an Anarchist."

Lips parted. Jaw slack. Winston shifted his confused eyes back to Adrian.

"That's who we want to talk about today." Adrian set one hand on the table, leaning forward, and Nova might have thought his attempts at being intimidating were borderline adorable if she hadn't been trembling with dread.

Her memory was replaying those moments in Winston's hot-air balloon as they drifted over the remains of the parade. Realizing they wouldn't clear the top of the next building. Choosing to sacrifice Winston to their enemies.

He had every reason to despise her now. He had every reason to betray her.

She swallowed.

"I'm sorry," Winston squeaked, gaping at Adrian. "But . . . come again?"

"Nightmare," said Adrian. "I'll begin with something simple. What is her real name?"

A deep crease seemed permanently etched between Winston's brows, and the way his mouth refused to close made it seem as though the mechanism attaching his marionette jaw to his marionette skull had broken. "Nightmare?" he croaked.

"Nightmare," Adrian confirmed. "You might remember her as the one that pushed you out of your own hot-air balloon. I want to know what her real name is."

Nova bit the inside of her cheek.

"No . . . ?" Winston started, but hesitated, letting the word drift off until his lips were puckered around that long, uncertain *o*. Nova's lungs squeezed, expelling any useful air.

"Excuse me?" said Adrian.

"No . . . no. Uh . . ." Winston glanced once, briefly, at Nova, then back at Adrian. "No . . . reen." He coughed. "Her name is Noreen."

Nova inhaled, long and deep. Everyone else, though, became motionless.

She knew that no one was fooled. But she didn't care. Winston had been given a choice to betray her, and he hadn't. A slim spark of hope flickered in her thoughts.

"Noreen," said Adrian, his voice thick with skepticism.

"Noreen," said Winston, with a determined, proud nod.

"Noreen what?"

"Hm?"

"Does she have a last name?"

"Oh, uh . . ." Winston glanced around, as if searching for inspiration, but then shrugged. "Nope. No last name. Just Noreen."

Adrian and Oscar exchanged a look, before Adrian cleared his throat. "We know that Nightmare obtained at least one of her weapons from the black-market dealer known as the Librarian. But we've witnessed her using a number of weapons and tools that don't resemble other things in the marketplace. Where does she get her supplies?"

Winston held his gaze. Blinked. Licked his lips. Opened his mouth. Hesitated. Swallowed. Coughed. Finally responded, "The hardware store?"

"The hardware store?"

"Yes." Winston's head bobbed. "That's where she gets her stuff."

"Is that code for something?"

"No? Just the hardware store."

Nova cringed inwardly, even though it was mostly true. She did get a lot of the items she used for her inventions from a local hardware store.

"Any specific hardware store?" asked Adrian.

"Hmmm." Winston seemed to consider this. Then, "Nope. She likes them all."

"Maybe," said Oscar, leaning forward on his elbow, "you could mention just *one* by name. Just to get us started."

Winston's lips stretched thin and he shrugged. "I don't know. Ask her."

Thankfully, his eyes did not shift back to Nova when he said this, though she could only imagine the restraint he was using to stay focused on his inquisitors.

"How about the names of any connections she might have had in the city," said Adrian. "Can you think of anyone she might have made contact with once the Anarchists abandoned the subway tunnels? Anywhere she might have gone?"

Winston looked down at the table, and he seemed to be giving actual consideration to this question. Finally, truthfully, he started to shake his head. "I don't know where they would have gone."

Adrian massaged his temple. "What about any other locations Nightmare likes to frequent? Any favorite . . . restaurants? Stores?"

Winston could not prevent his eyes from darting to Nova this time, though he quickly shifted them over to Ruby, then back to Adrian, as if to make up for the slip. "Rooftops?" he suggested.

Adrian's shoulders sagged. "Any particular rooftops?"

"I . . . I don't know. Honestly, I don't." Winston leaned forward, and his baffled face took on an edge of desperation. "I don't know where she is. Truthfully. I have no idea."

Adrian briefly closed his eyes. "It's all right, Winston. We're just trying—"

"No, it's *not* all right," said Oscar, slamming his fist on the table. "It's obvious you know something, and we're not leaving this room until you tell us what it is!"

Winston frowned. "They said we only had fifteen minutes."

"*That*—" started Oscar, holding up a finger. Then he deflated, clearing his throat. "—was actually true. But still, you can tell us what you know now, or we can come back and do this again tomorrow. And the next day. And the next! We're not giving up until you tell us what we need to know, so start talking, Mr. Pratt, or else . . . or else I will make sure that you don't get any tacos! Or, um, whatever it is they serve prisoners around here."

Adrian dragged his hand down the side of his face. "Okay," he said, "listen. She betrayed you. She literally threw you out of your own hot-air balloon and left you to be captured by your enemies. Right? You have no reason to protect her. Whereas, if you help us . . ." He hesitated, and Nova could see him struggling to find something he could offer to Winston, something that wouldn't break any of the Renegade codes. "I'll see about . . . I'll see if we can get you some books or something."

Nova pursed her lips, knowing that this bribe wouldn't get him far, and Winston's expression looked more confused by the offer than anything else. "Books?"

"Or . . . I don't know. Magazines? A deck of cards? Something to keep you entertained. It's got to be boring in that cell, right?"

Winston's eyes seemed to brighten. "Can you bring me a painting set? And a new marionette doll?"

Nova's shoulders tightened. No. *No.* He couldn't be swayed by them *now.*

"Uh . . . I'll have to get that approved by my supervisors," said Adrian. "But . . . I could ask?"

The hunger in Winston's eyes was inescapable, and for the first time Nova felt bad for how she had given so little thought to Winston since his arrest. He must not only have been bored, but lonely. Not that she could have done anything to help him, but . . . she could at least have spared him a thought.

"What was the question again?" said Winston.

"We want to know if there are any places Nightmare frequents," said Adrian. "Anywhere she might have gone."

Winston looked away, his thoughts warring across his face. The temptation Adrian had offered him fighting against whatever loyalty he still had for Nightmare and the Anarchists.

"She, um . . . she likes to go to . . . the . . . park?"

Disappointment fell across Adrian's face. "The park," he repeated dryly.

In contrast, Winston was all joviality for what he must have thought was a quick-witted, completely believable lie. "Yes. She really loves going to the park."

"City Park?"

"Oh no, no," said Winston enthusiastically, "*Cosmopolis* Park."

Nova coughed, covering her mouth to try to hide her amusement.

Adrian glanced back.

"Sorry," said Nova.

He sighed, returning his focus to Winston. "You're telling us that Nightmare likes to spend time at an amusement park."

"Oh yes. She goes there all the time. Particularly enjoys the, uh, the fun house." He giggled madly and shrugged, as if to suggest, *Those crazy kids, who knows what they'll be into next!*

"Can I ask a question?" said Ruby.

"Please do," said Adrian, stepping back from the table and gesturing for her to proceed. It was clear from the frustration in his eyes that this interrogation was not going how he'd hoped.

Ruby took a step forward, idly swinging her bloodstone back and forth like a pendulum. Winston followed it with his eyes, leaning slightly back as if afraid she was about to stab him with the thing. And quite possibly she was. "The Anarchists have been, let's say, *fairly* inactive for nine years, right? But Nightmare appears to be pretty young. Definitely younger than the rest of your gang. So what I want to know is how she came to join you all in the first place. Are you recruiting new members?"

"Oh," said Winston, apparently gleeful to be able to answer this question without having to strain himself too much to come up with a sensible lie. "Nope, no recruitment. Actually, Ace brought her."

"Ace?" said Oscar, with a disbelieving laugh. "Ace Anarchy?"

"Please," said Adrian, "she would have been a kid back then."

"Yes!" Winston said, his head bobbing in agreement. "She *was* just a kid."

They stared, speechless, for a long time. Finally, Adrian said simply, "Explain."

But by this time Winston seemed to have withdrawn back into his thoughts and was doubting his eager explanation. He looked again at Nova, and she shrugged at him, not really knowing how much trouble the truth would cause her at this point.

Winston, though, opted not to tell the truth, and again his face took on that fearful, uncertain look. "Ace found her . . . ," he started. After a long inhale, he continued, "At Cosmopolis Park!"

"Of course he did," said Oscar. "Where else?"

"No, no, it's the truth," Winston insisted. "I used to do business there, you know, before your Council made it so"—he grimaced—"*wholesome*. And one day, there was this kid. This girl. Wandering around after dark. The park had been closed for hours and, well, Ace found her and came to understand that her parents had left her there. Just . . . abandoned her. So he gave her some cotton candy, and . . . well, that was it. We had ourselves a little Nightmare." He started to smile—a real smile that stretched the dark lines on his chin. "She and I used to play together. When she was scared at night sometimes, I would entertain her with puppet shows. She especially liked shadow puppets, which are something of a specialty of mine. Remember that, N—" He hiccupped. Coughed. "Uh, I remember that Nightmare well. Little Nightmare. We were buds . . ." His brow creased, a sadness overshadowing the sudden burst of joy. "Back then, at least."

Nova felt like her heart was being torn apart. For the past number of years she'd thought of Winston as little more than a nuisance, but he was right. They had been friends when she was young. How had they lost that? How had she become such a . . . such an Anarchist?

She kept her eyes on him, wishing he would look up at her, wishing she could convey that she was sorry, and that she *did* remember those times, all those sleepless nights when he had made her laugh, and how much that had meant to her.

But this time, Winston kept his head down.

Behind him, the door clunked, and the guards returned.

The interrogation was over.

Walking back into the hallway outside the interrogation room, Nova felt as though a hundred Gargoyles were perched on her shoulders. She would have thought that to be leaving that room with her secret still intact would have left her buoyant and overjoyed, but she felt only guilt.

Not just guilt over Winston, but guilt over them all. The Anarchists were counting on her, and so far, what had she accomplished? Since she'd come here, they had been forced out of their home. Ingrid was exiled. The Librarian was dead. They were certainly no closer to destroying the Renegades.

"So," Ruby drawled, twirling her bloodstone like a pinwheel around her finger. "Do we think a single word out of his mouth was true?"

"I don't know," said Adrian. "Not most of it, that's for sure."

Oscar nodded. "I agree, but I think he was drawing on truth sometimes, do you know what I mean? Like . . . there might have been kernels of truth in it."

"Yeah, but which parts?" said Ruby.

Adrian paused and leaned against the wall, crossing his arms. "He mentioned Cosmopolis Park a few times, and we do know that he used to deal drugs there during the Age of Anarchy, right? Maybe there's something there."

"Wait," said Ruby, with a mild laugh. "Just think about that for a second. Can you really picture *Ace Anarchy* finding some lost kid at a theme park, feeding her cotton candy, and deciding to bring her home and . . . *raise* her? Come on."

Nova bristled, glowering at her, but then Adrian started to laugh too. "I know," he said, massaging his brow. "You're right. It's just . . . what else do we have to go on? Anything?"

"Nova," said Oscar, glancing at her, "you used to work at Cosmopolis Park."

It sounded like such an accusation that Nova stood straighter, ready to defend herself. "So?"

"If there is a connection between Nightmare and the park . . . I don't know. Did you ever see anything suspicious?"

Immediately her defensiveness started to retract. She exhaled. "You mean, did I ever see some girl walking around in a metal face mask? Um, no, can't say that I did."

"Not surprising," said Adrian. "If she does frequent the theme park, which I'm still really doubtful of, but if she did, she wouldn't be going there in full disguise, would she?"

"Still," said Ruby, "maybe Nova can talk to her old boss or something? Encourage people to be on the lookout?"

Nova forced a smile, trying to remember the name of her so-called boss and hoping no one bothered to ask. "Yeah. Sure. That wouldn't be a problem at all."

"Okay," said Adrian, scratching his jaw. "I'll get a transcript of the interrogation sent to each of you this afternoon. Let's all take the night to think on it, and discuss more tomorrow." He sighed. "He was obviously hiding something, but . . . I don't know. Something tells me he gave up more than we realize."

CHAPTER THIRTY-TWO

NONE OF THEM had come up with anything new or concrete the next day, or the next.

By the third night after the Puppeteer interrogation, Nova was beginning to relax. This might largely have been because she felt like she was making progress, learning things that might actually hold value, thanks to the cataloging job.

She found that she liked headquarters best at night. It was so quiet, after most everyone had gone home. Not entirely empty—there was always security staff monitoring the building, and late-night patrol units coming and going in between jobs, but the difference when compared with daytime was striking. The tranquillity was refreshing.

Nova had long had mixed emotions when it came to those most still hours of the night. The suspension of time in which all the world became lonely and shadowed. There had been periods in her childhood when she would frequent twenty-four-hour diners for no other purpose than to feel a sense of connection to whatever other sad souls were sleepless that night, where she would eat her stacks of blueberry pancakes and concoct life stories for the delivery man slurping black coffee at the bar, or the waitress who made up for her tired eyes with effusive perkiness. Eventually, though, someone always asked where Nova's parents were, and once their gazes turned to pitiful assumptions, she would have to leave.

There were other nights, though, when she craved that solitude. Nights when she would spend hours staring at the moon and imagining she was the last person alive on this planet. Imagining there was no one left to cause war or strife. No one struggling to claim power. No one left to fear or hate prodigies. No prodigies left to hate.

Being inside headquarters at three o'clock in the morning felt like a wholesome mix of both. The tranquillity that came with being alone, but also the knowledge that she wasn't, not really. Even if she was surrounded by her enemies, there was a strange sort of comfort in that thought.

She had been set up with her own little cubicle on the third floor, with a window that looked down onto the vast open lobby and a desk that she was told she could decorate with personal items, but so far all she'd thought to bring was a poster of the constellations that she picked up at a cheap print shop a few miles away, and then only because she worried they would think it was weird if she didn't bring in anything at all.

The assignment she'd been given wasn't exactly thrilling. She had spent three straight nights reviewing photographs that their forensics department had taken of all the destroyed artillery in the library, cataloging model numbers when they were available or otherwise scanning for identifying characteristics and comparing them with known weaponry in a global database. It wasn't exciting work, but it did give her an excellent opportunity to alter the metadata when she came across scans of a series of gas bombs that she recognized from Cyanide's laboratory, but which would now forever live in the Renegades' files as amateur-crafted explosives from an unknown source.

The assignment also gave her ample opportunity to delve further into the Renegades' system. Over the past nights, she had mapped out the locations of all security cameras and alarms within the headquarters building. Downloaded a full list of the weaponry and prodigy artifacts kept in their storerooms. Discovered the complete directory of current Renegades, with aliases, abilities, and even home addresses (including her own). And she had even, to her delight, found a folder titled "Concerns—For Future Consideration," which turned out to be full of public complaints lodged at the Council's ongoing failures and disappointments.

Nova finished entering the data on a box of ammunition—one of the few that hadn't exploded when exposed to the heat from the fire—and took a moment to stretch out her spine. A flicker caught her eye and she glanced out the window to see that the lights inside Max's quarantine were on, lighting up his glass city in a pale shade of yellow. She was sure it had been dark in there before. Was he having trouble sleeping?

She scooted closer to the window but could see no sign of the boy beyond the walls of his enclosure. Her eyes scanned the rest of the lobby. She could see one security guard pacing in front of the main entryway, but otherwise the place seemed as abandoned as it always did this time of night.

With a curious grunt, she leaned back in the sleek office chair, pulling her legs up until she was seated cross-legged. Checking the data list that had been provided for her, she decided to enter just three more items, and if Max's light was still on when she was done, she would go check on him.

Nova rolled her shoulders and pulled up the next batch of photos, showing a simple handgun taken from multiple angles. She discovered the serial number near the base of the barrel and punched it in to the database.

A window popped into view——ONE MATCH FOUND.

She clicked on it, pulling up the profile of the weapon, its manufacturer, and the year it had been produced, and at the bottom, a list of known criminals and gangs this or similar guns had been connected with over the years. Often this list was blank or contained only vague notes from the field when there was a match between a gun's serial number and a bullet casing found at a crime scene.

There was only one connection listed—not of this exact gun, but to another handgun of the same model. Reading the words felt like a kick to Nova's gut.

IN CONNECTION WITH MULTI-VICTIM MURDER——KINGSBOROUGH APARTMENTS. SEE SUMMARIZED REPORT.

Kingsborough Apartments.

She had lived in the Kingsborough Apartments.

Her hands were shaking as she opened the report.

It brought up a summary drafted by Hugh Everhart—Captain Chromium himself—dated the night of her family's murders. *The night of.* Mere hours after it happened.

Nova's heart thundered.

He had been there. He had been there that night.

But he had been too late.

> Four people found dead. David Artino: age
> 31. Tala Artino: age 30. Evie Artino: age

11 months. One unnamed man: age unknown. Suspected Anarchist or Roach affiliation.

Forensics confirm all deaths were a result of direct trauma from bullet wounds, without prodigy interference. Prints found on the gun matched both those of the unnamed man and also those of Alec Artino (alias: Ace Anarchy).

There is reason to suspect the deaths of the three family members were done as a killing for hire. The motive for the homicides remains under investigation. See the full report as filed by Hugh Everhart (Captain Chromium) <u>here</u>.

Additional notes: The eldest child, a six-year-old girl, was not found at the scene. Neighbors have reported no knowledge of her whereabouts. A report has been made to the Renegades missing persons unit.

An icon at the bottom of the report indicated a folder of pictures taken from the crime scene. Nova shuddered. She had been saved from seeing the bodies of her family all those years ago, and she would not look at them now. But to know they were out there . . . that such photos existed, mere clicks away, made her sick to her stomach.

With her heart feeling as though it were being squeezed in a clamp, Nova forced herself to click on the link to open the full report.

A small window popped into the center of the screen.

RESTRICTED ACCESS. ENTER PASSCODE: _ _ _ _ _ _

Nova stared at those words for a long time, in turns furious that something so personal to her could be kept confidential, but also in part relieved.

She knew what had happened to her family. She knew that the cowards in the Roaches had hired a hitman to kill them because her dad had refused to keep making weapons for them. She knew the Renegades hadn't been there to stop it, even after they'd promised to protect David's family, and neither had they been the ones to track down the gang and ensure justice was served. No—it was Ace who had destroyed them all in retaliation.

She stared at those words—RESTRICTED ACCESS—and felt new resentment smoldering inside her. The Renegades knew her family was being threatened. Captain Chromium *knew* they might be targeted, and yet he had failed to save them. He was too late. Could it be that the full report was confidential because he recognized his own ineptness? Was he so embarrassed to have failed to save this family that he would hide it from the world?

It was easy to believe. He hadn't protected them. He hadn't saved them. He'd only recorded their deaths, entering the information like notes on a ledger.

But people believed he was the world's greatest superhero. A hit like that to his reputation would be inconceivable to all the fools who idolized him.

With a shudder, Nova closed the summary report. She squeezed her eyes shut, pushing her chair back from the desk.

It was good she had found this, she told herself. It was a reminder of how the Council had betrayed her family's trust. How they had not been there when they were needed most.

They were not superheroes. They were frauds, and this whole system that was meant to protect and serve was nothing more than a failed social experiment. She could see now that many Renegades had good intentions—Adrian was proof enough—but it didn't change the fact that their society was not being run by strong, competent leaders, but by dictators who had put themselves in this position of power without cause, and now had no idea what to do with it.

The people would be better off on their own.

The world would be better off without them.

Nova waited for the tight knot in her gut to start to unravel, and peeled open her eyes. She was facing the window again, and her gaze immediately shifted toward Max's quarantine.

Her brow furrowed.

She rose from her chair and stepped closer to the window, trying to make sense of what she was seeing. A light was still on, but not the full overhead lights that had been on before. It was dimmer now, pale gold shimmering off the glass facades of his tiny skyscrapers.

And they were . . . floating.

Nova rubbed her eyes and looked again.

The same image greeted her. Not *every* building of the model city, but perhaps a few dozen of them, their glass spires hovering above the ground, bobbing like buoys on a calm lake. As she watched, larger bits of the city began to rise up too. Like a hundred shimmering missiles launching slowly into the air.

At their center sat Max, cross-legged and levitating.

Levitating.

"He's telekinetic," she whispered, but saying the words aloud did not make them any less surprising. Because . . . he *shouldn't* be telekinetic. She had seen his profile, when she found the directory. She struggled to recall what it had said—something that had been made intentionally vague, she recalled, because she'd been annoyed at the time that she didn't know what it meant.

Stooping over her desk, she minimized the weapons database

and tracked down the Renegade directory again. After a quick search, she found him.

Max Everhart. Alias: The Bandit. Ability: Absorption.

Absorption. That's right, she remembered it now, and how very frustrating it was that it meant nothing at all. Absorption of what? It offered no explanation for the quarantine or why people seemed to think he was dangerous.

But this . . .

She looked again. More of the buildings had risen up now, along with every miniature tree from City Park and the entire Sentry Bridge.

This, people might think was dangerous. Not because telekinesis was terribly rare, but because most telekinetics could only manage to move one or two objects at a time. Not *dozens* and certainly not while keeping themselves aloft as well. That sort of focus and mental aptitude had only been recorded in a handful of prodigies, so far as Nova knew.

And one of those prodigies was Ace Anarchy.

She returned to the window.

She even had a faint memory of seeing Ace in the cathedral, levitating just like Max was now—cross-legged and five feet in the air, one of the few times she'd seen him relaxed enough to go without his helmet. He had surrounded himself with candles in red glass votives, hundreds of them drifting around him, casting swirls of flickering light around the altar.

Seeing Max was so painfully familiar that she half doubted she wasn't hallucinating.

Down below, Max opened his eyes. For a moment he stared at nothing. Not his floating glass city. Not the lobby below. His expression was serene and still.

Nova pressed her palm against the window of her cubicle.

That small movement must have caught Max's eye, because he suddenly spotted her.

His concentration broke.

Nova saw it the moment it happened. His eyes widened, his lips parted, and his body dropped back to the ground, while all those sleek glass buildings crashed down around him.

Nova grimaced, embarrassed on his behalf.

But then she saw pain shooting through Max's expression. Not the sort of pain that accompanied a hard fall, but the sort of pain that was excruciating. She pressed her nose into the glass, her own breath misting against it, and tried to make out what had happened.

As soon as she saw the blood, she turned away from the window and started to run. Down the corridor, past the elevator bank, into the stairwell. She launched herself over the steps to the next landing, then down the next, her feet barely touching the ground. She burst out of the doorway and raced across the sky bridge. She could see Max through the quarantine walls. He was on his knees, bent forward, cradling his hand. His right arm was soaked in blood.

Nova rounded the side of the quarantine and yanked open the door to the tertiary chamber. She charged for the next door, pulled down the lever to release the air lock, and pried it open.

An atmosphere-controlled chamber waited for her. Screaming in frustration at all these barriers, she bolted forward and yanked open the second door.

Her breath hitched.

She was inside the quarantine.

Max hadn't moved. His back was to her, but he'd fallen onto

his hip. He looked back when he heard Nova enter. Pain was still drawn into his features, but his eyes widened in fear when he saw her. Fear and panic and desperation. Nova looked at his hand, which was covered in blood. Beside him, she saw the bloodied spire of the Woodrow Hotel.

"Sweet rot," she breathed, and already her mind was creating a checklist. Clean the wound. Bandage it up. Get him to the medical wing, or if no healers were available, get him to the hospital.

Nova started making her way through the glass city, kicking aside the fallen buildings in her path.

"No—" Max gasped.

"It's okay," said Nova. "You're fine. You might be in shock, but you're fine."

"No, Insomnia, stop!" he yelled. He started to back away from her until he collided with the wall of the arena. "Stay there!"

"You need medical attention," she said, halfway down Drury Avenue. "Just some basic first aid and then I'll get you to the heal . . . healers . . ."

Her body began to slow.

Her lungs contracted, expelling her last breath.

She stumbled, grabbing the model of Merchant Tower for support.

She blinked at Max, but her vision had blurred.

Terror crossing his features, Max stood and tried to step over the arena, but his ankle caught and he stumbled, knocking over one of the great standing floodlights. "Go back!" he screamed. "Get out!"

But Nova couldn't move. Her breaths wheezed as she slumped forward. Her eyelids were so heavy. Her brain was clouding over with . . . with *exhaustion*.

She felt like her limbs were full of sand. Like her skull was thick with fog.

She fell onto her side. Her shoulder smashed into the model of Gatlon City Hospital. Its north tower tipped over and shattered on the street, which was the last sound she heard before darkness engulfed her.

CHAPTER THIRTY-THREE

THERE WERE TWO all-night eateries within a one-mile radius of Renegade Headquarters, and Adrian and the team were frequent patrons at both. Sometimes they just seemed like a better option than coming back to HQ and getting something out of the vending machines or snacking off the cold salad bar in the cafeteria, which stopped serving hot food after nine. Fighting crime burned a lot of calories and sometimes a superhero needed a gooey grilled cheese sandwich or a giant chocolate chip waffle smothered in whipped cream.

He didn't know if cataloging data or whatever it was Nova was doing for the arms department burned a lot of calories, but Adrian did know that everyone needed to nosh when they were awake in the wee hours of the morning, and he doubted that an inability to sleep changed that.

As it was, he needed a distraction, anyway. Since the team was still technically on the Nightmare investigation case, which was fast becoming the Anarchist investigation case, they'd spent the last few days following every lead they could to try to find Ingrid Thompson, the Detonator. Frequenting any business she'd ever been known to visit. Calling on any citizen that might have had a connection to her, no matter how tenuous—a classmate from high school, a long-ago neighbor. So far, everything had led to dead ends, and Adrian couldn't help but feel like they were wasting their time. They needed something recent and concrete. Video footage or an eyewitness spotting or . . . he didn't know. Maybe a stash of glowing blue explosives discovered in an abandoned warehouse. Something *tangible*.

In lieu of something that would further the case, though, Adrian had three nights of restless sleep and, now, a bag full of sandwiches from Mama Stacey's Greasy Spoon. Since he didn't yet know Nova well enough to be able to guess her preferred sandwich order, he'd brought an assortment—a grilled cheese, a turkey club, a roast beef, and a southwest chicken wrap. He felt like he had the major bases covered, sandwich speaking, and Stacey had thrown in six bags of potato chips because, quote, "Gotta keep our heroes fed." Wink.

He still wasn't sure what the wink meant.

Anyway, he hoped Nova would think the gesture was thoughtful. He hoped she wouldn't be annoyed that he was interrupting her work. He hoped maybe they'd be able to sit and talk, because he kept thinking about the night spent in the office building across from the library and how it had been really nice to talk to her. To get to know her, at least a little.

The more he thought about it, the more he wanted to know her even better. Questions kept popping into his head when he wasn't around her, but then vanishing the moment they were together, and all the conversations turned toward the investigation again. Questions like, where did she get her ideas for her inventions?

And, what was the most bizarre thing she'd ever done to keep from being bored at three o'clock in the morning? And, did she have a boyfriend?

He was pretty sure he knew the answer to that last one. She'd never talked about a boyfriend. But then . . . she hadn't talked much about her personal life at all, so he couldn't be sure.

He'd even had this outrageous idea as he was leaving Mama Stacey's. This fantasy of sneaking into Nova's cubicle while she was gone and laying out the spread of sandwiches and napkins like a picnic. He could even draw some candles, except that would probably be too much, and he didn't want her to think this was, like, a *romantic* thing.

Except a part of him sort of did.

His palms were damp by the time he got to headquarters and he kept having to switch the paper to-go bag from hand to hand so he could rub them dry on his pants. The scanner near the door recognized the signal from his communicator band and unlocked with a clunk. He pushed through the revolving door and immediately heard someone yelling.

Adrian glanced at the security booth, where the guard on duty was screaming into his communicator. "—only two healers on night duty, and they're both on their way. But what was she thinking, going in there in the first place?"

Frowning, and wondering if something had happened to one of the patrol units, Adrian jogged down the steps into the lobby. His gaze shot up to the bay of windows where Nova had been working lately. He could see the light on in her cubicle, but her desk appeared to be empty.

His hair stood up on the back of his neck as he crossed the inlaid *R* in the tiled floor.

An erratic pounding made Adrian draw up short. He turned his gaze toward Max's quarantine, where a faint light was casting a glow across the lobby.

Max was standing at the quarantine wall. He was wearing plaid pajama pants but no shirt. One hand was wrapped up in cloth—perhaps the missing shirt—while he pounded the other fist against the glass. He was yelling, his face wild with panic, and it took Adrian a moment to understand him.

Adrian! Hurry!

The bag of sandwiches fell from his hand, hitting the floor with a crackle and thud, and then Adrian was sprinting up the stairs to the quarantine. As soon as he reached the sky bridge he saw a body lying inside the quarantine.

His heart jolted.

It was Nova.

She was unconscious.

She was *inside the quarantine.*

He slowed for only a second, but still—he did slow, and he knew it, and he would later feel like the biggest coward for that moment of hesitation. But then he was running again, as fast as he could. Before he could sort out what he was doing, his hand was grasping the handle of the quarantine door and yanking it open. He didn't know how long she'd been in there, but he knew that every second could make a difference. Every second that passed, her strength would be leaching from her, bit by bit.

Her power draining away, bit by bit.

But he would not be any safer if he didn't hurry.

Once past the door, his vision attached itself to Nova. He could reach her. He *had* to reach her.

On the far side of the quarantine, pressing his body against the glass wall, Max was panting as if he, too, had just dashed across the lobby and the stairs and the bridge. His thin, pale shoulders were shaking, and Adrian could see now that the shirt around his hand was soaked with blood. Glass buildings were toppled and broken everywhere he looked.

"I'm okay," said Max, before Adrian could speak. "I sent a message to security. The healers are on their way. But Nova! You have to get her out of here!"

Adrian gulped.

Whatever had happened, there was nothing he could do for Max. But Nova . . .

Gritting his teeth, he launched himself over the skyscrapers, careening down the streets of Gatlon City.

He was halfway across the quarantine when he felt it. Like someone had uncorked a drain in him and all his strength was seeping out.

Mostly he felt it in his hands. His fingers went cold. The muscles, the ligaments in his joints, they felt like they were atrophying with every step he took. Fingers curling inward, becoming useless and frail. Fingers that would never again hold a pen or a paintbrush . . . hands that would never again create reality from imagination . . .

Hurling himself over the hospital, he knelt beside Nova. His breaths were strangled wheezes as he scooped his arms beneath her. Her head fell against his chest and he turned and sought out the exit.

The door felt impossibly far. How many steps would it take to reach it? Thirty? *Fifty?* Adrian's head spun.

He wouldn't make it. Not if he had to stumble every step of the way.

He crushed Nova's body against him and crouched down. Though he didn't know if it would work. He couldn't be sure if that ability had already been sapped from him.

Still—he took in a deep breath and leaped.

His body sprang upward. Power coursed through his legs, sending him and Nova soaring over the skyline. For one delirious moment he thought, this is what it would be like. To fly over the city, to *really* fly . . .

Then the ground rushed up to meet them, the jagged glass buildings like hundreds of spikes jutting upward. Adrian adjusted his body with the lost momentum, and he and Nova crashed down onto Scatter Creek Row, mere steps away from the door.

His muscles were shaking from the effort to stand, but he did stand. His hands and arms were so numb he would have doubted they were still attached if he couldn't see them, and yet he still tucked them beneath Nova's armpits, locking his elbows beneath her shoulders. His legs felt like sodden rags, but he took a step back, then another. And another. Gasping. Dazed. His head swimming. His eyesight blurred.

He collapsed into the antechamber, dropping Nova beside him. With one final, pathetic lurch of his foot, he kicked the quarantine door shut.

And he lay there, panting. Choking. Dying, he would have thought, except he'd never heard of Max's ability actually killing someone. That's how it felt, though. Like all the life was flooding out of his body.

His head lolled to the side, and he peered at Nova. Her body was splayed across the floor beside him, but her face looked almost peaceful.

Was she unconscious . . . or asleep?

It was an important distinction, but he didn't know how to tell the difference.

His hands were still numb. There was no pain, only

nothingness, which seemed worse.

Rolling onto his side, he wriggled closer to her. "Nova," he said, patting her cheek. "Wake up."

She was breathing, at least. He felt for a pulse at her throat and it was steady and strong, and when he looked at her face he could see her eyes twitching beneath her eyelids.

Was it possible she was dreaming?

He decided in that moment that he wouldn't regret the decision to go in after her. Even if he never drew another picture, even if all the powers of the Sentinel were gone forever, he wouldn't regret it, so long as she was okay.

Because it's what any hero would have done.

"Nova?"

It seemed almost cruel to try to wake her, when she hadn't slept for so very long, but something told him she would understand.

He placed a hand against her cheek again, which was how he realized that sensation was returning to his fingertips, because he could feel the softness of her skin, the promise of warmth beneath his palm.

He turned her head to face him. "Please wake up."

And she did.

Not like a long-sleeping princess, who might have emerged from a leisurely nap with a refreshing stretch, a graceful arch of her back, eyelids flickering groggily from such a satisfying rest.

No. Nova McLain bolted upright and screamed.

Her glazed eyes fell on Adrian, and still shrieking, she scrambled to her feet and backed into a corner. Her breaths rattled, her head tossed from side to side, scanning the small antechamber.

"Where—what—" She gasped, her chest spasming with each labored breath.

"It's okay," said Adrian. Somehow, seeing Nova standing made him realize that strength had seeped back into his limbs, too, and he pulled himself to his feet. "You're okay, Nova. You just . . . you fell asleep."

"I did not," she spat. But then her expression turned from brutal and violent to terrified, and for a moment, Adrian thought he could see her on the verge of crying. Then she turned away, hiding her face against the wall, and pressed her palms over her ears. "Not again. Make it stop."

Adrian took a step closer. Her ragged breaths were slowing.

"It's all right," he said, hoping it was true. When he was close enough, he laid a hand on her back and, when she didn't flinch, he placed the other on her arm and turned her to face him. "You're at Renegade Headquarters," he said. "You're safe."

She swallowed. Though her breaths were uneven, she had stopped shaking by the time she pulled her hands away from her ears. She still looked bewildered.

"Max," she said. "Max fell. . . . He hurt himself. . . . I . . ." She hesitated, her voice going quiet and uncertain. "I went in to try to help him, but then . . ." She met Adrian's eyes. "Did you say I fell asleep?"

"I think so."

"Not passed out. Not fainted. Fell asleep. That's what you said. Why did you say that?"

He glanced beyond the antechamber windows and spotted two members from the medical staff rushing from the elevator bank, both in civilian clothing rather than their usual scrubs.

Turning, he pulled one of the hazard suits down from a hook on the wall. "We call Max the Bandit, right?" he said, undoing the zipper down the full length of the suit. "It's because he . . . he steals powers. When he gets close to a prodigy, they start to lose their abilities. Their powers just . . . fade away. The closer they get to Max, and the more time they spend in his presence, the more likely it is that . . ." He hesitated, watching the dawning realization on Nova's face, coupled with mounting horror. "That the effects will be permanent."

He held the hazard suit toward her and she took it dumbly, her gaze unfocused. "And I passed out," she whispered. "I never pass out."

Adrian took down the second suit and began preparing it too. When the two healers burst into the room a second later, he was already holding the suit out, ready for them to step into it.

"Security said—" started the first, a man Adrian had never learned the name of.

"I know," Adrian said. "Max needs help. I think he's lost a lot of blood."

"What about you? Do either of you require medical attention?"

"No," said Adrian. "We're both experiencing effects from being in the quarantine, but . . . that's it." He glanced at Nova. "Right? You weren't hurt otherwise?"

She shook her head, offering no resistance as the woman took the other suit from her and began stuffing her legs into the pants. "Stand back," she said, as they each pulled on the helmets and gloves.

Adrian pulled Nova out of the antechamber. They stood on the sky bridge, watching as the two healers forged their way through Max's city. The kid had sat down against the wall and his pallor was ghastly pale, his eyes shimmering with unshed tears as the doctors started to unwrap and inspect his wound.

"What happened?" said Adrian.

It seemed to take Nova a long time to answer. "He was levitating."

When nothing else followed, Adrian turned his focus on her. She was staring into the quarantine but he didn't think she was really seeing Max or the doctors or even the glass city. Her eyes were unfocused and haunted.

"Nova?"

"He saw me watching him, and I think it startled him. He fell and . . ." She gulped. "I think one of the buildings went through his hand."

Adrian flinched.

"That's when I ran in, to try to help. I didn't . . . I didn't know." She blinked, clearing whatever thoughts were clouding her mind. "How long was I in there for?"

"I don't know," said Adrian. "You were unconscious when I got here."

Nova fixed him with a look of disbelief. "Why *are* you here?"

He gulped, and realized then that he was still touching her, a hand on her arm, the other on her back. She hadn't moved away, but now that he could feel every sensation through his hands again, he became intensely aware of it. The soft fabric of the uniform. The warmth of her skin through the cloth. He remembered taking her hand at the parade, drawing on her wrist, and how he'd been so blithe about it at the time. How it had seemed like nothing at all— just something nice to do for a stranger.

But now the idea of drawing on the inside of her wrist seemed unforgivably personal.

"I brought you sandwiches," he said, and he knew it sounded ridiculous as he dropped his hands to his sides. "But I dropped them in the lobby."

Brow furrowing, Nova glanced over the side of the bridge, and there it was. The paper bag, tipped over, one paper-wrapped, toothpicked sandwich having tumbled out onto the tile.

"I thought maybe you'd be hungry?" Adrian added, somewhat lamely.

Nova stared silently at the lonesome bag for what felt like ages, before she finally turned back to him. Her expression seemed to have cleared somewhat. "People don't just lose their powers, do they? He steals them. He . . . *absorbs* them."

Adrian nodded.

"So why aren't you affected?"

He sagged against the rail. "I was. I am."

Her voice became weak as she said, "We're not prodigies anymore?"

"I don't know," he admitted. "We don't get a lot of willing test subjects to help us figure out exactly what Max's ability does, or how long it takes for it to become . . . permanent. But I do know there are people who have been around him and not lost their powers. At least, once they're able to get away from him."

Nova set her jaw and reached for Adrian, settling her hand firmly over his. There was something determined in the look, bordering on desperate. She reached behind him. Her fingers brushed against his low back and he jumped.

"Where's your marker?" she said.

Adrian blinked at her. *His marker?*

Feeling his cheeks warm, he fumbled for the hidden pocket sewn into the lining of his left sleeve. He pulled out the marker and tried to hand it to her.

"Not for *me*," she said, though she grabbed his hand anyway so she could hold it still while she ripped off the cap. "Draw something."

He stared at her, realizing what it was she wanted. Though

whether or not he'd lost his powers wouldn't prove whether or not *she* had, he could see it was important to her. And, truth be told, he needed to know too. Even if he was afraid the result wouldn't be what he wanted.

"What are you waiting for?"

"I'm scared," he said, and he started to laugh when he said it, because he knew what was done was done and avoiding the truth wouldn't change anything. But still. In this moment, for perhaps this last moment, he was still a superhero.

He and Nova both.

But Nova only let out an annoyed breath. "Don't be a dolt."

"A *dolt?*"

"Draw something!" she yelled, and her anxiety became clear, and for whatever reason, Adrian could see this was the thing she was latching on to, perhaps because her power wasn't something she could so easily test. Would she ever sleep again? Would she sleep like a normal person? It could be hours, even days, before she knew for sure.

Schooling his face, Adrian picked up her hand, like he had at the parade, and flipped it over so her palm was turned upward. He started to draw, not really thinking about what he was drawing, just allowing himself to sketch whatever came to mind first.

And what came to mind was a dinosaur. A tiny velociraptor, no bigger than her thumb.

Relatively small, but surprisingly ferocious.

When the hasty drawing was finished, he looked into Nova's face, but she was staring at the creature inked onto her palm. "He's adorable," she murmured.

He swallowed. "Here we go," he said, swirling the pad of his finger over the drawing.

The creature roared to life, peeling up from Nova's skin and perching there in the center of her hand. It looked eagerly in each direction, probably scouring the place for prey.

"He's a nice dinosaur," said Adrian, realizing that he was beaming only after he said it. "I'm pretty sure."

Nova's shoulders relaxed and she watched the beast scurry up her ring finger. It bent its head and nibbled at her fingertip, though it didn't appear to be hurting her.

"Okay," she breathed. Then again, "Okay. You're okay. I'm probably okay too."

Adrian didn't know what to say to this. He still wasn't sure how long she'd been in there.

The dinosaur leaped from Nova's hand onto the rail and dashed in the direction of the staircase. Adrian wondered how good its sense of smell was, and if perhaps it had already detected the fallen sandwiches.

"Adrian?"

He met her gaze.

"Where did he get telekinesis from?"

"Telekinesis?"

"Max. He was levitating. He was . . . he's powerful."

Adrian stared at her. "Max? Powerful?"

"He must have had sixty buildings hovering in the air, in addition to himself. Do you know how rare that is?"

"I . . . yes," he said, still frowning. "But Max can't. . . . He can only . . ." He trailed off. He had only ever seen Max lift one thing at a time with his thoughts, and usually not very well. "Are you sure?"

Nova gave him a frustrated look. "I'm sure."

His shoulders drooped. It was clear from Nova's expression that she knew exactly what she'd seen, and he had no reason to doubt her.

Besides, he knew exactly where that power had come from.

What he couldn't fathom, though, was why Max would hide it from him.

"Adrian?" she said again, more forcefully this time.

He swallowed. "Ace Anarchy," he said. "He stole that power from Ace Anarchy."

CHAPTER THIRTY-FOUR

NOVA HAD BEEN CONSTRAINED to a bed in the medical wing for nine hours already and she was anything but happy about it. She hadn't slept a wink, but the healers thought it was important to keep her for at least twenty-four hours and, ideally, up to as long as seventy-two hours, so they could see what sort of symptoms she might suffer from after being exposed to Max.

When they first told her that, she laughed. Seventy-two hours? Stuck, here, in a *bed*? Without sleeping? With nothing more to keep her busy than a stack of *Gatlon Gazette*s and a television screen that seemed to only show the news, which was itself a constant bombardment of negativity about how the Renegades had handled the situation at the library? When they couldn't even be bothered to give her one of the private rooms?

She thought not.

She insisted that she felt fine, but they kept impressing on her that she couldn't possibly know yet whether or not her powers were compromised. Even if she felt energized and awake now, it could be a result of adrenaline and her body's internal clock righting itself. Most people felt perfectly fine at one in the afternoon, and most people could will themselves to stay awake for days at a time before their body forced them to take the rest they needed. It was simply too early to tell whether or not Nova was still a prodigy.

While she understood this logic, it did not temper her frustration. If she could only get out of here, it would take her about five minutes to hop on a city bus, find some unsuspecting passenger, and use her real ability to put them to sleep. Then she would know for sure whether or not her powers were functional. It would be infinitely more efficient than being stuck here, doing nothing.

On top of that, Adrian didn't have to stay in the medical wing. They argued it was because he'd already demonstrated that his gift was intact, but Nova suspected he was being given some leeway from the rules because he was, you know, Adrian *Everhart*.

Nova was grumbling to herself, scanning over the newspaper headlines again in case there might be some she had skipped before but that had suddenly become more appealing in the face of her boredom, when a knock pulled her attention upward.

Monarch stood at the foot of her bed, her fist still raised against the metal framing that held the privacy curtains. "Hey," she said with a small, uncertain smile. "I heard about what happened last night. Thought I'd bring you a care package." She held up a paper bag.

Nova gaped at her. For a long time. Longer than was probably polite. It felt like a trap. So far, the only interaction she'd had with Danna was down in the training hall, and she'd left unsure whether or not Danna liked or trusted her.

Finally, she forced herself to sit up, pushing her back against the pillows. She eyed the bag warily. "Thanks?"

Danna started to laugh and came closer, plopping the bag on

the mattress against Nova's legs. "The food here isn't awful, but it's not exactly amazing, either. Ruby kept me well supplied while I was in recovery, so I thought I could pay it forward." She rummaged through the bag, pulling out a few choice items to show Nova. "I didn't know if you were sweet, salty, or none of the above, so I brought an assortment. Some pretzels, some chocolate, some dried fruit chips if that's your thing. And most important—reading material. Because one can only read the *Gazette* for so long before we are left bitter and disheartened." She reached into the depths of the bag and retrieved four paperback books, each with curling covers and flimsy spines, looking like they had been well loved over time. "One thriller, one romance, one nonfiction"—she lifted up the nonfiction book, which showed a large warship on the cover— "in case you like history. This was my dad's. I'm honestly not sure if it's any good. And lastly, my personal favorite." The final book depicted an armor-clad woman riding a dragon. "Don't judge the cheesy artwork. The story is genius."

She stacked the books on the tray beside Nova's bed.

"Thanks?" Nova said again, not quite sure how to handle this random show of kindness. "Are you fully healed now?"

Danna glanced down, rubbing her side. Beneath the uniform Nova could make out a slight bulge along her ribs, where there must still have been bandaging over the burns.

"Almost," said Danna, pushing back her dreadlocks. "They say I'll be able to go back on the field again in a couple days. Just a few more sessions with the healers and I should be back to . . . well, not a hundred percent, but as good as it's gonna get."

"Why not a hundred percent?" said Nova. "Everyone talks about the healers here like they're miracle workers."

"Well, they are—to a degree. I mean, having a doctor with

supernatural healing abilities is still better than . . . I don't know, applying ice packs and calendula oil, or whatever old-fashioned stuff they used to treat burns with. But they can't bring back the lepidopterans that were incinerated in the flames, and as a result, I'll always have some pretty gnarly scar tissue happening through here."

Nova lifted an eyebrow. "You call them *lepidopterans?*"

Grinning, Danna shrugged, only slightly self-conscious. "Sometimes I worry that calling them butterflies all the time undermines how remarkable of an ability it really is. Like saying, hey, I can turn into rainbows and daisies! Cool, huh?"

The corners of Nova's lips twitched upward, and Danna seemed to take this as a sign that it would be all right for her to sink into the visitor's chair.

"But I prefer it this way. Gets people to underestimate you, right? And that's an automatic advantage. You probably know what that's like too. I mean—obviously, no one thought you would beat the Gargoyle, which makes the win so much more satisfying."

Nova dropped the newspaper to the floor and shifted upward in the bed. "Do you ever use your gift for things beyond Renegade assignments?"

"Oh, all the time." Danna's grin became mischievous. "When I was a kid I was always sneaking into movie theaters. To this day I've never actually paid for a movie ticket." She cringed slightly and leaned forward. "Don't tell anyone, okay? That is definitely outside of our *code.*"

"Your secret is safe. But what about"—Nova glanced around, though she could see little of the medical wing beyond the enclosed curtains—"around here? There's so much going on, so many things the Renegades are trying to build and invent and . . . research. I bet they're coming up with things in R and D that would make the Sentinel look like child's play. Do you ever get curious about all that?"

Danna groaned. "Don't talk to me about the Sentinel. If I ever see that guy again, I'll show him where he can put those flames."

Nova smirked. "I know that feeling."

Danna brought her legs beneath her, sitting cross-legged as much as she could in the small chair, her knees sprouting over the arms. "I've never sneaked into R and D or the quarantine labs. They're serious about keeping their stuff confidential and even I'm not willing to risk their wrath. But"—she leaned forward conspiratorially— "when I first got here, I used to go sneaking through the air vents into the artifacts warehouse. If you ever get a chance to go inside, it's amazing. Like a catalog of every awesome prodigy weapon you've ever heard of. They have Ultrasonic's whip, and Magnetron's shield, and Trident's . . . well, trident."

"And you never got caught?" said Nova, surprised—and even a little hopeful—to think the security on such powerful objects might be lacking.

"I never formed," said Danna. "I mean, I stayed in swarm mode the whole time, and as long as I keep them spread out, it's pretty easy for a bunch of butterflies to go undetected. Lots of places to hide in there too. But actually, the best artifacts aren't even in the warehouse. A lot of people don't know this, but they keep a small collection upstairs, outside the Council's offices. In theory, anyone can go up and see them, but without an official appointment, not many people venture up there."

"What do they have?" said Nova.

Before Danna could respond, Genissa Clark—Frostbite— appeared framed in the curtains. She took one look at Nova and let out a peal of laughter.

"Great powers, I thought they were joking," she said, placing one hand on a jutting hip. "No one would be stupid enough to go into the quarantine. I mean, you do know what *quarantine* means, right, Miss McLain?"

Nova leaned back into her pillows, crossing her legs at the heels. "You're right, it was stupid. Clearly, when a superhero sees a ten-year-old kid put a glass spike through his hand, the correct response is to hang out and wait for someone else to come deal with it." She plastered a fake, encouraging smile to her face. "Yay, Renegades!"

"Actually," said Genissa with a haughty sigh, "the correct response would be to get someone who actually knows what they're doing. That way, when the experts arrive, they're not stuck dealing with *two* unconscious bodies."

"Here's an idea," said Danna. "How about you stab yourself with an ice pick, and Nova and I will make small talk while we wait for the healers to notice."

"In case you've both forgotten," said Genissa, lifting an eyebrow, "Nova didn't actually do anything to help Max. So, if you want to go on thinking you did some heroic act, by all means, stroke that ego. But all you really did was risk your own abilities and make yourself look like an idiot." Her voice turned singsong. "But lucky for you, we can always use a few more data-entry drones. I mean, that's what they had you doing, anyway. You do know what they call a Renegade without any superpowers, right?"

Nova pretended to think. "Someone who still beat your pet rock at the trials?"

Danna snorted.

"Cute," said Genissa, unperturbed. "But the correct answer is *administrator*. I know it's not the exciting Renegade position you've probably always dreamed about, but given that sleeplessness still isn't a real superpower, I feel like you were given a pretty good run while it lasted." She winked and turned away.

"Tell Gargoyle I said hi," Nova called after her.

Genissa's jaw twitched, but she didn't respond as she yanked the curtain shut around them.

"Charming," Danna muttered with a sneer. "Although, she does bring up an interesting point." She rested her elbow on the arm of her chair, cupping her chin. "You're one of the very few Renegades whose skill as part of a patrol unit wouldn't necessarily be impacted by losing your power." She shrugged. "Why wouldn't they let you stay on the team? I bet you could make a strong argument for it."

"I should certainly hope so," said Nova. She gestured to the curtain. "Be honest. Is she the worst of it—her and her team—or are there slews of Renegades who are far less noble than everyone wants to think?"

"Oh, there are definitely some patrol units who seem to be on a permanent power trip, but Genissa Clark is the worst. Most people here are pretty great. Though, between you and me, there is one person I try to avoid at all costs." Danna leaned forward, dropping her voice, and Nova couldn't help but lean toward her as well. "Thunderbird."

Nova blinked. "Really? A Council member?"

"Ugh, she's the worst." Danna covered her face with her hands, as if to hide. "I don't think she means to be scary, but I find the woman utterly terrifying. She's so serious, and every time she's around I feel like she's searching for any reason to oust me from headquarters. I don't know what it is, but I swear she hates me."

"She does seem . . ." Nova contemplated, unable to find the right word, before settling on, "Critical."

"Critical, terrifying, same thing." Danna screwed up her face, looking momentarily embarrassed. "Though, full disclosure, it could have something to do with my inherent fear of birds."

Nova's eyebrows lifted. "Birds."

Danna faked a shudder. "Ever since I was a kid. I mean, you know what one of the primary predators of butterflies is, right?"

Nova chuckled. "Okay, that makes sense." She pondered for a moment. "Did you know there are over forty species of waterfowl in this region?"

Danna gave her an incredulous look. "Seriously? Why would you tell me that? Are you trying to give me nightmares about being gobbled up by a flock of seagulls?"

"Great skies, no," said Nova emphatically. "If anything, you should be having nightmares about the royal albatross. Their wingspans can reach up to eleven feet across."

Danna fixed her with a cold glare. "I'm beginning to regret coming here."

"Too much information?" said Nova, feigning a sheepish look.

"Fine," Danna said, still glowering. "Your turn, Miss I'll-Fight-the-Gargoyle. Do you have any phobias, or are you always as calm in the face of fear as you were at the trials?"

Any phobias?

Nova couldn't keep her lips from stretching tight. "Just one. I have one phobia."

And he carries a scythe and is about a thousand times scarier than Tamaya Rae.

"Go on," said Danna. "I shared mine."

Nova shook her head. "I didn't ask for a full disclosure, and this is one I'm keeping secret."

Danna huffed, but Nova's attention caught on another figure moving past the curtains, a healer checking a clipboard as he walked past. She sighed. It had been hours since anyone had been to check on her. Clearly, they weren't as concerned as they were pretending to be.

"So, Adrian was bringing you sandwiches, huh?"

She startled. "What?"

Danna shot her a sly look. "At three o'clock in the morning. That's . . . *nice*." She drew out the word, hinting not so subtly that it was an act that went beyond nice.

"Oh. Yeah." Nova shrugged. "We didn't actually get to eat them, though."

"It's the thought that counts. And it doesn't hurt that he charged into a highly volatile situation in order to rescue you . . ."

Nova frowned. "Yep. He's a nice guy. I think that's been well established."

Danna folded her fingers over her stomach. "He really is. No one could argue that. But you know, in all the time we've spent on the same team together, he never brought *me* sandwiches."

Clearing her throat, Nova picked up the top book from the stack on the nightstand and started pawing through the pages. "He was just being friendly. He's really worked hard to make me feel like I fit in here."

This was true, she thought, though she also knew it didn't explain the warmth rushing into her face. Or why Danna's insinuations made her stomach flutter at the same time her jaw clenched.

The things was, when Adrian was around, she was finding it more and more difficult to keep her eyes scanning for exits and resources, or her senses attuned to potential threats, when all she really wanted to do was study him. She wanted to know how he managed to strike that balance between self-assured and humble. Relaxed, yet focused.

When he was drawing, she wanted only to watch the quick,

agile movements of his hands. When he was smiling, she found herself holding her breath to see if the smile would brighten enough to show off those elusive dimples. When he was looking at her, she felt compelled to look back. And also, illogically, to look away.

All of it combined made her far too annoyed with his presence.

It was attraction, pure and simple. It was hormones. It was . . . biology.

And it was not a part of her plan.

"You know," said Danna, "I don't think Adrian's ever had a girlfriend before. At least, no one serious. Not since I've known him."

Only when this comment brought a new surge of irritation did Nova realize how much, in the brief span of Danna's visit, she had almost started to like her.

So much for that.

But she did suddenly have an idea.

Narrowing her eyes, Nova leaned forward, inspecting Danna's face. "Are you feeling all right?"

Danna stiffened. "Fine. Why?"

Nova crooked her finger, urging her closer. "It might just be the temperature in here, but you look a little feverish." She reached out, setting her palm against Danna's brow. "Maybe you should get some more rest."

Her power flowed through her as easily and naturally as it ever had.

Danna's eyes closed. She slumped forward, her face planting onto the blankets.

Nova sat back with a sigh, casting her gaze toward the ceiling.

Proof, at last.

Her power was fine.

And every moment spent here was a waste of time.

Nova climbed out of the bed. "Nurse!"

A moment later, the nurse who had brought her lunch pulled back the curtain, surprised when she saw Nova lifting Danna out of the chair and settling her onto the mattress.

"I don't know what happened. She seemed fine one minute, then she just got really pale and passed out. You might want to get a healer in here. I think maybe she overexerted herself too soon?"

The nurse, bewildered, ran out to alert one of the healers.

By the time she came back, Nova was dressed again and nearly done pulling on her boots.

"And where do you think you're going?" the nurse asked as she felt for Danna's pulse.

"Home," said Nova.

The nurse barked a laugh. "Absolutely not, young lady. We'll have a new room made up for you in just a minute, but we do need you to stay put."

Nova glared at her. "Why?"

"Because!" the nurse said, as if this were a viable explanation. "We need to keep a close watch on you after—"

"After, what? Nearly having my superpower drained out of me by a ten-year-old?"

The nurse sighed. "Not too many people have ever come in contact with young Mr. Everhart. We must be cautious."

"Well," Nova said, finishing the latches on her boots, "if I die, I'll let you know. Until then, I have things to be dealing with. And"—she gestured at Danna—"apparently, so do you."

CHAPTER THIRTY-FIVE

———————■————————

"**O**KAY, THERE'S YOUR NEW HOSPITAL TOWER," said Adrian, pushing the building into Max's enclosure. "What else got broken?"

"Just those apartments you fell on," said Max, pointing toward the exit.

"Right," said Adrian, starting to sketch. Inside the quarantine, Max carried the new tower over to the hospital building. He set it down on the broken stump, working mostly single-handed, as his right hand was heavily bandaged. Adrian watched as Max used his forearm to hold the tower in place while wrapping his left hand around the break. Slowly, the glass began to melt together, forming a seal that wasn't perfect—a visible crack was still evident where the material had merged—but it seemed solid enough.

Adrian swallowed. He had seen Max use that particular gift a number of times, probably more than any other power he'd absorbed. It made him think about what Nova had seen—Max using his telekinesis to hold dozens of glass buildings in the air at once. Truthfully, that mental image had not left him since Nova had told him. He'd been trying all morning to find a way to ask Max about it, but he hadn't yet found a way to do it that didn't sound accusatory.

Instead of asking the question he really wanted to ask, he said, "How's the hand?"

"Could be worse." Max looked down at his bandaged palm. "They had to cauterize the artery—that's where all the blood was coming from. But the spire went through right here." He lifted his left hand so he could show Adrian. "In this meaty part between my thumb and finger. So it missed all the bones and tendons." He shrugged. "I guess it would have hurt a lot worse if the wound had been more central. And, you know, it hurt pretty bad as it was."

"With any luck, you'll have an epic scar to show for it."

A fleeting smile passed over Max's face. He stepped back to inspect the hospital, then picked his way back toward Adrian. He sat down at the edge of the bay while Adrian sketched out the crushed apartment building.

"Hey, Adrian?" he started, cradling his bandaged hand in his lap, picking at the edges of the wrapping.

Adrian looked up, immediately hesitant. It wasn't very often that he heard Max sounding worried about anything. "What's up?"

Max sat up a bit straighter, but still didn't meet Adrian's eye. "I have Ace Anarchy's power."

Adrian watched him, waiting for him to say something else, but this seemed to be the extent of his confession.

"Yeah," he finally responded. "I know."

Max shifted slightly, clearing his throat. "Do you think . . ." He trailed off.

"Do I think what?"

"Do you think I might be evil?"

Adrian's eyebrows shot up. He leaned back, pulling the marker's tip away from the unfinished drawing.

"Or . . . ," Max continued, "that I have some evil powers in me?"

Adrian waited for Max to look up at him, but the kid kept his gaze resolutely on the floor. "No, I don't."

Max's mouth puckered to one side, unconvinced. "I knew you'd say that."

"Because it's true," Adrian said with a laugh. "Is this why you pretend you're no good at it? Is this why you've hidden how strong you are, all these years?"

Max looked up, his face rife with regret. He didn't answer, but Adrian could see the truth written plainly on his face.

Sighing, Adrian capped the marker. "For starters, most of the horrible things Ace Anarchy did, he could only do because he had that helmet. Once they got the helmet, he was . . . I mean, for a telekinetic he was still pretty strong and all, but not nearly like before. And more important than that, what we do—what any of us do—it's just a series of choices, right? Take . . . take fire elementals. Every fire elemental has a choice. They can burn down buildings, or they can make s'mores."

He intended it to be funny, but Max frowned, looking unimpressed at Adrian's attempts at being clever.

"If you had the power to do everything Ace Anarchy could do, you would have chosen differently. You would build things, not tear them down." He gestured at the glass city. "Case in point."

This, finally, brought a small smile to Max's mouth.

"Speaking of building things," said Max, his eyes brightening. "I discovered something this morning. Want to see?"

Without waiting for an answer, he got up and bounded back to his rooms, returning a moment later with a slim red marker.

He crouched down in front of the wall and began to draw onto the glass. Soon he had completed a rudimentary sketch of a car. When he was finished, he capped the marker, then pressed his forefinger into the car's center and pushed.

Adrian was already grinning by the time the car popped out of the wall, landing in the palm of his hand. It was roughly the size of his palm. A little lopsided. The wheels did not turn. It also did not have the same solid feel that one of his own glass figurines had, but rather there was a softness inherent in the material. A malleability. Like glass that was on the verge of melting.

All that aside, it was real.

"Why, you little bandit," he said. "You stole my power."

Max grunted. He was staring at the car with obvious disapproval. "I'm not a very good artist. And there's something wrong with all the things I've made so far. They're not stable like yours. I did some things on paper first, and they just crumple like tissue paper as soon as I pull them out."

Adrian turned the car over, holding it by the hood, when the whole thing drooped down toward the floor, bending nearly in half. "Ah! Sorry."

Max shrugged. "You weren't in here for very long, so I didn't get much of your power. Which is good. If I'd gotten it all, then I'd be stuck making new buildings for the city, and they wouldn't be very good."

"Maybe at first, but I could give you drawing lessons." Adrian tried to bend the car back into shape, but it was quickly losing its form. Already it sat in his palm with the consistency of bread dough. Giving up, he set the clear blob down on the floor. "Do you know yet how much you got from Nova?"

Max shook his head. "She was in here for longer than you were, but . . . it still wasn't *that* long. You showed up right when it was happening. But I guess we'll see." His frown deepened. "I wish there was a way I could turn it off. I don't really want her power. The last thing I need is eight more hours of boredom every day."

Nodding in sympathy, Adrian drew his own version of Max's car onto the glass and pushed it through. Rather than picking it up, though, Max just scowled. "Show off."

"Can't help it."

Max's posture changed suddenly. His spine stiffened, his glower turned more thoughtful, but also hesitant.

"Adrian?"

The way he said it made Adrian tense up, too. "Yeah?"

"When you were in here . . . after you grabbed Nova . . ." His eyes narrowed and he wasn't looking at Adrian, but staring blankly at the glass car. "You *flew*."

Adrian's pulse thumped. The words hung between them, solid as the wall that divided them, for far too long before Adrian forced out a small chuckle. "I think you might have been seeing things. All that blood loss, probably."

Redness flooded Max's cheeks and when he did lift his eyes, they were flashing with anger. "I'm not stupid."

Adrian swallowed. "I didn't mean—"

"Okay, maybe it wasn't actual flying, but it wasn't normal, either, what you did. You jumped"—he glanced back, measuring the city with his eyes—"at least fourteen feet, and you weren't even running or anything at the time. You just took off."

Adrian stared at him as his mind searched for an explanation, but nothing came. The silence felt impermeable and Adrian wanted to break it, but he had nothing to say.

Finally, Max sank back onto his heels. "You know, I've seen videos of another prodigy that can jump like that too."

Adrian's pressed his lips tight together, as if the confession might emerge of its own accord. Already he was debating if it would really be so bad to tell Max the truth. He could be trusted with this secret, couldn't he? Clearly, he'd already figured it out—at least, *guessed*—so how much harm would there be in admitting it?

But still he hesitated. Because as much as he loved Max, he also knew that Max loved Captain Chromium, and Adrian couldn't be sure where most of his loyalties lay, and Adrian still wasn't ready for his dads to know that he was the Sentinel. Their expressions when they'd gotten to headquarters last night, after they heard about what happened in the quarantine, were burned into his memory. Fear and panic, relief coupled with concern. Not just for what had happened, but more for what could have happened. Adrian knew it wasn't just the fear that he might have lost his powers, which would be hard to come to terms with at first, but wouldn't have been the end of the world. But it was also the fact that he'd nearly died at the library that still had them shaken up. Perhaps, too, their nerves were running high from the Captain's brush with death at the parade, even if neither of them was admitting how close it had been.

Being a Renegade was dangerous. It had always been dangerous, and few superheroes tried to persuade themselves otherwise. It was just a fact of this life they had chosen—or that had chosen them.

But if his dads found out that Adrian was also the Sentinel . . . had taken on Nightmare at the parade, visited the Anarchists in their tunnels, faced off against the Detonator at the library, and charged headlong into the fire . . . their anxiety would skyrocket. He didn't need to put them through that.

At least, that's what he told himself. It was for them. He was keeping this secret for their own well-being, to protect them from their own worries.

But he also knew that it was a selfish decision. He wasn't ready to hang up the mantle of the Sentinel, and he knew they would ask him to.

What he didn't know was whether he would listen to the request or not. Right now, it seemed easier to stay silent.

"Okay, fine," said Max, once it became clear Adrian wasn't going to admit to his assumptions. "You don't have to answer. I saw what I saw."

Adrian looked away, his shoulders weighted down with guilt. He wished he could explain to Max that it wasn't personal. That he wasn't ready to tell *anyone*.

He said simply, "It's complicated."

Max guffawed. "Yeah, and I don't know anything about that."

Adrian cringed.

"But one thing did occur to me," said Max, tapping his marker into his palm. "This guy called the Sentinel . . . you might have heard of him? The Sentinel? He's kind of been in the news a lot lately."

Adrian shot him a wry look. "Sounds familiar."

"Right, so as far as I know, this guy they call the Sentinel and I might be the only prodigies alive who can claim to have more than one superpower. At least, we both have multiple, totally unrelated superpowers. Not like Tsunami, who can both create water from nothing and also manipulate existing water. But he can make fire and do the whole jumping thing and now they're saying he has some fancy new concussive energy beam. Whereas I have"—he tapped the pen against each fingertip as he counted—"telekinesis, metal manipulation, matter fusing, some invisibility, um . . ." He pondered. "Absorption, obviously, and now whatever it is you do. What do you call it, anyway?"

Adrian was smiling again. He knew Max was working to cross the divide caused by Adrian's secret and his unwillingness to talk about. It felt like a compromise, and he was grateful for it. "I just call it sketching," he said. "But I think it's listed as 'artwork genesis' in my profile."

"Artwork genesis. Cool. That's a good list, isn't it?"

"It's an awesome list." Truthfully, it was more impressive than Adrian realized. He rarely saw Max use any of the abilities he had gathered from prodigies, most of which had been absorbed when he was a child. Telekinesis from Ace Anarchy, metal manipulation and matter fusing from his birth parents, a bit of invisibility taken from the Dread Warden before they realized what it was he could do. Now, of course, Adrian's power, and maybe even some of Nova's. He may not have been powerful in all of these abilities, as demonstrated by the car that was now a jiggling pile by Adrian's ankle, but he was powerful enough. In fact, if he wasn't trapped inside this quarantine all the time, he would have made one hell of a superhero.

Adrian opened his mouth, ready to tell him just this, when Max blurted out, "Can the Sentinel give himself *any* power?"

Adrian blinked.

"Don't say that you don't know," Max continued hurriedly, "just . . . pretend you're guessing, or whatever. That is how it works, right? You're somehow . . . I mean, he's somehow drawing the powers into reality? Or . . . do you . . . does the Sentinel actually have power mimicry, and artwork genesis isn't the original power at all?"

Shutting his eyes, Adrian massaged his brow. "I don't . . ." He paused and sighed heavily. "Okay, if I had to *guess* . . ." He returned his focus to Max, peering at him intently, hoping to convey that should anyone else ask about this, ever, it was only a guess. "He's still figuring out how many powers he can give himself and the overall extent of the abilities. He's . . . sort of making it up as he goes along."

"I figured," said Max, in a tone that made Adrian bristle. "But do you think . . . has he tried invincibility yet?"

"Invincibility?"

"You know. Like the Captain."

Adrian leaned back on his hands. Somehow, he hadn't given much thought to replicating either of his dads' powers, or any of the Council's. Perhaps it felt too much like crossing an uncrossable boundary. He could never become Captain Chromium or the Dread Warden, he could never replace them—and that's not what any of this was about anyway. But to imbue himself with their abilities, especially the Captain's invincibility or superstrength, would have seemed almost disrespectful to everything Captain Chromium was, everything the world admired.

But at the same time, he knew precisely why Max had asked about *this* power, among all the superpowers of the world.

Because of his invincibility, Hugh Everhart was the only prodigy who could get close to Max. And though Max did a good job of hiding his loneliness, and Adrian largely tried not to think too much about it, in that moment it became clear how much he must yearn for interactions that weren't divided by a glass wall or a chromium-edged suit.

"I don't know," he said finally, slowly. "I honestly don't know."

Max nodded in understanding, and Adrian could tell he wasn't angry at this response. It was the truth. Adrian didn't know if he could bestow himself with invincibility, on any level, and certainly not to the level of his dad. Max must have recognized the honesty in his words.

But already Adrian's mind was swirling. Considering. *Wondering* . . .

"You should go check on Nova."

Adrian startled. "What?"

"I bet she's really freaked out still. It seemed like she actually enjoyed being awake all the time."

"I'm not sure *enjoyed* is the right word . . . ," said Adrian, trying to recall her exact words when they had talked about how she spends her time. "But I do think she's proud of what she accomplished because of it. She doesn't just read comics and draw, like I probably would. Instead, she made herself into a Renegade."

"Exactly," said Max, "and I might have taken that away from her."

Shaking his head, Adrian moved to stand. "Never. She's one of us now, whether she likes it or not."

CHAPTER THIRTY-SIX

T HE COUNCIL'S OFFICES had not been included in the initial tour of Renegades Headquarters on Nova's first day, but she was aware of their existence. The floor number was posted on the directory in the lobby, and Nova had been intending to come check them out, but she'd had no reason to. Nothing she could have used as an explanation, at least, in the event that someone asked her what she was doing.

As she stepped cautiously from the elevator, though, she realized she needn't have worried. On first arrival, the floor appeared to be deserted. At least, the central receptionist's desk was unoccupied and Nova could hear no signs of life coming from the open doorway behind it. Her gaze darted around to the security cameras tucked obscurely around the ceiling, and she reminded herself to act natural. To pretend that she had every right to be there.

Which she did. She *was* a Renegade, and this floor wasn't off-limits, according to the directory on the first floor. She wasn't even planning to do anything while she was there other than look around, but that knowledge did little to ease the sense of paranoia flitting around inside her head.

Nova stepped around the reception desk, noting the framed photos showing a handsome, gray-haired man with his arm around Prism, the prodigy who had taken them up to Council Hall after the library incident. She passed through the large doorway into a circular lobby with glossy white floors, an elaborate blown-glass chandelier, and vast windows that overlooked the sweeping views of the city and ocean beyond. A calming fountain burbled in the center, and artwork and glass display cases lined the walls. Five corridors sprouted from the lobby like spokes from a wheel, each with a decorative plaque hung above its entry, engraved with the aliases of the Council. Tsunami. Blacklight. Thunderbird. Dread Warden. Captain Chromium.

Nova paused to listen again. When still only silence greeted her, she started picking her way past the memorabilia on display. One case held a single green stone nestled into a bed of satin, and Nova didn't need the descriptive tag beneath it to recognize the Stone of Clairvoyance, which was credited with giving a prodigy named Fortuna the ability to describe for anyone the happiest and the saddest moments of their lives—even if they hadn't yet come to pass. Next was the golden fan that Whirlwind could use to cut an enemy up to fifty feet away. Then a collection of large fish bones, neatly laid out on a wooden plate. It was the skeleton of a razor fish, whose spirit was said to have haunted Sandprowler and imbued him with the ability to burrow quickly into almost any type of ground.

Nova paused when she came to a wall unencumbered by display cases, and instead hung with a large painting. Her stomach squeezed as she took in an artistic rendition of the Battle for Gatlon. She recognized the steps of the cathedral in the background, though the ground was littered with destruction and debris, bodies and blood. In the foreground, atop a mountain of rubble, stood Captain Chromium. He was gripping his chromium pike, with Ace's helmet speared at the tip.

At the bottom of the pile lay Ace Anarchy himself, his body broken over one of the shattered balustrades from the cathedral, his blood spilled across the dirt.

Nova's mouth ran dry. The artist had captured Ace's features perfectly—that horrible devastation, even in death. Dark eyes open to the sky, lips parted in disbelief.

It was not based on reality, she knew. This moment, caught in time, was nothing more than an artistic interpretation of what might have happened. Perhaps, in their mind, what *should* have happened. But in truth, there had been nothing left of Ace's body for them to lord their victory over.

That did not make the image any less disgusting, and in that moment Nova swore that, when she brought down the Renegades, she would find this painting again and she would destroy it.

Releasing a weakened breath, she forced herself to turn away. Her boots clipped against the hard floor as she passed the next corridor, but then she paused, her heart stuttering.

She stepped back, aligning herself with the entrance of the corridor—the Captain's corridor—and peered down its length.

Her jaw fell. Her skin tingled.

There, on a pedestal at the end of the hall, glowing copper-gold beneath a pale spotlight, was the helmet.

Ace's helmet.

Nova had barely taken a step forward when the communicator at her wrist hummed. She froze, sure in that moment the Renegades had discovered who she was and what she was planning, even though she wasn't entirely sure she was planning anything. She only knew that guilt and paranoia had flooded her system the moment the communicator went off.

Then she lifted her wrist, looked at the glowing text on the band, and released a long sigh. It was only Adrian—not accusing her of anything, just worried that she wasn't in the medical wing.

She allowed her racing pulse to calm before reading the full message.

> Insomnia, just because you never sleep doesn't mean
> you can get out of bed without the healers' permission!
> (Kidding. Sort of.) I just got to med wing and the nurse
> says you went home. Healers seem concerned—they
> say there could be side effects from being so close to
> Max that we don't know about yet. Can you come back
> to HQ? Or if you're passed out in a ditch somewhere,
> let me know so I can come find you, okay? (Kidding
> again. Not really.)
>
> —Sketch

Nova read through the message three times. The first time her thoughts were still tripping around the discovery of Ace's helmet and the majority of the message lost all meaning in the mad chaos inside her head. The second time she picked up only that there could be side effects and the healers were trying to order her around, and they were using Adrian to do it, which she found remarkably annoying.

The third time, though, she could see the message not just as glowing blue text, but she could also hear it in Adrian's voice, and by the time she got to the end she found that her irritation was gone, replaced with something almost like warm-hearted amusement. Because even if she was perfectly capable of taking care of herself and didn't need Adrian or the healers to watch out for her, there was something in his halfhearted attempts to disguise his concern that she couldn't help but find charming.

Then she looked up again, and all sense of charm and amusement vanished, like a fire doused in ice water.

Leaving the message unanswered, Nova lowered her wrist, took in a breath, and made her way down the length of the corridor.

Spot lighting was installed in a track on the ceiling, and the glint of light off the helmet's surface shifted as she came closer. She could see hints of her own reflection in the panels that curved around the face. The sharpness of the light snagged on the broken cranium where the Captain's pike had long ago broken through, leaving a gaping hole and deep cracks emanating outward. The helmet was set on a thin dowel, so that from certain angles it appeared suspended in air, the open slit where Ace's eyes had once peered through now nothing but a black hole. Unlike the artifacts in the main lobby, it was not protected by glass, but left out in the open. As if there were no fear of it ever being taken. As if no one worried that it might someday fall again into the hands of a villain.

And why should they fear it? That hole through the top was proof enough that it was destroyed. Whatever power it had once contained, whatever strength her father had worked into the fabric of this energy-turned-metal was long gone.

Nova stopped when she was an arm's length away from the helmet, overcome with memories.

Uncle Ace standing over the sleeping form of a murderer, looking at Nova with both sadness and awe.

Ace making the bells of the cathedral thunder and chime, just to bring a smile to Nova's face.

The moment she had seen the Council's parade float come into view, with the Captain showing off this helmet like a hunter proud of his conquest.

Tears pricked at the corners of her eyes as she lifted her hand, letting it hover an inch off the helmet's brow. She imagined faint vibrations coming off it, almost as though it could sense her presence. She felt sure some alarm would sound, but she couldn't quite resist the slow inhale of breath as she settled her hand onto the cool metal.

There were no alarms.

And the helmet felt like . . . a helmet. No shock of energy was sent through her skin. No faint pulse could be felt against her flesh. Just cool metal.

Looking at her own hand placed reverentially against the golden surface, Nova's eye landed on the slender bracelet dangling around her wrist.

Her brows drew together. Her head listed to one side. Reaching her other hand forward, she took hold of the delicate filigree and held it up to the light, wondering whether it was a trick of the shadows.

Her heart began to pound.

The bracelet and the helmet were not the same. There was a distinctive rosy tint to the bracelet, a beautiful but subtle vibrancy worked through the material that was missing from the helmet, which was itself a worn copper-gold.

Her frown deepened, as justifications worked their way to the surface. Surely the difference was because the helmet was ruined. Whatever power had once imbued the material was gone.

But then . . . her bracelet was broken too. The original clasp was missing entirely, and the prongs still hung empty, waiting for whatever jewel her father had intended for it. Should it not have also been relegated to this dull, muted tone?

Before she could doubt herself, Nova reached forward and plucked the helmet off its stand.

Still, not a single alarm blared. The corridor remained as quiet as ever as Nova pulled it closer, noting first how heavy it was, when she could remember her father's creations seeming impossibly light.

Nova turned it from side to side. She inspected the rupture in the top. Felt the edges along the back. Flipped it over and peered inside.

An abrupt laugh burbled from her mouth. For there, printed on the inside of the cranium, were the words MADE WITH 100% RECYCLED MATERIALS.

"Miss McLain?"

Her laugh turned into a yelp and she spun around. At first, she was faced with only an empty corridor, but then a form shimmered in the air and solidified.

The Dread Warden. He was not wearing his usual black cloak and domino mask, but blue jeans and a dress shirt. Nova's emotions were wound so tight, from her recent shocks, from the discovery of the helmet to the discovery of its being an impostor and now to the arrival of one of her archenemies dressed like a completely normal person, that they all combined into another frazzled, slightly delirious laugh pouring out of her again.

Simon Westwood frowned and Nova had to tuck the helmet against her side with one arm and clamp the other hand over her mouth to try to halt the giggling. "Sorry," she gasped. Gulped. Cleared her throat. "I'm so sorry. I didn't . . . I was just . . ." She looked down at the helmet and realized that perhaps an alarm had gone off after all, only not one she could hear. Perhaps any tampering with artifacts in these offices was announced to members of the Council in a more discreet manner. She'd just been caught in the act of taking Ace Anarchy's helmet—as far as anyone would know, she'd been trying to steal it.

She shook her head. "I wasn't trying to take it, I swear."

Simon's expression remained more curious than alarmed, and though he said nothing, she could sense him urging her to go on.

So she did, her thoughts scrambling to prove her innocence, until it occurred to her that . . . she was, in fact, innocent. She *wasn't* going to steal the helmet. For once, as far as the Renegades were concerned, she hadn't actually done anything wrong. Other than perhaps leaving fingerprints smudged on what she could only ascertain was a completely worthless relic.

A fake.

"I heard you had some neat artifacts up here, so I came to see them. I was told that was okay? That anyone could come and look?"

Simon nodded, just slightly.

"Um . . . and when I saw the helmet . . . I got curious. I mean, it's . . ." She barely refrained from laughing again. "It's *Ace Anarchy's* helmet. But then I got closer and . . . and it seemed . . . off."

"Off?" said Simon.

She swallowed. "It's a fake. This isn't Ace Anarchy's helmet."

Simon's dark eyes seemed to soften, just barely. "How could you tell?"

Nova looked down at the helmet. She gripped it in both hands again, holding it out so she could stare into the empty face. How could she tell?

"Every description I've ever heard, or read," she started, "said that the helmet had a sort of . . . an internal glow. But this is just . . . metal. Normal metal."

"Copper-plated aluminum," said Simon, drawing her gaze back up to him. He now wore a wan smile. "I'd heard you were observant, Miss McLain, but I must say, I'm impressed. I don't know that there's been anyone that helmet hasn't fooled yet."

"But why? Why is there a fake?"

Simon stepped forward and took the helmet out of her hands. He inspected it himself for a second, his lips tight, as if he might be reliving painful memories. "This is what we use when we want to put it on display. It's a great icon, you know—the defeat of humanity's worst villain. It's a visible reminder of how far we've come since the Day of Triumph, and how much we have to lose if we ever let humanity slide back to the way it was."

"But it's not real."

Shrugging, he set the helmet back on its stand, adjusting it so that it balanced just right. "It doesn't need to be."

"But—" Nova huffed, not sure how he could be so calm about this. She couldn't keep herself from sounding insistent when she asked, "But where's the real one?"

"Ah," said Simon, comprehension filtering through his expression. "Is that what you're worried about?"

She frowned. "I'm not worried."

Simon's eyebrows lifted. Though his olive-toned skin was light compared with Adrian's, everything else about him was dark. Thick, dark eyebrows. Thick, dark hair. Thick, dark beard. Somehow, it all served to make him seem more expressive, as if whole stories could be told with the curl of his lip or the crinkle of his eyes.

Nova didn't like it. Standing so close to him, she felt on display herself, like he could see right through her. The thought made her uncomfortable, especially when faced with the oft-invisible man.

"I'm not worried," she insisted. "I just don't understand

why there's a fake."

He hummed, and she could tell he didn't believe her. "The real helmet is kept under high security in the artifacts warehouse. We've never taken it out into public. It's not exactly the sort of thing you'd want falling into the wrong hands."

"Why not?" she said. "It's useless, isn't it? Captain Chromium destroyed it."

"Eh . . ." Simon rocked his head to the side, squinting one eye as if to say this one minor detail might have been a bit of an oversight. "That part of the legend might have been a bit embellished. We did claim the helmet during the Battle for Gatlon. And Hugh did try to destroy it, but . . ." He shrugged.

"But . . . what?" said Nova, suddenly breathless. "It's not destroyed?"

Simon gave her a sympathetic look. "Don't worry. No one is ever going to use that helmet to torment the people of this city again. We'll see to that."

Her fingers grasped at the air, as if the real helmet might be there, waiting for her to grab it. "So . . . can people go see it?"

"Ace Anarchy's helmet?

She nodded. "Renegades, I mean. Obviously not the public, but . . . if one of us wanted to see it, could we?"

The Dread Warden chuckled. "Maybe if you made a really great bribe to the people in weapons and artifacts. I hear Snapshot is a sucker for sour gummies. Hard to come by anymore, those are, but if you find some, she might let you take a peek."

Nova frowned, unable to tell if he was joking or not.

It didn't matter, though. She wanted more than just a peek, and he'd already given her so much more than she'd expected.

The helmet was intact. Ace's helmet was not destroyed, and it was here, in this very building, somewhere beneath her very feet.

Her communicator chimed again. She glanced down automatically, scanning the new message from Adrian.

> Seriously—you're not actually passed out in a ditch, are you?

She shook her head, unable to tell if he was trying to be funny. If so, the humor was lost on her jumbled thoughts.

"Everything all right?" said Simon.

"Oh yeah." She waved her hand, finding it a challenge to remain composed when it seemed that the foundation of everything she knew to be true had just shifted beneath her. "That's just the, uh . . . healers, wondering where I went. I'm supposed to be in the med wing, but . . . I get restless being cooped up in one spot for too long."

He nodded, as if this made perfect sense, and started heading back toward the central lobby. Sensing that she was intended to follow, Nova glanced one more time at the helmet then fell into step beside him.

"Adrian told us all about your run-in with Max. That was brave, what you did. I'm sorry you got hurt."

"Max was the one that got hurt. I just passed out for a bit."

Simon cast her a sideways look.

"Besides, I didn't actually know what would happen if I went in there, so I'm not sure we can call it brave."

His lips started to tick upward. "Would you prefer if I said it was reckless and dangerous?"

Nova held his gaze, unable to tell if he was teasing her or condemning her . . . or if this, too, was a compliment of sorts. Finally, she responded, "All in a day's work, right?"

Then, to her endless dismay, Simon Westwood laughed. A true, boisterous laugh, warm and guttural.

That was when it occurred to her that she was chatting with the Dread Warden. She had just made him *laugh*.

And not once had it crossed her mind that perhaps she should be using this chance to contemplate the best way of killing him.

Which was savvy, she told herself. She had counted the cameras when she stepped off the elevator. She knew there was no way to murder someone here and get away with it.

But still . . . shouldn't the thought at least have crossed her mind?

"Do you know how Max is doing?" she said, eager for a new topic of conversation.

"He's going to be fine," said Simon. "The amount of blood loss made the wound appear far worse than it really was. Of course, due to the nature of his gift we can't tend to him with prodigy healers, but even the normal doctors say that he will recover quickly. Perhaps with a scar, but what young man doesn't appreciate a new scar from time to time?"

They passed the painting of the Day of Triumph and Simon paused to look at it—not admiring so much as thoughtful.

"Perhaps," he continued, "this experience has taught Max to be a bit more careful when it comes to experimenting with powers he's not yet fully in control of. It's a hard lesson for any prodigy to learn, but I think him more so than most."

Nova's gaze traced the figures in the painting again. Captain Chromium holding up the helmet that she could now think of only as the impostor, knowing that pike had never been driven through it to begin with. Then she stared at Ace's body, fallen at the Captain's feet, and knew that this part of the legend, too, was a lie.

And also—

"Someone is missing from this picture," Nova said. "Max was there too, wasn't he?"

Simon did not look at her as he answered, "Did Adrian tell you, or did you figure it out for yourself?"

"A little bit of both." She tore her focus away from the painting. "What really happened? How did Max get Ace Anarchy's power?"

Simon scratched his beard. "Well. It was near the end of the fight. We couldn't bring Max into it before that, because his abilities would affect our allies as well as our enemies. But by that point, Ace Anarchy had separated himself from the rest of the gangs. He was standing up on one of the arcades of the cathedral, attacking those still on the ground. Of course, Hugh could withstand him more than anyone. Realizing this was our best chance, he went and got Max, who we'd hidden in a nearby cellar with a nurse to take care of him. Hugh strapped him to his back and returned to the battle. He's told me it was the most difficult thing he's ever done, knowing the danger he was putting Max into, but he didn't think there would be any other way."

Nova's jaw fell open as she listened, trying to picture the scene. The righteous, invincible Captain Chromium . . . charging into battle with a baby strapped to his back? She didn't know if she should find the image horrifying or hysterical.

"He scaled one of the side walls," said Simon, his voice having gone distant. "I remember looking up and seeing him at one point and realizing what he was going to do. Hugh reached the top, and Ace realized he was there. The closer he and Max got, the weaker Ace became, but he was still strong. He still tried to fight. He knew he couldn't hurt Hugh, so he focused his attacks on Max, knowing that must be the cause of his weakness." Simon paused, before adding, "I remember how remarkable it seemed at the time that Max didn't utter a sound—not a single cry."

Nova shuddered.

"Eventually, Ace lost enough power that he couldn't keep fighting. Hugh managed to wrestle the helmet away from him—and the moment he had the helmet, it was as if all the fight drained out of Ace Anarchy. A third of the church was destroyed by that point, one side of it was on fire, nearly all the Anarchists were dead, and Captain Chromium had his helmet. He must have known he'd lost. So . . . Hugh went to finish it, when Ace Anarchy simply . . . turned and jumped. He jumped from three stories up, right into the fire."

Nova was looking at the painting again, and found it astounding how a piece of art that had gotten so much wrong could still be here, in such a place of honor. Maybe it was testament to how much the truth, in this case, had never really mattered.

"Thank you for telling me," she murmured.

"No, thank you."

Brow crinkling, she looked up at the Dread Warden. He wasn't looking at her or the painting, but smiling softly into space. "I was never able to hold Max. Not when he was a baby, not now when he's hurt or sad. But I still love him. He's as much a son to me as Adrian is. So . . . thank you." He met Nova's gaze. "For trying to save him."

"Even if I had no idea what I was doing and really just ended up making things worse?"

His smile broadened. "Even if."

Nova cleared her throat and found herself unable to hold his gaze. "I should really get back to the medical wing."

"Please," he said, gesturing toward the elevator. "Don't let me keep you another minute. The healers can be dreadfully pushy when they feel they're in danger of being ignored."

Not entirely sure if she should say good-bye or thank you or something else entirely, Nova lifted her hand in an awkward wave, tucked her head down, and made her way back to the elevators. She passed the reception desk again, where Prism was now seated. She chirped a good-bye to Nova as she passed.

Once the elevator arrived, Nova stepped inside and leaned against the wall, rubbing her forehead. Her thoughts swam with the Dread Warden's recount of the Battle for Gatlon. Of Max's involvement—how Hugh Everhart had put that innocent baby's life at risk, and how Ace had done his best to kill him in order to protect himself.

Again and again, her thoughts circled back to that broken helmet on its pedestal, as dangerous as a child's dress-up toy.

While somewhere within Renegade Headquarters, they had the real thing. Ace Anarchy's helmet. Intact and waiting.

CHAPTER THIRTY-SEVEN

N OVA LET THE DOOR SLAM shut behind her. Not because she was angry, but because even after the long walk back to Wallowridge, she was still dazed from the discovery of Ace's helmet and all it meant. For her. For the Anarchists. For the Renegades, who probably had as much power contained within that one object as all their patrol units put together. They may have opted not to use it for their own purposes so far, but it still remained a possibility that they could at any time. So long as the helmet was in their possession, no one stood a chance to oppose them.

As Nova passed through the front room, Honey appeared in the doorway to the kitchen, digging a spoon into a mason jar full of golden honey. "That isn't your normal stealthy entrance," she said, lifting the spoon out. The honey began to drizzle down, before Honey deftly spun the spoon's handle to catch it. "Did something happen?" She shoved the spoon into her mouth, sucking on it like a lollipop.

Nova stared at her. *Did something happen? Did something happen?*

"Sort of," she said, squeezing past Honey and unwinding the communicator band from her wrist. She deposited it on the kitchen counter. It was the first time she'd taken it off since they had decided to leave their home in the subway tunnels, and her wrist felt bare without it. Bare—but also light and unencumbered.

"Uh-oh," said Honey, lifting a penciled eyebrow at the band. "You must be going somewhere the Renegades wouldn't approve of." She leaned saucily against the fridge. "Do tell."

"Later," said Nova. "There's something I need to do first."

She headed toward the back door and had just grabbed the knob when a small explosion vibrated through the walls. She looked up as a few drifts from the popcorn ceiling tumbled down onto the counters.

"Leroy is making up a new batch of something," Honey explained, dipping the spoon back into the honey. "Are you leaving already? You just got here."

Nova ignored her question. "You do realize we're trying to go unnoticed here, right?"

Honey smirked. "Sweetheart, some people just can't help being noticed."

Refraining from rolling her eyes, Nova asked, "Is Phobia here too?"

"No. Hasn't been all day. I think he spent the night back in the tunnels. He's better suited to the dankness and shadows, you know. Me? I'm so happy to be back in the sun." She sighed and cast a sweet smile at the small, dirty window over the kitchen sink.

Nova twisted the doorknob and pushed her way outside. "Don't get used to it," she muttered, stepping out onto the slim concrete porch.

She trekked through their small patch of weeds and thorns,

where Honey's bees were busy restoring their hives as fast as they could. The day before, Nova had noticed how their buzzing seemed happier than it ever had down in the tunnels, but now it served as little more than a distraction. She turned into the alleyway behind the house and started in the direction of Blackmire Way. It was nearing dusk, and the shadows from the surrounding row houses filled up the narrow spaces between buildings. She passed boarded-up windows and graffiti-covered fences and yards full of tufted dandelions. A flicker of light caught her eye and she glanced up to the second story of the corner house just as someone was throwing open the window sash. She paused in surprise. She'd gotten so used to thinking of the neighborhood as deserted, she was startled to find that they might have neighbors after all.

Or perhaps it was only the man she had kicked out of her own house before.

She was turning away when the hairs prickled on the back of her neck. Her stomach clenched and her hand fell instinctively on the shock-wave gun at her belt.

It was, she realized a second later, a distinctive scent that had caught her attention. The sweet aroma of coconut body oil mixed with the faintly rotten taint of sulfur and gunpowder.

She forced her shoulders to relax as she turned, letting her hand fall from the weapon.

Ingrid was leaning against the side of the building Nova had just passed, one heel casually pressed against the brick, her arms crossed over her chest. She was dressed in something that might have been intended to be a disguise: skinny black pants and a high-collared jacket that covered both her armbands and her midriff. Even her thick coils of hair had been imprisoned beneath a knit cap.

Otherwise, she did not look much different than she had the last time Nova had seen her, after they had fled from the tunnels. She was clean and did not seem to have gone hungry, at least, and only when Nova had the thought did she realize some part of her had been worried about her.

"How's life in the Renegades?" Ingrid said, her voice dripping with disdain. "Have you completely turned your back on us yet, or are you still holding on to the charade that you're on our side?"

Nova's jaw twitched. "You and the others knew exactly what my plan and intentions were from the first day I decided to go through with this. Perhaps you'll recall that you were the one who betrayed *me*, not the other way around."

Ingrid waved one hand languidly through the air, as if she had long ago tired of these ruminations, though Nova felt they still hadn't really had the chance to discuss what happened at the library. She understood that Ingrid had sought to exact some revenge against Captain Chromium and the Dread Warden by harming Adrian, and maybe even killing him. But she still couldn't fathom what had possessed Ingrid to keep it from her. To lead her into that trap along with the rest of the team.

Except she also knew that she would not have gone along with it. It wasn't in keeping with her mission, for one, and . . . she wasn't convinced that Adrian, Ruby, and Oscar deserved to be incinerated by one of the Detonator's bombs.

"What do you want?" said Nova. "Cyanide was the one who told you to leave, so if you're wanting to move in or something, it's not exactly up to me."

"Please," said Ingrid with a snort. "I've survived long enough without charity from you or Leroy Flinn or anyone else. The last thing I need is to be holed up in this ghost town." She shot a rueful look at the surrounding alley.

"Then why are you here?"

"I have a proposition for you, *Insomnia*. One that stands to serve us both."

Nova frowned. She knew Ingrid used her Renegade alias only to irritate her. The really irritating part, though, was that it worked.

"A proposition," Nova drawled.

Ingrid nodded, though a dark smirk had crossed her features. "If you're willing to hear it. Of course . . . you don't have much of a choice. Assuming you don't want all your new friends at Renegade Headquarters to find out exactly who Nova McLain really is."

Nova's brow furrowed, as much in dismay as anything. "Seriously, Ingrid? You're blackmailing me?" She cast her eyes toward the sky, which had darkened to a cool violet. "What is going on with you? Ever since the Renegade trials you've acted like I've somehow become the enemy." She took a few steps closer, tapping a finger against her own sternum. "I'm still Nightmare. I'm still the one you've been training for almost nine years, with one purpose. To destroy the Renegades. Not just Captain Chromium or the Council, not just a single patrol unit, but the whole lot of them. The entire organization. So *maybe*, instead of sneaking up on me in back alleys and threatening the one mission that might actually stand a chance in helping us accomplish that goal, you should take a moment and remember who we are. Who *I* am."

Pushing herself off the wall, Ingrid sauntered closer until she stood nearly toe to toe with Nova. "I hope you mean that. Because this is your chance to prove it. To show me that what happened at the library was just"—she shrugged wistfully—"an unfortunate but temporary lack of judgment."

Nova gawked at her. "Sure," she said slowly, "if you mean *your* lack of judgment. If you had trusted me from the start, the entire fiasco wouldn't have happened. The Librarian would be alive, we'd still have access to his stockpile and his distributors, and—oh yeah, we wouldn't have revealed ourselves to the Renegades and been driven out of our own home."

"Home?" said Ingrid, guffawing. "Those tunnels were never our home."

"So not the point," Nova shot back.

Ingrid peered down her nose at Nova, scrutinizing her. "Interesting you should mention the Librarian, given that the only reason I killed him was to protect *you*."

"Right," said Nova. "I'm sure you weren't at all concerned with him giving up any number of *your* secrets. Exactly how many explosives have you and Leroy sold to the Librarian for overseas buyers? It wouldn't surprise me if that's an actual war crime, come to think of it . . ."

Ingrid's lips curved. It was nowhere near a real smile, but it was a nice change from her scowl all the same. "There again, you and I have something in common. Although it doesn't much matter at this point if the Renegades discover my crimes, I sense you're still quite intent on keeping yours hidden. Now—picture this." She stepped closer and rested an elbow on Nova's shoulder, dropping her voice to a whisper. "Imagine a scenario in which the Renegades no longer cared to find the mysterious Nightmare. In which they lost interest in uncovering her identity. In which they left her completely alone."

Nova narrowed her eyes in suspicion. "Sounds unlikely."

"Not," said Ingrid, lifting a finger, "if they have every reason to believe that Nightmare is dead."

A chill swept down Nova's spine, and she did her best to conceal it by shaking Ingrid's arm off her shoulder. "Tell me this isn't some roundabout way of threatening to kill me in my sleep. Because, you know . . ." She gestured to her head. "Sleep. Not really my thing."

Ingrid let out a bellowing laugh, one that was far more boisterous than Nova felt her comment deserved. "You see?" she said. "Rooming with Honey has a tendency to make one just a little too melodramatic. No, no. I don't want to kill you. I just want to fight you. Publicly. And in the end, the whole world, especially the Renegades, will be watching as we tear each other apart . . ." She shrugged. "Metaphorically speaking."

Nova eyed her, struggling to parse out Ingrid's meaning from her words. "You want to fake our deaths?"

"Not exactly." Ingrid brightened. "I want to fake the deaths of Nightmare and the Detonator."

Nova's face must have been skeptical, because Ingrid ducked close to her again, her fingers painting an invisible picture into the air. "We'll stage it to appear as though Nightmare is furious over the death of the Librarian, and she blames me. Or—the Detonator."

"You are the Detonator."

"Keep up. We find a public place, and ensure at least one Renegade is present. Not too many. We don't want them getting in our way before we can finish. You and I fight, in full view of everyone, and in the end . . . you shoot me at the same time that I blow you up, and everyone sees it happen. Except you'll be using blanks and I . . . well, I won't really blow you up, but I can make it believable enough." She winked.

Nova was still frowning. "And when there are no bodies?"

"We'll stage it to appear that the explosions destroy us both. They won't be surprised if there's nothing left. Now, stop dwelling on insignificant details and focus on the big picture." Her eyes burned, suddenly intense. "They would stop hunting us. They would stop hunting *you*. How much easier would it be for you to continue with your work inside the Renegades if no one was investigating Nightmare anymore?"

Nova swallowed, unable to form a counterargument.

"Besides," Ingrid drawled, smirking, "you still owe me."

"Owe you? For what?"

"Killing the Librarian."

Nova laughed. "You didn't—"

"Yes, I did. Say what you want about what happened that day. He would have told the Sentinel everything, and the Sentinel would have taken it right back to the Council. I protected you."

"I wouldn't have needed protection if it wasn't for your asinine plan."

"You wouldn't need protection if you were capable of dealing with these situations when they come up. If you had the guts to take out Cronin yourself or Narcissa or even Captain Chromium for that matter. Face it, Nova. Despite all your talk, you're afraid to make the tough decisions when they need to be made. That's why you still need the Anarchists. That's why you still need me."

Nova clenched her jaw, angry sparks flickering across her vision. But her fury was overshadowed by the insecurities Ingrid's words stirred up. Because of her hesitation, she had failed to kill the Captain. She wouldn't have killed Cronin, even to save herself. She had chosen to let Narcissa go, knowing full well that she would endanger her mission going forward.

"You think about it," said Ingrid, rocking back on her heels. "I'm sure you'll make the right decision. How about I come back tonight and we can start hashing out the details? Right now . . ." She peered past Nova's shoulder. "It looks like you have company."

Nova glanced back.

Her heart launched into her throat.

Through a gap in the alley, past a chain-link fence and a half-disassembled car, a figure was strolling up the sidewalk.

She blinked rapidly, sure that the sight of him was some hallucination, some aftereffect of being in contact with Max, perhaps. Because what in this great city would bring Adrian Everhart *here*?

"Look at him, all distracted and nervous," said Ingrid with a subtle coo in her voice.

Cursing, Nova turned and shoved Ingrid toward the wall, trying to push her out of sight. "Get back before he sees you."

"Oh please. He's caught up in his own thoughts—talking to himself, probably planning out whatever adorably pathetic thing he's going to say when he sees you."

"What?" Nova glanced back, but Adrian had already passed out of view.

"I trust you've noticed how he looks at you, observant as you are." Ingrid's grin turned teasing. "Be careful, little Nightmare. Renegade runs in the blood of that one, maybe more than anyone else in this town."

Nova's heart was still drumming, panic thundering through her veins as she pictured Honey in the kitchen, Leroy upstairs . . . but still, something about the look on Ingrid's face gave her pause. "You know he's the son of Lady Indomitable."

Ingrid guffawed. "Of course I know that. She wasn't the first superhero we killed, but she might have been the first one that really mattered." Her cruel smirk made Nova's blood run cold.

"You killed her?"

"Not *me*," Ingrid said, as if this were obvious. "There was still something left of her, after all."

"But you know who did. Was it an Anarchist?"

Ingrid stilled and peered at Nova, her gaze darkening. "What does it matter to you?"

Nova took a step back and shook her head. "It doesn't."

Then she turned and started to sprint back to the house.

"See you tonight!" Ingrid called after her, and Nova would have shot her with the stun gun again just to make her be quiet, except she didn't have the time.

CHAPTER THIRTY-EIGHT

I T WASN'T A LONG RUN back to the house, and yet she was breathless as she barged through the back door into the kitchen, her pulse pounding in her ears.

The mason jar of honey had been left out on the counter, the sticky spoon balanced across the top, but Queen Bee was nowhere to be seen. Nova darted across to the staircase and was halfway up the steps when she heard a knock at the front door. She squeaked and barged into Leroy's room. His lab equipment took up half the space, some concoction left bubbling in a copper pot on an electric burner. But Leroy himself had disappeared.

Spinning around, Nova ran across the space into the second bedroom she now shared with Honey, but it, too, was empty but for their sleeping bags and Honey's air mattress and a few pieces of lingerie tossed haphazardly across the floor.

Nova's gaze swept up to the attic access door in the ceiling. It was meant to be Phobia's space up there, though she wasn't sure how much he'd actually been using it.

Another knock sounded at the door.

Gulping, Nova headed back down the stairs, stopping to peer behind every door and into every closet she passed, but there was no sign of Honey or Leroy.

She was still shaking when she finally opened the front door.

Her first impression of seeing Adrian standing on the stoop of the row house was that he was trying very, very hard not to appear awkward, and it wasn't working.

He smiled. Uncomfortable and uncertain. Nova was still far too frazzled to return it.

"Hi," he said.

"What are you doing here?" she blurted in response.

Adrian started, tucking his hands into his pockets. "I was worried about you."

Those simple words shattered Nova's mounting frustration with him, but did nothing to dissuade the panic of him being there. Her shoulders drooped slightly, but try as she might, she couldn't rearrange her features into something calm, confident, even welcoming. So instead, she just kept staring at him, her hand unable to release the doorknob.

"I sent you about a million messages . . . ," Adrian added, even as his gaze slipped down to her wrist. "Somehow it hadn't occurred to me that you might have just taken the band off." Taking one hand from his pocket, he scratched behind his ear. "I was having visions of you passed out in a gutter somewhere."

"Oh. Right," Nova stammered, remembering the concerned messages she'd gotten from him while she was still at headquarters. "I, um . . ." She searched for an explanation. "I take it off to . . . shower."

The moment she said it she became painfully aware of her

very dry, unwashed hair and the fact that she was still wearing the same clothes she'd been in last night when he found her inside the quarantine. She cleared her throat and gestured vaguely back toward the house. "I was going to . . . but then I got distracted with some stuff . . ." She inhaled sharply and finally managed something close to a smile. "But I'm fine. As you can see. Not passed out. Not in a gutter."

Adrian's gaze slipped past her, darting around the front room. The tattered furniture, the stained carpet, the peeling wallpaper. Though he said nothing and his expression remained perfectly neutral, Nova had the distinct sense that her real home wasn't adding up to be much better than the gutter he'd imagined.

Or maybe she was just being sensitive.

"Uh . . . you don't want to come in, do you?"

"Okay."

She gawked at him, horrified. "Really?"

Though he'd sounded eager before, Adrian now seemed to hesitate. "If that's all right?"

It was certainly, absolutely *not* all right, and Nova struggled to think of a reason, but it occurred to her that it might be just as suspicious to send him away as it was to let him inside. Pressing her lips, she stepped back out of the doorway, her mind scouring through every object and possession in the house and trying to determine how any of it could be traced back to Nightmare or the other Anarchists. They had done little to the place since claiming it for themselves, other than a bit of surface cleaning to make it somewhat habitable.

Adrian stepped inside. Nova gulped and shut the door.

His focus went to the arrangement of photographs on the wall. He reached out and straightened one of the frames.

"Are you hungry?" Nova asked, before he could ask who any of the strangers in the photographs were. She trotted past him without waiting for an answer. Swooped one of Honey's rhinestone hairpins off the coffee table as she passed, tucking it into her pocket. Gathered up Leroy's old copies of *Apothecary* magazine and shoved them into a drawer.

"We have . . ." Reaching the kitchen, she opened a cupboard and found herself staring at half a dozen mason jars. "Honey."

Adrian followed her into the kitchen and she could sense him behind her, staring into the mostly bare cupboard. She shut it and tried the next cupboard, discovering a box of unopened crackers and two cans of tuna fish. She dared not even pretend to look in the refrigerator—she'd opened it once when she first moved in and found the shelves mostly covered in mold. She hadn't bothered to open it since.

She grabbed the box of crackers and held them up for Adrian to see.

"I'm okay, actually," he said, and the look of confusion mixed with just a hint of pity was impossible not to notice.

Nova put the box back and shut the door. "We mostly eat out," she said, by way of explanation.

Adrian's eye caught on something through the back window and his brow furrowed.

Nova tensed, imagining that Ingrid was in the alley or that Honey or Leroy were in the yard. But when she looked, it was only . . .

Hives. And nests. And bees. Lots and lots of bees.

"That's . . . um. My uncle's?" she ventured. "He, uh . . . he heard there's good money to be made in beekeeping these days. I guess honey is a pretty desirable . . . commodity. It's"—she brushed a hand through the air—"sort of a new thing he's trying out."

Adrian's eyes were still narrowed, but now there was humor along with the curiosity. "I'm pretty sure honey bees are the only ones that actually produce honey."

She glanced out the window again. There were honey bees, but they were mixed together with a heady assortment of buzzing hornets and wasps, yellow jackets and even fat little bumblebees.

"I know. I know that," she said. Then she threw up her hands, as if exasperated. "That's what I keep trying to tell him, but he sort of does his own thing. Doesn't always like to listen to me."

"I'm very familiar with that feeling," said Adrian. He grinned, and she could tell it was a look intended to comfort her, as if to say that he wasn't judging her. That she could relax.

That, she thought, might be the funniest thing of all.

"Is your uncle home? I thought maybe I could introduce myself."

"Oh. No. He's . . . out."

Adrian nodded. His gaze darted toward the small card table they were using as a makeshift dining table, even though Nova suspected not one meal had yet to be eaten there. There were chairs, too, but she dared not ask him to sit.

"I'm sorry," Adrian said suddenly. "Maybe I shouldn't have come."

She stared at him, and though she could tell he was embarrassed, she wasn't sure what was causing it—the sad state of her so-called home or her obvious lack of hospitality skills?

He fidgeted, tapping one knuckle idly against the countertop. "I didn't mean to intrude. I just . . . was worried. When you weren't responding to the messages . . ." He trailed off. Clearing his throat, he finished lamely, "Are you all right?"

She felt the knots in her stomach tighten even more. "Yeah, fine. I'm just not used to having company." She was grateful that this, at least, was not a lie.

"No, I meant, are you feeling all right? The healers said they hadn't released you yet. They were worried there might still be side effects, or even . . . I mean, we still don't know for sure if . . ."

If Max took all your powers from you. We still don't know if you're a prodigy or not.

"I feel fine," she said, trying to sound convincing. "Completely normal." She attempted a more enthusiastic smile, eager to prove that everyone was concerned over nothing. "Wide-awake and full of energy!" She gave two encouraging thumbs-up.

Adrian grinned. "Well. If you do start to feel anything . . . not just tired, but . . . dizzy or weak or . . . anything. Just let me know. Or one of the healers."

"Yeah, sure. Of course."

He looked again at the card table and she could see him contemplating something. "Would you mind if I . . ." He took out his marker and motioned toward the table, as if this gesture adequately finished his question.

"If you what?"

Without responding, Adrian bent over the table and started to draw onto its dull gray surface. Nova cocked her head, mesmerized by the quick, confident movements of his hand. There was no hesitation, no uncertainty as to where to place the marker next, where to draw a line or a curve. Soon she saw a round vase emerge, overflowing with an arrangement of roses and lilies.

The moment he brought the flowers to life, their fragrance drifted through the room, pushing back the staleness of the house.

Adrian capped the marker and stepped back, frowning at the arrangement. "I really need to start carrying some more colors."

Nova laughed. It was true that the monochromatic shades of gray lifted from the table lent a muted aspect to the blooms, but they still brightened the little table, the little kitchen, the little home.

And it was clear, to her, at least, how much they did not belong there.

"Will they die?" she said, reaching forward to feel the soft outer petals of one of the roses.

"Just like real flowers," he said, though his mouth quirked as he glanced at her again. "But I can always make more."

That look made warmth spread across Nova's cheeks and she turned away, picking up the communicator band off the counter and busying herself by putting it back on. Ingrid's words came back to her. *I trust you've noticed how he looks at you* . . .

"So, um, I had a thought," said Adrian.

Nova lifted her eyebrows, but found she wasn't quite ready to turn back to him fully. "About?"

"Winston Pratt."

She stilled. Hesitated. Then straightened her spine, preparing for . . . what? An attack? An accusation?

She told herself she was being ridiculous. If Adrian had come here to cast accusations at her, it wouldn't have taken this long for him to get around to it. And he certainly wouldn't have drawn her a vase of flowers first.

"I think," Adrian continued, "we should look in to Cosmopolis Park."

One hand still tight around the band on her wrist, Nova forced herself to look at him. But Adrian was adjusting some of the blooms inside the vase.

"What?"

"Just to check it out." He pushed his glasses up the bridge of his nose. "I know Winston was lying about almost everything, but the carnival is one of the few possible clues he gave us. I thought maybe we could go and have a look around. Maybe you could talk to your old boss, see if he's ever heard anything about a . . . a girl being abandoned there. Or if he's ever seen anything suspicious, anything that might tie back to Nightmare or the Anarchists . . ." Finally, he looked up at her, and Nova couldn't quite read his expression. The self-assuredness from when he'd been drawing was gone, replaced with something uneasy, but . . . hopeful?

"You sure do want to find her, don't you?"

"Nightmare?" said Adrian, surprised. "She is Gatlon's most wanted. Well . . . her and the Detonator, I guess."

"Yeah, but . . . how did *you* get so involved with the investigation? Is it because Danna and the others fought her at the parade?"

"That's part of it," he said, that small crease forming between his eyebrows. "But also, she attacked the Council. She attacked my dad."

She looked away. "So why isn't he looking for her?"

"They don't really do field work anymore. The Council wants to find her as much as anyone, but that's part of why they built the Renegades. They can't do everything themselves. Either way, finding Nightmare is a priority for everyone." Adrian looked down, fidgeting with the marker. "It's been years since such a blatant attack was made. In broad daylight, surrounded by both civilians and Renegades. Plus, as far as I know, no one's ever come that close to actually killing the Captain. It shows that she's not to be underestimated."

Nova's chest tightened. In a way, she felt a surge of pride to think she'd gotten closer than anyone. But at the same time, it served as a reminder that *close* was not *success*. She had failed, and now she had every superhero in the city searching for her.

And Adrian . . . if he knew . . . if he ever found out . . .

The spark of pride quickly extinguished.

"So . . . ," said Adrian, his tone brightening a bit. "About the carnival. What do you think?"

She pondered, but could think of no reason to reject the idea. If anything, going to Cosmopolis Park might serve to lead Adrian and the Renegades further away from the truth of her identity and whereabouts.

At least, she didn't think there was any harm to it. Even if her paperwork said that she, Nova McLain, had worked there, Nightmare still had no real connection to the place.

"Sure. Okay."

"Cool. Great. Uh . . . we can meet, say . . . tomorrow? At noon? *If*," he amended, "I can get a release from the medical wing by then."

Nova rolled her eyes. "Just let them try to keep me back."

Adrian smiled, and Nova's heartbeat skipped to see the hint of dimples that were usually kept hidden. "Well, I guess I should let you . . . rest." His brow knitted. "Or whatever it is you're doing."

He did not move, though, and Nova had the distinct impression he was looking for an invitation. Some reason to linger.

She refused to give him one.

"Thanks for the flowers," she said, ushering him back toward the front door. "And for checking up on me. I'll see you tomorrow."

"Oh, hey," he said, stopping halfway out the door. "Are you planning to come back to headquarters tonight? Because I could, um, try bringing in some sandwiches again."

Her chest fluttered and Nova felt almost sad as she shook her head. "I think I might take the night off."

"Yeah. Of course. That's definitely the right plan."

He hesitated a moment more, then lifted a hand in a salute and stepped off the porch. Nova waited until his foot hit the sidewalk before closing the door.

She dropped her forehead against it with a groan, letting all the built-up frantic energy drain out of her.

"So that's the Everhart boy?"

Nova spun around. Honey and Leroy were both peering around the curve of the staircase's banner.

She waved her arms at them. "You couldn't stay hidden until he was at least off our street?"

Honey giggled. "We were just curious," she said. "It's a terrible shame he's a Renegade, isn't it? Otherwise, you could have asked him to stay for dinner."

CHAPTER THIRTY-NINE

◼

THE ENTRANCE TO COSMOPOLIS PARK was an enormous concrete archway molded into the shape of a giant carousel pony that seemed to stand guard over the old amusement park. The sculpture had once been painted in pretty peach and pearl white, but the paint had faded and chipped over the years. The proud beast had also lost one side of his face, probably due to vandalism during the Age of Anarchy, and no one had yet seen fit to repair it.

Nevertheless, the park was one of the many businesses in Gatlon City that had seen a resurgence since the Day of Triumph. It had never been out of operation, exactly, but under Anarchist rule, some villains had incurred a sizable fortune by turning the place into a haven for drug dealing, gambling, and brutal dogfights. Everyone knew the park was the domain of the Puppeteer, but he never bothered putting on any restrictions, so long as he was paid for using his space—whether in money or candy, as Nova had once heard.

When the Renegades reclaimed the city, it was one of the first areas they saw fit to revive—tearing down many of the ancient, weatherworn rides and constructing a fantasy land in its place, with a roller coaster, a Ferris wheel, and a vintage carousel surrounded by games of skill and chance and more than a few vendors of corn dogs and cotton candy. Yet, like so many of the Council's ongoing projects, they had stopped when the property was just shy of complete, leaving enough details lying around that one could easily recall what it had been, not all that long ago. The back few acres of the park remained fenced off and labeled with warning signs, informing visitors that this area was still under construction. Beyond the chain-link fence, guests could see a deteriorating fun house, grounded boats from the decrepit tunnel of love, and an entire row of carnival games left in shambles, their walls still hung with dozens of purple teddy bears that had been left to sag and grow mildew, abandoned to the elements.

Adrian was waiting beneath the horse statue's bridled mouth when Nova arrived. They hadn't discussed whether or not to wear their uniforms, and seeing him in jeans and a jacket made her instantly regret her choice to wear the gray bodysuit.

He grinned when he spotted her.

She glared back. "Seriously? You could have told me we were supposed to be incognito."

"I didn't think of it," he said. Reaching for the collar of his shirt, he pulled it down far enough to reveal the top of his own suit. "Would you feel better if I changed?"

"Not really," she muttered. "You draw enough attention as it is. Are you ready?"

"I already got our tickets," he said, pulling them from his pocket. He handed one to her, then cocked his head toward the gates. Nova's knuckles were white as she gripped the ticket, feeding it into the small machine beneath the horse's belly. A light flashed and she pushed through the rotating metal bars.

She cleared the entrance and paused on the other side, scanning the cacophony of lights and bodies, garish rides, chiming games, and booths full of cheap blow-up toys and glow-stick jewelry.

It was like a completely different place in the daytime.

"So?" said Adrian, joining her. "How are you feeling?"

A flurry of emotions responded in answer to the question. She was edgy, she was nervous, she was shaking with adrenaline as her body readied itself for what was coming.

But that wasn't what Adrian was asking. She turned to him with the brightest smile she could muster and said, "I didn't sleep a wink last night, so I feel amazing."

He chuckled, and his relief was evident. "Good. I'd hate to lose you after we just found you."

"You really think they would kick me off patrols, just because I'd be suddenly forced to sleep like everyone else does?"

"Not if I could help it."

They made their way through the crowds of squealing children and laughing parents, through the aromas of sugary sweet cotton candy and fried funnel cakes that wafted around them. When Adrian had first suggested coming to look around the park, Nova had known little about it, having only been taken there by Leroy and Winston one time, many years ago. But now she felt that she knew the place intimately.

While the city had slept last night, she had been here, preparing for the stunt she and Ingrid were going to pull off.

Here, today.

She had started to plot even before Ingrid had arrived late last night. Because as much as she refused to buy into the idea that she owed Ingrid anything, there was an undeniable appeal to faking her own death. No more Renegades hunting her. No more *Adrian* hunting her.

She wasn't sure they were ready. She would have preferred to take more time to prepare, but she also couldn't deny that the opportunity had presented itself and was too hard to pass up. Adrian and the Renegades had reason to suspect that Nightmare was associated with the carnival. She and Adrian were investigating that day.

It would be their best chance to make it believable.

"So," said Adrian, "where should we start?"

They both looked around again. There was a game of strength nearby, where kids were trying to swing a hammer bigger than themselves in order to get a weight to hit an alarm bell at the top. Beyond that was an abundance of games featuring everything from darts and balloons and bottles, to stacks of milk jugs, softballs, and hoops.

Nova was tempted to guide him straight toward the clues she'd spent the night placing strategically throughout the park, but she worried it would be suspicious if it was all too easy. Instead, she shrugged. "If you were a villain who spent most of your time at an amusement park, what would you do?"

"Games, probably."

She frowned. "Games?"

"We don't know much about Nightmare, but we do know she's a good shot. She has to practice, right?"

"And you think she practices with carnival games."

His eyes twinkled. "What's wrong? Are you afraid I might beat you?"

She pointed. "At *carnival* games? Hardly."

Laughing, Adrian dragged her toward a game where the goal was to hit a bull's-eye painted over the Puppeteer's face. "Good, because you really have nothing to fear."

And he was right.

Adrian might have been able to draw a functional rifle or illustrate a perfectly balanced blow dart, but he turned out to be a terrible shot himself. They made their way through the games and Nova defeated him at every shooting, aiming, throwing, and targeting contest the park had to offer, though Adrian easily bested her when it came to challenges of strength.

After nearly an hour, Adrian had won a small light-up wand that some marketing company had emblazoned with Blacklight's name, even though Blacklight had never used a wand so far as Nova knew. Meanwhile, she traded in all her mini prizes for a gigantic Dread Warden doll, which was almost as tall as she was. Adrian cracked up when the carnival worker handed it to her.

"Look, I won you a prize," she said, promptly passing it on to him.

"What? You don't want it?"

"I truly don't."

Adrian held the doll out at arm's length. "I should probably be flattered, but I can't help but feel that there might be something a little creepy about having a giant doll of your dad lying around."

"You think?"

He peered at her over the doll's head. "Will it hurt your feelings if I give it to him for his birthday? He will find it hysterical."

The doll *was* pretty hilarious, with its mop of felted hair and flimsy cape. "Do with it what you will," she said. "My feelings will survive."

He tucked the doll under one arm as they started to make their way through the carnival again.

"How weird is it?" Nova asked. "To know that so many people completely, blindly idolize your dads like that?"

"Honestly, the weirdest part is that you sort of get used to it after a while." Adrian shrugged. "And I'd rather people idolize them than want to kill them. Unfortunately, there doesn't seem to be much middle ground with how people feel about the Council."

She tore her gaze away.

"Luckily, these days, more people appreciate prodigies than despise them. I know there are still people out there who don't trust us, especially after all the things they went through under the villain gangs."

Nova knew it was true. Even today, walking around the carnival in her Renegade uniform, there wasn't much variety in the reactions she got from complete strangers. Either they stopped to stare at her with slack-jawed smiles and awestruck eyes, whispering giddily once she passed, or their expressions soured upon noticing the gray uniform and the red *R*, and they would promptly cross the path or turn another direction entirely.

She couldn't be sure, though, if that hatred was directed at Renegades, or all prodigies. People were still afraid of them, and rightly so. Even those who admired the Renegades, their supposed protectors, still seemed to harbor a respect that bordered on nervous insecurity.

Hero or villain, all prodigies were powerful. All prodigies were dangerous.

"—most people can see that we're not all like that," Adrian was saying, drawing her attention back to him. "Life is far better now than it ever was when Ace Anarchy was in charge, and that's because of the Renegades." He shook the doll. "And the Council."

Nova frowned. "Ace Anarchy wasn't actually in charge," she said, before she could restrain herself. "I mean, he . . . he was probably technically the ruler of the Anarchists, but I don't think he really wanted to *rule*, you know? He mostly . . . just . . . wanted the oppression of prodigies to stop." She swallowed. "At least that's what it always sounded like to me."

Adrian's lips quirked. "How forgiving does a person have to be in order to defend Ace Anarchy?"

"I'm not being forgiving. I'm just . . . I just think that he gets blamed for everything that happened during those years, when really . . . so much of it was because of the other gangs that rose to power in the absence of government. And that's not what he was trying to accomplish, either. He was all about personal freedom, personal responsibility, about taking care of yourself and your own, rather than expecting anyone to take care of you. He wanted to do away with oppression and regulations that only serve a small group of people, and . . . and . . . um." Her face flushed. "At least . . . that's . . . that's what some people say. About him."

Rather than looking at her like she had lost her mind, as Nova expected, Adrian's smile had grown. "Well, I have a feeling that if those people had ever actually met Ace Anarchy, they might feel a little differently."

Nova tensed. "Why? Have *you* met him?"

"Afraid not. And I'm not sorry that I'll never have the chance." His expression turned serious as he peered at her. "You don't actually think things are better now because of him. Do you?"

She considered her response for a long time. "I think a lot of horrible things happened during the Age of Anarchy, a lot of things that shouldn't have happened. But I also think that if Ace Anarchy hadn't done what he did . . . then *this*"—she tugged on the doll's cape—"wouldn't be possible. Prodigies would still be in hiding. People would still hate us."

Adrian's lips went taut, and Nova wondered if she had said too much.

But then he sighed. "I guess I can't argue that. But still, I can't help but believe that there was a better way to get from there to here."

Nova thought of all the buildings destroyed, all the people killed. Her sigh mimicked his. "I can't argue with that, either."

"One good thing that definitely came out of that time," said Adrian, opening his arms wide, "is that now, we have superheroes. Maybe that's the difference. Before, people saw us as freaks with scary powers. Now, they see us as . . . as inspirations."

"Inspirations?"

"Sure. Everyone wants to be a hero. When you think about it, it's a little sad that so few actually get to be one."

Nova couldn't contain a derisive sniff. "It would be sad, except they don't actually mean it."

Adrian cocked his head at her. "What do you mean?"

"There's no rule that says you have to be a prodigy to be a hero," she insisted. "If people wanted to stand up for themselves or protect their loved ones or do what they believe in their hearts is the *right* thing to do, then they would do it. If they wanted to be heroic, they would find ways to be heroic, even without supernatural powers." She waggled her fingers in mockery of said powers. "It's easy to say you want to be a hero, but the truth is most people are lazy and complacent. They have the Renegades to do all the rescuing and saving, so why should they bother? It's easier to just call the hotline, then turn the other way and pretend it's not your problem to solve."

Her words tasted bitter even on her own tongue, not because they were pessimistic, but because they were true.

Because of the Renegades, humanity was becoming weak and pathetic, as *she* had once been weak and pathetic. Waiting in the darkness of that closet, listening as her sister's cries were silenced. So hopeful, so trustworthy, believing with all her heart that the Renegades would come.

But they were false idols. Liars and cheats.

Maybe if she hadn't been waiting for the Renegades, she wouldn't have hidden in that closet. Maybe she could have put her parents' murderer to sleep sooner. Maybe she could have saved Evie.

Or maybe one of the neighbors would have heard the commotion and come to help, rather than assuming someone else would take care of it.

Maybe . . . just *maybe*.

"What do you propose?" said Adrian, slipping his free hand into his pocket as they meandered past a series of food vendors. "Should we open a hero-training course, open to non-prodigies? Teach them ethics and martial arts and . . . I don't know. Bravery. Do you think you can teach someone to be brave?"

Nova felt the side of her mouth lift, just a little, in some relief that he hadn't outright refuted her argument against heroes. "A hero-training course would be a start, but it would only go so far. As long as there are superheroes, there will be people who rely on them far too much. I think humanity would be better off if there were no . . . no prodigies at all."

For a moment, she'd almost said *Renegades*, before remembering who she was speaking to. But on further inspection, she realized it was true. It wasn't just Renegades who had caused so much trouble for humanity. It was the villains, too, though they'd only been reacting to centuries of hatred and discrimination.

How much better off would the world be if there were no prodigies at all?

"I agree that dependence might be a problem," said Adrian, with some amusement, "but no prodigies at all? That might be taking it a bit far."

"I don't think so."

"What about all the things the Council has built over the past nine years? All the things the Renegades do for this city, and the whole world, for that matter?"

"All things that non-prodigies would have built if we weren't around. All things that people would be doing *for themselves*. If there was no Council, they would have reestablished their own government by now, or at least be trying to. Putting together their own patrols and law enforcement, writing their own laws, building their own infrastructure . . ."

He cast a sideways look at her. "The world would be falling apart if it wasn't for us."

"The world was fine before prodigies got involved with it. It would be fine again. As it is, it's always going to be this way. Prodigies will always be at odds with one another, always fighting for power and dominance, and normal people will always suffer for it."

Adrian cocked his head and she could see him contemplating her words for a long time. "You're serious about this."

"Yeah, I am. Not that it matters, but I do believe humanity would be better off without us. Without prodigies or villains or the Renegades. Society would sort itself out, just like it has a hundred times throughout history, but it would do it a lot faster, and with a lot less turmoil, if it wasn't for our interference."

Adrien held her gaze for a long time. "That's bleak," he finally said.

Nova shrugged. "It's the truth."

They were quiet as they passed by the roller coaster, listening to the creak of the tracks and the screeches of the passengers.

Switching the doll to his other arm, Adrian finally released an exaggerated breath. "*Well.* Now that we have that important philosophical discussion out of the way . . . what next?" He pointed. "Roller coaster? Tilt-a-whirl? Are you hungry?"

Nova smiled, the knot in her chest quickly unwinding. "Correct me if I'm mistaken, but aren't we supposed to be looking for somebody?"

"You're absolutely right." Adrian tapped a finger against his lips. "And I think we should look for her"—he pointed—"on the Ferris wheel."

Nova followed his look to the colorful ride. "Yeah. That seems like a really likely hiding spot for a supervillain."

"Maybe not, but it will give us a good view of the park, and we can plot out a strategy from there."

It was an excuse, and not a particularly good one. Nova found her heart beginning to stutter as they made their way through the crowds. Because, for the first time since they'd arrived, she began to wonder why Ruby and Oscar and Danna hadn't joined them. She began to wonder why Adrian had asked *her* to join him, and not one of his more experienced teammates.

She began to wonder whether this whole day wasn't really about finding Nightmare at all.

But thinking that Adrian might have ulterior motives only led her thoughts down a path that made her palms sweat and her pulse flutter. She was picturing those small gondolas with her,

Adrian, and the doll crammed into one them. She was imagining their hips pressed against each other. His shoulder tucked against hers.

Or would it be so tight that he would put his arm around her? Her skin tingled with the very thought of it.

How was it that something that would have been unthinkable weeks ago was now so easy to imagine?

"Nova?"

"Ferris wheel," she said, then cleared her throat. "Sure. Okay."

They had not gone far, though, when there was a chorus of high-pitched screams: "*Renegade!*"

Nova turned to see a dozen children rushing toward them out of a yellow-striped circus tent, over which hung a sign that read PARTY CENTRAL. The kids themselves were wearing an assortment of masks and capes like those Nova had seen at the parade.

To her surprise, they did not run toward Adrian, but *her*, and it took her a moment to remember that she was the one in uniform.

"It's her! It's the one from the trials!" screamed a girl, to which a boy beside her responded, "Yeah, the one who beat the Gargoyle!"

She looked at Adrian, who appeared baffled himself, but the look quickly turned into a warm smile. "Hey, kids. You're right. This is Insomnia."

"Insomnia!" said the boy. "That's right! I was there that night—I gave you the Hero sign for sure."

"Oh. Thanks?" started Nova.

"Will you come to my birthday party?"

She looked down to see a small black-haired boy with a missing front tooth grinning up at them. He was the only kid in full superhero regalia—a Captain Chromium costume. His party hat read, in bold letters, CAPTAIN CHROMIUM'S SIDEKICK. "It's a superhero theme! Come on!"

Nova found herself being drawn toward the tent. She looked back at Adrian, bewildered, but relieved to find him trekking after them. He saw her expression and started to laugh.

They had just stepped into the overhang of the tent when Nova managed to shake the kids off her. "Hold on," she said, raising her hands. "Yes, I'm Insomnia. But he"—she pointed at Adrian—"is the real hero. You should definitely pester him instead."

Adrian lifted a challenging eyebrow at her, but it only took a heartbeat for the children to swarm around him. The birthday boy bounced on the balls of his feet. "You do look familiar. Are you a Renegade too?"

"I am," said Adrian, disgustingly composed.

Nova glared at him.

"What can you do?" asked one of the girls.

Adrian looked around and Nova followed the look. The small tent was crammed with long picnic tables covered in plastic cloths and folding chairs sporting clusters of balloons. On one table sat a homemade cake and a small stack of presents. There were adults too—the parents of all these children, Nova guessed, many of whom had ceased their conversations to stare at the new arrivals.

"What can I do?" said Adrian, and Nova saw his hand inching toward his pocket. His eyes brightened as he knelt down on one knee so he was eye to eye with the birthday boy. "Tell me, what's one present that you really, really want for your birthday this year?"

The boy immediately blurted out, "A bike."

"A bike?" Adrian glanced up at a woman who resembled the boy. "Is that all right with you?"

"All right with me?" said the woman, looking pained. "It's not exactly . . . I can't afford . . ." She looked helpless, like it broke her heart to not be able to answer this one wish for her child. "I would love to give him one, if I could."

"Well," said Adrian, pulling out the marker. "Let's see what we can do."

CHAPTER FORTY

NOVA FOUND HERSELF LOITERING on the edges of the tent, watching the party with a mix of delight at seeing the children's innocent enthusiasm, but also a fair amount of pity when she thought of how very misplaced that enthusiasm was.

Renegades, she wanted to tell them, *they'll break your heart in the end.*

Except she couldn't convince herself that *this* Renegade would.

The birthday boy had been wobbling on his bike for several minutes now and had even managed to lift his feet from the ground and take half a turn around the tent before he panicked and crashed into a table—unhurt, thankfully. And as soon as the other kids saw what Adrian could do, they began plying him with requests. *Draw me a teddy bear . . . a lollipop . . . an airplane!* Until the tent was full of gifts, all in matching canary yellow pulled straight from the walls of the canvas tent.

Adrian never said no, not even when the requests became more and more outlandish (*now a tree house . . . a tree house with cannons . . .*

a tree house with cannons and also a moat being guarded by a robotic shark!), and he never seemed annoyed, even as the kids pressed in around him, leaving him little space to actually draw the things they wanted.

"Excuse me?"

Nova glanced down. The birthday boy's older sister, perhaps eight or nine years old, stood at the table beside her.

"Don't look at me," said Nova, lifting her hands. "My abilities are negligible compared to his."

The girl blinked, and it occurred to Nova that she probably had no idea what the word *negligible* meant. She was trying to come up with a synonym when the girl asked, "I was at the trials."

Nova blinked. "Oh. That. Right."

"You were amazing," said the girl, a little breathless. "You didn't even use superpowers!"

"No. No, that's the thing, my power is . . . not . . ." She glanced at Adrian. "Not showy, like that."

"Yeah, but that's what was so great about it." The girl's ears had gone pink. "I'm not a prodigy, but . . . seeing you, it sort of made me think that maybe I could be a Renegade, too, you know?"

Nova opened her mouth, but hesitated, unsure how to respond. She doubted the Renegades would ever recruit someone who didn't have at least a little bit of a superpower, but Danna and Adrian had both suggested that she could stay on the team even if Max had stolen her ability. And if that was possible, maybe a non-prodigy could someday be accepted too.

She thought back to her conversation with Adrian. He thought they were inspirations to the people. He believed that the existence of superheroes could encourage everyone to be more heroic. Nova had been adamant that he was wrong, but seeing the way this girl was looking at her now, she had to wonder.

So instead of rejecting the girl's dream, she leaned forward. "Can I tell you a secret?"

The girl inched closer, nodding giddily.

"You don't need to be a Renegade to be a superhero."

The girl's head listed to one side. "That sounds like something my mom would say."

Nova laughed. "Sorry. I mean, it's true, but . . . it's also sort of a cop-out, isn't it?"

"Did you get any cake?"

Startled by the change of topic, Nova shook her head. "No, but I don't—"

"I'll bring you some! My mom made it. It's *really* good." The girl scurried off before Nova could decline the offer.

Nova watched her go, bewildered, when she heard Adrian's voice cutting through the giggles. "Absolutely not. No one's getting a life-size pony. I'm drawing the line, kids!"

He was holding his marker overhead as if *it* were the prize the children were grabbing for.

Despite the fake annoyance in his voice, he was grinning.

No—he was beaming, lit up from the inside.

He caught her eye, and Nova's insides clenched. She had been aware that he was handsome from the start, but something about him in that exact moment went far beyond handsome. She told herself it was the lighting in the tent. It was half delirium because she hadn't eaten any lunch yet. It was . . . it was just Adrian. With that ease that Nova couldn't comprehend. A brightness that seemed at odds with everything she'd ever known.

"Here you go!"

A piece of cake appeared in front of Nova's nose and she gladly diverted her attention, her cheeks burning. Never had she been more grateful for a piece of cake that she didn't actually want. "Thank you," she said more effusively than might have been necessary. She took the plate and stuffed a bite of cake into her mouth.

She checked the time on her communicator band. Ingrid would be in position soon.

She glanced back at Adrian, who had looked away from her, and was, of course, drawing a pony onto the tent walls. "Um . . . we actually have to go," she said, shooting a smile at the girl, then gobbling down one more bite of cake, which was, in fact, delicious. "Thanks again."

She rose from the bench and made her way through the cluster of children. Adrian spotted her and paused with the pony half finished.

"First," said Nova, "you might want to check with the parents before giving any of these kids an actual pony. Second, we should probably move on?"

"First," said Adrian, "you missed a sprinkle." He reached out and brushed a thumb across the corner of Nova's mouth. She froze, the touch sending a quiver through her insides. When he pulled back, a small orange sprinkle was resting on the pad of his thumb, which he popped into his mouth, eyes teasing. "Second, you're absolutely right."

He turned away and finished sketching the pony, but when he pulled it from the tent wall, it was not a living creature, but a simple toy horse. "And we're calling that my big finale, kids," he said, capping the marker and moving away from the tent walls to a chorus of disappointed groans.

"I know, I know. But heroism awaits!" He paused to wave at the birthday boy and the parents, thanking them for their hospitality, before grabbing Nova's wrist and pulling her from the tent, laughing.

"You're welcome," said Nova, still a little shaken, her cheek tingling where he'd touched her.

He beamed, shaking out his wrist. "Much appreciated. That was fun, though."

"It's hard not to have fun when you're so popular, I expect."

He scoffed. "Like you wouldn't know." He imitated a girly voice as he squealed, "It's Insomnia! She beat Gargoyle! We love her!"

Rolling her eyes, she smacked Adrian in the arm. "Hey, where's the Dread Warden?"

"I gave him to the birthday boy. Did you know, he *really* likes superheroes?"

"Truly? I couldn't tell."

He grinned at her, and against all her better judgment, Nova found herself grinning back. When she managed to look away, Nova saw that they'd reached some of the kiddie rides—tiny choo-choo trains and dinosaur-themed roller coasters on each side.

"Somehow," she said, "I don't think we're going to find Nightmare here."

Ignoring her, Adrian asked, "Which ride did you operate?"

"What? Oh, um. A lot of them. We would rotate."

"Have you seen anyone today that you used to work with?"

Gulping, Nova glanced at the ride operators. According to her paperwork, she had worked here as recently as a couple months ago. Surely, if that story were real, she should have recognized lots of the employees here.

"Not really," she stammered. "I, uh . . . didn't usually work Thursdays."

They circled around to the back corner of the carnival, where the old, deteriorating structures of the park could be seen beyond the chain-link fence. Nova's jaw tensed as she stared at the weedy walkways between carnival games, at the roof of the funhouse looking like it was close to caving in.

"Are you hungry?" said Adrian.

She nodded.

But they had come too far. All the food stands were back toward the more popular areas of the park.

Dragging in a breath, Nova pointed. "There's a popcorn stand this way. Past the . . ." She licked her lips. "Past the gallery."

The gallery was a long wooden tunnel that divided the children's corner of the park with the faster, more adventurous rides on the other side. The paneled walls of the tunnel were hung with old photos of the carnival's history, from when it had first been founded nearly seventy years ago. As they entered the tunnel, Nova gravitated toward the first collection of photographs, feigning curiosity as she read the caption beneath a photo that showed a clown posed behind a group of kids. The next photo showed the horse statue at the park's entrance from back when it was brand-new. The third photo, a woman in a paper hat handing a cone of cotton candy to a man in a suit. It was all very old-fashioned, very quaint. Before the Age of Anarchy. Before the rise of the Renegades. A different place, a different time.

"Amazing it's lasted this long, isn't it?" said Adrian, strolling along the opposite wall.

Nova stayed where she was, hoping he would see it. Hoping he would find it on his own . . .

"Amazing," she breathed. She continued down the row of photos. Slowly. Expectantly. She was no longer seeing the photos— she'd seen them plenty the night before, anyhow. Happy families boarding the rickety old roller coaster. Happy couples stepping into the gondolas in the Tunnel of Love. Happy children waving from the carousel.

"Nova."

She knew immediately by the tone of his voice that he'd found it.

She stilled, closing her eyes, and exhaled.

"Nova, look."

She turned and found him staring at the picture. *The* picture, the one that had taken her three hours to alter, using a photograph Honey had of the fun house, taken during Winston's time. She had carefully put it in the place of the original photograph the night before, when the carnival was silent and still.

For seventy years, the fun house that had been abandoned and left to rot in the back acre of the carnival had been called, simply and uninspired—THE FUN HOUSE.

But here, in this photo, painstakingly edited, the name had been changed.

Nova came to stand beside Adrian, peering at the framed black-and-white photograph, and the letters over the yawning entrance. Not THE FUN HOUSE, but THE NIGHTMARE.

"Coincidence?" said Adrian.

"Maybe," she responded.

"It's just called the Fun House now, right? I wonder when they decided to change it."

She said nothing.

He looked at her, and she could already see the conviction there. He did not think it was a coincidence at all. "Do you think we should go talk to your old boss about it? Maybe he could tell us when the name was changed, or . . ." He trailed off and it was clear he was grasping for any sources that might lead to a real clue, no matter how tenuous the evidence was.

"I doubt he would know much," said Nova. "It was the Fun House during the Age of Anarchy, so the name must have been changed a really long time ago." She swallowed, before adding, "I think we should just go check it out."

Adrian did not hesitate for long before he nodded. "You're right. Let's go."

"Are we supposed to call for backup?"

"We haven't found anything yet," he said, sounding almost—but not quite—amused. "But we will, at the first sign of trouble. Agreed?"

She curled her fingers at her sides. "Agreed."

As they left the gallery, Nova could sense that everything had changed. The lightness and ease that had been emanating from Adrian all day was replaced with tension and renewed focus. She saw that he was holding his marker again, almost like a weapon, though she wasn't sure when he had grabbed it. She found her own hand curling around the hoops of her belt, though why she should be anxious made no sense.

She knew exactly what they were about to find.

There was no gate that they could see along the perimeter of the chain-link fence, so Adrian clamped the marker between his teeth, clawed his fingers through the wire mesh, and climbed over. The metal rattled from his weight, but he was a nimble climber. He dropped down to the soft dirt on the other side and glanced back to check on Nova, but she was already to the top herself, perched delicately on the metal crossbar.

"Look," she whispered.

Adrian did. His body stilled for only a moment, before he walked forward and crouched down beneath a patch of soft dirt. He pulled back the weedy grass at its edges, revealing the crisscrossing paths of boot prints. The treads of thick rubber soles denoting a clear pathway between the far corner of the fence and the abandoned rides in the distance.

It had been the last clue Nova had decided to leave, early that morning, not an hour before the park was meant to open. Wearing the boots she'd found remarkably comfortable as Nightmare, even if she had to admit they were not on par with the footwear she'd received as part of her Renegade uniform, she had trudged back and forth, back and forth, hoping to suggest a path frequently traveled.

Nova hopped down to join him.

He took the marker from his teeth. "They're fresh," he said, standing and peering toward the fun house. She could see the debate evident on his features before he lifted his wrist toward his mouth. "Send team communication. Insomnia and I are at Cosmopolis Park. We think there might be a connection between Nightmare and the abandoned fun house on the back acre. We're going to investigate. So far there's been no sighting of the villain, but we're preparing for an altercation and might need reinforcements."

He ended the message and let his arm hang. "Do you think she's in there?"

"It would be a good place to lay low."

Adrian started trudging through the overgrown pathways. They passed a graveyard of broken-down rocket ships and cars from one of the original roller coasters, now with prickly blackberry bushes sprouting around their metal carcasses. Though their paint was faded, the bright colors were still at odds with the dreariness of this corner of the park—the rusted tracks and mechanical gears, the broken bits of fence rails and food carts.

Adrian paused at a ticket booth that had once been white but was now so covered in filth and water damage it was difficult to tell. He sketched two sets of handcuffs onto the wood siding. He handed one to Nova and tucked the other set into his pocket. It occurred to Nova that if this day had really been about finding Nightmare from the start, he already would have had these with him. She stared at his profile as he set the point of the marker against the ticket booth again.

"Adrian?"

Hand stilling, he turned his head to look at her.

She swallowed. "Was this a date?"

His lips parted, at first in surprise, but then in hesitation as he searched for a response. Pulling the marker away from the booth, he used the capped end to scratch behind his ear. "Well. This was the first time a girl's ever won me an enormous stuffed Dread Warden doll, so . . . you tell me."

Her cheek twitched. "That wasn't a real answer."

"I know."

They stared at each other, and Nova's heart started doing acrobatics inside her chest.

"Would you have said yes," said Adrian, "if it was?"

No, her brain said. Emphatic and aggressive. *No*.

While something else whispered back . . . *Maybe*.

But Nova, suddenly a coward, looked past Adrian's shoulder and plastered a startled frown to her face. "I think I just saw something."

Adrian spun around, simultaneously reaching his arm out to tuck her behind him, which was so obnoxiously gallant Nova found herself wanting to both shove the arm away and also take his hand into hers. In fact, as she stared down at the fingers that were just barely brushing against her own, she had the most absurd notion to lace her fingers through them and lift his hand to her mouth, to place one single kiss against those knuckles.

The flash of fantasy paralyzed her.

"Where?" said Adrian.

"Inside the fun house," said Nova, the words feeling robotic and rehearsed. "Oh, wait. I think it might have just been that creepy doll up on the balcony."

She lifted her eyes to the remains of a mannequin on the second floor. It was wearing a sodden clown costume—though someone had long ago taken its head.

They watched, unmoving, for a long while.

"Maybe we should go inside and look around?" she said.

Adrian nodded. "If we do see Nightmare, you know not to let her touch you, right?"

She shivered, looking again at his dark skin, his lithe fingers—touching her, but not really.

"I know," she murmured, and moved back just enough to break the hesitant contact.

Reaching up, Adrian began to draw onto the side of the ticket booth again. Nova closed her eyes while she waited. She focused on her breath, trying to drown out the surge of sensations flooding her body. She needed to stop thinking about handsome smiles and small touches and kisses and dates. If Adrian liked her—really liked her—it was only because he didn't really know her.

He would never like the girl beneath the lie. He would never like Nova Artino. And it didn't matter to her anyway, because she could never fall for a Renegade.

That word shattered the cloud of doubt that had gathered around her, and she opened her eyes, solid again in her resolve.

He was a Renegade.

He was her enemy.

He might have come here today with ulterior motives, but then, so had she.

"Ready?" he said.

She started, her skin prickling with apprehension. He had drawn himself a gun.

On closer inspection, she realized it was a tranquilizer gun. This alone might have given her pause, except she had so recently seen him shoot. She doubted she had much to worry about.

She gave him a fierce nod.

"I'm ready."

CHAPTER FORTY-ONE

THE FUN HOUSE—what the photograph had shown to once have been called The Nightmare—was a rickety two-story building covered in peeling white-and-orange paint. Its few windows sported crooked shutters and slatted boards long ago nailed across them. There was no glass. Spiderwebs, some as thick and dark as yarn, were strung across the overhang of the wraparound porch. As they passed beneath it, Adrian glanced up at the headless clown. He assumed it had once had a head, but it was hard to know for sure. The place was so creepy it was only with exaggerated imagination that he could picture what it must have once been—a place of amusement and whimsy. A place that people didn't enter while their stomachs filled with dread.

The porch groaned beneath his weight as he stepped up to the double-door entrance, where a mural of twin ballerinas had been painted to welcome in the visitors. One of them had a speech bubble that read, "Welcome to our fun house!" And the other, "Enjoy your stay!" And Adrian could just picture their little heads spinning around as he pushed open the doors, their tinny voices adding, with a haunting cackle——*Or else . . .*

But the mural was just a mural and there were no eerie voices when he and Nova stepped into the first chamber of the house. There was no noise at all beyond the distant carnival music coming from the amusement park they'd left behind.

This first room was without windows, and he held the door open long enough for them to get their bearings, though they could not see very far into the old attraction. A wall was built only six feet in front of the door, encouraging visitors to move quickly beyond the foyer and into whatever lay beyond.

"Someone's been here recently," said Nova, pointing at the ground, where clear footprints could be seen passing through the years of accumulated dust.

Nova reached into a pouch at her belt and pulled out a small device. She gave it a snap and it began to glow luminescent yellow. She tossed it into the next doorway.

"That's neat," said Adrian.

"Exothermic micro-flares. I make them myself."

He smiled at her. "If you happen to run out of them, I could also draw a flashlight."

She scowled as she stepped forward into the shadows.

Adrian let go of the door and it creaked loudly, then shut with a resounding click, trapping them inside with the stale, silent air. He followed Nova around the bend and through a series of switchback paths that looped back and around on each other a number of times. Nova left her micro-flare as they passed it, perhaps as a way to track the direction they'd come, lighting another and then another as they made their way through the narrow lanes. Adrian trailed his left hand against the wall to keep them from treading back over old ground, and though the maze seemed a little childish, he could imagine how disconcerting it would have been to try to traverse it in pitch-blackness.

After turning into two dead ends, they found themselves at the end of the maze, standing before a long hallway that was made up to look like the corridor of a quaint old house. Two small square windows donned lace curtains and the walls were covered in blue-checkered wallpaper.

They stepped out into the hallway, and the floor tilted beneath them.

Nova gasped and tumbled to the side, knocking into Adrian. He instinctively wrapped his arms around her as his back crashed into the wall.

They froze, neither daring to move while the hallway settled around them. He could feel Nova's heartbeat pounding, and when she met his gaze, her cheeks were flushed.

He couldn't keep his fingers from curling, just slightly, into the fabric of her uniform.

Nova let out a self-deprecating sigh. "Heads up—the floor moves."

Adrian grinned. "You don't say."

To his disappointment, Nova pulled herself away, leaning on the wall for support instead. "It's activated by weight," she said. "If we both stick to this side, we should be able to keep it pretty steady."

"Wow, you really are good at physics."

She glowered at him. "*Now* you decide to become sarcastic?"

Cheeks twitching, Adrian followed her through the corridor, each of them keeping their footsteps as close to the wall as possible to keep it from swaying beneath them again.

At the end of the undulating hall, they pushed through a hanging curtain and Adrian spotted two shadowed figures rushing toward them. He yelped and grabbed Nova's elbow to pull her behind him, when his brain caught up with his eyes and he realized he was staring at their own reflections.

At least, their own distorted reflections. One of the floor-to-ceiling mirrors was curved to make Adrian appear short and squat, while Nova's was altered to look eight feet tall.

He exhaled. "Sorry. This place might be making me a little jumpy."

Nova pulled her arm away and turned to face him, settling her hands on her hips. "For the record, while it's very charming that you keep trying to protect me, I would like to remind you that I actually know how defend myself."

He grimaced. "I know. It's just . . . instinct."

"Well, stop it."

He held his hands up. "Won't happen again." He hesitated. "I mean, unless I'm pretty sure you're about to die, then I'm absolutely going to rescue you, whether you like it or not."

Rolling her eyes, Nova headed into the hall of mirrors, which was another sequence of corridors that wound back and forth, so that at times they were surrounded by countless versions of themselves reflecting into infinity, and at other times the optical illusion of the hall made it impossible to see where the next break in the mirrors was, so that it felt as if there were no way out. At one point, Adrian found himself gaping at a version of himself in which his legs and head were shrunk to doll proportions, leaving his torso to stretch eternally between them, when from the corner of his eye he could have sworn he saw Nightmare herself dart past his view.

He gripped the tranquilizer gun and spun to chase after her, promptly crashing into a wall. When he did make it around the corner, he saw only Nova frowning at him. "What's wrong?"

Blinking, Adrian shook off the vision, realizing that it must have only been her that he'd seen, his own imagination getting carried away with another distorted reflection.

"Nothing," he said. "How do we get out of here?"

They fumbled around for another minute until they found a staircase. Adrian noticed small holes in the floor as they made their way up, and he suspected they were intended to blow bursts of air, probably up into the skirts of unsuspecting girls, but whatever mechanism had caused it must have been out of order, and they made their way to the top without incident.

Adrian stared down the next corridor. It was wider than the one downstairs. There were no windows here, just dark wood floors and a collection of framed oil paintings hung on the thick-striped wallpaper, mostly portraits of stoic-looking aristocrats. Stacked up against the nearest wall were dozens of burlap mats.

Adrian stepped out first this time, preparing to catch himself, but the floor held stable.

They made their way forward, side by side, waiting to discover what new surprise this room had to offer.

"I think they used those burlap mats for slides," said Adrian, peering at a painting of a man with a wiry gray beard. He frowned. There was something off about the picture. Something about his eyes that made Adrian pause. Had he imagined them moving, tracking him and Nova across the hall?

An optical illusion, probably, but he couldn't quite resist stepping closer to it, when he heard a loud *ka-thunk* and Nova screamed.

He spun around just in time to see Nova disappear through a square trap door. Adrian launched himself forward, trying to grab her, but the door snapped shut. All he'd caught was the sight of a metal slide leading back down to the floor below.

"Nova! *Nova!*" He fell to the floor where she had fallen through, trying to dig his fingers into the edges of the trapdoor, to no avail.

Standing, he stomped around in the same spot, but the door did not give. "Nova!"

From down below, he heard her calling, "I'm okay!"

At the same moment, the painting in front of Adrian popped open and a head launched itself forward. Adrian cried out, lifted the gun, and fired.

The tranquilizer dart shot past the disembodied head, clunking harmlessly into the wall beside it.

"*He-he-he-he!*" chortled a high-pitched mechanical voice. "*You've lost your pal, oh boo-hoo! But don't stop now . . . the only way out is through!*"

The head bobbed a second longer, and Adrian could see it was attached to a springy base, like a jack-in-the-box toy. It was painted like a clown, with garish red lips and a black diamond on its cheek, and he wondered if it was supposed to be the missing head from the doll outside.

The picture frame slammed shut. Inside the wall, he heard the click of gears as the mechanics reset themselves.

He swallowed, and realized he was shaking.

"Adrian?" Nova yelled from below.

Panic ebbing, he tucked the gun away and dug out his marker. "Hold on, I'm coming down to you." Kneeling over the floorboards again, he started to draw a trapdoor of his own.

"No—wait!"

He paused, tilting his head to listen more closely.

"I think there might be two routes through this place," Nova yelled. "We should keep going—check them both out."

He frowned. There was nothing appealing at all about being separated, especially when this really might be Nightmare's secret lair. Though the longer they stayed, the more Adrian questioned how anyone could stand to spend more time here than they had to.

Finally, Adrian forced his shoulders to release some of the mounting tension. "Okay," he yelled down to Nova. "I'll meet you at the exit."

She didn't respond. Perhaps she had already moved on.

Adrian took a moment to draw himself a new tranquilizer dart and loaded the gun before leaving the corridor. He opened the door at the end and froze as he found himself standing in a hexagonal room, where each wall bore an identical green door.

"Fine," he muttered. Letting the door shut behind him, he turned and marked it with an X, so he would know he'd already been this way. He pulled open the first door to his right, revealing a plain brick wall. He reached out and knocked and, determining that they were real bricks and not an optical illusion, shut the door and marked it.

He opened the next door and his pulse jumped.

The room before him was painted, floor, walls, and ceiling, in swirls of black and white, making it appear that the room got smaller and smaller as it stretched out before him.

But this was not what had given him pause.

Rather, the optical illusion was broken up by three things.

A sleeping bag. A pillow. And a large black duffel bag.

He stepped into the room, eyes darting over every surface. He half expected Nightmare to appear from some dark corner, but there was nowhere in here for her, or anyone, to hide.

Adrian crouched beside the duffel bag and pulled back the zipper. Inside, he found a change of clothes, a pair of sneakers, and the bazooka-size gun Nightmare had used to throw those ropes around him during their fight above the parade.

It was all the confirmation he needed.

Standing, he raised his wrist and sent a quick message to Nova, asking her to meet him back up on the second floor. Then he alerted the Council, informing them of what he and Insomnia had found.

He had just sent the message when he heard the squeak of floorboards. He stilled, holding his breath to listen. After a long silence, in which he could once again catch the tinny notes of faraway carnival music, he heard another groan of ancient floorboards.

Returning to the door, he peered into the hexagonal room. Trying to guess where the noise had come from, he adjusted his hold on the gun and stepped across to the opposite door. He opened it slowly. Silently. Grateful when it did not creak on its old hinges.

Inside was a narrow hall, just wide enough for one person to walk through. It was pitch-black, but for a series of tiny round holes on each wall, placed at varying heights in sets of two. Adrian stepped forward and the door shut behind him, throwing him into near blackness. He approached one set of holes and bent down to look through. On the other side of the wall, he recognized the corridor with the portraits, where Nova had fallen through the trapdoor, and quickly realized that he was staring through the eyes of one of the paintings.

His blood chilled as he recalled the peculiar sensation of one of the paintings watching them.

He turned to the other wall and found himself staring into another crooked room, where the walls were painted to trick the mind into thinking it was walking downward, and pitching to the left, while the floor itself was slanted the opposite direction. There were doors at each end of the strange room, and as he stared, the door to the left opened.

He waited for Nova to appear, but instead a figure in a black hood swept into the room.

He stifled a gasp, his lungs squeezing painfully in his chest.

Nightmare.

He had found her.

Without pause, Nightmare stalked purposefully to the next door and disappeared into the hexagonal room. Adrian listened as doors opened and slammed shut, then he thought he heard her shuffling things around in the room where he'd found her bag. His brow knitted. Did she know her location was compromised? Was she preparing to run?

He set his jaw, determined not to let her get away again.

Breaths coming in short bursts, he readied the gun and slipped back into the hexagonal room and paced across to the other door. His hand landed on the handle, but from the corner of his eye he noticed the black X he'd drawn onto the next door, and the next.

Wouldn't Nightmare have noticed—

The gun was yanked out of his hand, and a foot slammed into the back of Adrian's knee, knocking him to the ground.

He drove his elbow back, catching her in the stomach. Nightmare grunted and pitched forward, crashing into Adrian's shoulder. He went to shove her back, but in that same moment she had grabbed on to the hem of his own jacket and yanked it upward, trapping his arms in the sleeves. She shoved him to the floor and he landed hard on one side. As he struggled to rid himself of the restraining jacket, he heard a door open and slam shut, her footsteps pounding away as she ran.

With a furious cry, Adrian ripped his jacket off and threw it on the ground. He was panting, though more from frustration than anything else. Snarling, he grabbed for the door he thought she'd gone through and found himself staring down a long horizontal cylinder. There was no sign of Nightmare.

Snarling, he raised his communicator. "Sketch to HQ, calling for backup. I've located Nightmare. She's on the run—I'm pursuing her now."

He ripped off his T-shirt, then, revealing the top of the Renegade uniform, and ran. He stumbled through the cylinder, which didn't even surprise him when it started to pitch and roll under his feet, then through an obstacle course of swaying rope bridges and down a spiraling staircase. Through a gallery of animatronic marionettes that, thankfully, did not come to life as he weaved between them, then up another optical illusion ramp, until he finally shoved his way through a set of double doors and found himself outside.

It was darker now than when they had entered. Dusk came on fast this time of year, and already the shadow from the fun house stretched long across the overgrown grasses in front of him.

He paused, his eyes darting in each direction, searching and listening for any signs of Nightmare—or Nova, for that matter—but this desolate corner of the park seemed as abandoned as ever.

Nova.

He didn't want to worry about the fact that he hadn't seen or heard from her since they'd been separated, but now that he knew Nightmare was close, fears began to crowd into his mind. What if Nightmare had found her? What if . . .

What if.

There were too many what-ifs to waste time on any of them. Right now, he either had to find Nightmare or he had to find Nova.

He jogged down the exit steps and peered around to the back of the building. He saw nothing. Heard nothing.

Frowning, he turned back to the fun house. Was she still inside?

No sooner had he had this thought than his eye caught on the shadow of the fun house stretching across the ground, and the hooded figure standing at its peak.

Adrian's eyes shifted upward.

Nightmare stared down at him, calmly posed at the edge of the pitched roof. Her hood was pulled down low over her face, and with the sun behind her she appeared almost like a shadow herself. She had a weapon in each hand—his own tranquilizer gun and a revolver.

She lifted the revolver.

Adrian glared and crouched, preparing to launch himself up toward the roof, when she fired—

And missed.

By . . . a lot.

The gunshot was still ringing in his ears when it was replaced with an amused chuckle. "I thought I trained you better than that, Nightmare."

Adrian whirled around.

Directly across from the fun-house exit, perched on the stage of an old puppet theater, sat the Detonator.

CHAPTER FORTY-TWO

———◼——

NIGHTMARE'S BULLET HAD NOT HIT the Detonator, but rather, had struck one of two drooping marionettes that hung inside the theater, marking it right between its eyes. Though Nightmare hadn't hit either the Detonator or Adrian himself, he had a feeling she'd hit the exact target she'd been aiming for.

Whatever message she wanted to send, though, left him baffled.

"You have a lot of nerve showing your face here," said Nightmare, her voice low and muffled behind the mask.

Adrian felt his forearms tingling, as if the tattoos themselves were preparing themselves for a fight, though he still found himself reaching for his marker—habitually or instinctively, he wasn't sure. But when he lifted his gaze back to Nightmare, she appeared to be staring at the Detonator, not him.

"What?" said the Detonator, bobbing her crossed leg up and down. She wore the same outfit she had at the library, though Adrian saw that she had bandages wrapped around her upper arm where Nova had shot her as she tried to run. "I'm not allowed to stop and say hello to a dear friend?"

"*You*," Nightmare said, with a growl in her tone, "cost me a valuable connection when you went after the Librarian, and all the goods he'd stockpiled. Do you know how much work I put in to trading with him? How long it took me to cultivate that relationship? All for nothing, thanks to you."

Adrian took a step back, moving out of the path between them. When neither paid him any notice, he stepped back again, then again.

"Blame me all you want for your sorry misfortunes," said the Detonator with a one-shouldered shrug. "But let's not forget that you started this all when you decided to go after Captain Chromium. The head honcho himself. If you hadn't been so careless, the Renegades wouldn't be after us at all, now would they? They wouldn't have gotten your gun. They wouldn't have traced it back to the Librarian, and it would be business as usual, now wouldn't it?"

"Except they didn't attack us after the parade, did they? They took the Puppeteer and they let the rest of the Anarchists off the hook. It wasn't until you got lazy and impatient—when you decided to take a risk you shouldn't have. You know what I think?" Nightmare raised the gun again. "I think the Anarchists will be better off without you."

She fired again and the Detonator cried out and fell backward off the lip of the small wooden stage, disappearing into the tiny theater.

Adrian dived behind a rotting canoe, a leftover, he assumed, from the tunnel of love.

Nightmare kept shooting, letting off four more bullets until the revolver clicked over, spent.

When Adrian lifted his head, he saw that the front of the

wooden theater was peppered with holes and splintered wood. The marionettes were swaying on their strings and there was a splatter of something dark against the backdrop, but he couldn't tell if it was blood or dirt.

Nightmare holstered her gun and leaped from the roof, landing cat-like on the ground where Adrian had stood moments before. She hesitated, staring at the theater. Adrian couldn't see her face around the drape of the hood, but he sensed her waiting, bracing herself. His tranquilizer gun was still in her other hand.

Clenching his jaw, he uncapped his marker as quietly as he could and drew himself a new gun against the side of the canoe. It was a hasty drawing, made messy by years of dirt crusted onto the wood, but he was glad to be armed again when it was finished. He sketched out a handful of extra darts and stuffed them into his pocket.

He had just finished when he heard the melodic clunking of hollow wood. Looking up, he saw the Detonator pulling herself up, shoving the marionettes out of the way. She collapsed over the ledge of the theater booth. When she looked up, her face was contorted in pain, her eyes seething with fury.

She hauled herself up onto the ledge, then tumbled gracelessly down to the other side.

The entire front of her shirt was covered in blood. More was dripping down her midriff and coating the bands around her arms.

Her nostrils flared as she forced herself up onto shaky legs. She cursed, then spat into the dirt between her and Nightmare.

She stumbled forward. One shaky, plodding step.

Blue sparks began to crackle at her fingertips.

Nightmare shifted back, stepping up onto the bottom step of the fun house.

"Ace never should have taken you in," said the Detonator. The sparks began to converge into something no bigger than a tennis ball at first, but growing fast. "You might have had potential once, but now? You're nothing but a disappointment."

She took another step forward, then groaned, dropping hard to one knee.

Adrian brought up the gun, resting his hands on the edge of the canoe. He aimed first at the Detonator, then at Nightmare. He wasn't sure what to do. They were fighting each other. They might kill each other.

The Detonator, he suspected, wouldn't last long with those wounds.

But he still needed Nightmare alive.

Gritting his teeth, he targeted the Detonator again. The bomb hovering over her palm was as big as her head now, and still growing.

His eyes narrowed. Even at the library, he had never seen her compose an explosive device of that size. She was smiling now, a crazed, gleeful smile.

Adrian squeezed the trigger.

The dart disappeared into the grasses behind her. He cursed.

The Detonator laughed. "Now, you just wait your turn over there, sweetheart. I'll get to you next." The explosive was bigger than a basketball, glowing in bright, swirling blue.

"Ingrid?" said Nightmare, and the slight quiver to her voice brought Adrian's attention back to her, even as he hurried to load another dart. "What are you doing?"

Adrian hesitated. There was something familiar about her in that moment. Something that gnawed at him. Had she ever, for a moment, appeared vulnerable when he had fought her before? He didn't think so.

"If I'm going to die," said the Detonator, "it's not going to be alone."

Nightmare shifted—an almost imperceptible change. Her stance widened. Her head tilted down. Her shoulders tensed as she turned, ready to launch herself off the stairs and away from the fun house.

The Detonator hurled the bomb at her.

Nightmare was a moment too late.

The explosion knocked Adrian onto his back. A flash blinded him, washing out the sky overhead, leaving him trying to blink the shadowy stars from his eyes. His head rang. His whole body vibrated from the impact. The world smelled of smoke and dust.

Coughing, he rolled onto his side and took off his glasses, rubbing the lenses on his uniform to wipe away the dirt. He was still plagued with sparklers in his gaze when he put them back on and pushed himself up to his elbows. The canoe had been turned over onto its side, and he wondered how much it had protected him from the surge of shrapnel and flying rubble.

Half of the fun house was gone.

Broken floorboards and a few of the interior rooms were left exposed, including the metal slide and the hall of mirrors, which was now littered with broken glass. Wooden beams and siding and roof shingles were scattered across the ground in all directions. The pitched roof was toppling inward, ready to cave onto the mound of smoking wood and plaster beneath.

The Detonator had fallen forward onto her stomach. Her hair and clothing had turned chalky gray from all the dust, and the blood from her wounds was clumping in the dirt around her. She was not moving.

Adrian searched for any sign of Nightmare, who had been standing in the very spot where the great mountain of debris was smoldering. She could have been buried beneath, or, more likely, she could have been blown apart by the explosion.

Shaking, Adrian got back to his feet and tucked the gun into the back of his pants. He stared at the exposed insides of the fun house. A few small fires were scattered throughout the wreckage, sending plumes of black smoke toward the darkening sky. Somewhere inside he could hear the jack-in-the-box laughing.

His heart started to pound erratically. "Nova . . ."

His disbelief was quickly overcome with denial, and he lifted his wrist. "Nova—Insomnia, where are you? Report." Stumbling around the canoe, he picked his way through the remains of the building, searching the corners of its crumbling skeleton. "Nova!"

He was trying to navigate the destroyed outer wall when his eye caught on something shining beneath a fallen window shutter. He kicked the shutter out of the way, stooped, and picked up the slim, molded piece of steel.

Nightmare's face mask.

Turning it over, he saw that one side of it was streaked with blood.

A tittering laugh made his skin prickle. Adrian tossed the mask aside and turned to see the Detonator on her hands and knees, still chortling. She spat, then sat back on her heels and wiped the dirt from her mouth.

She was drenched in blood.

He stared at her, stunned. He wasn't surprised that she would survive the explosion. From what he'd seen at the library, she appeared to be immune to the blasts of her own bombs. But she had been shot so many times, she had lost so much blood . . .

How was she still alive? And . . . *laughing*?

With a delirious grin, the Detonator climbed to her feet. She seemed to wobble for a moment, but then she shook out her matted hair and her stance solidified. "I don't know who's more gullible," she said, rolling her shoulders. "Nightmare . . . or you."

Adrian was too distracted for her taunting. He found his attention constantly shifting around the park, hoping to see some sign of Nova.

The Detonator clapped her hands together, knocking off some of the dust. "That was fun, wasn't it? That little spat of ours. It was all staged for your benefit, you know, so I hope you were entertained."

He frowned. His pulse was beginning to race again, his instincts humming with warnings—but also curiosity.

"You see?" said the Detonator, swiping her fingers through the caked blood on her abdomen. "Fake blood. She was firing blanks. You know, Queen Bee thinks she's the only savvy actress around, but I think I've proved otherwise."

Adrian shook his head. "What are you talking about?"

"Don't you see? We planned this all, to make you think that we were both dead. So you would stop looking for us. Get it now?"

He stared at her.

"I know, I know. You're thinking . . . so why is Nightmare *actually* dead, then? And why am I giving up our villainous plan now, when we almost got away with it?" She staggered forward, and though she didn't seem to be in pain, she wasn't moving as gracefully as normal, either. Adrian wondered if creating a bomb that size had drained her. "It's too bad, really. I liked Nightmare. Always have. She was a lot like me in a lot of ways—always willing to do what had to be done. But I could see the writing on the wall. It was only a matter of time before she betrayed us, betrayed all of us. And I couldn't have that. So . . . she had to go. Problem solved."

Adrian was still frowning, still confused. "Is this . . . ," he started, dismayed, "a *villain* speech?"

Ingrid laughed. "Maybe so. It's horrible to go through all this plotting and have no one around to appreciate it. Besides, you'll be dead soon, too, so it's not really going to matter."

Adrian reached for the gun, but he had barely gotten his fingers around the handle when a glowing blue marble smashed into the ground at his feet, blowing a small crater into the earth and knocking him onto a pile of splintered siding and wooden studs. A sharp pain tore through his tricep and he cried out, tearing his arm away from the nail that was sticking up through one of old trim boards.

Hissing, he scrambled to sit up.

The Detonator sauntered closer, gathering more power around her hands. "It's time to finish what we started at the library."

Adrian snarled and clenched his fist, drawing on the power of the cylindrical tattoo on his forearm. Within seconds, his arm from fingers to elbow had begun to glow molten white.

The Detonator paused.

Before Adrian was entirely sure this would work without being in the Sentinel's armor, a long metal cylinder emerged from his skin. He fired, striking the villain in the chest with a single bolt of blinding energy. She was blown back, smacking hard into the puppet theater. The mannequins trembled and clacked together.

The cylinder retreated into his flesh and Adrian clambered to his feet, trying to find purchase on the shifting piles of wreckage beneath him. He staggered forward, retrieving his gun.

The Detonator coughed and placed a hand over her chest, where the beam had hit her. Her breathing was raspy and labored as she met his eyes.

"Fine. Let's finish what we started at the library," said Adrian. "No—actually, let's finish what started ten years ago." He came to stand half a dozen feet away from her and raised the gun, confident that even he could hit her from this distance. "Nightmare knew who killed my mother, and you just took that one lead away from me. But you're an Anarchist, so maybe you have some answers too."

In response, she began to laugh again. Dazed and maniacal. "The Sentinel," she gasped. "You're the Sentinel. Oh, that's *rich.*"

His eyebrow began to twitch. "Who killed Lady Indomitable?"

Her cackle turned to a wheeze as she studied him. "You're going to threaten me into submission with . . . what? A tranquilizer? Life imprisonment?" She smirked. "I seem to recall you were eager to negotiate with the Librarian. Don't I get the same treatment?"

He held her gaze, considering, trying to discern if she really had the information he wanted, or if this was just her trying to play him again.

And even if she did know, could he really bargain with her, after everything?

"No," he said. "The Renegades are done negotiating with Anarchists."

Stepping forward, he dug the handcuffs from his pocket and yanked the Detonator's wrists forward, binding them together. He could just see the amused twinge enter her eye when he pulled out his marker and began to draw lines crisscrossing her hands.

"What are you doing?"

Rather than answering, he finished his work, then pulled the chains from her skin, securing her hands and fingers tight enough that she would be unable to produce any more explosives.

She peered up at him, her lip curling. "And how do you plan on keeping me silent about your little secret?"

"I don't," he said. "The Sentinel's mission was to find Nightmare. With her dead, it no longer matters who knows the truth."

He didn't entirely mean it—his secret had turned out to be more complicated than he would have imagined when he'd first concocted the idea. But he wouldn't allow this Anarchist to lord the knowledge over him. He wouldn't allow her to have any power over him at all.

"Adrian!"

He looked up as the sound of wingbeats thrummed in the air. Thunderbird dropped out of the sky, a lightning bolt crackling in one fist. She eyed the Detonator with surprise. "Your message said you found Nightmare!"

"I did," said Adrian. "She's dead. And . . . Nova . . ." He turned back to the fun house again, or what was left of it, as more chunks of material broke off and crashed down to the rubble below.

It had been ages since he'd seen her. He wanted there to be some explanation . . . maybe she'd gone for help. Maybe the effects of being near Max had finally caught up to her and she'd fallen asleep in some safe, secure alcove somewhere.

But he knew it was desperation talking.

"Oh, *Nova*," said the Detonator, dragging his attention back to her. "I already dealt with her."

He tensed, unwilling to believe her. She was only taunting him, only trying to get a reaction. But that haughty look . . . that careless smirk . . .

Adrian roared and threw himself at her, seeing nothing but livid flashes as those words repeated in his head. *I already dealt with her.*

Thunderbird caught him by the arm and slowed him down just

long enough for another, infinitely stronger arm to clamp around Adrian's chest and haul him backward. He fought to free himself, but was spun around. Two hands clapped onto his shoulders and he found himself staring into his dad's eyes. Captain Chromium's eyes.

"Adrian!" he yelled, scanning him up and down. "What happened? Are you all right?"

"No!" he yelled back, because shouldn't it have been obvious? Had he not heard what she just said?

But he knew his frantic, furious thoughts weren't really what his dad was asking about. Hugh Everhart pulled one hand away, looking down at his fingers wet with blood. Adrian had already forgotten about the scratch from the nail. It was nothing. Nothing. Not when Nova . . . when Nova was . . .

Where is Nova?

He yanked himself away and spun in circles, seeing Evander as he shot a series of white lights into the air, brightening the field surrounding the fun house. Then he spotted Kasumi and, a moment later, Simon, too, shifting into visibility. The Council. The whole Council was there. Was it for Nightmare . . . or for him?

Then, too, he spotted Ruby and Oscar and Danna, running through the abandoned park, calling his name.

"Mercy mine," said the Detonator. "What an all-star show this turned out to be. It's so very nice of you all to join us." Though she was slumped against the wooden theater, her arms latched securely on top of her stomach, she was still grinning as she peered around at all the new arrivals. "Why, this has worked out even better than I expected. All *five* Council members." She clicked her tongue. "What will people say once they realize that you were right here? You were *so close* . . . and you still couldn't save them?"

"What is she talking about?" said Hugh.

Adrian shook his head, frowning. "I don't know. This was all a setup—she killed Nightmare, something about how she thought Nightmare would betray the Anarchists. And she tried to kill me. But I don't—"

A distant explosion rumbled the ground beneath their feet. They all turned to see a plume of black smoke erupting from the amusement park on the other side of the fence.

Oscar and the others froze and turned. They were the closest to the explosion, and they hesitated for only a moment before Danna burst into a swarm of butterflies and soared back toward the fence, Ruby and Oscar chasing after her as screams spread through the park.

Adrian stumbled forward a few steps, blinking in disbelief. The sun had set. The carnival was alight with twinkling lights and flashes of colors from the rides and booths, and it was almost impossible to tell at first, but as he stared he could detect a faint blue haze emanating from the whole carnival. Dozens—maybe hundreds—of small blue spheres blending in with the cacophony of twinkling lightbulbs. Even as he watched, they continued to brighten, their vibrant sapphire glow gradually overwhelming the multicolored hues of the park.

But . . . she was *here*. The Detonator was here, she was captured, she was bound. How could she . . .

His thoughts trailed off, answering themselves.

She had done it at the library too. She had set a bomb against the basement wall and detonated it from the other side of the room, with nothing but a snap of her fingers. She didn't just make bombs to be tossed around and used up like hand grenades. She could be much sneakier, much more calculating than that. *The Detonator.* It was right there in her alias.

Adrian looked at her confined hands, his gut sinking in horror.

The snap had been for show.

She could detonate those bombs with nothing but her thoughts.

Tsunami sprinted off toward the park while Thunderbird took to the sky, soaring in the direction of the explosion. A second later, another blast shook the earth and, in the distance, the pillar that held the giant swings toppled over mid-rotation. It spun out like a top, launching hapless riders into the fence and across the pavement.

The Detonator was laughing again, staring up at the sky, dazed and content. "By tomorrow morning, they are going to *hate* you . . . ," she sang.

Another explosion destroyed a leg of track on the rollercoaster. Thunderbird changed direction, rushing to get to the coaster before the riders plummeted off the edge.

And that faint blue haze grew brighter.

Bombs, everywhere he looked.

What if she set them all off at once?

Adrian clenched his fists and felt a surge of power rush into his forearm again. But the energy beam had been designed to stun, not to kill. And the only way to stop her, to be sure the rest of those bombs would never be detonated, was—

A gunshot rang across the grass. The Detonator's head snapped back, hitting the boards of the theater.

The world seemed to still, hovering in a space without time. Then the Detonator slumped down. Adrian released his breath and watched her topple onto her side, leaving a smear of blood on the wood.

Real blood.

Adrian flexed his fingers, dissipating the building energy, and peered into the shadows of the fun house.

Nova pushed aside a blockade of wood scraps and crawled out of the rotating cylinder that had crashed down from the second floor and landed not far from the exit doors—or where the exit doors had once stood. She was holding a handgun. Her hair and skin and the iconic gray bodysuit were caked with dust.

"I found this," she stammered, shaking the gun a little. "In a . . . a duffel bag." She sounded worried, as if anyone would care that she'd stolen the gun that had stopped the Detonator.

Breathless, Adrian glanced back out toward the park. Thunderbird was at the crest of the rollercoaster, holding back the train of carts only a few feet from the gap in the tracks.

The rest of the carnival was in pandemonium, with civilians screaming and running in all directions, though he could imagine Danna and the others had reached the sites of the first two explosions by now.

Clouds of smoke were still swelling over the park, but the blue glow was gone. The rest of the spheres had extinguished, evaporating back into the atmosphere.

"All right, everyone," said Simon, always the first to snap out of his shock. "Let's get as many patrol units as we can here, pronto, to help with the injured and start getting this place cleaned up."

Adrian ignored the order, turning back to Nova. His entire body was trembling with relief. "Nova . . ."

She stood amid the debris and tried to shake some of the filth from her hair. Then she looked at him and stumbled down the steps—tripping on a fallen beam. Adrian leaped forward, catching her before she collapsed into the wreckage. It was, he thought, a reasonable jump, even if he had used the springs on his feet a tiny bit.

But if anyone noticed, he wouldn't care.

"You were in there the whole time? Great skies, Nova, do you know how worried I was?"

She dropped the gun and sagged into him. Her expression was dumbfounded. "I pulled the trigger," she murmured.

Captain Chromium barged his way toward them, clearing a path in the rubble. "You thought faster than any of us. For all the times I went up against the Detonator during the Age of Anarchy, I never knew she could pull a stunt like that. By the time I realized how to stop it, I suspect a lot more people would have been hurt."

Nova peered up at the Captain and swallowed.

"Nova?" said Adrian.

She switched her attention at him.

"I'm going to be chivalrous right now and carry you to safety."

Her expression softened. "Okay," she breathed.

"Really? You're not going to fight me on that?"

Her only response was to slump into his arms.

Adrian set his cheek against the top of her head, briefly enjoying the closeness of her, the knowledge that she was okay. That they were both okay. Then he bent down and lifted her into his arms.

"You know," said Evander, casting orbs of white light in Adrian's path so he could see clearly as night settled over the park, "this is proof that not every prodigy deserves their powers. It's because of villains like her that we need Agent N."

Nova pressed a hand against Adrian's chest, swiveling her body to peer at Blacklight. "Agent N? Is that what you call the Sentinel?"

"The Sentinel?" Evander smiled secretively and shook his head. "No, no. It's not a person. It's more like an antidote. And once it's ready . . ." He crossed his arms and glared at the Detonator's body. "The world will become a much safer place."

Nova shifted again and Adrian sensed her trying to squirm out of his hold, but he tightened his arms in response. "Nova, what's wrong?"

"Nothing," she said quickly. "I just want to know what he means."

"What he means is confidential," said Simon, sending a warning look at Evander, who returned an exaggerated roll of his eyes.

"Oh, honestly, they'll all know soon enough."

"It isn't ready," said Simon. He looked apologetically at Nova.

"Fine," said Evander. "Just suffice to say that we will never have to worry about these villains ever again. Pretty soon, all prodigies will be Renegades . . . or their powers won't be tolerated at all."

Nova cocked her head. "What are you—"

"No, that's enough," Hugh interrupted. "Simon is right. It's still confidential. And besides . . . you all look like you could use some rest." He fixed a stern look on Nova. "That goes for you, too, Insomnia."

The drone of vehicles drew their attention toward the fence, and Adrian saw squads of media vehicles rushing past the delivery gate of the carnival. Journalists began to pile out.

The remaining members of the Council released a collective groan.

"I'll fend off the reporters," said Hugh. "Let's get something to cover the Detonator before they get any photos of the body. Adrian, Nova, you head back to HQ, get some medical attention. You can give us your report tomorrow."

Nodding, Adrian began striding in the opposite direction, away from the media vans, but they had barely cleared the graveyard of roller coaster carts when Nova stopped him and scrambled out of his arms.

"This Agent N," she said, startling him. "Do you know what it is?"

He blinked at her. His mind was still exhausted, still trying to compute everything that had happened.

"No," he said slowly.

Nova crossed her arms and glared at him.

Adrian sighed. "I've heard them mention it a few times. I know it has something to do with Max . . . something to do with all those tests they run on him. But that's it. That's all I know. I swear." He reached for her hand. "Nova, are you all right? Were you hurt at all?"

She looked down at their hands, and after a moment, Adrian did as well. Though he'd spent the first half of that afternoon trying to work up the courage to hold her hand, this was the first time he actually had.

When she didn't move away, he inched closer to her and dared to take her other hand too.

"I thought you were dead," he said, saying the words that he'd refused to admit in his own mind. But he realized now that it was true. Beneath the denial and the refusal, he'd thought she was dead.

Nova licked her lips, drawing his gaze toward them.

"You never answered my question," he said.

"What question?"

"If I asked you on a real date, would you say yes?"

She seemed to tense. Her fingers tightened around his. "Are you asking?"

Adrian hesitated. She was watching him closely, her blue eyes curious, but also nervous.

Nervous.

Somehow, seeing his own uncertainty mirrored back at him helped to ease the anxiety knotted inside his chest. He tugged her closer, until their toes were nearly touching. She didn't resist. She didn't look away.

"I'm asking," he said.

Rather than wait for an answer, he craned his head and closed his eyes.

Nova stepped back, jerking her hands away.

Adrian's eyes snapped open.

Even from the faint light coming from the carnival, he could see that her cheeks had gone red. She wasn't looking at him anymore, but staring back toward the fun house. "My uncle will probably be watching the news," she stammered. "He'll be worried. I . . . I should get home."

Before Adrian could venture a response or offer to walk her back, she turned, scaled the nearest fence in half a heartbeat, and was gone.

CHAPTER FORTY-THREE

C AUTION TAPE HAD BEEN STRUNG across the entrance to the Blackmire Way subway station, where Ingrid had blown a gaping hole into the wall the day the Anarchists had fled. Nova ducked beneath it and pressed one hand to the side of the stairwell as she made her way into the shadows. Her feet felt heavy; her body ached. But she had a singularity of purpose now. Something she should have done twenty-four hours ago, before she was distracted with plotting fake deaths and Renegade investigations and the all-encompassing hunt for Nightmare.

Nightmare, her alter ego.

Who had been officially declared dead, according to the accounts she'd picked up peering into apartment windows and staring at the news on their TV screens. Her death was headlining the news that night, though it was almost matched by reports of the casualties at Cosmopolis Park—so far, thirty-six casualties were confirmed, but no fatalities. Thunderbird was being heralded as a hero for rescuing the riders aboard the rollercoaster. Ironically,

Insomnia was receiving praise, too, for having killed the Detonator before she could cause more destruction. The rest of the Renegade organization, however, was already being criticized for not having responded quickly enough to the threat.

Once it became too dark to see even the faint gleam of the metal rails, Nova pulled a micro-flare from her pocket, snapped it with her teeth, and tossed it over the edge to the platform below. It hit concrete and rolled for a bit before coming to a stop feet away from the ledge.

This had been Winston's platform, but his tents were gone, carted away by the Renegades. Evidence of some sort.

Probably Nova would be expected to tag them for data and catalog them in the database one of these nights. She wondered whether they'd ever found Honey's trunk of clothes or what they had decided to do with all the chemicals and poisons Leroy had left behind. Had they been confiscated, or destroyed? Perhaps they were all at headquarters. Probably, if she'd been doing her due diligence as an adequate spy, she would have known the answers to these questions by now.

Her boots hit the bottom of the steps, crunching on chunks of gravel and debris from the tunnel that had been collapsed by another of Ingrid's bombs, while Renegades chased after them. Dust covered the space, so thick that it almost felt like entering a lost tomb.

Tomb.

The word stuck in her head and might have made her laugh at the irony if she wasn't so drained. So ready to do what she had come here to do and start preparing for what would come next.

What would have to come next.

A new plan. A new strategy. A new focus going forward.

Her stomach had been in knots since she'd left Adrian. The day had wreaked havoc on her state of mind. There had been far too many moments when she'd been caught up in his spell. His charming smiles, that adorable wrinkle between his brows, his infuriating, impeccable *goodness*.

For a short time, she'd almost enjoyed being with him. And not just that . . . she'd enjoyed being a Renegade.

But the words uttered so casually by Evander Wade had brought reality crashing back down around her.

Not every prodigy deserves their powers. It's because of villains like her that we need Agent N.

Agent N.

An antidote, he'd called it.

An antidote that had to do with Max. The Bandit. The kid who could steal powers . . . who had stolen *Ace's* power.

And suddenly, she had known. She knew why they were running so many tests on Max. She knew what they were developing behind closed doors. The Renegades wanted a way to rid prodigies of their powers. A way to punish any prodigy who didn't join them.

The very idea of it made her blood run cold. Because, yes, maybe someone like Ingrid Thompson caused more harm than good, especially after a night like tonight. But where would that line be drawn? When someone refused to join the Renegades or attend the trials? Or when a prodigy disobeyed a law enforced by the Council, though the people had yet to receive any sort of vote or representation? Or maybe they would decide to remove powers based on the potential for violence or damage or even disloyalty?

She did not know where the line would be drawn, and she did not trust the Renegades to draw it.

Especially knowing that the Anarchists would be the first to be targeted.

She couldn't allow it to happen. Ace had fought to save prodigies from oppression, and here the Renegades wanted to force them into a new type of harassment. A new form of persecution.

Nova had long believed that the world would be better off if there were no prodigies at all. Superpowers would always lead to conflict—the weak versus the strong. And so long as the people relied on superheroes to take care of them, they would never learn to stand on their own again. It was a downward spiral she feared they would never get out of.

And maybe, just maybe, this all would have been fine, except the Renegades hadn't held up their end of the bargain. They promised to protect people, but crimes still happened every day. People were still hurt. People were still killed. And yes, the Renegades must shoulder the responsibility for this, but the people didn't even seem to understand that their own despondency was as much at fault. They saw the Renegades as heroes, the Anarchists as villains. They saw prodigies themselves as only good or only evil, leaving the rest of humanity somewhere in the realm of neutral.

There was the potential for evil everywhere, and the only way to combat it was if more people chose goodness. If more people chose heroism.

Not laziness. Not apathy. Not indifference.

But nothing would change so long as the Council was in charge. This, she knew. They would go on getting stronger. The people would go on getting weaker. And no one else would recognize how flawed this system was until it was too late.

During her time with the Renegades, Nova had started to lose herself.

But not anymore.

Years ago, there had been a little girl who believed the Renegades would come. How had she strayed so far from the betrayed hopes of that little girl? How had she forgotten the dreams and intentions of Ace Anarchy, who had saved her, who had dreamed of a society in which all people were free of tyranny?

He had failed.

But so had the Renegades. They had failed her family. They had failed *her*.

And they would go on failing until someone stopped them.

Nova made her way back through the tunnels as these thoughts crowded and tangled inside her head, occasionally lighting a new flare to guide her way. She had just reached her old train car when the darkness began to converge before her. Rivulets of inky blackness seeped down the curved concrete walls, dripping into the languid shape of a long cloak, a hood, a scythe.

Nova paused. She had seen little of Phobia since they had fled from the tunnels, and at times she wondered if he had chosen to return to the one place he felt most at home once the Renegades had given up their search.

Though she could not see his eyes beneath the overhang of the hood, she could feel him studying her, his breaths making the fabric of the hood flutter ominously.

"You have always feared failure," he said, and his voice seemed even raspier than normal, "but it is an especially strong fear tonight."

"Not really interested in the psychoanalysis," she said, moving to pass him.

He shifted the scythe, hooking her with the blade.

Nova scowled.

"And also a fear that all will be for naught . . ."

Nova rolled her eyes and waited for him to finish.

"The Detonator is dead." His voice quieted. "You fear that you will come to regret this."

"You just let me know when you're done."

Phobia brought the tip of the blade up to Nova's cheek and used it to turn her face toward him. "These doubts . . . these insecurities . . . they will come to serve you well, Nightmare." He listed his head toward her. "After all, one cannot be brave who has no fear."

She stared into the shadows where a face should have been. Utter nothingness stared back.

Leroy had once told her that Phobia did not need a body, because he was the embodiment of fear. She still wasn't sure what that meant.

"Yeah," she said, taking hold of the scythe handle and pushing it away. "You've said that before."

She walked past her train car, and when she dared to give a cursory glance back, Phobia had dissolved back into shadows.

Nova turned her back on the car that had been her home for so many years and paused to gather herself. Her hands had begun to shake, but she wasn't sure why. She wasn't afraid. At least, she didn't think so. Surely Phobia would have deigned to tell her if she was.

Nervousness, perhaps. Or even dread, to have to confess all the ways she had failed up until now.

Phobia was right about that, at least. She had always been afraid to fail.

Which is why she wasn't going to let it happen.

Sucking in a deep breath, she approached the old graffitied poster and angled it away from the wall. She slipped into the tunnel. This time she did not bother to turn on any flares. There was only one path here—she could find her way just fine by the feel of rough stone scraping against her elbows.

The journey through this narrow, damp passageway had seemed

to take eons when she was a fearful little girl fleeing from the cathedral, but in the years since, the journey seemed to get shorter every time she made it. Perhaps knowing that it wouldn't go on forever, that there was indeed an end to this cramped, filthy passage made all the difference.

She knew she was getting close when the air stopped smelling of stagnant water and rats, and started to smell like death and slow decay instead.

She reached the end of the tunnel and pressed her hand against the simple wooden crate that served as a makeshift door, shoving it aside just enough for her to slip into the cathedral's tombs. Inside the door, a tray had been set with a meal for one. A goblet of red wine and a cloth napkin, a china plate holding a triangle of hard white cheese, a sprig of grapes, a hunk of bread. A white taper candle was burning in a silver candlestick. She could taste the sulfuric tang of a recently lit match, and the candle was tall enough still that Nova could guess the meal had not been left there for long. She wondered if Phobia had delivered it, or if one of the others had been making pilgrimages too.

She felt guilty that this was the first time she'd come since they had abandoned the tunnels.

Stepping over the tray, she passed the familiar stacks of old stone sarcophagi, their inscriptions so covered with cobwebs and dust they were impossible to read. She passed beneath an arched doorway that had words from a dead language carved into the top, past the wall of rubble and broken stones where Ingrid had long ago closed these tombs off from the cathedral above.

She arrived at the bones, stacked so thick and deep they made a wall from floor to ceiling. Mostly skulls, but there were other things too. Femurs and ribs and even the tiny little finger bones that, for whatever reason, had scared Nova the most when she was young.

Nova looked into the empty eye sockets of those countless skulls of saints and clergymen and warriors, or whoever all these people were. She found herself wondering, as she had countless times before, if any of them had been prodigies. If so, had they dared to use their powers, or had they kept them secret? In their time, had their gifts been seen as miracles, or did even the devout feel the need to disguise who and what they truly were?

That was one thing that everyone had to agree on when it came to Ace Anarchy. Because of him, prodigies no longer had to hide.

At least, most prodigies no longer had to hide.

Nova settled down onto the floor, folding her legs beneath her. She stared into the faces of death and felt death peering back at her.

She took in a shaky breath and said the words that seemed impossibly simple for all that they meant.

"The helmet isn't destroyed."

The words echoed in the chamber and though it was an almost imperceptible change, she could have sworn that some of the skulls turned to look at her with increased interest.

"The Renegades have it. They keep it locked up because . . . because it's still intact, and they're worried that someone will try to use it again. But I think . . ." Her voice dropped to a whisper. "I think I can get it back."

The wall of bones began to tremble. Softly at first, enough to dislodge bits of dust. To send a couple of those tiny digits rolling across the floor toward Nova's knees.

As one, the bones pulled back, like the curtains framing the stage of a grand production. They moved quietly, languidly.

The chamber beyond had little in it, but what it did have was luxurious. A four-poster bed draped in velvet. A writing desk stocked with linen paper and the finest pens. And books. So many books, the Librarian would have wept with joy to have seen them.

Though Ace had loved the cathedral, he had always felt happiest when he was down here. It was not so macabre as people liked to believe, he said. He liked the peace of it. The solitude and the quiet. He had told her once, his eyes twinkling, that being here kept him grounded.

And so, it was with some irony that Nova looked into the small chamber and saw Uncle Ace levitating three feet in the air, legs crossed and face serene. He reminded her of a monk in the middle of a meditation, except that his eyes were open, gazing at her with the same softness and warmth that had always served to remind her of her father.

"I knew you would do well," he said, his lips curling into a smile, "my little nightmare."

ACKNOWLEDGMENTS

WRITING THIS BOOK turned out to be a much more treacherous journey than I expected when I first set out to write about superheroes and supervillains, and I am so grateful to have had the support of so many remarkable people to guide me and cheer me on.

To my agent, Jill Grinberg, who really saved me (and Nova and Adrian!) by shedding light on the heart of their story when I had lost sight of it. And also for all the excellent visualizations. They totally worked! In truth, you don't know what your steadiness and reassurance has meant to me over the years. And of course to Cheryl, Katelyn, and Denise, for being such incredible rock stars, all day, every day.

To everyone—and I do mean everyone!—at Macmillan Children's. First and foremost, my outstanding editor, Liz Szabla, for your guidance, serenity, cheerleading (*we've got this!*), and mostly for all the chocolate. Seriously, thank you for all the chocolate. Thank you to Jean Feiwel, who always puts her authors first. To "Clever Master" Mary, along with Jo, Caitlin, and the entire publicity and marketing team, who consistently blow me away with their genius ideas. To Rich, for yet another jaw-dropping cover (*I love it so much!*). To Mariel, for everything you do, but mostly for my banner. Great skies, that banner! And to Jon, Allison, Angus, and countless, *countless* others who work so hard to make wonderful, beautiful books and put them into the hands of readers, which might just be the world's most effective way of fighting against evil.

To my amazing, brilliant, dedicated, and oh-so-patient beta readers, Tamara, Meghan, and Jojo, who had to suffer through an absurdly rough early draft (Tamara actually suffered through two of them . . . sorry!), yet their support and encouragement never wavered. Thank you for believing in me and always helping me see the story and characters in ways I never would have considered.

To my fellow writers who kept me sane through a number of long café writing dates and writing retreats (we have really got to do more of those): Anna Banks, Kendare Blake, Jennifer Chushcoff, Kimberly Derting, Corry Lee, Lish McBride, Ayesha Patel, Rori Shay, and Breeana Shields. And also to Leilani and Emily, who always seem to have a word of kindness just when I need it most.

To my parents, who always remind me to take a moment for self-care, and to my big brother, Jeff, who introduced me to superheroes via *X-Men* comics when we were kids, and who was able to describe for me *exactly* what it's like to be stabbed through the hand with a semi-blunt object. Who knew that accident would someday have a silver lining? Yay, research!

And in the name of the Moon, I have to thank all the (Sailor) Moonies and the Lunartics! I couldn't possibly express how much your enthusiasm has meant to me over the years.

Finally, to my own little Renegades, Sloane and Delaney, who have brought more joy into my life than I ever thought possible.

And also thanks to Sarah and all the grandparents who were willing to take on last-minute childcare duties as my deadlines crept ever closer.

And—always, always—to my amazing husband, Jesse, who is as gallant as they come. (Truly, if you ever meet him, ask him about the time he chased down that purse snatcher in London. He would *love* to tell you the story.) Beyond literal heroics, though, he has rescued me countless times in the writing of this book. I can't even begin to list all the ways I'm grateful for you and everything you do—as a man, a husband, and a father.

ABOUT THE AUTHOR

MARISSA MEYER is *The New York Times*-bestselling author of The Lunar Chronicles. She lives in Tacoma, Washington, with her husband and three demanding cats. She's a fan of most things geeky (Sailor Moon, *Firefly*, any occasion that requires a costume) and has been in love with fairy tales since she was a child.

RENEGADES

HEARTLESS

MARISSA MEYER

BEFORE SHE WAS THE
QUEEN OF HEARTS
SHE WAS JUST A GIRL WHO
WANTED TO FALL IN LOVE

LONG BEFORE ALICE FELL
DOWN THE RABBIT HOLE . . .

AND BEFORE THE ROSES
WERE PAINTED RED . . .

THE QUEEN OF HEARTS WAS
JUST A GIRL, IN LOVE FOR
THE FIRST TIME.